Christina Dodd's romantic suspense
Trouble in High Heels
Tongue in Chic

Christina Dodd's *Darkness Chosen* series
Scent of Darkness
Touch of Darkness

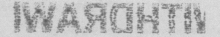

Christina Dodd

Thigh High

A SIGNET BOOK

SIGNET
Published by New American Library, a division of
Penguin Group (USA) Inc., 375 Hudson Street,
New York, New York 10014, USA
Penguin Group (Canada), 90 Eglinton Avenue East, Suite 700, Toronto,
Ontario M4P 2Y3, Canada (a division of Pearson Penguin Canada Inc.)
Penguin Books Ltd., 80 Strand, London WC2R 0RL, England
Penguin Ireland, 25 St. Stephen's Green, Dublin 2,
Ireland (a division of Penguin Books Ltd.)
Penguin Group (Australia), 250 Camberwell Road, Camberwell, Victoria 3124,
Australia (a division of Pearson Australia Group Pty. Ltd.)
Penguin Books India Pvt. Ltd., 11 Community Centre, Panchsheel Park,
New Delhi - 110 017, India
Penguin Group (NZ), 67 Apollo Drive, Rosedale, North Shore 0632,
New Zealand (a division of Pearson New Zealand Ltd.)
Penguin Books (South Africa) (Pty.) Ltd., 24 Sturdee Avenue,
Rosebank, Johannesburg 2196, South Africa

Penguin Books Ltd., Registered Offices:
80 Strand, London WC2R 0RL, England

First published by Signet, an imprint of New American Library,
a division of Penguin Group (USA) Inc.

First Printing, March 2008
10 9 8 7 6 5 4 3 2 1

On August 27, 2005, I had a plane reservation for New Orleans. There I intended to do research for the book I was writing, a book filled with the eccentricities, the joy, the larceny, the pleasures, and the madness of the Big Easy.

The flight was cancelled. On August 29, Hurricane Katrina made landfall, changing the face of the city forever.

This is my book, a little later than planned, but dedicated with affection and admiration to the resilient people of New Orleans and to the city itself.

Here's to the Big Easy. Long may she reign!

Acknowledgments

With thanks to Connie Brockway.
A great idea delayed is still a great idea,
And this one was brilliant.

Thank you to the people who keep me honest:
my editor, Kara Cesare, and the whole gang at NAL;
my agent, Mel Berger;
my family; and my friends.

One

Mrs. Bertha Freytag, as imposing and efficient an executive assistant as Mac MacNaught could find, opened his office door and stepped inside, using her broad body to guard his privacy. "Mr. Reed is here, sir."

"Send him in." MacNaught stood, remote in hand, before a bank of video screens that marched like soldiers across his wall. Each featured a live feed of Japanese bankers, men and women like him, intent on victory over the world of finance—and they all worked for him.

"Come in, please." Mrs. Freytag gestured Reed into the room.

The private investigator was a scrawny guy with a nondescript face, a droopy, graying mustache, and a fringe of hair around his ears. He blended into his surroundings, took no discernable pleasure in human company, and was incredibly patient. That made him the best at what he did, and that was why Mac used him.

Looking back to the screens, Mac spoke in quick, crisp Japanese. Heads bobbed. MacNaught bowed. With one click, he cut off their farewells.

"Good to see you." Reed stepped forward to shake MacNaught's hand.

MacNaught shook, then gestured. "Sit down. Give your report."

Reed sat, as instructed, in the uncomfortably hard chair positioned in front of MacNaught's steel and glass desk. "As you instructed, I went to New Orleans to investigate the Beaded Bandits."

"Who?" Mac scrutinized Reed. He looked different somehow. Tanned. Relaxed.

"The guys who have been robbing your banks. That's what they call them down there." Reed got a foolish half smile on his face. "The Beaded Bandits."

"Why would they call them that?" Reed had gained weight, too. And come to think of it, instead of his usual shuffle, he walked with a spring in his step.

"Because they dress in such elaborate costumes, write those quaint little demand notes, and they don't shoot anyone or take too much money. And they only do it once a year during Mardi Gras. They're not seen as a threat."

"So . . . I . . . gathered." MacNaught walked behind the desk and lowered himself into the well-padded, adjustable leather chair. With elaborate sarcasm, he asked, "Why would four bank robberies committed during Mardi Gras by the same perpetrators be taken seriously?"

Reed lost the smile, started talking, and talking fast.

"As you instructed, I focused my investigation on Miss Dahl. I followed her to work, watched her with her friends, interviewed a couple of the boarders living in the Dahl House."

"Excuse me? The *Dahl House*?" Mac tapped his pen on the desk and stared, heavy-lidded, at his formerly invulnerable investigator.

"That's what they called it in New Orleans. The Dahl House. Because the Dahls have lived there for, um, generations." Reed was smiling again.

Mac was not.

Reed swallowed loudly.

Good. He retained enough sense to realize the interview was not going well.

"Anyway, Miss Dahl participated in no suspicious activity. She works hard, she goes out for coffee and drinks. She likes jazz, and she's a good dancer."

The pen stopped. "You danced with her?"

"Only in the line of duty. Really! In New Orleans, things are different. If you *don't* dance, you'll stand out, and I wanted to blend in." Like a damn statue, Reed lifted one finger. "*Laissez le bon temps rouler!*"

"What the hell does that mean?" Mac snapped.

"Let the good times roll! Surely you've heard the saying."

"No." Mac got back to business. "Who are her friends?"

"One's a cop, Miss Georgia Able. Nessa—"

"Nessa?" Mac's eyes narrowed.

"That's what everyone calls her. Nessa." Reed fidgeted with the crease in his trousers. "Anyway, Nessa gets along well with the tellers, but she's not close to any of them, I think because it's not good policy."

"Who else?"

"Everyone likes her. Everyone speaks highly of her. She has a *lot* of friends."

Slowly, with a patently false tolerance, Mac asked, "Are any of them of interest as conspirators?"

"There's this Pootie person. She's one of the boarders at the Dahl House." Reed pulled a long face. "Man, is that one weird woman."

"We decided the perps were men dressing in women's costumes."

"I'm not sure Pootie's not a guy," Reed said thoughtfully. "She's from New York, and I don't know why she hangs around New Orleans, because she sticks out like a sore thumb. She works in the attic, doing God knows what. She doesn't like anybody. No one ever visits her."

Mac made a note. "Pootie who?"

"Pootie DiStefano. I did a fast Internet search on her and came up with no trace. Fake name."

"Or a hacker who's wiped her record clean. Who else?"

"There are a couple of musicians living in the Dahl House. Incredible losers, Ryan Wright and Skeeter Graves." Reed watched as Mac wrote down their names, too. "They both have the hots for Nessa, but in my considered judgment, neither of them is smart enough to pull off these robberies."

"Is either of them smart enough to do it if she told them how?"

"Yes, but I don't think she . . ." Reed's voice dwindled as he remembered that it wasn't his job to decide whether Ionessa was guilty, only to gather information about her. "Anyway, you said the Beaded Bandits were accomplished cross-dressers. Wright and Graves couldn't fake it in a million years."

"Are any of her friends accomplished cross-dressers?"

"Maybe, um, Daniel Friendly." Reed shifted uncomfortably in his chair.

"What about him?"

"He's an entertainer known as Dana, and he is really good. If I hadn't known better, I would have been convinced." Reed's papery skin flushed, and Mac knew he *had* been convinced.

"Could this Dana be one of the sonsabitches who is robbing my banks?"

"He's not tall enough."

"How nimble is he in heels?" Mac's voice rasped as it always did when he was irritated.

Reed inclined his head. "Okay, so it's possible."

"Did you speak directly to Miss Dahl?"

"Actually, *she* spoke to *me*," Reed said sheepishly.

"Well, now, isn't that a coincidence?" Mac drawled with heavy sarcasm. "I send a private investigator down to look into the possible involvement of one of my assistant managers in the annual Mardi Gras robberies, and she picks him out of a crowd to talk to."

"It wasn't like that. Down there, hospitality is a way of life, and I was hanging around a lot."

Staring at Ionessa, Mac would bet.

Reed continued, "She noticed and invited me over, and I thought it was a good way to, you know, get her confidence. So we went out a couple of times—"

"You *dated* her?" Mac could barely keep a lid on his simmering outrage.

"No, not like that!" Reed looked horrified—and

pleased. "I mean she welcomed me into her group. I went out to dinner with them, dined at the Dahl House, met her great-aunts—what a kooky couple of old ladies they are!—and I really got to know Nessa."

"You mean you compromised your investigation."

Reed stiffened. "Not at all. You wanted to know the dirt on Miss Dahl, and I've got it. She's frustrated with her job, hates her manager. She doesn't like having the boarders live in the house and she wants them out, but the family needs the income. She's the most charming person I ever met, but underneath, she's restless, looking for something more. . . ." Reed stared over Mac's shoulder, lost in his dream of Ionessa Dahl.

"All right." Mac came to his feet, decision made. "That's it. You're discharged. Pick up your check from Mrs. Freytag. And Reed—don't you dare screw this up." He spoke clearly and slowly, letting his true meaning bleed through his speech.

Reed paled, and Mac knew he comprehended perfectly.

If Reed let Ionessa know about Mac's suspicions, Mac would ruin him and his business.

Reed got out of the office in one hell of a hurry, leaving Mac staring at the closed door, fighting the urge that overcame him so often lately.

He didn't understand it. He was a self-made man, a man who enjoyed the brutality of corporate takeover, a cold, unfeeling bastard. He dressed in expensive, conservative suits. He kept his black hair severely trimmed. He wore his broken nose and the scars on his head and throat proudly, never considering plastic surgery to soften the impact.

His office provided him with a fitting background.

The floor was polished concrete. What artwork hung there was stark, modern, splashes of black and red. No flowers or plants softened the industrial feel of the large room. The hum of his three computers was the only music he needed. Behind him, outside the giant window, the view showed a city of concrete and steel, while down below, snow covered the sidewalks and turned to slush on the streets.

So what was it about *her* that made him watch her, over and over again?

The same thing that made poor, stupid Reed fall in love. The same thing that lured other men into Ionessa Dahl's web.

Almost without his volition, he reached for the remote and flipped on a single video screen.

An overhead camera showed him what he'd seen so many times before: a traditional bank lobby, rich with marble and polished wood, customers standing in line, tellers conversing as they accepted deposit slips and counted out money. A problem developed, the customer argued vehemently, and into the picture stepped a young woman, tall, slender, leggy, calm. She wore the conservative blue jacket and skirt of a woman in charge. Her hair was black and styled back from her face.

MacNaught caught her in the crosshairs and zoomed in.

She was pale, with a hint of pink on her lips and cheeks, but she wore large, glittering sapphires in her ears—and she didn't look like the type to wear fakes.

When Mac adjusted the focus, her down-turned head filled the monitor. She looked up, and he froze the frame.

Leaning forward, his elbows on his knees, he stared compulsively.

The long-distance shot didn't do her justice. She wasn't more than pretty, with stark cheekbones, a dramatic chin, and smooth, smiling lips. But the corners of her wide blue eyes slanted up (Mac believed the sooty lashes were real), and the way she gazed at that customer, as if his every word was gold, made the poor sucker stammer and falter and finally wriggle like a puppy.

She was Ionessa Dahl. Graduate of the Goizueta Business School at Emory University in Atlanta, summa cum laude.

She was the woman Mac suspected had planned and executed the robberies in his banks.

She was his obsession.

Two

The guidebooks claimed the Dahl House in the Garden District represented the finest in New Orleans architecture as well as the finest in New Orleans families—the Dahl family had built the gracious old mansion in 1847 and owned it ever since.

The guidebooks didn't mention that the most recent remodel had occurred in 1901, when indoor plumbing had been added and electrical wire run, or that the air-conditioning unit, added in 1971, was on its last legs. The Dahl House was the sort of behemoth that wove the noble family (rumored to be long-ago exiled French aristocrats) into the fabric of New Orleans, giving them such distinction that everyone from the first black mayor to the newest grocery store clerk knew and revered it and its current owners, Hestia and Calista Dahl.

Affectionately known as the Dahl girls, Hestia and Calista were eighty and eighty-two, tall women with the characteristic Dahl tremor in their arthritic fingers.

Hestia's hair was snowy white, short, and styled in that old-lady poodle permanent that enabled to her to get up in the morning, take a shower, and run down to the kitchen to start breakfast without ever lifting a comb. She wore polyester pants with elastic around her skinny waist, and shirts that didn't quite match the pants and sweater vests she picked up at resale shops.

Calista's brown hair sported chunky auburn highlights and, close to the end of the month, gray roots. When dressed in the size-fourteen jeans she bought at Wal-Mart, she reported proudly that people told her she looked younger than her age, and laughed when Hestia asked, "How young would that be, darling? Seventy-eight?"

The Dahl girls were almost the last of the Dahls. Almost.

The honor of being last, and of rescuing her heritage and her great-aunts from an ignoble slide into oblivion, fell to Ionessa Dahl.

As she had done every day since she was four and came to live with her great-aunts, Ionessa descended the wide, curved stairway into the foyer. Standing before the gilt-framed mirror, she straightened the crisp white button-front shirt, the single-button jacket, the straight-cut skirt. She carried an umbrella—in New Orleans, the chance of downpours always existed, and it had been a warm, wet February. She squared her shoulders and, pleased with her image as a conservative, successful banker, she nodded at herself.

Of course, in this house, her image wasn't worth a damn.

"How is business, Daniel?" Aunt Hestia's voice, high, clear, and lilting with the accent of metro New

Orleans, mixed with the clink of silverware and china from the dining room.

The alluring scent of bacon wafted into the foyer. Daniel's voice, hoarse from breathing too much cigarette smoke and singing too many shows, answered, "We're off a little this year. The tourists aren't drinking as much as usual, and they're not tipping because it's storming and they're wet."

"You ought to give out towels before the show. A dry tourist is a happy tourist." Ryan Wright was from Texas or maybe Oklahoma—no one had quite figured it out—with an accent that grated on the ear and a superior attitude totally unjustified by his success or intelligence. Luckily for him, he was handsome and played the saxophone, and in New Orleans, those were two attributes that would keep a street musician from starving.

"Brilliant idea," Daniel said with a much-feted club singer's irony. "Why didn't I think of that?"

Slipping into the dining room, Nessa poured herself a cup of coffee from the marble-topped antique sideboard and turned to face the long table. One hundred and fifty years of hard use pitted the mahogany surface, but the rich wood shone with the patina of age and beauty. The placemats were plastic, the plates scratched Corelle, but the Mardi Gras runner of purple, green, and gold added a festive touch.

"Morning, sweet girl." Calista bent and offered Nessa her soft, wrinkled cheek.

"Morning, Aunt Calista. Tonight's the big night!" Nessa gave her a hug and a kiss. Calista always smelled brisk and sweet, like key lime pie.

"I know. I just can't wait." Calista glanced at the clock.

Hestia called from the kitchen, "Come and get the eggs!"

"Later, Nessa." With a pat on Nessa's cheek, Calista bustled away.

The boarders were eating a sumptuous Southern breakfast of ham and eggs, grits swimming in butter, and biscuits and gravy. Nessa figured the cholesterol was going to kill them all—but they were going to die happy.

Certainly, Skeeter Graves was happy. With his arm wrapped around his plate, he shoveled in scrambled eggs with the speed of someone convinced that if he didn't eat quickly, they'd be stolen. And Skeeter wasn't even a boarder; he was just a bass-player friend of Ryan's who mooched a meal as often as he could.

Ryan sat next to him, gauntly handsome with good, broad shoulders and a buff chest displayed by a Hawaiian shirt he buttoned only halfway. He winked at Nessa, the wink of a man who knew and depended on his seductive abilities. "Hey, gorgeous." He developed a husky growl when he spoke to Nessa—indeed, to any woman, sort of like Gaston in Disney's *Beauty and the Beast*. Nessa half expected to see him tear his shirt open the rest of the way to show off his six-pack.

Debbie Voytilla sat next to him. Debbie was fun, cute, enthusiastic, and clever, a middle-aged divorcée, and a woman frankly enjoying her infatuation with Ryan. Putting her hand on his arm, she smiled into his face. "The coffee's hot. Do you want me to freshen your cup?"

"Thanks, Debbie, but Nessa's up. She can do it." He held out his cup.

All of her life, Nessa had taken this kind of nonsense from men, but with a smile rather than making a scene. Guys with small . . . egos . . . liked to be waited on, so she humored them. But lately, she hadn't been herself. She was tired of people—men and women—taking advantage of her good nature, lying to her, using her. She blamed the last seven years; purgatory had curdled the milk of her human kindness into something else. The cottage cheese of bitterness, she guessed.

Grabbing the coffeepot, she carried it over to Ryan's outstretched cup—and poured a stream onto his wrist.

"Son of a bitch!" He dropped the cup, splashing the floor with the dregs of coffee.

Aunt Hestia stepped into the doorway. "Mr. Wright, we do not encourage that kind of language in the dining room!" But her eyes twinkled.

"I'm so sorry." Nessa put the pot back on the burner.

"Really, Nessa! You're clumsy this morning." Debbie pulled an ice cube from her tea, wrapped it in a napkin, and put it on his wrist.

"That's so much better." Ryan gave a dramatic sigh, caught her hand, and kissed it. "Thank you, Debbie. You're an angel."

Debbie dimpled and blushed.

Ryan waited until she turned back to her meal. Then he glanced at Nessa and rolled his eyes.

Nessa wished she had poured the coffee in his lap.

"Nessa, darling, you look so professional in that suit. A touch of red around your neck would make quite a power statement," Daniel Friendly said.

Nessa slipped into a chair beside him. "I've got a scarf in my bag."

"Do you want me to tie it for you?" Daniel asked.

Nessa grinned at him. "I can tie a knot."

"I don't tie knots, darling. I make artistic statements in silk." Daniel was bronze sequins, white feathers and rhinestones. Pale skin, expertly applied makeup, and wide brown eyes. A swirl of blond hair and sensuous lips. And a figure that made men suck in their stomachs and the women pinch their husbands—until they discovered he was a guy in drag.

Nessa only knew when she stood next to Daniel—Dana to his audience—that she felt like half a woman. In his gestures, his mannerisms, and his appearance, Daniel was ultrafeminine. Only his speaking voice gave him away.

Aunt Calista bustled over to place a heaping plate of eggs, ham, and biscuits in front of Nessa. "Eat. You need sustenance to work in That Bank."

"With That Woman," Aunt Hestia added as she popped more bread in the toaster.

The aunts always said it like that, in capital letters—That Bank, That Woman—and accompanied the words with glares of disapproval.

Nessa smoothed her napkin in her lap. "My promotion is finally coming through."

"About time," Daniel said.

"When I think how That Woman has spread ugly rumors about how you're soft—you, the descendent of Althea Dahl!" Calista said.

"I don't have a lot in common with Althea Dahl," Nessa said.

"No, it's not as if you've ever poisoned your husband. Not that you have a husband. Not that that's a concern, you're still young, but the occasional date wouldn't hurt." Hestia blinked at Nessa. "Are you bringing someone tonight?"

Maddy stuck her head in from the kitchen. Their cook was black, four-foot-ten inches tall, ninety pounds soaking wet, older than God, and wielded as much authority.

All conversation stopped while Maddy announced, "The McHauers sent a tomato aspic—where am I going to find room in the refrigerator for that?—and Mr. Richarme came by with an envelope, and Mrs. Bagnet made her pralines." Maddy's black eyes swept the room and lingered on Calista. "I counted 'em, so no one's going to sneak one. And there is *another* mouse in the kitchen!"

"Oh, dear." Calista headed for the door Maddy held open.

"You girls have got to get the exterminator. That is no place to cut corners. Ever since the flood, the little devils have been all over the city, gnawing in the pantry, making me jump, and all you do is catch them. . . ." Maddy's voice faded as the door closed behind them.

Hestia turned in surprise as their very first boarder trudged into the room, pulling a carry-on suitcase. "Pootie, you came downstairs! You should have told us you wanted breakfast. All we've got is frozen bagels."

"S'okay." Pootie DiStefano's Bronx mumble made it sound like one word.

"Where are you off to this beautiful morning?" Hestia chirped.

"N'York."

"Oh, but Pootie. Tonight's our party, you know it is!" Hestia cried.

Pootie gave her a weary look.

"Now, Pootie, you should try it once," Hestia said persuasively. "All of New Orleans comes. It's so much fun. I'm sure you'd like it!"

"No." Pootie settled herself at the table and eyed the food balefully.

"Maddy has been cooking day and night," Hestia continued. "She's making shrimp étouffée in puff pastry shells. You know that's your favorite."

Pootie visibly wavered for a minute, then shook her head. "Gotta go see my family. But thanks."

Tall, stout, taciturn, and middle-aged, she was without vanity or social skills. She smoked until she was hoarse; her once black hair was salt-and-pepper; and Nessa doubted she'd ever applied mascara or dressed in anything except khaki shorts, T-shirts, and sandals. For ten years she had lived in their attic, but even the inquisitive aunts knew nothing about her except that she was Italian and so antisocial she had never, not once, had a visitor of any kind.

To Nessa, the sight of Pootie grated painfully. She served as a constant reminder of Nessa's failure.

Calista returned, and as the kitchen door closed behind her, they could hear Maddy's voice shouting, "What if the guests see a mouse tonight? Can you imagine? All the fancy ladies shrieking and spilling their drinks on the carpet . . . ?"

Calista placed a split toasted bagel, cream cheese, and a circle of warm blueberry crumble at Pootie's elbow. "I caught the mouse," she announced.

"Horrid little things!" Debbie looked truculent. "I

swear I hear them squeaking in the attic at night. The first time I see one in my bedroom, Miss Calista, no one will sleep that night."

"Don't worry," Hestia said. "We'll be rid of them by the end of the week."

Calista took her seat at the head of the table. "Nessa, you were going to tell us about your promotion."

"That Woman has held you back." Hestia's eyebrows snapped into an angry V at the thought of Stephanie Decker. "She's jealous of you."

"I wish she would let me help her with her makeup." Daniel was frankly distressed. "She's beige. Just beige. Does she think it's enough to wear good clothes? Doesn't she know she needs to be seen, not overlooked?"

"She's a woman in a man's world." Nessa snapped her napkin open. "She has to be a—"

"Bitch?" Pootie asked through a bite of bagel.

"Not a doormat," Nessa corrected.

"You're too kind, Nessa." Hestia put the spoon in the warm glass pan full of blueberry crumble and passed it around the table, and took her seat. "The way she's treated you, making you do all the work."

Pootie took a huge helping.

"She's the manager. I'm supposed to do the grunt work." Nessa ran the bank, but that was her weakness—she couldn't bear to let Stephanie out on the floor to make the tellers and the customers mad. "Yesterday she had me get the big corner office ready. When I asked her why, she refused to say. She hasn't hired anyone, but there has been an unsigned communication from Philadelphia, and you know what that means. Mr. MacNaught is taking a hand."

Everyone tossed troubled glances across the table at each other, then at her.

"No, it's good!" Nessa assured them. "Stephanie was unhappy, so it must be good news for me. I'll get a raise, a real raise this time, one big enough to make a difference." To allow her aunts to live as they should, alone in their house without the need to cook and clean for a bunch of boarders.

"That means you can get your own apartment," Hestia said.

"But she's happy living here," Calista said.

"I am." No matter how much she would like to have a private conversation with her aunts without boarders listening in and expressing their opinions, Nessa couldn't get an apartment and pay off the mortgage on the aunts' house, too. So she would stay

"But Calista, that's not the point," Hestia explained. "Other than college, she's never lived anywhere else with anyone else. She's twenty-seven years old and I'm very much afraid she's still a virgin."

Nessa lifted her gaze from her plate to see every eye in the dining room fixed upon her.

Calista looked horrified.

Even Hestia looked surprised.

"Am not," Nessa muttered. "I did go to college, you know."

"Oh, dear," Debbie murmured, and offered Nessa a sympathetic smile.

Ryan's gaze moved from one person to another, obviously fascinated.

Pulling his head out of his plate, Skeeter offered Nessa a wide-lipped simper that made her skin crawl.

Pootie stood. "Fascinating as this discussion is, I

have to go." She trudged toward the door, then backed up and stopped behind Nessa's chair. "Kid, if you ever have the guts to get out of that stupid bank, come to me. You've got the smarts. I could teach you."

Nessa turned in her chair and stared as Pootie stalked out. The front door slammed shut with the sound of solid wood.

"That was nice." Hestia's impressive eyebrows knit. "I guess."

"What does she *do*?" Debbie asked.

"We don't know," Calista said.

"Then you don't want Nessa doing it, do you?" Daniel asked.

"I suppose not." But Hestia thoughtfully tapped her finger to her lips.

"Yeah, who'd want to work with her? I mean, it's one thing to be queer, but even her name is weird, and her legs are white and she never shaves them." Ryan wiped his hands on his chest as if wiping away slime.

"*Mr.* Wright." Hestia fixed Ryan with a stern gaze. "We don't rent to scalawags and certainly not to men who make ungentlemanly remarks. Please remember that before we change our minds about *you*. You, too, Mr. Graves."

Skeeter looked at his plate with alarm, then back up at Hestia. Like any child of the South, he said, "Yes, ma'am!"

Ryan's truculent expression gave way to abashed boyishness. "Sorry. I shouldn't spread rumors. It's not like *she's* one of the Beaded Bandits."

"I should say not." Hestia was clearly offended. "Pootie is a dear, but neither one of the Beaded Bandits is a damned *Yankee*."

Nessa couldn't help it—she laughed softly. "Certainly. Only people from New Orleans are mad enough to successfully rob banks every year for such ridiculously small amounts."

"Not mad, chère." Calista tapped her forehead. "Clever."

"Crazy," Skeeter mumbled.

"Well, my darlings, I've got to go to the club." With a whoosh of sequins and perfume, Daniel tossed his boa around his neck. "I used my seniority to grab the afternoon show so I could be here for the party. Oh, and—" He slid an envelope out of his décolletage. "Here's a little something to make it extra special."

Embarrassed, Nessa turned her head away.

"You shouldn't have, Daniel!" But Calista took the envelope and kissed his cheek.

"Can't wait, darlings!" he called.

"We've got to go hit the streets, too. Mardi Gras is one hell of a"—Ryan observed the aunts' reproving stares—"one heck of a lot of work, but the tips could keep me for half a year." He stood.

So did Debbie. "Wait, Ryan. I'll walk with you."

"That would be great." Ryan tugged on Skeeter's arm.

Skeeter stuffed a biscuit into his pocket and bobbed his head at the aunts. "Thank you, Miss Hestia, Miss Calista. It was wonderful!"

The front door slammed repeatedly, a solid sound of two-inch-thick mahogany against a massive door frame, before silence fell over the dining room.

Hestia put her hand over Nessa's. "I'm so sorry."

"Hestia, what got into you? I almost fainted when

you said that. . . . About Nessa's . . ." Words failed
Calista.

"For a moment"—Hestia squeezed Nessa's fingers—"it seemed as if we were sitting here with our
family."

"They are *not* our family," Nessa said fiercely.

"I know, dear. It's just that they're familiar now, and
I remember so well those days when all our sisters
dined here, and little Buddie and Daddy and Mama."
Hestia turned to Nessa. "Little Buddie, that was your
grandpa."

"I know, Aunt Hestia."

"I remember, too," Calista said. "We'd sit around
this table, little Buddie in his high chair, having the
most marvelous breakfasts, teasing each other—"

"About your *virginity*?" Nessa's voice rose.

"Well, no, not that." Yet Hestia smiled.

Calista smiled, too. "But almost. We could tell our
mother anything, so when Daddy got up to go to work,
we would laugh about our gentlemen callers and ask
advice and—oh! it was wonderful. Lots of times we
had company—relatives or friends—and they'd stay
for days. We used to complain about going to see the
same sights over and over again, but before the war
and that wicked hurricane, New Orleans was a grand
city, and we were awfully proud of it."

"I don't understand how we could have been so
many and dwindled to so few." Hestia shook her head
in bewilderment.

"We Dahls don't breed well," Calista said.

"Daddy and Mama did."

"Yes, but Daddy was always chasing Mama around
the kitchen."

"Lucky Mama!"

The aunts were lost in their memories.

But Nessa could think of only one thing worse than talking about her great-aunts' sexual history, and that was talking about her great-grandparents' kitchen romps. "Whatever! But while you're near to my heart, aunts, I don't even want to talk about it with you!"

"You can! It's not as if *we're* virgins," Calista said.

"Of course, I was married," Hestia said.

Nessa wanted to stop her ears with her fingers. "Yes, so I assumed you—"

"And my young man didn't make it back from the war." Calista's smile crooked with remembered pain.

Hestia put her veined hand over Calista's and gently squeezed.

Nessa took Calista's hand, too. "I'm sorry."

"It was a long time ago," Calista said, "but I've always been glad I didn't wait. Ever since I got that phone call from his parents, I've tried to live my life so that I had no regrets. You need to do that, too, Nessa!"

"For once, Calista's right!" Hestia said. "You listen to her, Nessa."

"What regrets could I have? I have the two best aunts in the entire world." Nessa stood hastily before Hestia and Calista could point out that a young woman should have more in her life than her family and her career.

Because maybe that was true, but Nessa had a goal.

Her darling aunts had mortgaged the house to pay for Nessa's expensive education. They claimed it was well worth it, that she'd brought them such pleasure they were in debt to her.

But Nessa knew better. Every day her aunts got up

and spent the day cleaning, changing sheets, shopping for groceries, and the hundreds of tasks necessary to run their boarding house.

So she would pay them back, get the boarders out, and her aunts would never have to change another bed or make another breakfast.

"Now I'm off to work and a fabulous new promotion." Nessa kissed her aunts on their papery cheeks. "And tonight we party!"

Three

Easter was late this year, so Mardi Gras was late, too, and Nessa walked outside and into a humidity so dense she could taste it. Or maybe it was New Orleans she could taste. She caught the streetcar to the French Quarter, and hopped off at the Canal and St. Charles streets stop.

Eight o'clock was early enough that she could see only the exhausted shopkeepers sweeping the debris of last night's party into the gutter, the occasional tourist staggering toward his hotel, and Georgia Able, Nessa's best friend from grade school and a police officer for the New Orleans police department.

Georgia's family had been in New Orleans as long as Nessa's, at first as slaves, then as free blacks, and she knew every inch of the city. Her wide, melting brown eyes, slow drawl, and curvaceous figure hid a steel-magnolia personality that she used as skillfully as she used her service revolver.

Now she perched on a police horse, a riding helmet on her head, grimly surveying the streets from behind dark glasses, but at the sight of Nessa she smiled and lifted a hand.

Nessa stopped to pet Goliath. "The parades start today."

"Don't I know it!" Georgia said fervently.

"Are you still on shift from last night or are you going on now?"

"I'm going on shift now, but they called me in last night because the crowds were out of control. I'm working on four hours' sleep, and I'm about this far"—Georgia showed Nessa an inch between her thumb and forefinger—"from strangling the first tourist who throws their beads at Goliath." Leaning down, she patted his neck. "Poor boy, he's as tired as I am."

"Fat Tuesday is only nineteen days away." Nessa gestured toward a cart. "Want me to get you a café au lait?"

"No, thanks. I've had so much coffee I'm sloshing." Georgia lowered her warm, gentle voice to a whisper only Nessa could hear. "And I'm on the rag so I have to pee all the time, anyway."

Nessa grinned. "Want me to make a sign? OFFICER WITH CRAMPS AND BLOATING. GO AHEAD, MAKE HER DAY."

"Can you tell I'm bloated?" Georgia slid her dark glasses down her nose, aimed a lethal glance at Nessa, and fingered her pistol.

"I didn't say that!" Nessa said in fake alarm. "Your bulletproof vest makes you look dangerous, not bloated."

"For true?"

"For true. Just keep saying—only nineteen more days. Nineteen more days and the parades will be over, the tourists will be gone, and it'll be Lent once more."

"Nineteen more days, seven hundred more arrests for public intoxication and lewdness, and, God help us all, Fat Tuesday looming at the end of it all."

"I'm glad I work in a bank," Nessa said with heartfelt sincerity.

"As long as you're not the bank that gets hit *this* Mardi Gras."

"Hit? Oh. You mean the Beaded Bandits. No leads?"

Nessa's fond tone seemed to aggravate Georgia. "Sure, you and everyone else in New Orleans think they're captivating, and the press has come up with *such* a cutesy name for them. But how do you get leads with robberies like that?"

"Don't forget that they steal from a coldhearted corporation based in Philadelphia."

"There's that." With an alertness that belied her complaints of exhaustion, Georgia scrutinized a group of tourists who straggled out of a bar, looking as if the night before had been long and difficult, and shook her head. Returning her attention to Nessa, she added, "We're getting pressure from the CEO to stay on top of the situation, but it's Mardi Gras. I can barely stay on my horse."

"Is ol' MacNaught being a jerk?"

Georgia leaned on the saddle horn. "From the top of his balding head to the tip of his shiny black shoes."

"I heard a rumor that he looks like Danny DeVito."

"Could be. I heard he's a hermit who hides from the press."

"Yankees." Nessa sighed.

"Bless their hearts."

The women exchanged understanding grins.

"Where y'at?" Georgia asked.

In the New Orleans patois, she was asking how Nessa was, and Nessa could hardly contain her sarcasm. "Great. Just great. This morning, I've been talking about sex with my aunts."

Georgia straightened up. "Did you learn anything?"

"Yes. I learned neither of them are virgins."

Georgia winced. "I thought you were talking about *your* sex life."

"God, yes, that, too. Nothing is sacred anymore. Are you coming to the party tonight?"

"Are you kidding? I don't care what riot occurs today. I wouldn't miss the party at the Dahl House." Georgia lowered her voice. "I don't know how many of the cops are going to be able to drop by, but we took up a collection. Not much, just a little to help with the expenses. I'll bring you the envelope tonight."

"Thank you. Thank the others." The tradition of giving the Dahl girls a few dollars in an envelope to offset party expenses had started long before Nessa's birth, and she felt no false pride in admitting, "We couldn't do it without your help, and if we couldn't have the party, it would break my aunts' hearts."

"The party at the Dahl House *is* Mardi Gras," Georgia said.

"Are you bringing a date?"

"No." Georgia was brief to the point of curtness.

Which didn't stop Nessa. "Why not? You could stand to see some action."

"Civilians can't deal with a woman who can knock them down and beat them up, and they really can't deal with the hours I work during Mardi Gras." Georgia patted her horse and stared down the street.

"That leaves only cops, and they're all married or jerks."

"Except for—"

"*All* of them are married or jerks." Georgia glared at Nessa.

"Okay. If you say so. But I like Antoine, and I know for a fact he's available."

"I don't know why you're so hung up on Antoine Valteau." Everything about Georgia—her expression, her posture, her movements—radiated irritation.

That didn't impress Nessa. "I'm not. You are. And he likes you, Georgia."

"I'm not interested in a one-nighter." Georgia held up her hand. "Just drop it, Nessa. Just . . . drop it. I'll tell the aunts I had a date, but he couldn't get off work. . . ."

Nessa narrowed her eyes in thought. "Maybe that's what I should say. He couldn't get off work. . . ."

"Who couldn't get off work?" Georgia must be tired. She wasn't following.

"I don't know. Some mythical guy."

"*You're* not bringing a date tonight?"

With an exasperated glance at the officer on the horse, Nessa asked, "Remember three years ago when I brought Brad Oglesby, he looked around, decided he liked the Dahl House, and moved in? A single date became a yearlong ordeal of me locking my door every night to keep him out."

"I'd forgotten that one." Georgia relaxed. "That was great."

"Yeah. Great. Not to mention two years ago when Rafe Cabello got drunk and spent the whole evening throwing up in the bathroom."

"He's still pining after you, you know." Georgia visibly perked up at Nessa's recital of the past horrors. "You have to stop rejecting these guys. They take it so badly."

"And last year was the worst ever. The weatherman from Channel 6." Nessa shuddered in real horror.

"Rayburn Pluche brought the TV cameras, and proposed." Georgia burst into laughter. In between gasps, she asked, "Remember the Elvis costume? And the blue suede shoes? My God, Nessa, the look on your face when you realized . . ."

Nessa watched her friend in disgust. "This is what I live for. To entertain you."

"No. Really. Sorry." Georgia wiped at her face and tried to control herself. "I'm just . . . worn out . . . and when I remember the sequins on his collar . . . the sideburns . . . it was so . . ." She went off into another gale of laughter.

"If you're entirely done"—Nessa gave Goliath a last pat—"I have to get to work." She started toward the bank.

"Hey, Nessa?" Georgia called.

Nessa turned back.

"Are you bringing a date?"

Four

Nessa shot Georgia the one-fingered salute, then walked through the French Quarter to the distinguished old bank on Chartres Street. At eight thirty, she climbed the steps and tapped on the glass door.

Their uniformed guard let her in, and the blast of air-conditioning felt like heaven. "Good morning, Miss Dahl."

"Morning, Eric." The old-fashioned lobby gleamed with marble floors and polished wood counters, and glittered with Mardi Gras tinsel hanging from the lights and masks decorating the walls.

She put her purse away in the locked drawer in her desk, the one that sat against the wall in the lobby—the one she would soon be leaving behind forever—then made her way behind the counter to the vault. She punched her code into the electronic panel, and the round steel door silently opened.

Last Friday, she had checked the amounts in the tellers' cash drawers and put the totals into individual bank bags. She placed the bags on the shelves and the drawers on the table. Today, soon, the armored car would come and take most of the cash, the bank would open, and the banking cycle would begin again.

Now Nessa took the stacks of bills off the shelves, counted them, then filled the drawers for the tellers. Stacking the drawers, she hefted them in her arms and marched out to the counter. One by one, she distributed them, waited until the teller counted and confirmed the amounts, and glanced at the clock.

Eight fifty a.m. The system of checks and balances took a while, but with that one mistake she'd made seven years ago, she had proven how necessary it was to take the time and do it properly.

Five women and one man stood waiting at their stations. Each one wore a costume that represented a period in New Orleans history. The older tellers, Julia, Donna, and Mary, had been through this bank promotion the year before. Julia and Donna wore gowns from the roaring twenties. Mary wore a nineteenth-century serving maid's black-and-white costume. Jeffrey wore the formal suit of a Southern planter, grew his sideburns down his cheeks, and greatly enjoyed the irony of his attire; Jeffrey was black. Those four looked cool and comfortable.

Lisa and Carol, new to the bank, young and attractive, had both opted for glamorous costumes from the old South. They were now paying for their vanity in misery and discomfort.

"Hey, Carol, how's it going?" Nessa asked the most pitiful-looking teller, a slender Cajun with large, doe-brown eyes, a glorious fall of glossy brown hair, and a low-cut, lacy gown with a massive antebellum hoop skirt.

"Scarlett O'Hara my ass. This corset is killing

me." Carol grabbed her waist and tugged. "No air-conditioning, all these petticoats—how could those poor women stand these things?"

"That's why they fainted so much," Julia said.

"And had the vapors." Carol watched Julia with envious eyes.

"You'd have the vapors, too, if your waist was cinched so tight you couldn't pass gas." Donna, old enough to be everyone's grandmother and frank to a fault, grinned at Carol's expression of horror.

"Makes you long for the good old days, doesn't it?" Mary checked her supply of hand disinfectant.

"Not me," Jeffrey said.

"Me, neither." Dainty, tanned Lisa shook her head, and the lacy widow's cap perched atop her curls slid sideways.

"Here, honey, let me." While Lisa squirmed, Donna briskly took the pins out of her hair, rearranged the cap, and stuck it back on.

"What about you, Nessa?" Lisa asked. "You're not dressed up at all."

"Here." Eric hustled over with a couple of strings of beads. "Better get them on before the Stephabeast sees you. You know how she is."

The others concealed grins at the nickname and waited for Nessa to reprimand Eric. With her stiff-necked demands and her grim surveillance, Stephanie had earned their enmity.

Instead Nessa cranked her neck toward the open door of Stephanie's corner office. "She's here already?" Stephanie usually didn't arrive until a minute before the bank opened. Or a minute after.

"Oh, she's here." Eric did the Frankenstein walk.

"With a stick up her behind. But that means good news for you, right, Miss Dahl?"

Nessa supposed Stephanie's secretary had spread the news about Nessa's new office. She showed everyone her crossed fingers.

"We hope you get that promotion this time, Miss Dahl," Julia said.

The others nodded.

"I know not to get my hopes up." Yet Nessa invariably got her hopes up. She couldn't help it. She was the kind of optimist who not only saw the glass half-full, but knew it was lead crystal.

With a glance at the clock, Nessa moved behind the counter and paced the line of tellers. "It's one minute to nine. Do you need anything? Are you ready?"

"We're ready." Mary squared her shoulders.

"Another day in paradise," Donna said.

"All we have to do is get through today, and we have the party at the Dahl House tonight." Jeffrey smiled.

Nessa glanced toward the door and saw the tall, narrow figure of a man dressed in a rumpled black suit. His gaze darted from one teller to the other, the tip of his long nose fogging the glass. "Mr. Miller's waiting for us to open."

The tellers groaned.

"After that, the day can't get worse," Mary said cheerfully.

"You're just saying that because he won't come to you," Carol said.

"Nope, he sure won't. He's one of those guys who loves to fall into that trap of yours." Mary nodded at Carol's cleavage.

"It's nine." Nessa signaled Eric. "Open the doors."

Eric did as he was told.

As always, the line of customers waiting for the bank to open was long, and as always on Friday, Mr. Miller led the way. He disappeared into the men's room, coming out with a roll of toilet paper beneath his arm.

Carol flashed a smile and some cleavage at the first man in line, and she was busy when Mr. Miller stepped forward.

He headed for Julia, who muttered, "Guess I drew the short straw."

"Good morning." Mr. Miller claimed to be a minister, was inevitably friendly, and perfectly polite. He should have been the ideal customer, but in a disagreeable ritual, he unwound a strip of toilet paper and used it to thoroughly wipe his nose before counting out his money and making his deposit.

Julia took him in her stride, waiting until he had left the bank to use the disinfectant to clean her hands and her counter. Then she welcomed the next customer, and they were off on another day at the bank.

But this wasn't a normal day.

Today Nessa moved on with her life.

"Ionessa!" The high-pitched shriek from Stephanie's office made even the customers flinch.

Nessa passed Stephanie's secretary, who muttered, "Take the promotion, but don't get your fingers close to her mouth. Those big teeth can snap right through bone."

As Nessa entered, Stephanie made a show of shuffling papers. She was thirty-one, the valedictorian of her class in Tulane, of medium height and weight, well groomed and, as Daniel said, beige. Her hair was a dirty blond, she never wore bright colors, and even her eyes were an indeterminate hazel. She attended business breakfasts at Toastmasters and bored everyone silly. She dated, but only on Saturday night and only if the guy took her somewhere she could be seen. She kept her desk clean of photos and used her e-mail for official bank communications. She was dedicated to her career, the perfect middle manager.

"I got a phone call last week from the big man himself." Stephanie lifted her gaze and glared. "Yes, Ionessa, it's true. Mr. MacNaught himself called me. He's taking a personal interest in catching the Beaded Bandits."

"The CEO of Premier Central is concerned with Beaded Bandits?" Had Stephanie cracked under the pressure of running the bank? For the past three years, Mr. MacNaught had made the "I'm the richest, nanner, nanner," list in *Fortune* magazine. "Don't they steal a thousand dollars or less? Why would he care about such an insignificant amount?"

And why were they discussing this now?

"He has a reputation for despising thieves, and it would seem that that's true." Stephanie crumpled the paper she held, then, seeing Nessa's gaze on her clawed fingers, made an effort to straighten them and the paper. "He's sending an insurance investigator to track down the thieves and arrest them."

"Okay." Nessa was still floundering. Why was Stephanie telling her this stuff? "What does he think an insurance investigator is going to be able to do?"

"He's not impressed with the NOPD's work on this

case, and thinks this guy who's coming in will light a fire under their collective lazy asses."

"Hm." Nessa knew most of the police department personally. They visited at the Dahl House. She took care of their banking needs. She doubted that some stiff-necked Yankee was going to help by stomping into the police department and demanding they investigate his way.

"He ordered that I prepare him an office here in the bank—"

Shock sent a jolt down Nessa's spine. She snapped to attention.

"—and get him someone who knew the city and the officials well to ease this guy's way. I offered myself—I grew up here, I went to school here, I know everybody—but *no.* He already had someone in mind."

The newly cleaned office. The orders to get ready to move. The aunts were right. None of this was about Nessa and her promotion. This was about Mr. MacNaught's insurance investigator. Nessa's lips were stiff as she said, "Mr. MacNaught wants me."

"Of course he wants *you.* Somehow word of your charm and your connections got all the way up to Philadelphia, and Mr. MacNaught demands that *you* assist his man." The rancor and jealousy that marred Stephanie's personality burned like acid in her tone. "I don't understand why *you're* always the one who gets the commendations, why *you're* always the one the customers write glowing letters about. *I'm* the manager. If it weren't for *me*—"

Nessa lifted her eyebrows.

Stephanie snapped her lips shut. Not even she

had the nerve to claim the bank ran smoothly because of her.

"What am I supposed to do for this insurance investigator?" Nessa spoke carefully, keeping her tone even, allowing none of her frustration to seep through. Stephanie would enjoy it far too much.

"Get him coffee. Take notes. The usual things a secretary does for her boss." Stephanie smirked. "You've been demoted to a secretary."

"I believe they're called administrative assistants now." Then, because Stephanie had so clearly wanted to show off for MacNaught's man, Nessa added, "I hope to do a good enough job to call myself to Mr. MacNaught's attention."

Nessa's shot must have struck home, for Stephanie crumpled the paper again, and this time she didn't bother to straighten it out. Her pale eyes narrowed. She must have seen a crack in Nessa's disciplined coolness, for she exclaimed, "Poor Ionessa! Did you think that office was for you?"

Stephanie had the knack of hitting where it hurt, but in a battle of wits, Nessa carried the greater ammunition. "I assume you'll be taking my place in customer service?"

Stephanie hated helping the clients with loans and investments, and the clients reciprocated. "Yes, of course I will be," she snapped. "There's no one else qualified."

And whose fault is that? Nessa wanted to ask. Stephanie wouldn't promote anyone else for fear that person would overshadow her.

The phone rang. Stephanie picked it up, spoke

briefly, then hung up and told Nessa, "He's on his way."

Nessa came to her feet. "Does he have a name?"

"Jeremiah Mac." Stephanie leaned back in her chair. "I imagine he's an old fart, don't you? After all, he's an insurance investigator, and that's nothing more than a glorified accountant."

"I've never dated an insurance investigator or an accountant, so I wouldn't know. *Are* they all old farts?" Nessa waited for the delicate moment when the insult sank in, then as Stephanie's lips lifted in a snarl, she walked out of the office.

She dusted her fingertips together. She adjusted the lapels on her jacket. She smiled evilly.

Stephabeast, indeed.

Stephanie picked up the vase behind her desk, weighed it in her hand, then reluctantly put it down again. No matter how much she wanted to throw it against the wall, she would not. It was the bank's. Now, if it were Ionessa's . . .

She didn't understand why everybody liked Nessa so much. Everybody talked about her—how nice she was and how good to her aunts and how efficient she was. . . .

Yeah, well, she was none too smart, or she would have realized how Stephanie had used her. Seven years ago, they'd both started at the bank as assistant managers. Nessa had realized they were in competition for the top spot—after all, she was no dummy—but she was a soft touch. One of the tellers had given her a sob story about a sick kid, Nessa had let her leave without counting her drawer, and five hundred dollars had walked out with her.

The mistake of a lifetime. Stephanie had secured the position of bank manager, and right away she got an e-mail from Mr. MacNaught himself. *Keep an eye on Ionessa Dahl.*

That was all it took. Stephanie had done just that. She'd kept an eye on Ionessa when she improved the efficiency of the tellers, and Stephanie took credit for the idea. She'd kept an eye on Ionessa when she secured accounts from some of the most influential people in New Orleans, and Stephanie took credit for the jump in savings. She'd kept an eye on Ionessa when she provided the most home loans of any officer in Premier Central history, and Stephanie took credit for every one.

Mr. MacNaught had a reputation as a real son of a bitch who stomped on people without even noticing the crunch of their bones beneath his boots.

But he did give rewards for efficiency, for self-motivation, for ingenuity. According to a *Business News Monthly,* Premier Central Banks was one of the top one hundred companies to work for, as long as one stayed clean and smart.

Mr. MacNaught had been duly impressed by Stephanie's performance, and he'd given her huge bonuses.

Stephanie had been careful to dole out the occasional faint praise for Ionessa—not enough to get her promoted, but enough to keep her on. Because the last thing Stephanie Decker wanted was to have to run this bank herself.

And until this damned investigator was finished, that was exactly what she was going to have to do.

Picking up the vase, she slammed it against the wall. It shattered into a million pieces, and she took a long breath.

The cleaning people were so careless.

Five

Before she stepped back into the lobby, Nessa allowed the air-conditioning to cool her hot cheeks.

While Nessa had won the battle, Stephabeast had won the war. She always did, because no matter how sternly Nessa lectured herself about shrugging off Stephanie's insults and slurs, Nessa reacted. Nessa handled bad boyfriends, eccentric aunts, nosy boarders, never allowing them to disrupt her sleep or serenity. But there was something about Stephanie's smug malice that made Nessa want to chop her down to size—and today her disappointment had overcome her good sense. Now she had a bitter taste in her mouth and the clear knowledge that Stephanie would thoroughly enjoy taking her revenge.

The line had dwindled down to Mrs. Fasset, a girlhood friend of her aunts, and George Broussard, the middle-aged, overworked bartender at Mike's Brew Pub two blocks down. The morning rush was over. Thank God. Right now, Nessa couldn't have managed a crisis—because all eyes were on her. Everyone in the bank—the customers, the tellers, and Eric the guard—waited to hear her good news.

Thankfully, she had experience with ironic smiles.

And at that moment, the door of the bank opened. A man stepped just inside, a big man, blocking the intense New Orleans sunshine.

Nessa glanced up, then did a double-take. *Wow.*

She would have sworn she only mouthed the word, but Julia gave it voice. "Wow."

He was tall. Very tall. His broad shoulders tapered down to a narrow waist, and his hands were massive. One gripped a bulging leather briefcase. He wore a dark suit, a white shirt, and a red tie that should have fixed the eye, but didn't. It was his face that riveted her . . . His handsome, battered face. He reminded Nessa of Russell Crowe in *Gladiator*, broken and rising like a phoenix from the ashes of his life.

He exemplified tragedy.

He exuded power.

He looked at the small group of stunned tellers, his gaze moving from face to face, memorizing each feature, his face impassive. . . . Until he reached Nessa. There his gaze lingered, a slow interest kindling in his green eyes.

Nessa took a small, involuntary step back.

Then, with the fluid grace of an athlete, long strides and swinging arms, he continued on his way into the newly arranged office and shut the door behind him.

"I just came," Julia whispered.

"Sh!" Donna whispered, and nudged her. "You horny old broad!"

"Oh, like you didn't," Julia said.

"Yeah, but I don't talk about it."

"Whew!" Mrs. Fasset's open mouth snapped shut, and she sagged against the countertop.

Carol, who was waiting on her, nodded. "That was spectacular. Miss Dahl, who do you suppose he is? The guy who's going to give you your raise ... so to speak?"

Laughter swept the small group.

"I don't get it. What are you women talking about?" Mr. Broussard asked. "He looked like the kind of guy it takes five of us to toss out of the bar, and we're lucky if he doesn't come roaring back for more."

"Yeah, that guy's not good-looking," Eric agreed.

"He sure isn't," Julia said with enthusiasm. "He's more than good-looking."

Donna let out a long sigh of pleasure. "He's a god."

"Well, he scared the hell out of me." Lisa stood with her hand pressed against her flat chest. "I wanted to tell Eric to take out his gun and shoot him."

Nessa smiled, a raw twist to her lips. "He's the insurance investigator who's going to solve the mystery of the Beaded Bandits."

"But what's he doing in your office?" Lisa asked.

"That's not my office. That's his office." Nessa could almost taste the bitterness. "All I'm doing is assisting him in gathering the evidence."

Donna took an audible breath. Nessa shook her head at the shocked, pitying expressions directed at her. "Don't. I told you I don't hope anymore. And neither should you." She smiled at them, mocking them gently. "Because Stephabeast will be directing operations at the bank until further notice."

"Son of a bitch." Carol strung the swear words together like beads on a rosary.

Mrs. Fasset slapped Carol's wrist. "That is enough, young lady!"

Yes, Nessa thought as she made her way to Mr. Mac's office. That was the way to distract them from her sudden plunge in prospects. Point out their own.

Knowing she'd left them wallowing in their misery and human enough to enjoy it, she walked to her office.

Oh, pardon me. Mr. Mac's office.

She paused in the open doorway. "Mr. Mac? I'm Nessa Dahl. I'm to assist you with your investigation."

Mr. Mac looked up from the files he had scattered across his desk, scrutinized her, looking for fault where she knew there was none. "Come in," he said. "Shut the door behind you."

She did as she was told, cynically aware that she'd dressed the part of an executive to play the part of a sycophant.

"Sit down." He indicated the chair before the desk.

Her resentment at his command was savage and surprising. She had been disappointed too many times to take this setback with her usual equanimity.

What was she going to tell her aunts? And the boarders—oh, God, she'd told all the boarders she expected a promotion. So many people to bear witness to her failure . . .

"Miss Dahl." Mr. Mac said her name so sharply she jumped.

"Yes, sir." She would brood later. For now, she focused on him.

His eyes were so richly green, his hair so dark, his face so unabashedly masculine, he should have been handsome. But he looked more like a street thug than an insurance investigator. The guy was probably thirty-six years old, and probably six-foot-three or -four. He wore his dark hair in a short military cut. At some point in his past, his face had been used as a battering ram. An expensive suit had been altered to fit him perfectly, yet nothing could conceal the heavily muscled shoulders and arms. When he turned his head, she could see a scar almost hidden along his jawline, as if some skilled surgeon had done repairs. He wore his hair combed to one side with a drape of bangs over his forehead, but white scars mottled the skin along his hairline. It looked as if someone had knocked him down and kicked him—and as big as he was, she didn't want to run into the guy who'd done it.

No wonder the older tellers swooned and young Lisa shivered. When he watched Nessa as he did now, with eyes as green and cold as glacial ice, she wondered what work he'd done before taking the mundane job of insurance investigator. Put a machine gun in his hands, and this guy looked like the Valentine's Day massacre come to life.

When he spoke, his voice was deep and rough, as if he had a cold—or that beating had done damage to his throat. "I have heard that tact is the ability to tell a person to go to hell and make him look forward to the trip."

Whatever she'd expected, that wasn't it. She blinked at him, then said cautiously, "So I've heard."

"And I've been told in no uncertain terms I don't have that ability."

She hated to agree after an acquaintance of thirty seconds, but as abrupt as he was, she guessed he was right.

"That's why you've been tapped to help me with

this investigation. You're known for your ability to handle difficult people."

"I'm to handle you?" *Bitchy, Nessa. It's not his fault you can't fight your way up the food chain.*

He lifted his eyebrows as if her response surprised him. "I'm not difficult. It's other people who are."

She almost laughed. Not difficult? Perhaps not. Demanding. Intelligent. Intense. She suspected he was all of those things and more. If she remembered that, she could handle him.

But just once, she wished someone would take the trouble to handle her.

"You are familiar with the crimes, aren't you?" he asked.

"Pretty much everyone who lives here is familiar with the Beaded Bandits."

"I thought so, but you looked so perturbed, I thought perhaps I'd confused you."

"Not at all. I was . . ." What could she say? "I wondering how an investigator from somewhere North—"

"Philadelphia."

"Of course. From Philadelphia, discovered I was known for my ability to handle people."

"That's why they call me an investigator." He delivered the line deadpan, as if he didn't know he was funny—or as if he had no sense of humor.

Oh, dear. "Where would you like to start?"

"I need to see the banks here in the city where the crimes occurred. I've watched the videos, but nothing is the same as walking up the steps, standing inside, and surveying the situation. I assume I'll see the Mardi Gras celebration?"

"You won't be able to get away from it." *In fact, you're alone in the city. Come to the party at the Dahl House tonight.* The words hovered on her tongue. Every hospitable instinct urged her to speak. But an innate caution stopped her. The party was famous, fun, overwhelming, with friends dropping in and leaving all evening long. But to Nessa it seemed as if Jeremiah Mac would move through the crowd like a black hole and suck all the life from the party.

With his hands full of files, he went to the cabinet and opened the top drawer.

Well. Stephabeast might consider Nessa his secretary, but apparently he did not. Nessa tested him. "Would you like me to get you some coffee?"

"When we go out, we'll stop at Starbucks."

She had been tense; sitting here watching a man work relaxed her to no end. "This is New Orleans. We'll stop at Deaux." Oh! And she liked directing him, too.

"As you say." He placed the manila folders in their proper position. "Are you familiar with the other branches?"

"Certainly. There's the occasional emergency that requires me to visit them to help out."

"I want to interview all the tellers who were robbed."

"This morning?"

"Of course."

"I'll need to schedule them."

"Pick some place neutral. Deaux, if you like it." He shut the drawer and faced her. "Then I need to talk to the policeman in charge of the investigation."

"That would be Chief Cutter."

"You know him."

"He's an old friend of the family."

He nodded as if that confirmed some perception he held of her. "I was told you knew everyone in New Orleans."

She was tense again. "Who told you that?"

"Is it true?"

"Yes, but . . ." But it was almost spooky how well he knew her, as if he'd been studying her from afar.

"Then I chose my associate wisely."

Associate. She was flattered. Yet she wanted to question him further, to find out who'd talked to him about her. But he'd already proved he wouldn't answer her queries if he didn't wish to. She supposed that was the investigator part of his job; he had to protect his sources.

But what sources would talk so freely about her?

"So wherever we go, you'll do the talking?" he asked.

"I will." When he looked at her as he did now, as if he knew what color panties she was wearing, the hair rose on the back of her head. She stood, a quick, uncomfortable leap to her feet. "I'll make the calls right now."

"Do it here."

No wonder he needed someone to help him out. He was the oddest, most abrupt man she'd ever met. Furthermore, although he worked while she made the calls, unloading his briefcase, loading DVDs into the new changer that had been placed there for his convenience, she was quite sure he was eavesdropping. Why, she didn't know. Calling the banks and sweet-talking the managers into releasing their employees for an hour was not that interesting. Nor were her calls to the tellers who had gone on to other jobs. When she put down the phone, she felt on edge. "We're set. Do we need to tell anybody we're leaving?"

"No."

She waited, but apparently Jeremiah Mac saw no reason to explain himself—to her or to anyone.

Well, all right.

"I'll get my purse, Mr. Mac."

"Call me Jeremiah."

"All right, Jeremiah." Stephabeast would hate that Nessa called him by his first name. She would hate that Nessa could leave during bank hours. She would hate that Nessa no longer reported to her—and she wouldn't say a word. Mr. MacNaught himself had demanded Nessa's cooperation.

Nessa found herself liking this assignment.

She got her purse out of her desk—the desk she'd said farewell to this morning, the one that sported an invisible and apparently unbreakable ball and chain—and with a cheerful wave at the tellers, walked across the lobby and out of the bank, Jeremiah Mac on her heels.

The heat and humidity had intensified. The street was getting busy. In the distance Nessa could hear the roar of the endless party on Bourbon Street. "Let's go to the corner. We can catch a cab there."

Jeremiah walked a few steps away, then stopped to look back at the bank. "It looks like a house."

"You would be right, sir." Nessa listened in amusement as her Southern accent strengthened in response to the plain, flat notes of Jeremiah's Yankee voice. "This branch of Premier Central has a history. It was

originally built before the War between the States by
the prosperous Steve Williams family. The Williamses,
being a New Orleans family of proper sentiment,
backed the Confederacy, and by the time the war
ended, their fortune had vanished."

"It pays to back the winning side," Jeremiah said
without inflection.

"So it does, although some would say honor and integrity are more important than winning."

"The some who say that—they've never held the
shit end of the stick."

An involuntary gust of amusement caught her by
surprise, and she shook with laughter.

He watched her. "Right?"

"You most definitely are right." So while he gave off
the aura of wealth, at one time, he'd been poor. Poor
enough to understand how poverty could grind one
down, trap one in a dead-end job, and eat away at one's
confidence until that person feared to make a move because disaster loomed so high.

"What would you do if you had to make the decision between honor and a meal on the table?" he asked.

She thought of her aunts, and the tight ball of worry
in her stomach twisted tighter. "I'd feed my family. But
don't tell anyone I said so."

"The Civil War is long over."

"The War between the States," she corrected. "And
it isn't over here."

He looked down at her. Just looked, and she caught
a sudden glimpse of how those long-ago Southern
belles must have felt when the conquering Yankee
troops marched into town. "Mardi Gras keeps the cabs
busy. We won't get one standing here. Let's go up to

Esplanade Avenue—it borders the French Quarter, and we've got a better chance." She walked.

He followed. "You were telling me about the history of the bank."

"Right." She slid off her jacket and wished for a breeze. "A wealthy carpetbagger, a Mr. Frederick Vycor, bought the house next. He lived there for eighteen years, and it was he who turned the lower floor of the house into a bank. He built the vault to hold the fortune he collected by foreclosing on war widows and their children. He grew paranoid about his safety and would lock himself in with his money at night."

"A legend."

"Maybe. But as it turned out, Mr. Vycor was right to be paranoid. One morning he didn't make his appearance in the bank. When the browbeaten workers finally unlocked the vault, they found him inside, bludgeoned to death." She lowered her voice to a mysterious hush. "Money was scattered across the floor. But not a dime was missing." She had told the story before, and she told it well.

But rather than the usual expressions of horror and surprise, Jeremiah again stopped and looked back at the bank, studying every inch of its structure. "Then one of two things happened. He let his attacker in. That's the most likely scenario. Or he built an escape hatch, and someone found their way in."

"Fine. Ruin a great tale," she muttered.

"It's a tale that's impossible to ruin." He lowered his voice to the same mysterious hush she'd used. "Because no matter what the means of his demise, his greedy ghost still haunts the vault."

"You've already heard this one?" she asked, disappointed.

"I already know how to play this game."

She laughed. "I am properly abashed. And yes, his ghost does haunt the vault. I've been told an encounter is unforgettable, because at the time of his death he weighed four hundred pounds and smoked Cuban cigars."

"And indulged in wild sex?"

"In the vault? No, I never heard that."

"So it's a virgin vault?"

If she wasn't careful, she would come to like this Yankee. "New Orleans would have liked him better if he had indulged in wild sex—of any kind. We understand dissipation. No one understands a man who chooses to separate himself from his kind to better justify his cruelties."

"Was he cruel?"

"Widows and children were left homeless on his behest." A fate she intimately feared, if not for herself, for her great-aunts. "He owned property all over this city, beautiful homes, some of them—and he slept in a vault. He was a vampire."

"Another creature for which New Orleans is famous." Jeremiah obviously knew his Anne Rice. "But why do you say that?"

"He sucked the life from people."

"Dramatic." Jeremiah condemned her with one word.

"I'm not being dramatic. Think about it. Families with their hopes and dreams crushed, their respectability destroyed, their security stolen . . . what kind of monster ruthlessly steals those qualities from a family?"

"One who owns a well-run bank and recognizes the need to foreclose when, and only when, payments have been consistently missed?" Jeremiah suggested.

"Mr. Vycor allowed for no late payments. Ever. Even the CEO of Premier Central gives people a second chance on their loans. Of course," she added reflectively, "those chances are mandated by the government."

"And it's bad publicity for the bank if he seizes property without allowing a second chance."

They reached Esplanade. The traffic was thicker, pedestrians strolled the streets looking at the houses, and cabs raced past. A street musician played warm, rich jazz on his trumpet, and collected tips from the passing tourists.

"Do you know Mr. MacNaught?" She picked out a cab, smiled at the driver, and waved her arm.

The cab screeched to a halt.

"Yes." Jeremiah held the door while she climbed in.

When he'd settled himself beside her, she asked, "Is he as ruthless as they say?"

"Yes."

"Great," she said gloomily. "I work for the devil."

He turned sideways in the seat and examined her until she wanted to squirm in discomfort. "Yes," he said. "In this case, I believe you do."

Six

"It was three years before the flood. Before Hurricane Katrina." Melissa Rosewell accepted the cup of decaf Jeremiah set down in front of her with a nervous smile of thanks. "I'd never been robbed before. For that matter, never been robbed since. But the bank trains tellers in what we should do. Cooperate with the thieves. If possible, activate the silent alarm. Don't get killed. I really paid attention to the last part."

Nessa sat across the tiny table in the Deaux Bakery, not far from the Barracks Street branch of Premier Central, and divided her interest between Melissa and Jeremiah.

They were as different as two people could be.

Melissa was beautiful, full-figured, black, and a native of Shreveport, Louisiana. She had a bit of a lisp, large, soft brown eyes, and she was hugely pregnant. She was the first teller ever robbed by the Beaded Bandits, and had agreed to this interview not because she liked being the center of attention, but because Nessa had asked her to.

She most certainly hadn't done it for Jeremiah.

Jeremiah, stern, big, and oozing authority, made Melissa shift in her seat, and look everywhere but at him.

So Nessa reached across and patted Melissa's hand. "You bet, honey. Staying alive is the most important part of the job."

Melissa focused on Nessa. "That afternoon, having to stay alive was the farthest thing from my mind."

"Do you remember what afternoon it was?" Jeremiah shoved Nessa's café au lait across the table at her and placed a plate of beignets between the two women.

Nessa inhaled deeply. The scent of chicory, warm fried dough, and powdered sugar made her close her eyes in delight.

She opened them to find Jeremiah scrutinizing her, his eyes mesmerizing in a way she had not expected from the conservative Yankee investigator.

Why did he look at her as if he knew her?

Melissa's voice broke them apart. "It was just a typical Friday afternoon during Mardi Gras, packed with people draped in purple, green, and gold beads. Half of them wore fancy costumes, the other half were almost naked. I . . . I know it's not true, but it seemed as if all of them were drunk. For sure they were all desperate to withdraw a few bucks before the weekend. So I didn't think anything when *those* two people stepped into the bank."

"I've been there." Nessa patted Melissa's hand again. "Friday afternoon during Mardi Gras. What a mess."

"I don't like to work Fridays during Mardi Gras

anymore." Closing her eyes, Melissa rubbed her lower back as if it ached.

"Are you uncomfortable, Mrs. Rosewell?" Jeremiah asked. "Because we can do this later."

Melissa put her hand back into her lap. "No. Please. I always felt guilty because . . . because I let it happen."

"You did *not* let it happen." Jeremiah broke off a piece of the warm beignet, shook off the mound of powdered sugar, and offered it to her. "I've seen the security videos. You behaved exactly as you should have."

Melissa cautiously took it, then her gaze shifted to Jeremiah and stuck there. "Thank you, Mr. Mac. You're sweet."

Nessa blinked. Her instincts told a lot of things about Jeremiah Mac. That he was gifted, grim, with surprising flashes of humor. That the Beaded Bandits were doomed, because he would never let up until he caught whomever he was after. That his authority was absolute.

But sweet? No.

He performed the same service for Nessa, shaking off the beignet's excess powdered sugar and offering it to her.

She took it easily, smiling at Melissa, trying to convey an ease with the situation when, in fact, Jeremiah Mac put her on edge. He observed Melissa, the city, and Nessa with vivid curiosity, as if everything were new and different. And of course, New Orleans was unique, but Nessa would have thought that in his line of work he'd interviewed many crime victims and acquired and discarded many assistants. What did he seem so poised and eager to hear?

"I want to help you if I can," Melissa said. "I want you to catch them. And yeah, I know that note changed my life, and they didn't do any harm, and they only asked for a little money, but those guys—well, I mean, I think they're guys—they scared me."

"Then I want you to tell me every detail of that first robbery. Everything you can think of, no matter how minor, no matter how silly. Everything you thought and did, anything that's occurred to you since. I want to hear it all. Sometimes it's the littlest element that solves the crime." Jeremiah shifted forward.

Nessa thought if he looked at Melissa with half the intensity he'd used on Nessa, Melissa would gladly share every detail of the crime, her thoughts, and her life, plus make him dinner and give him the keys to the city.

And, in fact, Melissa sat up straight, as if he'd cured her backache. "When they came in, I didn't have any inkling of trouble. The two guys wore dresses—"

"What made you think they were guys?" Jeremiah pushed her to reveal every detail.

"They were tall. I'd say six feet, maybe a little less, and they walked stiffly, as if they weren't easy with their bodies, so I figured it was a shift change at the April in Paris nightclub on the corner, because why else would the drag act be on the streets then?"

Nessa had seen the clips on TV. They were grainy, shot at a bad angle, and in black-and-white. But she was used to Daniel's polished professionalism, and in a town where a lot of men made a good living dressing up as women, only the best worked at April in Paris.

"One man was wearing a purple silk gown that swept the floor, and there was a bustle, you know, that stuck out over his butt as he walked." Melissa gestured as she showed them the wiggle at the back, then lifted her hands to her head. "He wore this swooping broad-brimmed hat—huge, I don't know, twenty inches across—and tilted over his eyes, with a black veil that swept from the brim all the way down to his chest. He looked strict, like a guy who wields the whip. He was so dramatic, I almost didn't notice the other one."

"What was he doing? The one in the purple gown?" Jeremiah brushed his hand over his forehead, pushing the bangs away, exposing the scars Nessa had glimpsed there.

"He hung around by the door," Melissa answered.

Jeremiah was testing Melissa's memory, Nessa realized, making her recall every detail.

"Okay, what about the other one?" Nessa asked.

"The other wore a simpler costume, long powder blue silk dress, bits of gold stuck here and there." Melissa gestured at her bosom and her ears. "The look was more like a debutante. Both guys wore elbow-length gloves."

"Oh." That filled in an important element for Nessa. Men's hands were distinctly different from women's, and gloves covered a hundred sins. "It sounds like a prom a hundred years ago."

"Yes, exactly!" Melissa leaned back in her chair as if relieved to have conveyed so much so accurately. She took a sip of her decaf, ate a bite of beignet. "It was hot that day, humidity was eighty or ninety percent."

"Like today," Jeremiah said.

"Sort of like today." Melissa frowned as she glanced outside, and she rubbed her swollen belly as if calming the turbulence inside. "I couldn't figure out how those guys could stand the corset and the petticoats. But I was going to a party that night, so I forgot about them and concentrated on three things—remaining civil, doing the transactions correctly and quickly, and the number of minutes, fourteen, until closing time."

"Exactly right." Jeremiah gave his approval freely.

"The guy in blue waited for probably a dozen people in front of him to collect their money and leave. He was very patient, didn't huff and puff like some customers do. When his chance came to be helped by the first available cashier, he indicated he'd wait for me."

Nessa swallowed her coffee too fast and burned her tongue. "Did you recognize him at all?"

"No, my only thought was that this guy knew me and I didn't have a clue who he was. You know how sometimes that makes for difficulties—some people want me to remember them, even if I've served them once three months ago." Melissa grimaced. "Not to mention Mr. Dewy Debutante wore an elaborate mask of feathers and sequins that covered his face from his forehead to his chin."

"A mask?" Jeremiah turned positively dour.

Nessa and Melissa exchanged glances.

"Everybody dresses up for Mardi Gras," Melissa said.

"The robbery caused a change in policy at the bank. The security guards at the bank don't allow customers to wear masks anymore," Nessa explained gently.

"The possibility of robbery—" Jeremiah began

"Had occurred to us, but had never happened," Nessa finished.

Jeremiah inclined his head. He knew this, obviously, but was still irked.

Nessa pushed the plate toward him. "It's a crime to come to Deaux's and not try the beignets, Mr. Mac."

"I don't eat doughnuts." He sounded impatient. Abrupt.

She raised her eyebrows at him, and allowed her tone to grow softer, slower, more Southern. "Bless your heart, Mr. Mac. They're not doughnuts. They're beignets."

"What's the difference?"

"Try them and find out," she said.

He examined the two women, Melissa with her hands resting on her belly, and Nessa wearing a slight, fake smile. Something about them must have penetrated his thick Yankee hide, because he growled, actually growled in annoyance, and popped a piece in his mouth.

He choked.

"Be careful with that powdered sugar, Mr. Mac," Melissa advised.

He caught his breath and chewed.

Beignets were nothing more than deep-fried pastry dough covered with powdered sugar. . . . And nothing less than heaven. He finished one still-warm beignet and started on another.

Nessa lifted three fingers at the cook behind the counter, and more dough went in the fryer. The second batch landed on the table while he was licking his fingers.

He looked up at Nessa. "All right. They're wonderful. Satisfied?"

"We like to feed our men." Nessa was still drawling out the accent. "We find that makes them almost civilized."

"I am always almost civilized," he answered.

Melissa covered her laugh with her hand.

"Now that I've been handled . . . I was handled, was I not?" he asked. "I'd like to hear the rest of Mrs. Rosewell's story."

Melissa wiped the smile from her face. Cleared her throat. "Mr. Dewy Debutante stepped up to my window, laid his beaded evening bag on the counter, opened the clasp, and pulled out a deposit slip, and I thought, *Oh, good. I'll glance at his name and refresh my memory.* So I was chatting with him."

"What did you say?" Jeremiah ate another beignet, but more slowly.

"Something like, *Wonderful costume. Big night for all of us. Are you going to a party tonight?* You know, the usual." Melissa and Nessa nodded at each other. "He didn't say anything, but I thought he was smiling."

"Why did you think that?" Jeremiah asked.

"His eyes were sort of twinkling." Melissa seemed to remember that he wanted the details, and she added, "Blue eyes. They were both white guys."

"According to the experts who have studied the tapes, both were white guys, neither were more than six feet," Jeremiah confirmed.

"He pushed the deposit slip at me. It was one of ours, and I looked for a name, but there wasn't one, and instead of numbers, there was this message printed on it. Big type, easy to read. My first thought when I saw that it said, "'Dear Miss Melissa,'" was that I'd been right, this guy did know me, and I still didn't know him." Melissa continued to hold the cup, but now her hand trembled.

Nessa started to comfort her, but Jeremiah caught her eye and shook his head.

"What did the note say?" His voice was smooth, unobtrusive.

"Dear Miss Melissa," she recited, *"That particular shade of peacock blue you're wearing today compliments your beautiful brown eyes and the warmth of your skin. The blouse in the window of Chere's on Madison Street would look marvelous on you—get it and your Mr. Rosewell will be unable to take his eyes off you. He has been very lonely since his wife died, but with a little nudge, he could count himself a lucky man to court such a sweet girl as you."*

"You were Melissa Jude then." His words seemed innocuous, but both women clearly heard the accusation.

"Yes, but I swear, Brad and I hadn't dated or talked or anything. There was no reason for those guys to think—"

"And yet, here you are, married to Mr. Rosewell," Jeremiah said.

"I liked him. Sure I did. He's a good man. But he was the bank manager. I was a teller. He hadn't noticed me. Or at least, I hadn't thought so." Melissa put a hand to her cheek. "But as soon as he realized I'd been robbed, he was there for me. He made them send me to the hospital—"

"You were shot?" Nessa hadn't remembered that.

"No, but when I flung myself on the floor, I cracked my head on the desk. I was bleeding, the cops were yelling at me, and Brad yelled back at them."

"So the police thought you were in on the robbery," Jeremiah said.

"I wasn't," Melissa answered him fiercely. "Once the

contents of that note were released, I was humiliated. Can you imagine . . . well, no, *you* can't." She turned to Nessa. "Can you imagine having a secret crush and having the whole city find out about it? Do you know Chere sent me that blouse, then released the information to the press? It was a nightmare. Every time Brad said anything to me, every time I glanced his way, every time I wore a blue blouse, everybody grinned and nudged each other. We barely looked at each other for the next year. *God.*" She put her hands over her eyes.

"What happened?" Nessa asked.

"The second robbery." Nessa didn't remember, but clearly Melissa recalled every bitter detail. "The gossip had died down, then the next year, the Beaded Bandits struck again at a different bank. That changed things. There was another note to another teller giving fashion advice and demanding money. They got away again, but it was much more exciting—the police caught a guy wearing one of the gowns, the news reported that one of the Bandits was caught. It turned out the guy had an alibi—he'd been drinking in Norton's all day, was too drunk to have committed the crime, and he told the police he'd found the costume in a Dumpster behind House of Blues. They checked, and the other costume was in there. When all that happened, I couldn't take it anymore. I quit to go back to college." Melissa smiled. "That night, the doorbell rang, I opened the door, and there was Brad. He asked if I gave a damn about the gossip. I said no, and we went out." Her eyes were clear as she looked at Jeremiah. "That's all."

Nessa knew Brad Rosewell. She liked him and

Melissa. She had attended their wedding. But for the first time, she realized what the note meant. "So you liked Mr. Rosewell. You hadn't told him. You hadn't told *anyone*?"

"No one," Melissa agreed.

"How did the Beaded Bandits *know*?" Nessa asked.

Jeremiah's face looked hard, unyielding, like one of the masks he deplored. "They timed everything perfectly. They came during the busiest time of the week, when everyone was distracted and wanted to go home. They wore costumes that both disguised them and, during Mardi Gras, attracted no attention. They deliberately picked Melissa and used her secret to slow her reaction time. Everything about the robbery proves they coolly plotted each move—and they observed Melissa enough to know what she believed was secret. Everyone in New Orleans seems to be under the impression, because the thieves don't steal large amounts and they write adorable little notes, that they are spontaneous. They are not." For one second, his mask cracked.

He was coldly furious. He took these robberies personally.

Interesting. Nessa wouldn't have thought an insurance investigator would care so much.

"Mrs. Rosewell, tell Miss Dahl what else the note said," he prompted.

"Please, without making a fuss, deposit $1,192.45 in small bills in the bag," Melissa recited.

"I vaguely remember hearing that is the most money taken," Nessa said.

"The amount of money demanded has not escalated. In fact, the other robberies were for less." Mac's frustration sounded like ground glass.

"I didn't know what to do. I was so stunned. I didn't think to hit the alarm button." Melissa pushed the coffee away. "I didn't do anything, just stood there. Mr. Debutante reached into his purse. He pulled out a tiny silver pistol and he pointed it at me. I just . . . I thought . . . I still stood there, and the guy said, 'Now.'"

Fascinated, Nessa hitched her chair forward. "What did his voice sound like?"

"Low. Husky."

"Accent?" Jeremiah asked.

"Sir, *you* have an accent," Melissa snapped.

Nessa smothered a grin.

Jeremiah said nothing, waiting patiently for the young women to get back on track.

"I didn't notice an accent," Melissa said, "but I was scared. No one realized what was going on. The line was as long as ever. The other cashiers were busy. Cooper, our security guard, was dealing with the usual cranks who had arrived too late to get in, turning them away at the door. The other transvestite . . . the other transvestite held a much larger pistol in the folds of her skirt. His skirt. The skirt. Mr. Debutante said, 'Don't push the silent alarm. Don't make me shoot you. Just put the money in my bag.' I knew if he shot me at this range, even with that tiny pistol, I would die. I didn't want to die. So I put the deposit slip in the machine, typed in $1,192.45, popped open my drawer, and pulled a handful of hundreds out." She gripped the edge of the table. "The guy told me to count it out exactly. Didn't want more, didn't want less. I was counting, 'One hundred, two hundred . . .' And all the while

I kept thinking that the silent alarm button was right there by my knee, and if I scooted over a little, I could set it off. It was like he knew what I was thinking. He made a tiny circle with the pistol and said, 'Don't do it.'" She stopped, gasping.

Scooting over, Jeremiah put his arm around Melissa. "Take deep breaths. It's over. You did the right thing. You're alive, and you're helping with the investigation. When you get scared, think of that."

"I have nightmares sometimes," Melissa admitted.

"Revenge will cure your nightmares. I promise."

Nessa almost jumped when he smiled into Melissa's face.

Wow. He could turn on the magic. And . . . sweet? Yeah. Maybe sweet.

Melissa visibly calmed. "I would like revenge." She smiled a little and straightened. "This is when it got really weird."

"As opposed to being robbed by well-dressed transvestites." Jeremiah was still smiling.

"Right. I said to Mr. Debutante, 'I really need this job.' And Mr. Debutante said, 'You need to finish college.' He sounded stern, like my mother. I finished counting out the cash, put it in an envelope, and shoved it across the counter. He took the money, said, 'You don't want to work as a teller your whole life. You might run into someone like me again.' When he said, 'Now step back from the window,' he glanced behind him, so I pushed the silent alarm, screamed, and threw myself on the floor." Melissa glanced over Nessa's shoulder. "Brad!"

"Are you done questioning my wife?" Brad Rosewell spoke from behind Nessa.

She heard the anxiety hidden behind the hostility in his tone, and as she turned, she said lightly, "Almost done. I don't think we've taxed her too much. Have you met Mr. Mac?"

Jeremiah rose and the two men shook hands, measuring each other.

They were, in one way, almost identical. Both were tall, distinguished-looking men in dark suits, white shirts, red ties. Both sported an air of authority, but there the resemblance ended.

Brad Rosewell looked like a bank manager, a man who understood numbers and who worked well with employees and customers.

Jeremiah Mac looked like a thug in a designer suit.

"Mrs. Rosewell has been very helpful," Jeremiah said. "Won't you sit down while we finish up?"

Brad slid a chair close to his wife and took her hand.

"I'm fine," she said. "Really."

Brad didn't relax, but leaned toward Jeremiah. "I want you to understand, I want those Beaded Bandits caught. At the same time, I hate rehashing that day. I almost lost my job, and worse, I almost lost Melissa."

"What do you mean, you almost lost your job?" Nessa asked.

Mac sat back and crossed his arms over his chest.

"That night, I got a phone call from Mr. MacNaught. That guy is psychotic about losing money. I mean, he's a banker, we're all psychotic about money, but he was over the edge. He pounded on me, asked me all kinds of questions." Melissa rubbed Brad's arm as he talked. "I know he'd already received the security tape from the bank, so I don't know what he thought he could find out, but I thought for sure he was going to fire me."

"Because your bank got robbed?" Nessa was incredulous.

" 'The buck stops here,' he said." Brad blotted his forehead with a napkin. "Every Mardi Gras, I think, *Please don't let them hit my bank again.*"

"Mr. MacNaught sent me to find the culprits, so with your wife's help, you don't need to worry anymore." Sitting in the shadowy coffee shop, Jeremiah looked like a stone carving.

"Thank you, sir." Brad Rosewell stood and shook Jeremiah's hand again. "I'm glad to hear that." Putting his hand under Melissa's arm, he hoisted her to her feet. "Come on, honey, I'll take you home."

Jeremiah got to his feet also. "One more question, Mrs. Rosewell. Is there other information you want to pass on? Anything at all?"

She took a breath. Looked at her husband. At Jeremiah's stern face. And shook her head. "No. Nothing."

Seven

The noise, scents, and appearance of the New Orleans streets spilled into the cramped lobby of the NOPD. Accents of every kind assaulted Mac's ears—French, Italian, Spanish, and Cajun. People smelled of sweat, perfume, and beer. They wore elaborate costumes. They wore masks. One guy wore tennis shoes and nothing else. A woman cried because her pocket had been picked. Another cried because she'd been caught picking pockets. A line of a dozen people stood waiting to talk to a frazzled-looking police officer. Policemen moved among the crowd, coercing, comforting, cajoling.

"They need a bigger building," Mac said.

Nessa snorted. "They're lucky to have this. Since the hurricane, most of the fire departments are working out of trailers.

"Now, here's what we're going to do." Nessa slid her sunglasses off her nose and hung them on the V of her blouse. "I'm going to get you in to talk to the chief of police. Chief Cutter's been involved in the investigation, and he's taken a lot of heat for not making any arrests."

"I would hope so." Mac removed his sunglasses and placed them in the sunglass case in the left inner pocket of his suit jacket, and used the excuse to look at Nessa.

He wouldn't have thought it possible, but she was prettier in person than on the video, with more charisma and a soft, warm voice that made his libido race like a Chevy 427. She reminded Mac of sex performed in the sunshine, of passion before a roaring fire, of love. . . . Pure, glorious, everlasting love.

She continued, "So you can ask questions, but when you do, smile. You can talk to whoever you want, but if I nudge you or kick you or step on your foot, you smile."

"Right. Smile," he repeated.

She could make any man lose his head, and Mac figured she did—once a year without fail.

She didn't suspect him of being anything but what he said, a guy investigating the Beaded Bandits, and she gave him her complete assistance. Why wouldn't she? Being in control of the investigator gave her the illusion of being in control of the investigation.

"I'm sure we could have gotten more information out of Melissa Rosewell if you hadn't been standing there with that big ol' stone face."

"Mrs. Rosewell was very helpful," he answered austerely.

Austere was a good description for him, he felt, especially in New Orleans during the wild celebration that was Mardi Gras.

"But she didn't give us that last juicy little detail because you made her feel dumb," Nessa lectured.

"All right. I got it. I'll smile!" Nessa was irritating, like a mosquito buzzing around his head—but he also thought she was right. Melissa Rosewell had had something else to tell them, and between her husband and Mac, she'd faltered.

"Practice your smile on me," she suggested.

He manipulated his lips in that unfamiliar upward tilt.

She studied him quizzically. "Maybe you'll get better with practice."

This was their last stop of the day. So far, they'd visited every bank that had suffered a robbery, met the managers, met the tellers, and eaten lunch. Now Mac followed her through the lobby to the long line that led to the desk sergeant.

Officer Ernie Rippon stood behind bulletproof glass. He looked ready for retirement, and more than that, he looked as if he'd heard every story and believed none of them. His sagging, bulldog face sagely observed every person who stepped up. He handed out forms, gave directions, and called for assistance with quiet efficiency.

But when Mac and Nessa reached the front of the line, Nessa smiled at him as if he were her best friend. Of course. "Ernie, you are looking debonair today."

Ernie glared, then laughed. "Yeah, chère, I look debonair today. You can't find a more debonair officer on the force. But that's because"—he glared again from bloodshot eyes—"it's Mardi Gras!"

"Are the tourists crazier than normal?" she asked sympathetically.

"No. Yes. I don't know." Ernie observed Mac in one

sweeping glance. "You pick yourself up a tourist? Because I have to tell you, Miss Dahl, he's a big one."

"I didn't pick him up. He was given to me." She injected amusement and friendship in her tone. "This is Mr. Jeremiah Mac. Through no fault of his own, he is an insurance investigator."

Mac nodded a greeting.

"Welcome to our fair city, Mr. Mac." Ernie might be world weary, but he was courteous. "Are you here to celebrate or investigate?"

"He's here to investigate," Nessa said firmly.

"Let the man talk," Ernie said.

"No, he's not allowed." She put her hand on Mac's arm as if holding him back. "Also through no fault of his own, he's a Yankee."

Ernie laughed until he coughed, a smoker's hack that sounded as if he were bringing up a lung. "I do not kill Yankees for less than a misdemeanor."

Nessa laughed, too, and dug her heel into Mac's instep.

Mac smiled.

"Mr. Mac wishes to see the tapes and transcripts of the Mardi Gras robberies," Nessa said.

"Now?" Ernie's wide eyes bulged. "Miss Dahl, Chief Cutter hasn't got time now. After Easter, he can—"

Nessa smoothly interrupted his rant. "We can't wait until after Easter—you know that. By then there'll be another successful robbery, and the bank's insurance company will be angrier than they already are."

That made sense to Mac, but Ernie almost spat with fury. "It's not the insurance company, is it? It's that

CEO, that head of your lousy bank. He has made the chief's life miserable—"

"I know, Ernie." Nessa verbally patted Ernie's hand. "But Mr. Mac is merely the poor man who works for the insurance company, and he is very sorry to be a bother—aren't you, Jeremiah?"

"Very sorry," Mac repeated.

"But he has a job to do. And, Ernie, I promised to help him." Nessa managed to look both sorrowful and determined.

"No choice, eh?" Ernie glanced at the ever-growing line behind them. "I'll call Rav Woodland to take you back. Might as well give the boy a thrill." He winked at her. "And, chère, I'll see you tonight."

She flopped a vague hand in his direction and walked toward the door that led into the inner sanctum.

Mac didn't understand what Ernie meant about Rav Woodland until the young redheaded officer stepped into the lobby, caught sight of Nessa, and blushed all the way to the tips of his ears.

The kid was maybe twenty-one, and he was in love.

Had one of the thieves hid red hair beneath his wig?

"Rav!" Nessa stood on tiptoe and kissed his cheek. "How's your daddy?"

Mac thought she was using slang until the kid answered, "He's good, Miss Nessa. That surgery cleared the pipes and he's golfing again. How are Miss Hestia and Miss Calista?"

"Busy as always."

"That's right. Tonight's the big party!" The kid's eyes snapped with excitement as he led them through the locked door and into the depths of New Orleans law enforcement.

The big party. Nessa's big party?

Mac observed her discomforted glance at him.

Yes. Definitely Nessa's party. If ever a woman showed signs of guilt, it was Nessa.

"You see, Jeremiah, when Chief Cutter hires his officers, he tells them he's giving them a pen, a club, and a pistol, and during Mardi Gras, they're to use them all at the same time, all the time." Nessa walked backward through the maze of desks and partitions. "The first year makes them or breaks them. Isn't that right, Rav?"

"Last Mardi Gras almost killed me," Rav agreed.

Mac observed that the chaos was organized back here, with handcuffed prostitutes and criminals being led through the paperwork of arrest, and every officer writing on a stack of forms or walking rapidly toward some unknown goal or scowling intently at a computer screen.

No wonder Nessa had been eager to bring him here. She wanted him to see the relentless pace Mardi Gras forced on the police department.

"Mardi Gras madness is why no one pays attention to the Beaded Bandits. I've got it." Mac looked directly into her eyes. "But let me remind you that most thieves are not benign, and when they realize the weakness in my banks, they'll do the job and do it right. We'll be out a fortune, the insurance company will ask for my head, and the investors will scream bloody murder."

She watched him with a half smile. "*Your* banks?"

Mistake. "I represent those banks."

"Okay. Point taken," she said.

"Let me tell the chief you're here." Rav knocked on

a door and at a muffled call, leaned in to say, "It's Miss Nessa Dahl with some guy wanting to know about the Mardi Gras Robberies."

"Oh, for cripes sake. Send them in." Just like everyone from New Orleans, Chief Cutter had an accent. But if Nessa's voice was warm butter, the chief's voice was grated horseradish.

Rav backed out at a speed that told Mac how quickly that horseradish could bring tears to the eyes. "See you tonight, Miss Dahl."

Nessa performed that same vague wave she'd used on Ernie, and strode in as if she hadn't a care in the world. She walked around the desk, leaned down to the dashing forty-year-old in the police uniform, and kissed his cheek, then danced backward as he made a grab for her. "No, you don't, Chief. Last time you had an affair, your wife aimed your service pistol at you and shot a hole in your refrigerator, and I know for a fact she's been taking lessons so that next time she doesn't miss."

"But, darlin', a taste of you would be worth death." Chief Cutter had narrow brown eyes surrounded by laugh lines, a face tanned by years in the sun, and rumpled blond hair.

When he eyed Nessa seductively, Mac wanted to jerk him right out of his polished black shoes.

Odd. Every guy they'd met today had hit on her. Why did Cutter's attentions bother Mac?

Because Cutter was the kind of man with the experience and ability to entice a woman.

"That would be fine if she was satisfied with *your* death. But I'm afraid she'd want to kill me, too." Nessa put the desk between her and the chief. "I'd like you to meet Jeremiah Mac, the insurance investigator for—"

"Yeah, I heard you were coming. Take a look, Mr. Mac." Chief Cutter brusquely switched out of amiable mode. He waved a remote at the television set up in his office, hooked up to a five-disk DVD player. "Robbery number one. New Orleans, Mardi Gras. The thieves wore masks." He flicked the remote. The picture changed. "Robbery number two. New Orleans, Mardi Gras. The thieves wore latex masks that looked lifelike." He flicked the remote again. "And robbery number three, Baton Rouge, Mardi Gras. Lifelike masks again."

Mac had seen it all before. Seen it many times. But, as always, the images on the screen commanded his attention. The on-screen robbers appeared in costume, passed a note, pointed a gun, collected the cash, and disappeared into the crowd outside.

"Hurricane Katrina comes through. Wrecks the city." Chief Cutter was grim, telling the story as if he weren't sure Mac had heard about the greatest natural disaster in American history. "The first year, Mardi Gras proceeded in defiance of fate. The next year, Mardi Gras was bigger, bolder. The Big Easy was back."

"Well. At least . . . it had recovered a wisp of its old spirit." Nessa pulled up a chair and watched the screen in apparent fascination.

"Those two years, the banks saw no action," the chief said. "Then robbery number four, New Orleans, Mardi Gras. You'll recognize the bank branch on Burgundy Street, the branch that got struck the second year. The same thieves, the same MO."

"Two men, dressed as women, entered the bank and handed the teller a note demanding money"—Mac watched Nessa now, not the videos—"and giving fashion advice. Then they disappeared onto the street and they were invisible in the crowds."

"While everyone in the bank claims to be bewildered and shocked." Chief Cutter used the remote to stab at the screen. "Someone somewhere knows what's going on."

"That's what *I've* been saying," Mac said in profound satisfaction.

"Isn't robbing a bank is a federal crime?" Nessa asked—as if she didn't know.

The two men nodded.

"Why isn't the FBI involved?" Nessa looked from one to the other.

"The FBI has given some time to it, but they put a low priority on the case because of the lack of violence and the small amount of cash involved. As far as they're concerned, our robberies are about one step above a raid on a kid's piggy bank." Chief Cutter was disgusted.

"In addition," Mac said, "Agent Adams claims that when Mardi Gras rolls around, every professional criminal in the country heads for New Orleans for the easy pickings and a chance to party, and they're too busy cleaning *them* off the streets."

"That, at least, is true." Chief Cutter gestured toward the packed lobby. "When I've got every cop on the force working as many hours as I can squeeze out of them simply to keep control over the crowd and deal with the vicious crimes, it's damned hard to give these robberies top priority."

"I've heard that one before," Mac said.

"Yeah, yeah." Chief Cutter ran through the DVDs again. "I still don't know what that CEO, that piece of dog doo you work for—pardon my French, Miss Nessa—wants me to do. He has every bit of information I have."

"Good to know." Certainly Mac recognized every piece of paper he picked up. "For a piece of dog doo, he's very thorough."

"Chief. Mr. Mac knows the, um, piece of dog doo," Nessa said gently.

"Do I look like I care? What does that idiot think I'm doing here? Not solving the crime so I look stupid?" The chief's voice rose with each question.

"Mr. MacNaught's frustration is as great as your own," Mac said in a clipped tone.

"I doubt that," Chief Cutter snapped back.

Mac picked up a sheet of paper covered with scribbles going in all directions. "What's this?"

"Whenever something occurs to me about the Mardi Gras robberies, I write it down."

"Interesting stuff." Mac turned the paper back and forth as he read.

"It seems as if I'm one step away from figuring it all out, but I can't make that leap." Chief Cutter leaned back in his chair and sounded truly frustrated. "For the first couple of years, I was sure it was a couple of tourists. Then came the Baton Rouge robbery. Now I think they have to be Louisiana people."

"Because . . . ?" Mac lifted his eyebrows.

"Did you know that Baton Rouge has a Mardi Gras, Mr. Mac?" Chief Cutter asked.

"Call me Jeremiah," Mac said. "And no, until I

started studying the case, I didn't know that Baton Rouge had a Mardi Gras."

"For most of the country, Jeremiah, Mardi Gras *is* New Orleans. Not Baton Rouge, not Galveston, Texas, sure as hell not Biloxi, Mississippi." Chief Cutter stood up and paced back and forth behind his desk. "So I called in a linguistics specialist from Tulane, and put up with an hour listening to the most pompous bore in the entire world while he expounded on the number of foreign flags that have flown over the city and how the different languages formed the unique patois that is our accent today. Or some such horse pucky—pardon my French, Miss Nessa."

"What did you find out?" Nessa asked.

"That when I isolated the voices, he definitely, positively, almost completely believed they were native New Orleans speakers." The chief ran his hand through his thick blond hair, ruffling it in a way Mac thought both pretentious and potentially attractive to Nessa.

"Let *me* hear them," Nessa said.

"You bet, darlin'." Chief Cutter smiled at her and hustled over to the table. He located an iPod and earbuds.

"Can I make a copy of these?" Mac indicated the scribbled sheets of paper.

"Over there." Chief Cutter waved a distracted hand toward the printer/copy machine. "Nessa, darlin', my headphones would be better, but that scoundrel daughter of mine took them to school and left them in her locker. Or so she said. I hope she's telling the truth." He tried to help Nessa put the earbuds in.

Nessa briskly removed them from his hands. "If you

come near me, not only would your wife shoot you, but if she missed, that daughter of yours would finish the job."

"You're a hard woman, Ionessa Dahl," the chief said sorrowfully.

Mac listened as Nessa handled Cutter. Everyone in the damned police station either loved her as a niece or a girlfriend. To Mac's surprise, that irritated the crap out of him. "Assuming the thieves are New Orleans natives—what good does that do us?" he asked.

"It narrows down the number of people who could be the perps to, oh, one-point-two million." Chief Cutter peered over Mac's shoulder as he made the copies.

"They have to be oddballs to study the layouts at the bank so thoroughly and then steal such quirky amounts every year." The copies were light but serviceable.

Both Nessa and the chief laughed with varying degrees of attitude, and Cutter said, "We in New Orleans *pride* ourselves on our oddballs and eccentrics."

"I'm related to a couple of them." Nessa smiled fondly as she popped the earbuds in and started the iPod.

Mac thought of his mother and her dedication to maintaining her hard-won middle-class image, of his grandparents and their stiff-necked horror at scandal—specifically the scandal his birth had brought on them—and he tried to decide how he felt about this casual tolerance for peculiar conduct. He was not seduced; these madmen were making a fool of him. On the other hand, if he gave in to his wholehearted disapproval, was he not just like the rest of his miserable, narrow-minded family?

When he turned back to the room, Nessa sat listening to the iPod, a slight smile on her face. "What do you think?" he asked. "Are the thieves from New Orleans?"

"I think Jeannine did not get Chief Cutter's propensity for harmless curse words," she answered.

"What do you mean?" The chief snatched the iPod.

Nessa offered the earbuds. "Your daughter appears to have recorded over the thieves."

He pushed one in his ear, listened, and groaned. "Drat the girl! Where was she when she attended a party like this?"

"Probably your house." Nessa stood up.

Cutter's eyes widened. "You don't suppose that while I took Dorothy to the Bahamas to, you know, smooth things over, she had a party?"

"I don't know, Chief. She's your daughter. At that age, what would you have done?" At Cutter's stricken expression, Nessa burst into laughter. Her dancing eyes met Mac's, expecting him to share the joke.

And he had to admit, he liked the idea that the official Casanova of New Orleans had problems with his daughter.

"Do you have everything you came for, Mac?" Nessa asked.

"For the moment." He rattled the papers in his hand. "I'd like to study all Chief Cutter's thoughts and discuss them with him later."

"Sure. Anytime," Chief Cutter said. "We can do it tonight if you want."

"Tonight?" Mac asked . . . as if he hadn't already figured it out.

"At the Dahl House for the annual—" The chief stopped suddenly.

Out of the corner of his eye, Mac saw Nessa shake her head.

"Take the weekend, Jeremiah," Chief Cutter said.

"Good. I'll spend the weekend in my hotel room. Alone. Studying your notes. Chief, I'll see you . . . Monday. Have a wonderful weekend." Mac took possession of Nessa's arm. As he led her toward the door, he reflected that if all went as he planned—and things always went as he planned—before this Mardi Gras was over, he would have proved the guilt of his primary suspect.

And he would personally oversee Chief Cutter as he arrested Ionessa Dahl for the crime of organizing and directing the annual robberies of the Premier Central Banks. Then this weird obsession of his would be cured, and he could go back to being Mac MacNaught, the meanest bastard in banking.

The warm scent of Nessa's vanilla perfume rose to encircle him.

He only hoped that the arrest didn't come too soon.

Eight

Nessa and Jeremiah stepped out of the police station into the late afternoon, heavy with humidity and unseasonable heat. Only a few blocks down, Bourbon Street was in full swing, with music and screams of laughter.

"I'll get a cab." Nessa pulled out her cell phone.

"How far is it?" Jeremiah asked.

"Fifteen blocks."

"It would be faster to walk."

In one short day, he'd discovered the truths about travel within New Orleans; during Mardi Gras, cabs were hard to hail, they had to take the long way around to get anywhere, and they frequently got stuck in traffic. "You're right—the parades start at six. But we have to cross Bourbon Street to get back to the bank."

"Great." As they walked, Jeremiah loosened his tie. "How do you stand this day after day?"

Nessa didn't like his tone. She didn't like it at all. Typical Northerner. Judgmental, convinced his way was superior, and rude. So rude. At the police station, he'd bothered to smile only when she prompted her.

But as the aunts always said, "Honey, you have to make allowances. Yankees are barbarians and don't know any better."

So Nessa said pleasantly, "Stand what? The weather or the celebration?"

He glanced at the sky. Clouds were clabbering toward the west; the heat would break soon. "You can't do anything about the weather."

"Well, bless your heart." *Damn you and your shriveled, nasty-minded little self*, she meant.

But he didn't understand. Yankees never did. "How do you stand the noise? The smells? The parades blocking the streets? The constant celebration?" He observed the steady stream of policemen who led men who staggered and women draped in beads.

"It doesn't happen day after day. This is Mardi Gras."

"The weeks between Epiphany and Lent."

"The tourists come from everywhere to drink, dance, listen to the music, and, frankly, after Hurricane Katrina, New Orleans needs the revenue." The crowds got thicker, rowdier. "But my family has been here since long before the War Between the States, and we live the tradition."

"I see."

She didn't believe he did. Everything about him declared he understood nothing of celebration, or joy. She'd never seen a man so stern, so at odds with the spirit of the Big Easy.

The increasing crowds and the raucous noise made it impossible to carry on a conversation, and she was glad. Glad, because no matter how hard she justified her reluctance to invite him to the Dahl House party, a shred of guilt tugged at her conscience. Leaving a stranger to fend for himself during Mardi Gras was the antithesis of everything she'd been taught. Yet if she invited him to the Dahl party, he would cast a damper on the festivities. She'd be the one responsible for trying to make him part of the celebration, and this year, she didn't have the spirit. When she remembered how this morning she had foolishly hoped her promotion had come through at last, she knew she would need to concentrate merely to maintain a happy facade.

Taking his hand, she led him across Bourbon Street.

He seemed the sort of man who would take direction badly, but he clasped her fingers and let her forge a path.

She smiled into the crowd, touched shoulders, and said, "Excuse me." She steered clear of the gangs of obnoxious young men, dodged a spilled drink, winced when an extremely drunk woman flashed them. Scantily clad transvestites carried signs advertising their nightclub acts. Brock's Famous Dancing Monks performed their routine on the teeming sidewalks.

Nessa wanted to explain that Bourbon Street wasn't really Mardi Gras. Mardi Gras was the parties, the parades, the family time. But what was the point? Jeremiah wouldn't believe her, anyway.

She glanced back once, and found him intently observing her.

He was a very odd man. He sent a prickle down her spine and up the back of her neck, and she was *glad* she hadn't invited him to the Dahl party.

On the other side of Bourbon Street, they broke through the worst of the mob. The crowd thinned enough to hear the lone wail of an unseen musician playing sad, bluesy notes on the saxophone.

She raised her voice to be heard above the music. "Okay, Jeremiah, the bank's probably twelve blocks from here. Are you sure you don't want me to try and get a cab?"

"I can walk it if you can," he said.

The saxophone wailed a sour note. The music died, then stumbled to a start again.

"The musicians have to learn somewhere," she said, and kept walking.

The music and the noise was fading behind them, all except for the rumble of a street cleaner or . . . the sun went out, and she glanced at the sky. "Oh, no."

The rumble was thunder. The cloud was tall and black. The heat was about to break in a spectacular collision of Northern cold front and warm Gulf air. And she was stuck here with Mr. Sourpuss, who would undoubtedly be as snotty about the storm as he was about the heat and about Mardi Gras. She needed to get rid of him as rapidly as possible, and that meant cutting through a few alleys. Not the best part of New Orleans to show a tourist, but Jeremiah Mac had formed his opinion before he got off the plane.

She tried to free her hand, but he didn't let go.

Interesting. He seemed tough, not like the kind of guy who would want to hold hands. In fact, not like an insurance investigator at all. More like a bodyguard. Or a hitman.

Amused at herself, she glanced back at him.

His gaze flicked around them, observing the thinning crowds, inspecting one brawny beggar who squatted on the street corner. His gaze found her.

Rather sternly, he asked, "How often do you use this route? The area seems risky for a woman alone."

"But I have you with me." And she never told her aunts or Georgia when she walked this route, because he was right. It paid to stay alert.

She increased her pace.

He moved up beside her.

The first fat drops fell, hitting the sidewalk hard and steaming from the heat. "Bad timing," she said. "We're in for a soaking."

Faintly she heard cries of dismay from the Mardi Gras crowd. People here glanced up, grimaced, pulled out umbrellas, and hurried on their ways. The street suddenly became lonely.

All day, she'd been with Jeremiah Mac, but not alone with him. Now she glanced at him, and he was watching her.

Eric and Mr. Broussard were right; Jeremiah wasn't really handsome, but he looked like a man who always won, always succeeded, always got what he wanted. He would keep a woman safe from any threat, and demand his payment in bed. And it would be payment, with no obligations on his part. He would want no talk of love or future. He would tell no pretty lies. He'd want good sex, he'd give good sex, and he'd be gone. The man was cold as ice, and if she was going to break her long, very long, too long, almost fatal case of virtue, she wasn't going to do it with a Popsicle.

Abruptly, the rain increased. The streets grew dark. The temperature dropped.

"Let's run for it." She started forward.

Catching her arm, he used her momentum to swing her into an alley. "Or not." He shoved her onto a back step, against a door covered in peeling paint with a sign that said, CLAUDE'S AUTO PARTS—DELIVERIES RING BELL.

Instant panic set in. She felt threatened. Threatened and . . . smothered. She put out a hand to hold him off. "What? Hey, mister . . ."

"Listen." He looked out toward the street.

She heard it. Hail. Sweeping toward them, slamming into the asphalt, the tile roofs, the garbage cans. The wave of the black rain changed, became a sheet of white as chunks of ice fell from the sky, exploding on the streets.

She felt stupid. How could she have not heard that? She blinked, trying to see, but the storm was at its height, black, raging, and frothing. The freezing air nipped at the edges of her flesh, but Mac stood between her and the worst of the storm, protecting her with his shoulders, his body, his legs.

Why did she feel breathless and feminine? He wasn't her type. She'd spent the whole day not inviting him to the aunts' party. Yes, he was tall and broad shouldered, but that was no reason to suddenly feel dainty and clumsy.

She strained to see his face, but all she could see was two glittering eyes, examining her. . . .

Lightning flashed right overhead. Simultaneously, the thunder shook the ground. In the white blaze, she saw Jeremiah Mac. His features looked carved from bleak rock and stark desolation.

The light vanished.

Dark enveloped them.

He stood close, almost touching but not quite. His body radiated heat; the fine hairs on her skin lifted as if he sent an electrical current through her. She felt him flinch as hail bounced off the street and hit him. Yet he didn't move; he was like a wall, protecting her from the elements.

Chivalry. From a Yankee.

She wanted to say something, but for once her gift for meaningless Southern courtesies had deserted her. His silence was so heavy, so thick, enveloping her like a living blanket, smothering her.

Except that it wasn't really his silence that enveloped her.

It was his desire.

He wanted her and she . . . oh, *no*. She wanted him.

What was she thinking?

Okay, she wasn't thinking. She was . . . feeling. Feeling the tension rising from deep inside, taking control of her heart, her mind, her nerves. She trembled from the dampness that seeped through her jacket to her skin, from the cool air that broke the heat like a sledgehammer.

She took a long breath, trying to get control. She could smell the rain, but she could also smell him— soap and a faint scent of, um, well . . . he made her think of sex.

He must be throwing off pheromones. That was the only explanation for the way her lids fluttered and drooped, the way the blood in her veins slowed and heated, the way she bit at her lip to stop a flirtatious smile.

As if it mattered. He couldn't see her, not unless he had a cat's vision. The darkness grew blacker. The storm shattered the air, hail denting plastic garbage cans, lightning striking hard and white, thunder cracking over their heads.

He was a stranger. He was everything a Yankee could be—blunt, impatient, rude, large, bold, rough . . . all domineering male. And he made her aware, for the first time in too long, that she was a female ripe for mating.

My God, if she didn't seize control of herself, she'd soon be fluttering her fan and drawling endearments to him.

Yet her body didn't care. Her hands lifted. She was going to put her palms on his chest, see if the promises he made with his still body and his unexpected chivalry were as solid as they felt.

Then, as roughly as it started, the hail stopped. The thunder still rolled, but farther to the east. The rain continued, but after the cacophony of the hail, that seemed like silence.

She dropped her wayward hands to the clasp of her purse, hoping he hadn't noticed their journey toward his chest.

With a blast, the Southern sunlight hit the streets.

She blinked and found herself staring into a set of dark eyes.

He *scrutinized* her, stripping her down to her bare emotions. Stripped her naked—and he didn't like what he saw.

With a jolt, she realized he didn't like her. She didn't know why, but clearly he didn't.

So he was a fool, for she knew very well her own worth.

"We can go now." She stepped out from behind him.

He moved aside easily, without hesitation, and the thick sexual tension dissipated in the cool air.

It hadn't really existed. It had been the imagination of a woman who'd deprived herself of a relationship for far too long. Maybe the aunts had a point. Maybe it was time for her to get out a little. After all, dedicating herself to the bank wasn't giving her any satisfaction.

The sun went back behind the clouds. Blazed out again. Went behind the clouds. Steam rose from the street.

"We need to get back to the . . . the bank." So she could go home and get ready for the party. "The weather's not usually like this. So unsettled." In the alley, she bent down and picked up a hailstone in each hand. They were uneven, jagged, both about the size of a golf ball. She balanced them, marveled at them. "I've never seen them so big before." That sounds sexual. "I mean—" She caught herself before she could say another word.

What was it about him that made her lose her glib good sense? She had to get him back to the bank *now*. Taking one step, she slipped on the hail-covered street.

He caught her arm, held her up when she would have done an ignominious case of the splits.

She glanced up at him and he looked dangerous, like a mugger far too familiar with the streets, like a man who took what he wanted.

Then, slowly, his head turned. He looked right at the rusting Dumpster.

A man with a hat pushed low over his eyes and a scarf wrapped over his mouth stepped out. He pointed a handgun at them. At Mac. "Gimme your wallet."

Frustration hit her first.

New Orleans was really showing off her tricks.

Then rage rose in her, caught at her throat.

Her wallet? *Not even.*

Without thought, she flung the hailstones at their mugger.

He ducked.

One struck his shoulder. The other glanced off his head with satisfying thunk.

Before the mugger had recovered, Mac launched himself into the air, kicking out right at the guy.

The pistol fired.

Mac booted it out of the mugger's hand.

The mugger hit the wall behind him, hard enough to knock the air out of him.

Mac landed on his feet. Started toward him. Slipped on the hail and ended up on his butt.

He didn't curse. He got up, but the mugger wasn't waiting around to see if Mac could get in a second kick. He ran, his legs rolling out from underneath like a marionette.

Mac collapsed back onto the ground and took a deep breath.

"You okay?" She fumbled her cell phone out of her purse.

"What are you doing?" Mac asked sharply.

"Calling the police."

He caught her hand. "Don't bother. He's long gone."

"But there's a gun. They could get fingerprints—"

"And do what? Catch some drug user who is already on parole? As has been pointed out to me multiple times today, during Mardi Gras, the police don't have time to do more than herd people." With a grimace, Mac rose to his feet, then fixed his dark eyes on her. "Why in the hell did you throw those hailstones? Don't you know you're not supposed to resist a mugging?"

"Why the hell did you kick him?" She mimicked him. "Don't you know you're not supposed to resist a mugging?"

He didn't answer. He used his silence to demand an explanation, and she found herself muttering, "I hate thieves."

He laughed, a brief bark of amusement.

That startled her. She didn't know he *could* laugh. "I don't see what's so funny. I hate being robbed. I work too hard for my money to hand it over."

"You could have been hurt."

"*I* could have been hurt? What about you? *I* didn't do an imitation of Bruce Lee. Not to mention—" A tear on his jacket caught her attention. On the side, under his arm, right through the fabric. She could see light through it. "What did you do? Did you—"

The pistol had gone off. The pistol had discharged.

"Damn it, he shot you." She lifted the material.

She expected to see that the bullet had struck only the coat. Because otherwise, how was he standing?

But a red stain spread across his white shirt.

"My God, he shot you," she repeated, her voice rising. She caught at him. "Sit down. Let me—"

"It's nothing."

"Nothing? You're bleeding."

He pulled his handkerchief out of his pocket and pressed it to his side. "The bullet nicked me, that's all."

"I'll call an ambulance."

Again, as she lifted her phone to her ear, he caught her hand. "No."

"You've been shot." Didn't he understand how serious this was?

"I'll go back to my hotel and wrap it up."

"Wrap it . . . it's a gunshot wound. You can't just wrap it up!"

He was starting to look amused. "The bullet didn't even puncture an organ."

"Oh, well, then. As long as it didn't take out a kidney or anything," she said sarcastically.

"If I'd been a little quicker on the kick, he wouldn't have gotten the shot off at all."

"Shame on you! You're not up on your karate!"

He seemed to take her seriously. "I work on it three times a week, but I was in my twenties when I started lessons. I was too old to have developed the necessary speed."

She didn't understand his pigheaded insistence about not going to the hospital, but then, she never understood this stiff-upper-lip stuff. "You are such a guy." She lifted her phone, and when he would have caught her hand again, she glared. "I'm calling in a favor with the cab company. They'll figure out a way to come and get us."

He lifted his brows. "Where are we going?"

"I'm taking you to my house."

You are a dumb shit, boy.

Russell Whipple ran, aiming his steps for the spots without hailstones.

You couldn't hit your butt with both hands.

The breath seared his lungs. Sweat dribbled from under his hat and the scarf over his face.

Stop whimpering, boy, and take your lickings.

His hand throbbed from that kick. He knew plenty about broken bones, and nothing was broken, but God damn, who knew that big bastard could jump like that? And that bitch—she'd hit him hard enough with that hailstone to cut his head.

You clumsy little shit, you can't do anything right.

He took a chance and glanced behind him.

He was alone. Well, except for a couple of tourists wandering along, looking lost, and a busboy smoking at the back door of a restaurant.

Panting, Russell leaned against the wall, pulled off the hat, used the scarf to wipe the sweat off his face, and made himself relive the scene.

It had started when he caught a glimpse of Jeremiah MacNaught.

He hadn't believed it. He thought for a moment that he'd been concentrating on him so hard, his mind had conjured him up. But there he was, walking along, head and shoulders above the tourists. Then the crowd had parted, and Russell saw who held him by the hand.

Ionessa Dahl.

Mugging them had been a whim, a whim brought on by too much work and too little sleep. He hadn't planned it.

You little shit, you're a screwup.

But his revenge on Mac was perfectly designed. He'd spent months putting everything in place, and the fact that Mac was in town. . . . Well, one more plan had to be implemented.

Because the way Russell saw it, Mac had to die.

This time, he would stay dead.

Nine

If Mac had planned it, it couldn't have worked out better. He was stepping out of a cab at the Dahl House, assisted by Ionessa Dahl herself.

He let her pay the driver, then slip her arm around his back and help him up the front walk.

He appraised the house as he walked. No wonder the thing was on the National Registry. It looked like the old mansions in Philadelphia, the kind he'd visited while earning his way through college.

The wraparound front porch was six feet off the ground, the steps leading up to it broad and worn. The house, handsome, brick, with all the trim painted white, rose two stories with an attic above that. Yet the paint was peeling, and even from here he could see rot on the exposed wood.

Still, this was Southern grandeur at its most attractive. "Nice place," he said in deliberate understatement.

She laughed, a brief gurgle of surprised amusement. "We like it."

"We?"

"My aunts and I."

"So you have family." In his experience, family was nothing to brag about.

But her smile crooked up fondly. "My great-aunts Hestia and Calista. When my parents were killed, they took me in."

"That's a good deed." One, in his experience, she'd had to pay for, over and over again.

"They're good people, born and raised in the city. Everyone knows them. Everyone loves them. The Dahl Girls and the Dahl House are legend in New Orleans." She scanned the outside as if looking for something, then let out a sigh of relief. "At least it didn't hail here."

"How do you know?"

"The roof isn't damaged. We had to get a new one after Katrina. The hurricane ripped the shingles off."

"The Garden District is high ground, I've heard."

"It is. That's why the house survived with no flood damage." She helped him up the stairs. "But once the roof went, it leaked and we had to repair damages inside. Not to mention every window was broken."

He remembered the troubles New Orleans suffered after the hurricane. "Looters?"

"Oh, no. My aunts refused to leave the house, and they had guns. Looters didn't stand a chance. The windows went during the hurricane—flying debris." Nessa pointed at the giant live oak in the side yard, then opened the front door and maneuvered him inside. "They told me branches snapped off like twigs and flew around the yard."

"You didn't stay?" The entry way was huge, with

doors leading off it and a magnificent stair made of gleaming wood and polished within an inch of its life.

"They wouldn't let me." That obviously didn't sit well with Nessa.

An elderly woman, tall and straight, dressed in a vintage fifties-style purple silk dress, with a turban wrapped around her head, came bustling out of the dining room. "Of course we couldn't let you stay, dear girl. You're young. We're old. Someone has to carry on the family line." She eyed Mac, appraising first Nessa's arm around him, then his face and body, as a suitable candidate.

Clearly annoyed, Nessa said, "*Not* right *now*, Aunt Hestia. I'm too busy trying to get Mr. Jeremiah Mac somewhere where I can bandage his gunshot wound." She pulled his jacket back.

Vaguely, Hestia blinked at the bloodied shirt, then at him. "Young man, are you in danger of dying?"

"No, the bullet only took a bit of skin." He would be sore, but not unduly so.

"Then, Nessa, don't let him bleed on the rug," Hestia scolded. "The guests will start arriving in an hour."

On one side of the entry, large double doors were flung open. Inside, he could see a small ballroom, and in the corner a band was setting up. On the other side, he saw the dining room where white-coated caterers decorated a long table and the sideboard. Rich odors of sausage, garlic, and peppers permeated the air. His stomach took notice and growled. "You're having a party," he said.

"Yes." Nessa's jaw set in annoyance. "It's the Dahl House Mardi Gras party."

"It is a social event of some magnitude," he suggested, and watched in amusement for her reaction.

"Of course it is," Hestia said vigorously. "Guests fight for an invitation. I'm so glad Nessa has a date, and one that seems so . . . well, Mr. Mac, don't be insulted, but you seem almost normal."

"Have I disappointed you?" She certainly acted as if he had.

"No, the band is good—we probably don't need any more entertainment tonight." Hestia beamed at him as if she were talking sense.

"Mr. Mac is not my date," Nessa snapped. "He arrived in New Orleans today."

"Then of course you had to bring him. Our hospitality is legendary." Hestia placed her hand on his arm and confided, "It would be a disgrace if she didn't ask you."

Nessa's face turned the color of his brightest red power tie.

Busted! Oh, this could be played to his advantage.

"He's the insurance investigator for the bank, and he's looking into the Mardi Gras robberies," Nessa said.

"Really. How interesting. Mr. Mac, you may call me Miss Hestia—everyone does." She shooed them toward an open corridor. "Nessa, take him to the utility room and bandage him up, then bring him back—he looks like he knows how to dance." She bustled into the ballroom.

Nessa had claimed her aunts were some of the renowned eccentrics in New Orleans, but he hadn't expected . . . Miss Hestia. "Why does it matter if I dance?"

"The aunts love to dance, and there are never enough men who can." Nessa led him through a short hallway to the bustling kitchen.

He had found the source of the enticing smells.

A tiny black woman, so old she made Miss Hestia look like a teenager and so short she could walk under his outstretched arm, bellowed directions at an entire team of food preparers and chefs.

There was nothing wrong with her lungs.

The bustling crew arranged hors d'oeuvres, stirred bubbling pots, and placed raw biscuits on baking sheets.

Nessa waved. "Hi, Miss Maddy. This is Jeremiah Mac."

"Good to meet you, Mr. Mac. What are you doing in here, child, and dressed like that? You'll be late!" Maddy scowled so heavily Mac stopped in his tracks.

"We got mugged. He's shot. Aunt Hestia said to bandage him up in the utility room—"

"Do it fast, because we need that sink."

As casual as these women were, Mac wondered if gunshot victims appeared at the Dahl House every day.

"Yes, ma'am." Nessa hustled him into the large utility room and shut the door. "On party day, it's a good idea to stay out of Miss Maddy's way. She's been running this show so long, we couldn't do it without her."

Remembering the deep wrinkles around Maddy's mouth, he said, "She looks ancient."

"She is. We just don't know how ancient. Aunt Hestia and Aunt Calista remember her cooking when they were little, but Miss Maddy won't hear of retiring. She says sitting around would kill her." Gently

Nessa pushed him down on a low, battered stool. "Personally, I think if the hurricane didn't do it, nothing will."

"She was caught in the hurricane?"

"She lost everything. She lost all the mementos of her son, killed in WWII. Thank God the aunts had a couple of snapshots in their photo albums." Nessa sadly looked into space. "Can you imagine the pain of having no family?"

He snorted.

Nessa blinked at him. "What's wrong?"

"Sorry." He hadn't meant to betray himself like that. "Sometimes family can be a pain in the ass."

"Yes, but it beats the alternative. Take off your shirt."

"It's stuck." He tugged lightly on the bloody material.

She winced as if his wound were hers. Getting a towel, she wet it in warm water, then folded it into a pad and handed it to him. "Soak your shirt loose."

Going to the large cupboard in the corner, she opened the doors and rummaged inside. "Who's a pain in the ass?" she asked.

"In my family? All of them, pretty much." As he waited, he looked around. The room had once been a porch. Now the walls were pale pink, the floor cracking linoleum.

"Siblings?"

"A stepbrother. Joe. He's fourteen years younger, though, in the military." A washer and dryer and a big, old, deep sink occupied one wall. Another wall was floor-to-ceiling drawers and cupboards, and between them, a hanging rod full of kitchen towels.

"He sounds like he's okay," Nessa said.

"I barely know him." If he didn't give her something, she wouldn't quit. "My mom is never going to win the prize for Mother of the Year. My grandparents don't much care for me." An understatement—when his mother popped up pregnant, her working-class family had been deeply ashamed, and they'd never forgiven him for being born. "My stepfather . . . he doesn't like me much."

"But your mother . . . wasn't she on your side?"

"Don't get the wrong idea. My mom tried. She really did. It was just a difficult situation"—and that was an understatement—"and she didn't have intestinal fortitude to stick by me. Most people aren't like Miss Maddy or your great-aunts. Most people, when put to the test, fail. My mom was no different."

"That is such a terrible attitude. So cynical. I wish that you . . . well, there's no use saying that, after what happened today."

"You wish that I what?" he asked softly.

"I wish that you could have a family like mine. My great-aunts always do what they think is right, no matter what the consequences."

"It's great that you have so much faith in them." Not that he believed what she said, but it was nice she did.

Nessa really wasn't the kind of woman he'd expected.

Even if he'd never seen her on the video, he would have known she came from money. She wasn't as tall as he'd expected, only about five-seven, but her legs were long and slender, and somehow, rich women always had delicate bones and striking faces.

Not that she was rich; he knew the amount in her

bank account to the last penny, and a pitiful amount it was.

She didn't seem the type to sell that body for money, not even in marriage. Too bad, because if she weren't an accomplice in these robberies, he'd be willing to plunk the money and a ring to get her in his bed and keep her there. He knew himself well enough to admit he'd never tire of having her beneath him in bed, making her abandon all that proper gentility, making her sweat and move and scream while he—

"Is that doing it?" she asked.

He stared. "What?"

She came over and lifted the damp towel away from his side and peeled the material away from his side. "There you go. Now you can take off your shirt."

"Right." He'd pay to hear her say that in the bedroom.

He unbuttoned, tossed the shirt on the washer, and waited.

Nessa tucked a stack of clean rags under her arm, then opened a drawer and took out ointment and a roll of gauze. She turned back to him. . . . And stopped cold, her eyes wide and shocked.

"What's wrong?" As if he didn't know.

His body had been knit from his grandfather's muscles and bones, and his grandfather had worked on the docks, then in the mills. Like him, Mac had broad shoulders, a massive chest, big arms, and huge hands. Ashley Wilkes he was not.

More to the point, old, pale white scars from the knife attack covered the left side of his body, and although the gunshot wound was twenty years old, it still formed a pale pink scar on the right shoulder.

"Wow," she said. "You must work out a lot."

For once he was grateful for the much-vaunted Southern tact that praised his attributes and ignored his blemishes.

"Karate, of course," she said, "but you lift weights, too."

"And run." Interesting. He was strutting and he wasn't even on his feet.

She put her supplies down on the floor. She shed her jacket, unbuttoned the top two buttons of her white shirt, and rolled up her sleeves. She was all business, without a hint of coquetry, yet as she knelt beside him, he looked down at her profile: at her smooth cheek, her generous lips, at the hint of cleavage from the previously buttoned-up assistant manager—and he wished she were performing another task for him, one less onerous and more . . . erotic.

Taking a deep breath, he erased the thought from his mind. He'd managed to inveigle himself into her home; he most definitely did not need an erection now.

With the aim of furthering her guilt, he said, "I'm sorry to get shot and mess things up."

She smoothed a damp cloth across the wound, rinsed the cloth, then did it again. With her fingertips, she pressed carefully on the edge of the wound, and sighed with relief. "It's not bad."

He looked. A lucky shot for him. The bullet had sliced a two-inch gash through his skin. "I told you so."

Exasperated, she said, "Mr. Mac, has no woman explained that those are the most noxious words ever spoken by a man?"

"I've certainly heard enough women say them."

"But then they're true."

Those gloriously shaped lips tilted upward in a quirky smile, and she made him want to smile back. Odd. He'd expected to feel desire, but never to discover such humor in her.

Of course, there was a sort of wicked humor in once a year robbing the bank where she worked of such a small amount the police failed to pursue the matter.

She was intelligent. She'd proved that today in her dealings with the police, her staff, and more important, with him. He had come here to keep an eye on her; two eyes would be better. "So this is the Dahl House," he said.

"Yes. We're very proud of it. Of course, it's old, it's big, and the upkeep so massive."

"How do you do it?"

"I make enough to pay the insurance and taxes and pay the bills, and I put a little away every month. The repairs from the hurricane wiped out my savings, but once I work my way into management . . ."

"Yes? What happens then?"

"The aunts started taking in boarders to pay for my school loans, and once that got going, it just never stopped."

"Do the boarders bother you?" The sudden sting as she used a pre-moistened pad to sterilize the area made him hiss and then straighten.

He knew better. Never let them see you in pain.

But if she noticed his weakness, she gave no indication. "I think it would be lovely to someday come down to breakfast and have only family at the table." With the scissors, she cut a series of butterfly bandages out of the tape, and her forehead puckered with concentration as she pulled the edges of the wound together and taped it tightly. "And I don't like my aunts cooking and cleaning and caring for strangers."

"How long have you been working for the bank?"

"Seven years."

"How long does it usually take to become a manager?" *Did she know?*

She shifted her knees as if she were uncomfortable. "The average is maybe . . . five years."

He drove the point home. "So if you're not a manager yet, you probably never will be. How much longer are you going to wait around to see if someone at the bank gets wise?"

"I don't know."

"Do you have any other experience? What else can you do?" *Rob a bank, maybe?*

"I can repair gunshot wounds." She took the roll of gauze and folded a pad to fit over the wound, placed it over the gash, and taped it in place.

Shit. She was giving him the silent treatment. He was going to have to apologize again.

But no, when she had finished, she sat back on her heels and examined her work. "I wish you had gone to the hospital. My Girl Scout first-aid badge is hardly up to this."

"You did a great job." Taking her hand, he lifted it to his lips and pressed a kiss on her fingers.

Her wide, startled gaze flew to his.

"What's wrong?" he asked.

"You don't seem like the Continental-kiss-on-the-hand sort of guy."

"You're right." Turning her hand palm up, he pressed his lips to her wrist. A mixture of scents—her perfume and her skin—filled his nose with the suggestions of vanilla, orange blossom, and warm, willing female. His smile sent her heart thundering in her veins. "I'm not." Leaning over, he wrapped an arm around her waist, pulled her up on her knees, and leaned down to meet her lips.

Ten

He kissed her.

Mac kissed her, and in that first touch of mouth to mouth, all the lies fell away.

Nessa *did* want him.

And she hadn't been wrong in that alley while the thunder rumbled and the hail fell.

He wanted her. She tasted the desire in him.

But he despised himself for it.

Because it was her? Or because passion was an emotion beyond his control?

For a man with a build like a WWE wrestler and scars like a New Orleans gang member, his touch was delicate. So delicate. He held her lightly, his arm loose around her waist, his hand clasping her wrist. He felt her caution, respected it, for his lips caressed hers lightly, making no move to deepen the kiss, satisfied to explore the contours of her mouth.

After a first minute of indecision, she relaxed.

After all, it was only a kiss. And he was only an insurance investigator, one who would be leaving town in a week or so. In a way, he would be perfect for her.

He lingered over her mouth, taking advantage of his strength and her mindless acquiescence to learn her desires. One large hand stroked her hip, her waist, her spine. The other rubbed her neck, smoothing tension until she moaned and curled closer.

He smelled . . . so good. He felt . . . so strong. His heat warmed the cold places of her body, and her heart expanded with the pleasure of having a man she could lean on.

A man she could lean on.

Where had that thought come from?

This was just a kiss—one she should end *now*.

He must have felt her stiffen, for abruptly, the kiss became more. More heated, more intimate, just . . . *more*. He no longer tasted her. He absorbed her, enjoyed her, used his lips and tongue to savor her. He placed her hand on his bare shoulder. He lifted her up and into his arms.

Her bottom rested in his lap. Her breasts flattened against his chest. He slid his fingers under her hair at the base of her neck. Muscle upon muscle rippled across his chest, and with each breath he pressed her closer.

And she felt suddenly surrounded. Threatened. He was *big*, his shoulder heavily corded and so massive her hand couldn't encompass it. This man was the size of a caveman and kissed like the most skilled lover—a frightening combination.

He lifted his head, waited until she focused on him. "Stop thinking," he whispered. "Let me show you how to feel."

Her head rested in the crook of his arm. She was close enough to see the dark stubble on his chin, the thin white scars against his tanned forehead and cheek, and, most important, his beautiful, enigmatic green eyes. He had taken control of her, and she should struggle. But she was in her own home. Maddy and the caterers were in the next room. Today, he'd been shot fighting their mugger. And really, he'd done nothing shocking. It was just a kiss. *Just a kiss.*

He pressed his lips over her eyelids, shutting them. His lips caressed her cheek, her ear, her jaw . . . and found her mouth. He teased her lips open, slid his tongue inside. . . . And precipitously, she fell out of prudence and into passion. Without a sound or a struggle, the dark surface of madness closed over her, taking her breath, stealing her will, leaving her with only one lifeline—Jeremiah Mac.

This was no longer just a kiss. It was sex. Slow, hot, wet sex.

With each push inside her, he stole her will, made her move restlessly, try to get closer, press her aching breasts against him. She wanted to take the lead, wrap her legs around him, make him want, make him hurry.

She'd experienced passion before, but all her memories were driven onto the rocks of *now* and smashed beyond recognition.

Just as she reached the greatest depths, ready to take the plunge into submission, he murmured against her lips, "Someone's knocking on the door."

"What?" Nessa opened her eyes. She stared at him in confusion.

Gently he sat her up on his lap. "Someone's knocking on the door."

"Oh." His eyes were very intent, his lids heavy. His lips looked swollen.

His lips looked delicious.

The door swung open. "Miss Nessa. Miss Hestia sent a shirt down for Mr. Mac to wear."

Nessa snapped to attention—but not in time.

Maddy stuck her head in. "Here it is. . . . Oh, Miss Nessa." She took in the scene: Nessa scrambling to her feet, Nessa's well-kissed mouth. . . . Jeremiah's wide, bare chest. Her brown eyes twinkled. "Well! This will make your aunts very happy."

Nessa straightened her skirt. "Come on, Miss Maddy. Don't tell them."

"I won't have to." Maddy shook out a white linen shirt with ruffles at the cuffs and a front that laced up from the breastbone to the neck.

Jeremiah stared at it, his eyes narrowing.

"I know what you're thinking, Mr. Mac. You're thinking you're going to look like a damned fool. But Miss Nessa's grandfather wore this for Mardi Gras, and so did her father. They were supposed to be a pirate, Jean Lafitte to be exact, and those two were the only men big enough to loan clothes to you." Maddy looked him over. "You'll look like a big brawn of a man in anything you wear."

Wasn't that the truth? Most men—straight men, anyway—wouldn't be able to carry off the pirate shirt, but the thought of Jeremiah in ruffled sleeves made Nessa drool.

She took a long breath. She needed to remember— sex wasn't on the menu. Not for her. Not tonight. Not with him . . .

Jeremiah rose and walked to the door, and as he reached for the shirt, the muscles of his back flexed in an intricate, glorious network. "Thank you, Miss

Maddy. I would be honored to wear Mr. Dahl's costume." His voice was deep, warm, respectful.

Tiny Maddy smiled at him, the wrinkles on her soft old face deepening as she took in the magnificent sternum right before her nose. "You're welcome, young man. Now, hurry up and get dressed. The caterers need that sink!" She whisked away, leaving the door open.

The noise of kitchen work filled the room, dispelling the intimacy—but not the desire.

The desire would subside soon. It always did. But Nessa knew damned good and well that until Jeremiah left, this desire would nag at her like a toothache that wouldn't go away.

"I'm afraid I'm going to need help getting into this shirt," he said.

"Well, of course you need help." Because when every instinct was screaming at her to get away, she had to touch him, stare at that broad chest, get within range of those long arms again.

She approached him cautiously.

He stood waiting docilely.

Docilely. Sort of like a bull mastiff trained to attack but waiting for the command.

Just a kiss, huh?

Then why did she feel like this was the morning after? It hadn't been sex. It had been . . . just a kiss— and far too intimate for a first time.

Not that he'd groped her boob or made a grab for her butt.

No, she'd been the one who'd responded too completely.

And why? She dated. She exchanged kisses; good

ones, too. But not one of them ever sent her out of her mind with lust.

In fact, none of them ever distracted her from the next day's schedule.

So it was Jeremiah. His fault. He'd done something to her. And he'd better not try to do it again.

Because she might . . . um, she might not be able to stop, and if one taste of him made her that hungry, she'd hate to try the whole tamale. For the first time, Nessa realized she would have to put her brain to work to help solve the Mardi Gras robberies. If she didn't, she'd be drawn into an affair with a Yankee from Philadelphia who fought like a hero, looked like a trucker, and kissed all too well.

He was, she feared, an unforgettable combination.

Mac stood in the foyer, watched Nessa scurry up the stairs, and smiled the kind of smile that, if she had seen it, would have made her very nervous.

Some people would say he was a lucky man. He would agree, if luck consisted of knowing what he wanted, putting himself in the right spot at the right time, and making split-second decisions that took advantage of every opportunity that came his way. And if lucky was getting shot by a mugger on his first day in New Orleans.

He breathed in the scent of Old English furniture polish and lilies arranged in a crystal vase, and glanced around at the Dahl House.

Helluva place. The carpets were threadbare, but man, they had cost a bundle when they were new. The floor shone, but over the years, so many feet had walked across the threshold they'd worn a slope into the wood. Gilt frames hung on the walls, filled with nineteenth-century paintings and mirrors so old the reflective backing had worn away in patches. Two sets of double doors stood wide open on the left. One room was a living room with an antique desk, two sagging couches, and a window seat that looked onto the street. The other was a huge, bare, elegant room that sparkled with crystal chandeliers—the ballroom. Since an eight-piece band was setting up in there, he wandered into the living room and over to the oil portrait that hung over the fireplace. The lady was clad in mid-nineteenth-century splendor, sitting stiffly upright in her blue silk dress. Her jet-black hair framed her pale skin, and her exotically slanted sapphire eyes clearly insinuated he had no business sullying her home with his uncouth presence.

"My God," he said.

From the corner, an elderly lady's voice piped up, "It *is* amazing, isn't it?"

He turned to see a plump woman curled up in a large, worn easy chair, a book open in her lap. She studied him with a frankness that gave him leave to return the favor. She wore a fringed flapper dress and a turban wrapped around her head, her thick glasses made her blue eyes exorbitantly large, and she had such a marked resemblance to her sister he could safely assume she was Nessa's aunt Calista. "What's amazing?" he asked.

"How much Nessa looks like Althea Dahl. That is what you were saying, 'My God,' about, wasn't it?" Removing her reading glasses, she carefully folded them, placed them on the table, and rose.

He looked up at the Dahl ancestor. "Yeah."

Calista came to his side and stared up at the portrait with him. "People in New Orleans say Nessa resembles Hestia in her figure and me in her face, but all you have to do is look at that picture of Althea Dahl, and Nessa's face looks back at you." She turned to him and offered her hand. "You're Jeremiah Mac. I'm Miss Calista."

"Good to meet you." He gently shook the fragile-looking fingers. "With looks like those, Althea must have been very popular."

"Before the war, she was the belle of New Orleans. She was also the woman who sacrificed herself by marrying the rich Yankee invader, John Dahl, and thus saved her family from ruin."

Sounded like crap to Mac. "It couldn't have been much of a sacrifice. Not if he was rich."

"Well." Without an ounce of compassion, Calista grinned. "It turned out *he* was the sacrifice, since the rumor claims that after she'd secured her Yankee husband's fortune, she poisoned him and lived to a ripe old age as a cane-wielding matriarch."

"Wow." He was impressed. "Don't mess with Althea."

"Don't mess with any of the Dahl women," Calista warned, and he understood she was talking directly to him. Then she added thoughtfully, "Although Nessa has none of the malice necessary to poison anyone."

"*Does* she draw the line at murder?" He thought he sounded pleasant enough.

But Calista must have discerned an undertone in his voice, for she whipped around and attacked. "*Nessa?* Nessa is a dear girl. My sister and I wish she were a little tougher—if she were, she wouldn't allow That

Woman at That Bank to take advantage of her the way she does—"

He reeled from the unexpected attack from the gentle-looking lady. "Who's That Woman?"

"Stephanie Decker, the manager. *Nessa's* the one who keeps things running smoothly. *Nessa's* the reason customers prefer Premier Central over any other. *Nessa's* the officer who secures the loans and brings in the savings accounts. That bullheaded man who runs the bank, Mr. MacNaught, has done Nessa a disservice, and he doesn't realize it. Or care." Calista's voice dipped below freezing.

Obviously, if her aunts knew all this, Nessa had done plenty of griping about her job. "She's ambitious."

"Of course she's ambitious."

Everything Calista said solidified the suspicions in Mac's mind. "She *could* change jobs."

"When Nessa was just starting, she made a mistake. Now she's nothing but a dogsbody for Stephanie Decker. She has tried to get another job, but That Woman has made sure everyone in New Orleans knows she'd messed up."

"In banking, news travels fast."

"It's not fair. Nessa is honest. She's loyal. She'll do anything for her friends and relatives, and even though the bank doesn't treat her right, she does everything for it."

"But she resents the bank."

"She's not stupid. Of course she resents the bank. It's been seven years since she made her mistake, and she hasn't made one since." Calista's blue eyes snapped as she leveled them on him, demanding he agree.

"If everything you say is true, then . . . no, it's not fair." But if Nessa was taking her revenge by robbing Premier Central banks, that was even less fair.

"If that sweet girl would leave New Orleans, she could have the job of her dreams." Calista clasped her hands below her chin. "But she won't leave Hestia and me."

"You want her to go?" He liked Hestia and Calista, but he could hardly believe they'd want to lose their living wallet.

"No, we don't want her to go. But we want her to have a life! Just this morning, Hestia said . . ." A pang of . . . something—horror? Amusement?— brought Calista to a firm stop. "Well, what Hestia said doesn't matter. The point is, Nessa feels responsible for us, and we Dahl girls want her to spread her wings."

Calista sounded as if she believed it. And maybe she did, especially since Nessa showed no signs of leaving. "Maybe she's afraid."

"Of course she's afraid. When a child loses both her parents at a young age, it's not a blow from which she can easily recover, and Nessa is—was always—a sensitive child."

He lifted his eyebrows, a silent command for Calista to go on.

She stared back, not a bit cowed.

"I didn't know any of that," he said. "You could tell me."

"That depends. What's your interest in Nessa?"

In astonishment, he realized he was being interrogated. Interrogated by an eighty-year-old woman about his intentions for her niece.

Had he fallen into a time warp?

No. He'd arrived in New Orleans.

"I met her this morning. She's smart. She's attractive."

"You kissed her."

He would not discuss his inexplicable passion for Nessa with anyone. "If I did, it is my business and hers. But not yours. Not Miss Hestia's. Not Miss Maddy's or the caterer's or the mugger's. Just Nessa's and mine."

"You know where to draw the line." Calista studied him. "You'll do."

The doorbell rang.

"The guests are arriving!" she said.

"Tell me about Nessa," he insisted.

"Ah, but I know where to draw the line, too. If you want to know about Nessa, you'll have to ask her." Calista smiled, hooked her hand in his arm, and started toward the foyer. "Mr. Mac, I understand you dance."

Eleven

Throughout the ground floor, guests in the Dahl House, resplendent in costumes and masks, held filled plates and half-filled glasses. Music from the ballroom wove its way through the crowd, animating them in conversation, dance and laughter.

As Nessa made her entrance at the top of the curving stairway, cries of delight greeted her.

"Brava, darling, brava." Daniel tossed his boa around his neck and clapped in appreciation. "You look dashing!"

Nessa smiled mechanically. She knew she looked dashing, the image of a World War II movie star in her red jacket with her matching red skirt, and a hat with a great spiked feather. She wore her hair up, seams in the back of her hose, basic red pumps, and shoulder pads. Huge shoulder pads. She'd scavenged in the attics of the Dahl House for this outfit, altered the skirt and the jacket, and searched the Internet for the hose. She'd spent a year, ever since last year's party, planning her entrance—and she didn't even glance in the mirror as she descended the curving staircase. All that occupied her mind was Jeremiah.

Where was he? What was he doing? Was this Yankee, at the most traditional carnival party, holding his own with the people of her city?

"As always, Ionessa, the Dahl girls have outdone themselves." Nessa's sophomore science teacher kissed her cheek. "Do you know my bride, Angelina?"

Nessa shook hands with the twenty-two-year-old he'd married. "I've heard so much about you." About how, when Mr. LeJeune inherited a small fortune from his aunt, Angelina had broken up a four-kid marriage.

"Yeah, a lot of people say that." Angelina took a deep breath and her impressive breasts quivered beneath her low-cut, sequined gown.

Nessa wanted to cover her eyes and yell, *I've been blinded!* Instead, as Mr. LeJeune handed her a half case of wine, she said, "We'll enjoy these." She handed the wine to a passing caterer. "Have a good time."

"Laissez les bons temps rouler!" Angelina tripped off toward the ballroom, Mr. LeJeune on her heels.

And Nessa still hadn't caught sight of Jeremiah. She started for the ballroom when Maddy caught her. "Child, you look grand. Look at that! That idiot Gauthier Lavache is spiking the punch bowl! As if it wasn't flammable enough!" She plowed fiercely through the crowd.

Nessa felt sorry for the unfortunate Gauthier Lavache.

"Hey, chère." Ernie Rippon stood before her in his police uniform. "I can only stay for a few minutes. They called me back in to help with crowd control down in the Vieux Carre."

"Go pick out a pretty girl and dance one dance."

"I can't. The only pretty girl is standing here greeting her guests." He grinned at her with all his old-guy charm.

"You are so sweet." She shoved his shoulder, then kissed his cheek. "You be careful out there tonight, Ernie."

"Always." He headed for the dining room.

Debbie Voytilla circled the foyer, looking worried. "Nessa, I haven't seen Ryan. Have you?"

"I just came down." Nessa glanced around, but not because she cared about Ryan. She wanted to see Jeremiah. "Is Skeeter here?"

"I haven't seen him, either."

"Then I suppose they're still playing. The tips must be good tonight."

Debbie floated across the floor, a wonder of lingerie in chiffon and feathers, toward the clump of people blocking the door to the ballroom. "I wonder what's going on in here."

Nessa's fertile imagination immediately conjured a multitude of scenarios, all of them involving Jeremiah, all of them involving some kind of strife. She elbowed her way through the throng to the front—and stopped short at the sight that met her eyes. "I don't believe it," she whispered.

"Believe it," Aunt Hestia said.

Jeremiah and Aunt Calista glided smoothly across the polished wood of the Dahl House ballroom floor, their waltz perfectly in sync with the music provided by the jazz quartet. They were beautiful together, the elderly woman in flapper outfit and the tall, rugged, scarred man in the white pirate shirt.

The other dancing couples had moved aside to give them room. The walls were packed, and the double doors that opened to the outside held a crowd.

"Who is that gorgeous man?" Georgia's gaze was plastered on the dancing couple.

"Jeremiah Mac. Insurance inspector for the bank. Investigating the Mardi Gras Robberies." Nessa took a breath. "I'm his assistant."

Georgia turned on her like a furious wolverine. "His *assistant*? You had this fabulous beast of a man this morning and you didn't tell me?"

By Georgia's slight sway and the slur of her speech, Nessa judged that her friend had already celebrated with one too many glasses of punch. Nessa only wished *she'd* had time to soften the edges of reality with a good, stiff drink, but patching up Jeremiah . . . and kissing him . . . had made her late for the party. Now she yearned for a milk punch or a mimosa or a hurricane. . . . Or that she was in Jeremiah's arms as he smoothly led *her* through the waltz.

"I didn't know him this morning," Nessa told Georgia.

"Can I have him?" Georgia asked.

"No. If you don't want Antoine, then you most certainly do not deserve Jeremiah." Nessa's gaze returned to the dance floor, to the couple swirling in glorious unison.

"My God. He already got to you." Georgia flung her arm around Nessa's neck. "He already got to you!"

"Would you lower your voice?" Nessa hissed.

Aunt Hestia moved closer. "How did he do it?"

"He didn't do anything," Nessa said.

"You're looking flustered, Ionessa Dahl, and nothing

flusters you. So what did he do that got to you?" Georgia insisted.

Nessa backed out of the crowd, around the corner, and into the living room, where a few people had found chairs and sat quietly to eat.

Nessa's great-aunt and best friend followed close behind, their gazes focused on her.

When she was sure they were private, Nessa quietly admitted, "He kissed me."

"Tongues?" Aunt Hestia asked.

"For the love of God . . ." Nessa began.

Aunt Hestia lifted her eyebrows.

Nessa surrendered. "All right. Yes. Tongues."

"Glory hallelujah!" Aunt Hestia lifted her arms in praise.

"Fast mover. And with *you*. I'm impressed. It's been so long since you've been kissed you've got dust on your lips." Georgia looked closely at Nessa. "Yep. Now all the dust has turned stardust in your eyes."

"Shut up." But Nessa laughed.

"I want to hear every last detail, and I'm not leaving your side until—" Aunt Hestia stopped in midsentence.

They heard applause from inside the ballroom.

"I want the next dance. But I'll be back. Don't say a word without me." She decamped so fast, Nessa and Georgia grinned.

Then Nessa sobered and confided, "He's good with a kiss, Georgia, but there's something about him that makes me uneasy. He's intense and scary, and I think he's dangerous."

"Good. You've spent too many hours dating safe

guys and leaving them because they bore you to death—or not dating at all."

"That's not true." At a look from Georgia, Nessa reminded her, "I've also dated my fair share of madmen."

"You do attract them, don't you?" Georgia chuckled.

"And why are *you* picking on *me?* You're here alone, too."

An officer of the NOPD with a rugged, lived-in face and sad, hound-dog eyes walked past the door of the library and stopped. Antoine Valteau. He and Georgia exchanged a long look.

Then he strolled on, and Georgia flinched. "Coonass," she muttered.

Nessa watched, and ached for her friend. "He's a good man."

"In case it's escaped your notice, he's Cajun. I'm black. That doesn't work. Not ever."

"I tell you, Georgia, he's not a boy who's afraid of a little controversy. He knows what he's getting into when he gets you. He wants *you.*"

Georgia took a good, long drink from an almost empty glass. "Did that look he gave me give you the impression he still wants me?"

"No, he looks like he's mad at you. *How* many times have you rejected him?"

Significantly, Georgia dodged the question. "My parents would kill me."

"They'd come around." Nessa jostled Georgia. "Besides, it would just be a date."

"It would just be a heartache. I can't date a guy I work with." Georgia looked right at Nessa. "Isn't that one of the reasons you've got lined up to tell me why you shouldn't sleep with Jeremiah?"

"It's a good one!"

"I agree." But Georgia stared into the foyer where Antoine had disappeared.

"Other than this investigation, I don't think I ought to have anything else to do with him," Nessa said.

Georgia turned to her friend and smiled, a slow, pleased curl of the lips. "I don't know, dear Nessa—he doesn't look to me like the kind of man who'll leave that decision in your hands."

Twelve

The music ended.

Mac stepped away from Calista and bowed. "Ma'am, you're light on your feet."

"You are, too, young man. Dancing with someone so capable is a pleasure I've not enjoyed for many a long year." Calista glowed with delight. "Look, here comes Hestia. I know her. She wants her turn."

Calista was a delightful woman: tall, well upholstered, and funny. She made him think of family, the kind of family that cheered for each other in *It's a Wonderful Life.*

Yeah, right. Like he believed in those kinds of fairy tales.

But he could be pleasant, at least to older women, so he said, "I've just met the woman I've been waiting for all my life, and now she wants me to dance with her sister."

Calista beamed and let Hestia cut in, then caught her sister's arm. "When you're done with him, I get him back."

"Shouldn't we let Nessa have a turn?" Hestia asked.

"Nessa who?" Calista sashayed off the dance floor like a woman whose every dream had come true.

"I haven't tangoed in thirty years." Hestia looked up at Mac. "Do you tango?"

"Of course." He looked into her faded blue eyes, the eyes so much like Nessa's. "But there is a price."

"A price? Ten cents a dance?" She dimpled.

"Something like that. You have to tell me all about Nessa."

"No, dear." She patted his cheek. "The cost is too high." She turned away.

Damn. These aunts were like lionesses protecting their cub.

He caught her arm. "Come on. Dance." He walked to the band, spoke to the band leader, and purposefully strode back to Hestia.

"You're direct."

"It gets me what I want."

She allowed him to clasp her in his arms, and she fit well: tall, so thin she was bony . . . and graceful.

The compelling beat took the ballroom, and he took control of the dance, with precision and close attention, leading Hestia through the moves with a power that echoed his training (from the other women) and his respect for any female who wouldn't gossip about her niece just for the pleasure of sharing a treat that came all too rarely.

He got his reward. When they finished to a nice round of applause, he caught Nessa's approving gaze on him. Her friend, a lovely black woman, was poking her in the ribs and grinning. And Nessa was blushing.

Yes, the dance had done its job. Nessa's aunts liked him, and Nessa liked him even more.

He would have worked his way toward Nessa, but
Hestia caught his hand and led him off the dance floor,
past Calista, who joined their little cavalcade, and up
the grand curving stairs in the foyer. Here they were
above the main action of the party, out of the way, out
of earshot, yet not out of sight.

Calista seated herself on the top step, looked up at
him, and said, "I remember when Ionessa first came to
live with us. She was five."

He released a pent-up breath. They were giving him
a glimpse of Nessa's past, one he had not requested,
but one that they thought was important.

"Barely. She had just turned five." Hestia leaned her
elbow against the banister.

"Her parents were killed on her birthday." Calista
gestured down the stairs. "In a plane crash."

"Good God." So Ionessa Dahl wasn't quite the privileged daughter of society she appeared to be. In her
way, she'd suffered. And sadly, that made him like her
better.

"We were her only relations, and we hadn't seen
Nessa since she was a baby. But as soon as we heard the
news, we went for her." Hestia's mobile face grew
quiet with anguish. "Pitiful little thing, that first night,
she was so quiet."

"She was in shock," he said.

"And in pain. I'll never forget those sad, lonely
eyes." Calista sighed.

Yes, he'd seen something similar in Nessa's eyes,
too.

"The next morning, Calista brought her downstairs," Hestia said. "As Nessa descended those stairs,

she burst into the most awful wails of childish anguish."

The two women were silent as they recalled that long-ago morning.

"I just sat down on the steps, put my arm around that poor, skinny child, and pointed to that mirror." Calista gestured at the gold-framed mirror on the wall. "I asked, 'Do you see yourself there, Ionessa?' and Nessa stopped in midwail and looked at herself. Her complexion was blotchy red, and she shut her mouth as if to spare us her honest distress."

Hestia sniffled, and Mac handed her his handkerchief. She dabbed at her nose, took a breath, and closed her eyes in remembrance. "So I asked her, 'Who would you like to be today?'"

"She said, 'I want my mommy. I want my daddy. I want to go home.'" Calista's eyes filled, too. "She was ready to burst into tears again, so *I* told her, 'I think you're a princess going to a ball.'"

"I held out my hands"—lost in her reminisces, Hestia followed the script—"and said, 'I think you're Princess Ionessa of Greece. We should dance.'"

"Remember, sister?" Calista smiled a wobbly smile at Hestia. "She came down the stairs so cautiously, put her hands in yours, and you danced across the foyer."

"While you belted out 'Ramblin' Rose.'" Hestia smiled back. "Afterward, she looked at us as if we were crazy. Five years old, and already she thought we were crazy."

The two old women laughed and shook their heads.

"When she was older, she told us she liked us, but she didn't know what to think." Calista wrapped her arms around her knees. "So many people don't know what to think of us, either, but we have our reasons for what we do, Mr. Mac. We remember what we were taught as girls, about honor and kindness and what's required of people who have had privileged lives such as ours."

Remembering Nessa's litany of what was wrong with the house, he glanced around.

Hestia correctly interpreted his gesture. "We know. We're barely scraping by, but we have always had a home. We had a loving family. We had a good education. We know who we are and what our place is in life. So many people do not. Displaced people, homeless people, people without family or roots."

Was she talking about him? *Did she know . . . ?* "I don't understand."

"No, I don't think you do." Calista caught sight of Nessa, working her way through the crowd in the foyer toward them, and waved. "Having that child in the house to care for gave us so much warmth and affection."

Nessa waved back, then got stopped by a lady of enormous girth. They hugged and exclaimed, and the lady carted Nessa off to be surrounded by her family.

"She kept us young," Hestia added.

Mac didn't know what to say. The old women seemed so . . . well, almost kind. They'd taken in a child they barely knew, arranged their whole lives around her.

Hell, even his mother had broken under the pressure of having Nathan Manly's son, and she was his *mother*. How did mere great-aunts manage so difficult a task as taking in a small, anguished child?

A woman's scream cut the music and babble.

Mac straightened, focused.

The aunts stiffened and peered down.

Everyone below in the entry turned toward the library. Four guests burst through the door and scattered in different directions.

Six policemen, uniformed and not, armed with service pistols, appeared and stalked forward.

Nessa's friend was one of them.

Nessa walked at her side.

A well-endowed young woman in a sequined gown bounced out of the library, eyes wide and frantic. "It's a mouse!" Her high shriek almost broke glass.

The policemen and their revolvers disappeared.

Nessa covered her eyes with her hands.

"Oh, for heaven's sake," Hestia said in disgust, and started down the stairs.

"It's that silly twit Angelina." Calista offered Mac her hand, and he pulled her to her feet. "Afraid of a little mouse."

As Calista started after her sister, Mac said, "Miss Calista, if there's a problem, I can pay for the exterminator."

Calista whirled around. "We're taking care of it!" She seemed to collect herself. She gentled her voice. "I mean . . . it's not a problem. We're taking care of it."

He watched her descend. These women—tall, dignified—were Southern to the core, steeped in pride, the kind of women who cured the sick, fed the hungry, took matters in their own hands.

Hestia and Calista were the women who had raised Nessa. He would do well to remember that.

The great-aunts disappeared into the library, then reappeared.

Calista held a small cage covered in a napkin. "Lagniappe for our party," she called with a laugh.

Most of the guests laughed with her.

Angelina shuddered, her fist pressed to her lips. "It's a mouse. It's disgusting."

With the situation defused, the aunts hurried toward the back of the house. Toward Maddy, who stood, her hands on her skinny hips, and glared up at them. "I warned you girls about those mice. Didn't I warn you girls about those mice?"

"Yes, Miss Maddy," they said in unison, and, cage in hand, Calista disappeared behind a closed door.

The chatter was muted as the guests returned to their conversations, but Mac clearly heard a petite forty-year-old say, "I board here, you know, and at night I hear them squeaking up in the attic. When the first one of the little monsters runs across my pillow—"

The swelling music and the rising tide of conversation cut her off.

Maddy caught a glimpse of him and hollered, "Mr. Mac, you need to eat something before you start satisfying the ladies."

He lifted an eyebrow. "Satisfying the ladies?"

"They all want to dance with you. Best get on with it." Maddy glanced toward one of the servers as he walked past with a tray of hors d'oeuvres, made a growling noise, and whisked after him.

Mac descended the stairs.

Hestia stood waiting for him. "Calista tells me you offered to pay for an exterminator. I want to thank you for your offer, but we couldn't use your friendship so shabbily."

"Men were put on this earth for women to use." His gaze found Nessa. "And use them they do."

"Well, bless your heart."

He heard a note in Hestia's voice that told him somehow he'd put a foot wrong. But he didn't know how. He'd said no more than the truth. Yet women had a way of getting offended over nothing, and most women kept their mouths shut about it because of what he could give them.

Hestia didn't know who he was, and even if she did, he suspected she would say what she wanted and spit on what he could give them.

"If only you carried on a conversation as well as you danced." Her faded blue eyes watched him shrewdly.

"Which would you rather I do?"

"Lots of men have the skill of conversation."

"That's what I figure."

"Yet I wonder where you learned one skill so well and the other so ill."

"It's one of my unsavory secrets." He offered his arm.

She took it, and they walked into the throng. "Yes, you have the look of a man with secrets." She glanced toward a glorious, shapely creature as she made her way through the crowd toward them.

The tall woman commanded the room. Her makeup was far too dramatic for Mac's taste, with black-rimmed eyes and skin that looked untouchable. She wore elbow-length fingerless black gloves, and her sleek, sequined, flesh-colored gown hugged her curvaceous figure. Each feather on the chocolate brown boa around her neck had been dipped in sequins.

Many of the guests stopped her, spoke to her,

smiling intimately or with amusement. She spoke graciously to each one, but her process toward them was steady.

"A man without secrets is like gumbo without Tabasco. Dull. Flavorless." Hestia hugged the lady who stood taller than Hestia's imposing height. "Daniel, that outfit is marvelous."

Mac did a double take.

"Daring, aren't I?" Daniel spread his arms and spun in a slow circle.

"It's what we expect of you." Hestia's eyes danced as she made the introduction. "Mr. Mac, this is Daniel Friendly, one of our longtime boarders."

The cross-dresser.

Hestia placed her hand on Mac's arm and in a confidential tone said, "Mr. Mac is Nessa's date."

"Really?" Daniel cocked his head.

"This afternoon, he was shot rescuing her from a mugger."

"Really?" Daniel repeated, and examined Mac from head to toe.

Hestia concluded, "He is also the man investigating the Beaded Bandits."

"Really?" This time, Daniel drew out the question.

Had Mac found one of his bank robbers? Up close, Daniel wasn't as young as he first appeared. But he had no stubble on his chin, his hands were beautifully manicured, and his glorious fall of blond hair was clearly real.

Yes. This could be one of the guys.

"An investigator. How fascinating!" Daniel pressed a long red nail into the weave of Mac's linen shirt. "Whatever made you become an investigator?"

"I'm nosy," Mac said bluntly.

"I can attest to that." Hestia laughed. "Gentlemen, I'll leave you to get acquainted."

Daniel slid his arm through Mac's. "Don't worry about us, darling. We're going to do just fine."

With a wave, Hestia went off.

"You intrigue me," Daniel said. "I look at you and I wonder how you managed to catch our little Ionessa's attention. You're not her usual kind of man."

"No?" At the mention of Nessa and other men, Mac discovered his ire slowly rising. "What kind of man does she usually date?"

"Nobody important. Just guys like . . . Alan Arsenault. Look, there he is."

Mac turned to see Nessa throw her arms around the celebrated crooner, as famous for his talent as he was infamous for his affairs.

Alan bent Nessa backward in a kiss, and when he stood her on her feet, she was flushed and laughing.

"What's he doing here?" Mac asked, hostility rising.

"He's an old friend of the family," Daniel said.

"Why is he kissing her? He's got to be twice her age."

"But look at him. He's gorgeous. He's got it for her, too, but she doesn't want him. Maybe tonight she'll get smart and grab him." Daniel smirked. "It wouldn't be the first time a Dahl has married for money."

"What kind of man would marry a woman who only wanted him for his money?"

Daniel gave him a disbelieving look. "The kind of man who wants Ionessa Dahl badly enough to take her for any reason."

Mac snorted and went to lean against the wall.

Daniel joined him. "When a woman like that wants you, you dance to her tune and pay the band, too."

He spoke right to the heart of Mac's suspicion. Was Daniel dancing to Nessa's tune?

She was in for a shock if she thought she could sucker Mac the same way she suckered these other guys.

Daniel continued, "She thinks she's so smart about people, but underneath, she's as soft as butter."

Or hard as diamonds. Mac craned his neck as Alan swept Nessa into the ballroom and out of view.

It was better that way. Mac could bend all his attention on Daniel. "You like Nessa."

"I do. I like her a lot. But don't we all?" Daniel watched him, challenging him with his attitude and his mockery. "Miss Hestia and Miss Calista are my real sweethearts. They've done more for me than any other human beings, so I do my best to watch out for them and for Nessa."

"You're indebted to them?" Had Daniel helped Nessa out of gratitude? Remembering Nessa's instructions, Mac tried a smile.

Laughing, Daniel shielded his eyes. "Shit, man, if you promise not to do that, I'll tell you all about it."

Relieved, Mac wiped the smile away.

"But first"—Daniel tugged Mac toward the dining room—"I'm on a diet, and I'm starving. Let's eat."

Mac was starving, too. It had been one hell of a long day.

They moved toward the dining room, and Mac had just caught his first glimpse of the completely laden buffet table when he heard someone say "Oh, for the love of God" in such tones of disgust, he turned back toward the foyer, expecting to see some judgmental asshole making a nasty comment about Daniel. And maybe the short, stout, badly dressed female was a judgmental asshole, but she was glaring at *him*.

Mac searched his mind. Did he know her?

More important, did she know him? Because if she did, his masquerade was finished before it started. "Who's that? And what did I ever do to her?" he asked aloud and with, he hoped, convincing innocence. Of course, the only trouble with that was he couldn't act worth a damn.

"That's Pootie DiStefano. She lives in the attic," Daniel said.

Pootie DiStephano. Reed had mentioned her as a possible bandit, and when Mac had ordered his resources to get her personal information, they'd run into a stone wall. This Pootie was either psychotic about her privacy—or guilty as hell.

Lowering his voice, Daniel said, "Look at her. I've tried to help her, but she ignores me. She always wears the same crummy clothes. She won't do anything about the mustache. She is the most antisocial person I've ever met, and in normal circumstances, we'd never see her at a party."

Mac scrutinized her.

Pootie looked back, bristling with hostility.

"Wow. Is she ever looking you over!" Daniel sounded thoughtful, and he appraised Mac once more. "She doesn't like you much, does she?"

"I'm a great guy," Mac said.

"Pootie!" Calista rushed forward and tried to take Pootie's luggage. "What happened, dear? I thought you'd be in New York by now."

Daniel lingered to hear the answer.

Pootie snapped the suitcase back into her control. "Flight got delayed because of technical difficulties, then cancelled because of the goddamned storm."

"You've spent the whole day at the airport?"

"Yeah. They wouldn't let me smoke." Pootie coughed from deep down in her lungs.

"Poor dear," Calista said. "You must be starving! Come in and get something to eat."

With obvious distaste, Pootie's gaze swept the gathering, then settled once more on Mac in a way that made the hair stand up on the back of his head. "Good idea. Let me put away my suitcase first."

As she trudged toward the stairs, Daniel walked on. In an undertone, he said, "That's . . . weird. Must have been a really bad day at the airport."

"None of us are strangers to that." Mac watched her disappear into the upper reaches of the house, then joined Daniel in the buffet line.

Daniel rubbed his hands in the first masculine gesture Mac had seen from him. "Try the andouille sausage," he advised. "It'll teach you a new respect for cayenne."

"Okay." Mac picked up a plate. "You were telling me about Nessa."

"I was?" Daniel loaded up his plate. "Oh yeah. Nessa and her aunts. They're good people."

Damn Pootie and her lousy timing. Another fifteen minutes at the airport and Mac would have heard Daniel's version of his story. And somewhere in the midst of that story, Mac suspected, there was a clue to the robberies and how they were committed.

"So tell me why they're so good," Mac said.

"Miss Calista and Miss Hestia . . . when I had money problems, they managed to arrange a loan from a bank." Daniel chose his words very carefully, as if he walked through a minefield and a single wrong syllable could make it blow up in his face.

"How?"

"They have connections you can't imagine."

Mac glanced around at the guests, coming and going, laughing, talking, eating. He saw Chief Cutter trailing after a gorgeous woman he hoped was his wife. He recognized the mayor, a famous trumpet player, a jazz band leader, and Hollywood's newest celebrity.

Connections? Yeah. Now, that he could believe.

"I couldn't have done it on my own. They saved my life." Daniel stood, lifted his glass, and in a toast that effectively stopped all Mac's questions, shouted, "To the Dahl girls, long may they reign as the leading ladies of New Orleans!"

"To the Dahl girls!" the guests shouted back.

Clearly, Mac wasn't getting any more information out of Daniel. But that didn't mean Daniel wasn't front and center on the list of suspects.

"Come on, Mac," Daniel said. "Let's go rescue Nessa from Alan."

"I thought you said she should take Alan."

"She doesn't care what I think." Daniel grimaced. "I'm pretty sure she only likes *you*."

Thirteen

Nessa saw them coming, and with a kiss on Alan's cheek, she left him standing alone and started toward them. Toward Mac.

His breath hitched when he remembered the kiss they'd exchanged; she'd been cautious at first, and he'd compelled her when he should have wooed her. Next time, he'd keep his lust in check, use a little finesse, show her he wasn't really a brute with a scarred face and no neck—even if that's who he really was.

"Shit!" he said as Rav Woodland stepped into her path. The young cop was weaving a little, half-drunk, and trembling as he offered her his embrace.

The kid wanted to dance, and Mac already knew what she would do.

Nessa stepped into the boy's arms and let him sweep her away, but before she disappeared onto the dance floor, she gave Mac a shrug and a smile.

"Watching you two is like watching two trains on a single track heading for a collision," Daniel said. "It's inevitable, it's going to be colossal, and it's impossible to pull my gaze away."

From beside them, a hoarse voice said, "Yeah, and it's gonna be disaster."

Mac looked at Pootie DiStephano.

She stood at his side. She smelled like cigarettes, she looked like hell, and she challenged him like a large, aggressive bulldog.

"Why disaster?" he asked coolly.

"Because you don't get it."

"Get what?" He sure as hell didn't get her.

"If you two are going to fight, I'm going to leave," Daniel warned them.

Mac paid him no heed.

Neither did Pootie. "You don't understand these people. People in New Orleans. People in the South. Every time they talk slow, you deduct ten points from their IQ."

"I don't think they're stupid."

"You just think you're smarter."

"I'm out of here." Daniel disappeared into the crowd with a swish and a rustle of feathers.

"I *am* smarter than almost everyone." Maybe that made him an arrogant ass, but it was true and Mac didn't mind saying so, especially to this short, stout, crew-cut and pierced fifty-year-old. *Did* she know who he was? And if she did, why didn't she come out and say it?

Was she one of the Beaded Bandits? And if she was . . . was this her way of meeting the challenge of an investigator? "I don't understand people in New Orleans, if that's what you mean. How can I? They don't say what they mean."

"Yeah, they do. They just say it a little more gently than we do. You gotta know the code." She waved fingers stained with nicotine. "Like they'll tell you that *I'm* playing for the opposing team."

"You're a lesbian."

"Right. You're catching on." She glanced around. "See that good ol' boy over there? The one with the droopy pants and a belly the size of a stove?"

"The fat one."

"No." Pootie held up an admonishing hand. "Never *fat*. Short for his weight. And of course, there's the ever-popular, 'Bless your heart.'"

He took a long, slow breath. "Bless your heart?" He'd heard that phrase before. He'd heard it from Nessa. And she'd been talking to him.

"Sort of an all-purpose phrase." Pootie indicated a matron wearing a midriff-bearing shirt and low-cut jeans. "You'll hear them say it when someone has bad plastic surgery, or someone dyes her hair an off shade, or she wears something inappropriate. 'Bless her heart, the mirror in her room had a malfunction.'" She smirked as Mr. LeJeune hurried through, trying to corral his inebriated young wife. "They'll say it about guys who divorce their wives and marry a trophy and think that makes them young. 'Bless his heart, he's trying to stuff a wet noodle in a wildcat.'" She looked directly at him. "They say it about Yankees. 'Yankees can't help it if they were born north of civilization, bless their hearts.'"

He could almost hear Nessa laughing in his head.

Pootie continued, "If they say it right to you—*Bless your heart*—it means you've mortally offended and been told to go to hell."

His gaze settled on Nessa. "Really."

Nessa caught him watching her, disentangled herself from Rav's too-tight grasp, excused herself, and started toward him.

He watched her stroll forward, willing her to come into his arms without a care for anyone else. "Anyway, Miss DiStephano, why do you care what I think about people in New Orleans?"

"Listen, I've lived here fifteen years. It's different from N'York, from Chicago, from Philly. Doesn't mean it's wrong, it's simply different. Kinder." A smile softened Pootie's tough features. "A place where it's more important to be happy than right. I like it. I like the heat, I like the humidity, I like manners. If you don't like it—if you don't like Nessa—then get the hell out. I don't need a damn Yankee shitting in my nest." She stomped off, clear proof that living among the mannered folks of New Orleans hadn't rubbed off on her.

Nessa arrived in time to see her go. "What'd you do to Miss Pootie?"

"Nothing." He saw heads turning, saw people start their way. People who wanted to talk to Nessa, to dance with Nessa, to be with Nessa. So Mac tucked his hand around her waist, pulled her close, and turned her toward the dining room. "Sometimes people from New York are easier to anger than most people."

"Really? You think that?"

"Don't you?"

"Yes, but it seems to be true of most people from the North. Must be breathing all that cold air when you're young that makes you irascible." As she spoke, she rested her hand on his sleeve, looked up at him, and smiled.

Keeping Pootie's lecture in mind, he asked, "Irascible? Is that a polite way of saying I'm mean?"

She chuckled, a deep, joyous sound of enjoyment. "You catch on fast."

"I've always been a fast learner." He guided her through the dining room, dodging one guy wearing a high school football uniform and an infatuated grin. Mac got Nessa through the kitchen without incident, and out the back door onto the porch.

The backyard was empty of people, dark except for the light from the windows, silent except for the sound of the music wafting out the door of the ballroom. The freshly washed half-moon slid its light across the hard, shiny leaves of the magnolia tree. A series of arbors lifted their arms, laden with clematis and rose, over the flagstone walk, and a wall enclosed the flowers, the benches, the herb garden.

"Much better." He had Nessa to himself. He walked her down the steps and under the arbor. "There's only one woman at this party I want to dance with now."

"You've danced with my aunts, and you've made them very happy. Thank you."

Was she evading him? Did she really think that was going to work? "Your aunts are a pleasure. But now, I want to dance with *you*."

"Really. You don't have to dance with me. It's all right." She massaged his arm. "You must be tired."

"Listen to the band. They're playing a slow dance. That won't tire either one of us." With a whimsical smile, he offered his hand, palm up, and waited.

She was out of excuses to stay out of his arms. She placed her hand in his, and slowly he reeled her in.

Fourteen

Jeremiah's gaze locked with hers. And he smiled invitingly, telling Nessa without words that he was harmless.

He lied.

"You dance very well for a . . ." She hesitated too long.

"For a thug?"

"Not at all," she said, and wondered at his choice of words. "I was going to say . . . for a man."

"Men don't dance?"

"Seldom, and unwillingly. At least in my experience." And most certainly never this movement of thighs against thighs, of hips against hips, this slow, smoky seduction that tangled their bodies and created a heat unlike any she'd ever experienced . . . except during sex.

Dancing with Jeremiah was better than sex, and the motion, the friction, the sharing, pressed her to wonder what sex with him would be like.

She laughed at herself. Like she wasn't already wondering that.

"You've been hanging around with the wrong kind of men," he said.

"That's probably true. But the only men I know who enjoy dancing are gay, and while I dearly love their company, I find I like that tiny fillip that happens between a man who's interested and a woman who's tantalized."

"I am very interested, and I assure you, it's not tiny."

"What isn't tiny?" She realized what he meant one beat too late.

"My fillip."

She struggled to answer with some wit and no discomfort. "I . . . never thought it was. Why do you dance so well?"

"I worked my way through college as an escort to wealthy old women."

"No, really."

"No. Really."

He sounded serious, but she couldn't believe that. "What? You couldn't get a scholarship?"

"I had an . . . accident when I was thirteen, fell behind in my grades, dropped out of school."

She winced, wanted to ask about his accident.

But he whirled her in a circle, moved her under the second arbor and onto the flagstone patio, where the fountain splashed water against old, slick stone.

He continued, "I got a GED, which knocks you right out of the running for most college scholarships. But I always knew that somehow I was going to get through college, and one very wealthy, single woman offered to show me how to make a good wad of money while attending classes and making good grades."

She didn't believe him. She couldn't believe him.

She knew stuff like that went on, of course. But not to Jeremiah. Not to this man who defined self-confidence. "So you learned to dance."

"To dance . . . and other things. I learned how to dress. I learned how to kiss." He slid his hand under her chin and lifted her face to his. "And I learned how to make love to a woman to bring her the ultimate pleasure."

He took her breath away. "You were a gigolo?"

"That's one way of putting it."

"If you learned so much, how come you need me to be tactful for you?" She was trying to ground this conversation in reality, in the events of a long, hot, New Orleans day. But the shadows caressed his features, the play of dark and light emphasizing the heaviness of his lids, the glints in his eyes, his crooked nose and strong jaw.

"Those women never required conversation."

Nessa didn't know whether to laugh in amusement or snort in disbelief.

"I was taught certain pat phrases. 'Your eyes are ravishing tonight.'"

She started to thank him, then comprehended that he was reeling off a series of compliments.

"'That dress accentuates your fine figure,'" he said in one tone deeper than normal. "'Your voice reminds me of a nightingale.'"

"Have you ever even heard a nightingale?"

"No, but apparently it didn't matter. I finished college clear of debt, and with a recommendation from my original patroness, I landed a job at . . . at my company. I've never looked back."

"Do you own your company?" she asked.

"Why do you ask?"

"Because you seem the kind of man who would not take orders from anyone."

"You're right." He spanned her waist between his two hands and swung her so that her back rested against the wall. "You're so right." He kissed her.

No pressing of lips was this kiss, but a slow penetration of her mouth, a sweet meeting of tongues, of flavors, of heat. He kissed like a man with all the time in the world, like a man who pleasured women for a living. Nessa's breath caught again and again as his tongue slid in and out, tasting her, luring her.

The music sounded faintly through the air. The fountain played its own tune. The scent of lilies rose like heady perfume from the warm, damp earth. The seconds slid smoothly, one to another, becoming minutes marked by blissful sensuality.

If only she weren't already too relaxed, blindly trusting him to lead her where he wished, trusting him to care for her. Dimly, she knew she was a fool to feel this way about a man she'd only met this morning. But that man had protected her from the storm, saved her from a mugger, kissed her like a lover. In twelve hours, they'd been through more than most couples lived in a month.

He nipped her, his teeth closing on her lower lip, teasing, just on the edge of pain, and she forgot to breathe. Her body jolted, each muscle tightened as if he'd shot an electric current right to her clit. God. God, she teetered on the edge of orgasm, fighting against a surrender too precipitous and too soon.

Rescue came when something—something big—

fell off the wall and landed a few feet away in the flower bed.

Nessa jumped and shrank back against the wall.

Jeremiah put her behind him and faced the intruder. It was a guy. He blundered around and cursed.

"What were you doing up there?" Jeremiah asked sharply.

"Whoa, you guys were really going at it." Ryan Wright's drunken voice blared, and he brayed with laughter.

She flinched at his coarse hilarity. Had he been *watching* them?

"Go away." Jeremiah's tone left Ryan—and her—in no doubt of his intentions if Ryan disobeyed.

"You think you're so smart." Ryan slurred every word. "You piece of shit."

Jeremiah moved toward him, a large, threatening hunk of a man.

Ryan stumbled back, whirled, and raced toward the house.

Jeremiah started forward.

Nessa caught his sleeve. "Jeremiah, please. Let him go."

He halted. He looked down at his fists, then turned and took her in his arms again.

But it was too late. Ryan's vulgar taunt echoed in her mind.

Going at it? Yes, they'd been going at it, and for a long time. Ten minutes? Twenty? She didn't know. She only knew her back was against the wall, her body trembling with heat and need. One of his arms held her close to him, belly to belly, and his erection pressed in the cup between her thigh and her pelvis. His thumb brushed her nipple in small circles, each movement creating a greater tension, a greater intimacy. . . . With a man she barely knew. For Nessa, who had worked so hard all these years while ignoring her libido, Jeremiah was a temptation in which she never should have indulged.

Worse, one of her hands clutched the sleeve of his shirt over his bicep; the other wrapped his waist. She embraced him as if she couldn't stand without him—and right now, she wasn't sure she could. Shadows clung to one side of him, caressing him like velvet, turning his skin dusky. The sweep of his dark eyelashes hid all but the glint of his eyes.

"I'll spend the night." His voice was low, coaxing. He didn't wait for an invitation. He made a demand.

"What? No. No, you . . . that's impossible, here, with my great-aunts in the house." Then she thought, *I'm presuming too much*, and babbled, "I mean, you can stay, of course you can. We always have a lot of people who stay because they're too intoxicated to go home, and you were shot, so you should stay. But . . ."

He stroked his forefinger across her lips. "But you won't let me in your bed, which was really what I was asking."

Okay. She hadn't presumed. Which made her feel less stupid, and yet more pressured.

Lots more pressure. He was leaning over her. Brooding over her. Holding her as if they'd not been sharing a dance but having sex. Every breath she inhaled was filled with his scent, and all she felt, still, was the intense pressure of desire pushed too close to the brink of climax. "We're working together. We've known each other less than twenty-four hours. We shouldn't even be . . . kissing."

"Or dancing."

"Exactly." Was he laughing at her? "Probably this is all a response to the storm and the danger of the mugging and the, um, liquor we've consumed. No one gets this aroused merely standing in the garden in the honeysuckle."

He chuckled, low and deep in his chest. "Honey, I'm a man. I get horny about the word *honeysuckle*. You know, *honey . . . suckle*."

When he said it that way, he made *her* horny. She plucked at the laces on his shirt. "So you're not mad?" *Nice, Nessa. Right back to high school.*

"I have the Garden Suite at the Olivier House. Going back tonight is no hardship—"

No hardship? She guessed not. The Garden Suite was one of the city's premier rooms, and the fact that he stayed there told her all too clearly how much his company valued him.

"—But I don't believe this desire is the result of the honeysuckle or the mugging or the storm or the liquor. The first time I saw you, I thought—" He stopped.

"What did you think?" She desperately wanted to know what he thought. About anything. And everything. Because although he had just shared a part of himself, deep in her bones she knew he hid secrets he had never revealed. . . . To anyone.

"Someday, I'll tell you."

Someday . . . all his secrets . . . but what would he require in payment?

In a slow, torturous motion, he pulled away from

her. "So I'll go away tonight. What time should I pick you up tomorrow?"

"Tomorrow?"

"We'll go on a . . . date."

The way he said *date* made her think he meant something entirely different. Her temperature rose, measured not in mercury but in increments of passion. "No, really. We can't . . . date. It's too soon. It's not right." She expected he would point out that those were two different arguments completely.

Instead, he bent to kiss her, and pulled back at the last minute. "Then I'll see you Monday morning. We'll work on the case and pretend tonight never happened."

"Yes. That's exactly what I want."

"I thought it was."

Fifteen

Saturday morning, Mac sat downstairs in the Garden Suite at the Olivier House, watching one of the robbery DVDs and going through Chief Cutter's notes. His cell phone rang, he glanced at the number, his eyebrows rose, but he muted the TV and answered at once.

No use hesitating. She couldn't help what she was, and he didn't care anymore.

"Hi, Mom. What's up?"

His mother's voice, hesitant as always, said, "Hi, Jeremiah. How are you?"

"Good. Busy." Although he'd reviewed the videos a hundred times, he still kept an eye on the TV. "How are you? And how's Mitch?"

"He's good. He sends his love," she said in a rush.

Right. His love was the last thing his stepfather wanted to send to Mac. "So what do you need?"

"I don't need anything." She sounded anxious now. "But your brother's coming home on leave in a couple of weeks and I was hoping . . . I mean, I know you're busy, but it would be great if you could be here. For him, you know. He's always admired you."

"He's a good kid." Mac meant it. For all that he and Joe shared a mom with a less-than-stellar character, and his father was Mitch, the most easily irritated asshole Mac had ever met, Joe was a good kid.

"Not such a kid anymore." Her voice trembled. "After his leave, he's going back for a second tour of duty."

Mac sobered. "Good Lord, why?"

"He says he's good at what he does, and they need him."

"What does he do?"

"He won't say."

One of *those* jobs. "All right. I'll be there."

"Good! Your stepfather said you wouldn't, but I knew you'd come for Joseph." She sounded pathetically grateful.

Mac felt a twinge of guilt, and the twinge made him irritable and cruel. "Yeah. I'll come for Joe."

As if he'd slapped her, his mother caught her breath. "Jeremiah, you don't come home enough, and *I* want to see you, too."

For about a year now, his mother had been trying to talk to him about . . . stuff. Their relationship, he guessed, and what happened when he was thirteen. He didn't want to rehash old problems. Not now. Not ever. He should have shut up while he had the chance.

"I know, Mom. Listen, I've got to go. There's somebody at the door." As if his words had power, someone knocked.

If he were really lucky, it was Nessa come to seduce him into doing her bidding.

He looked through the keyhole.

He wasn't really lucky.

Jerking open the door, he asked, "What are you doing here?"

Gabriel Prescott countered, "What are *you* doing here?"

"I guess it's important business?" Mac's mother said in his ear.

"It's my security man paying me a surprise visit, so I suppose it is important business." He stepped back and let Gabriel walk through the door.

Gabriel's dark tan, black hair, and high cheekbones proved his Hispanic heritage. His strong body and lithe motions betrayed a skill with self-defense. His narrowed green eyes betrayed something entirely different—a European legacy and a fair amount of irritation.

"How did he get up to your penthouse without you knowing?" Mac's mother asked.

"I'm not in my penthouse. I'm in a hotel in New Orleans."

"New Orleans? Why are you in New Orleans?" Her voice rose in excitement. "Are you in New Orleans for Mardi Gras? Did you actually take a vacation?"

Her enthusiasm made Mac grind his teeth. "No, Mom. It's not a vacation. It's definitely business."

Gabriel dropped his overnight bag with a thump.

Mom's enthusiasm was undimmed. "I've always wanted to go to New Orleans. Please, Jeremiah, take a little time for yourself. Eat and drink and dance. Have some fun for a change!"

Remembering the party the night before, Mac said, "I already have, Mom."

"That's good. So good. You don't take care of yourself enough."

Whatever else she was, he guessed she remained enough of his mother to worry about him. "I gotta go. I'll let you know when I'm coming in. Tell Joe I'm looking forward to seeing him."

"Okay."

"Okay." He hung up. He had to. If he didn't, she'd draw out the good-byes like some sort of ceremonial mother/son ritual. "What *are* you doing here, Gabe?"

"You wanted an immediate security upgrade at your banks. I came to check on my boys, the ones installing it. And what do I see on the security video? Mac MacNaught. Only they tell me you're not Mac MacNaught, but Jeremiah Mac, the insurance investigator come to get to the bottom of the Mardi Gras Robberies." Gabriel threw out his arms. "Have you lost your mind? You're the CEO of Premier Central Banks. Shouldn't you be directing a board meeting? Don't you have anything better to do than chase after bank robbers?"

"No. How's the upgrade going?"

"Okay."

"Just okay?" That was irritating.

"The wiring in the banks is ancient. We've run into termites. Hurricane Katrina did a lot of damage. Everything's taking twice as long as it should. I should have doubled my estimate." Gabriel peeled out of his suit jacket.

"Tough."

"Ain't it?" Gabriel collapsed on the couch.

"Make yourself at home."

"Thanks. So why are you down here pretending to be an insurance investigator?"

"Because my last investigator fell in love with my primary suspect."

Gabriel lifted his eyebrows. "Male or female?"

It took no more urging than that for Mac to find Nessa on the video and zoom in on her face.

"Wow. She's hot." Gabriel sat forward, elbows on his knees, and stared.

So did Mac. "She blew it seven years ago, lost five hundred dollars—"

"She stole it?"

"No, the teller did, but Nessa didn't get the promotion she wanted. Right away, she goes in and arranges to have my bank robbed."

"Far-fetched."

Gabriel didn't worry about making his opinion known, Mac noted, and as blunt as he was, he reminded Mac of . . . himself.

"It would have been easier to change jobs," Gabriel said.

"Not in New Orleans. She's a native, daughter of one of their oldest, most respected families. Apparently, that's important here."

"Then why not steal a *lot* of money and be done with it?"

"Because then she's got the attention of the police and the Feds, and she's screwed."

"If she gets caught, she's screwed, anyway. She might as well be hung for a sheep as a lamb."

"That's not what it's about with her. She does it to irritate me." And Mac *was* irritated. Irritated and intrigued.

"She doesn't know *you*." Although Gabriel seemed to. It was like he'd researched Mac's background. "She doesn't know the CEO of Premier Central would pay any attention to such insignificant robberies. She doesn't know how much you hate thieves. Nothing about this theory makes sense."

"What about these robberies *does* make sense?"

"Well. There you've got a point. Senseless crimes are always a problem. I can follow the logic of crime for money or for passion. But delinquency like this, with no rhyme or reason, leaves me with no direction." Gabriel flexed his fists.

"I don't put my face out there," Mac said. "There aren't any pictures of me hanging in the lobby. But I make my feelings known. Everyone who works for me knows I demand exemplary honesty and integrity from my people."

Gabriel nodded. "Yet you still haven't convinced me Nessa Dahl is guilty, and if she is—who is this woman from one of New Orleans's oldest families manipulating for the trigger men?"

"That's the beauty of it. She's got a drag queen living in the boarding house with her. He's flawless."

Obviously, Gabriel was turning it over in his mind. "So the cross-dresser recruits a compatriot to rob your banks. . . . All right. You've made your point. There is a possibility that she's at least close to the source of the problem. What are your impressions of her?"

"She's as smart as I thought. She and her aunts plead poverty, but they spend a lot of money on parties. Men would commit theft and worse for a chance between her legs." And that was really what had Mac convinced.

Mac could see the question forming on Gabriel's lips.

Would you?

So Mac changed the subject. "There's a way into the Chartres Street branch vault."

That brought Gabriel to his feet. "What?"

"A hundred years ago, the guy that built it was killed in there, the crime was never solved, and no one ever figured out how he got in."

"You are kidding."

"I just spent the morning going over the newspaper records online and reading every available account of the crime." With a wave of the hand, MacNaught indicated his laptop. "Although they searched, they found no way in. They walled off the vault and turned the place into a store, and for years the area around it went to hell. When the French Quarter revival came in the sixties, some smart son of a bitch restored it as a bank. In the eighties he sold it to Security Corp, who sold it to Prime Finances International, who sold it to us. Never was I told the history of the bank."

"You wouldn't have cared if you had been."

"You're right." Mac never hesitated to admit a possible fault.

"Do you have reason to think someone's using unauthorized access?"

"No, but I want that hole plugged, anyway, and discreetly, too."

"Right. Talk about bad publicity." Gabriel pulled his planner from his pocket and flipped through the calendar. "I'm only going to trust my top people with this one. . . . And they're not available. On a scale of one to ten, how do you assess the danger?"

"A one. It's been a bank for fifty years without a

robbery in the vault. But if I can figure it out, someone else can. You need to deal with this right away."

"It's not possible," Gabriel said coolly.

"You're doing a big job for me, and I've got a lot of influence in the banking world. If I insinuate I'm not happy with your firm . . ."

Gabriel snorted, not a bit impressed. "My reputation is solid—and so's yours as a curmudgeon."

Mac almost grinned. But that wouldn't do.

"Better to do it after Mardi Gras, anyway, when the streets are empty. So—in twelve days you need to clean out the vault. I'll be back for that."

"How long are you staying this time?"

"I fly out tonight."

"Right." Mac flicked off the TV. "Come on. I'll take you out for coffee and beignets, and you can bring me up to date on the security upgrades."

"Sounds good." As they headed out the door, Gabriel said, "So, you're masquerading as an insurance investigator, hoping no one recognizes you, to infiltrate Ionessa Dahl's life and catch her in the act."

"I want Nessa's head on a platter—or proof that she's innocent. And no matter what, I want the men who commit the robberies."

"You could get hurt."

"Do I look like someone who's afraid?" Mac checked the door of his suite to make sure it locked.

"No. You look like someone who knows how to fight."

"Better than that." MacNaught led the way onto the crowded street. "I always win."

*　　*　　*

Russell Whipple slid into a tiny sidewalk table at the French Coffeeshop across from Deaux Bakery. "Coffee," he told the waitress.

"Beignets?" She dimpled at him. "They're fresh and hot."

"God, no." Deaux had the best beignets, but he couldn't go there, could he? Mac MacNaught and his boyfriend were over there.

His waitress made a face and turned away.

He grabbed her hand. "Make it Bailey's coffee."

"Right!" She dimpled again. He would have liked to think it was because she liked him, but he knew she anticipated a better tip.

Keeping his sunglasses on and his hat pulled low over his eyes, he watched the two guys talk. Their waitress obviously pegged them as hot shits; she was fawning over them. She made Russell sick. The whole setup made Russell sick.

"Here you go, sir!" The waitress set the coffee down, all sweet smiles and Southern charm. "With extra cream!"

"Great. Thanks." He took a sip and burned his mouth. "Ouch. Shit, goddamn!"

"Are you okay?" She hovered sympathetically, but when he glanced up, she was grinning.

"Yeah, very funny. Get me some ice water."

Her grin disappeared, and so did she.

She'd just seen her tip evaporate, and he bet she was going to forget the ice water. That bitch.

You're so skinny, the women will never notice you, boy. Are you sure you're not a faggot?

"Shut up," Russell whispered, and flicked the thought away like he would flick away a fly.

The guys in prison thought you were pretty enough.

"Shut up!" he said.

"What?" The waitress stood beside him, dripping water on the table. She slammed the glass down. "You don't need to be a jerk!"

Across the street, Mac and his friend stood up.

Russell never took his gaze off them. "Gimme the bill."

"It's eight bucks."

He took a swig of the coffee, burned his mouth again, put a ten on the table, and followed them down the street.

Last night, he'd checked out MacNaught's whole setup.

In one day, that bastard MacNaught had managed to check into one of the best rooms in New Orleans, visit all his banks, and impress Nessa Dahl so much she invited him to the annual Dahl House party.

Of course, Russell had been invited, too, but the gossips never thought he was worth mentioning. They never talked about how he dazzled the old Dahl ladies, or spoke in awe of how he got shot defending Nessa from a mugger. They never called him Nessa Dahl's date, or whispered that he'd been seen kissing her in the garden. Nobody ever noticed him.

But they were going to. When he was finished making a fool of Mac MacNaught, he would be rich, he would be famous, and Mac MacNaught would be bleeding on the ground.

Just like before.

Sixteen

All weekend long, Nessa heard not one word from Jeremiah Mac—a good sign that he'd seen the sense of her argument and withdrawn from his pursuit.

She was very pleased. She could only imagine how uncomfortable she would feel now, at eight thirty a.m. on Monday morning, as she walked into the bank dressed in her most conservative black suit with the one-button jacket, the straight skirt, and the heels. . . . Well, her heels weren't at all conservative. They were tall, open-toed, and red. Bright, stunning red.

Some people might say she was in conflict with herself.

Some people were jerks.

"Hey, Miss Dahl, congratulations on escaping from the Stephabeast!" Carol gave Nessa a big thumbs-up.

Nessa responded with a grin and a wave at the tellers, all of them once again dressed in their Mardi Gras costumes, all of them pleased that she had broken free, at least temporarily, of the grind of making sure the bank ran smoothly. Which was damned generous of them, considering that meant they were stuck with Stephabeast as their real, day-to-day manager.

"Miss Dahl, can you open the vault so we can get our drawers?" Jeffrey asked. "The beast isn't here yet—"

"Duh," Julia said.

Jeffrey continued, "And with you gone, she's the vault teller. But if we don't get those drawers counted, we're not opening on time. And you know what that means." He lifted the imaginary noose around his neck, tilted his head, and bugged out his eyes.

"I know." Nessa dropped her purse in her drawer and locked it. Walking behind the counter, she punched her code into the vault, counted out the bills into the cash drawers, took them to the tellers, and watched as they confirmed her count.

As always, it took twenty minutes, and she wondered what Stephanie would have done when she strolled in at one minute to nine and none of the tellers were ready to work. What would that have done to her impeccable record?

"Is, um, Mr. Mac here?" she asked Carol.

"He came in plenty early. So I came, too." Carol grinned.

"Carol, men are not meat. They deserve the respect accorded to another breathing, sentient being." Nessa observed Carol's smirk of delight, and shoved her shoulder. "Okay, listen—men are carbon-based life forms, and they deserve to be fed dinner occasionally."

"Hey!" Jeffrey feigned insult.

The women laughed, and Nessa hurried toward Jeremiah's office. Not because she wanted to see him after his easy abandonment of his pursuit. That this guy had slipped away just because she said *no* . . . that surprised her. Most men faded away as soon as a woman expressed an interest, or a lack of interest, or wanted to have a conversation, or didn't like their football team, or ate something expensive on the menu, or offered to pay for dinner. . . . But she would have sworn Jeremiah wasn't a normal, easily intimidated kind of guy. She had thought he seemed a real man, the type who made up his mind what he wanted, planned how to achieve his goal, and wasn't dissuaded by mere practicalities such as the fact that they were working together or that they had nothing in common.

So. She was disappointed in his character. Better now than later, when she'd invested time and emotion in him.

Right, Nessa. Don't invest time and emotion in him. Pretend like you didn't lust after him the first moment he walked into the bank.

She stopped in the doorway of his office.

He stood gazing at the sheets of paper spread out on his desk, his jacket unbuttoned, his hands on his hips.

He looked good.

He glanced up at her, and with no greeting whatsoever started a consultation. "You're here. Good. Have you seen all the security videos from the robberies start to finish?"

Wonderful to see you, too. "No, just clips on the news and what was playing at the police station Friday."

"Right. I've had them put on one DVD. What I want you to do is sit down and watch them, make notes on what you see." He pointed at the new flat-screen TV hung on the wall and the two plush chairs sitting before it.

Do you like my shoes? "You know I'm not a trained observer or anything."

"But you have a good eye and you're a sensible woman."

Ooh, those were love words every girl wanted to hear. But hey, if she wanted to hear his love words, all she had to do was lie prone on a bed and he was a veritable fountain of compliments, lovingly prepared by the patronesses who had put him through college.

An escort. He'd been an escort to older, wealthy women.

She still didn't know if she believed him, but why would he lie? It wasn't the kind of thing most men would brag about. Certainly not this guy, with his intense gaze and grim face that hid so many secrets.

He continued, "I want to know if you spot collusion between any of the customers or tellers. I want to know if you recognize anyone or think you recognize anyone. I want to know if you see something in common between the personnel before, after, and during."

Did he remember what he'd told her? Did he remember that he'd kissed her?

"Play them as many times as you like," he said. "Take notes."

"All right." Thanks to him, she now realized she was totally resistible, not to mention the most boring female ever to walk this earth, and a pair of red, open-toed pumps was not going to change that immutable fact.

"What are you waiting for? Come in. Get started!"

"All right." She walked in, took the remote he offered, and gathered a notebook and two pens. "Are you going to watch with me?"

"No. I've seen them enough. I need a new eye—

yours." He picked up his briefcase. "I'll use Miss Decker's office. I've got business in my office that needs to be taken care of."

"Where is she going to be?"

"On the floor, of course." With a frown, he glanced at his watch. "If she ever gets here."

It was ten minutes to nine.

As Nessa seated herself, she deliberately kept her expression bland.

He left and shut the door behind him.

She loosened her control and grinned. She might be the most boring female on earth, but Jeremiah Mac had just reduced Stephabeast to a joke in her own bank. . . . And Nessa was human enough to enjoy it.

Mac placed his briefcase in the middle of Stephanie Decker's pristine desk. He glanced at the clock on the shelf—a gold clock, one the bank had sent Stephanie Decker for winning the contest for the most loans secured in one year.

It read one minute to nine.

He heard her heels slapping hard on the marble floor, past the office where he'd left Nessa viewing the videos.

Decker stopped. She backed up. He heard her give a huff of disgust, then her heels rapidly and loudly came toward her office.

She walked in muttering, "Always did like her better, and now—" She caught sight of him. She jumped guiltily, then stopped cold. "I was rehearsing a play."

He didn't care what stupid excuse she made—she'd been complaining about his decisions at a moment when he'd begun to wonder if she had been entirely straight in her annual assessments of Nessa's character and actions. "Miss Dahl is using my office today, so I'll be using your office to conduct my business."

She blinked at him, trying to comprehend and failing. "Where am I supposed to sit?"

"There are desks in the lobby to make bank officers available to the customers. I believe Miss Dahl has one. Sit there, where you'll be cognizant of any problems that arise on the floor."

As he hooked his Bluetooth headset over his ear, he observed the ugly red flush as it slid from Decker's collar, crept up her cheeks, and rose to her forehead, giving her complexion a sunburned, mottled look.

"Is that a problem, Decker?"

"No." But she clenched her fists as if she wanted to hit him.

Briefly, he wondered if she believed her fury carried weight with him. Then, dismissing her from his mind, he sat down in her chair and went to work.

She turned on her heel and started out.

He didn't look up. "Shut the door behind you, please."

She did, with less control than he would expect from one of his bank managers.

Placing his laptop before him, he opened it as he placed the call to his private line.

Mrs. Freytag answered at once, and together they began the process of answering the hundreds of e-mails that she deemed important enough to require his attention. As they worked, he kept an eye on his in-box, and within ten minutes an e-mail arrived, the one he half expected to see.

Stephanie Decker had written him a personal note.

"Excuse me, Mrs. Freytag." He put her on hold and opened the e-mail. He read:

Mr. MacNaught,
As much as I hate to bother you when you've gone to such lengths to place your insurance investigator in the best possible circumstances to crack the case of the Mardi Gras Robberies, I reluctantly must inform you that he's obstructing the normal workings of the bank. I believe he's simply ignorant of the delicate balance required to maintain good service between customers, tellers, and officers, and perhaps he fails to realize that in this case, service is my first priority. Also—and I hesitate to suggest this—I believe Miss Dahl may have used her privileged position as his assistant to behave less than professionally with Mr. Mac. While I certainly hope this is not true, I'm afraid past experience will prove me right.

Okay, Stephanie was a malicious bitch. Okay, she was a tattletale and a troublemaker.

But she had a point. That stupid investigator he'd hired had fallen in love with Nessa without even realizing how easily she'd manipulated him. . . .

Worse, since Mac had met her, he no longer wanted to remember his own suspicions.

He returned to the e-mail.

I'm not in any way criticizing your arrangements, but perhaps in the future it might be better if Mr. Mac worked somewhere else with someone else.
Sincerely, Stephanie Decker

Mac typed:

Miss Decker,
Thank you so much for keeping me up to date with the
situation. I'm afraid Mr. Jeremiah Mac has been placed
there by the insurance company and there's nothing I
can do to change that. However, as always, I appreci-
ate your clear-sighted assessment and will be inter-
ested in any further comments you might have.
M.

Mac hit *Send*, briefly wondered what Decker would
do next.

Dismissing her from his mind, he opened the line to
Mrs. Freytag and went back to work.

Seventeen

After a morning spent watching security videos and taking notes, Nessa was glad to go to lunch—alone, for Jeremiah absently asked her to bring him a sandwich.

She hadn't seen anything particularly interesting on the DVDs. She'd spotted a few familiar faces: neighbors, friends, customers. She'd noted the clever methods employed by the robbers, methods that changed with each robbery and made each unique. But she hadn't uncovered anything helpful to the investigation, and that made her feel as if she'd failed.

As she left, she expected Stephanie to be in one of her rip-roaring snits that caused secretaries, tellers, and bank officers to quit, and customers to take their money to another bank in a huff.

Instead, Stephanie smiled pleasantly as Nessa made her exit, so pleasantly Nessa was put in mind of a serial killer gloating over her next hapless victim. Not that Nessa was a victim, but . . . Stephanie's smiles tended to be the prelude to another of Nessa's crushing disappointments.

Oddly, Pootie's offer of a job leaped to her mind, and

wasn't easily dismissed. Nessa supposed it was because Pootie was so independent; nothing and nobody (except for her family in N'York) gave her any trouble. And right now, Nessa would enjoy having troubles that were her own and only her own. She didn't want to remember the tellers and their uneasy expressions, or the way old Mr. Carnation stopped her on the way out of the bank and quavered a greeting. Her aunts said she took too much on her shoulders; maybe they were right.

The rest of the afternoon was spent rerunning the DVD, trying to concentrate on what she'd seen half a dozen times when the events of Friday evening were so much more interesting.

Once, she thought she saw a familiar gesture, but she couldn't put it together with anyone she knew. Once, she thought she recognized a walk, then realized she was mistaken. The truth was, she *wanted* to see something more, strained to put clues together, anything that would impress him, end this case, put them on equal footing. . . . And then what?

Then he'd leave, that's what.

But it didn't matter. No matter how hard she tried, she couldn't see anything conclusive on this DVD.

At closing time, she turned off the TV and stretched, sprawling with her legs out and her arms over her head.

The door opened.

She leaped to her feet.

It was Jeremiah. Of course, it had to be Jeremiah.

"Any luck?" he asked.

"No." She ripped a sheet off her tablet and handed

him her list. "That's everything I noted, but I don't think there's anything that's helpful."

Without bothering to glance at her scribblings, he placed it on one of the piles on his desk. "I'll decide that." Taking her arm, he walked her into the reception area.

The last customers stood at the counter in front of Lisa, Carol, and Mary. Eric stood before the door, key in the lock, letting them out one by one. Jeffrey, Julia and Donna were finished for the day, counting out their drawers. Stephanie waited to swoop on them as soon as they finished. The bank echoed with too much cold marble and the gust of air-conditioning, and the Mardi Gras decorations hung limply, showing their age, waiting for Lent.

Everyone looked up, took note of Jeremiah's hand on Nessa's arm, and looked back down. Carol was grinning, but the rest managed not to smirk.

Well, except for the Stephabeast, who scowled.

Jeremiah didn't notice. Of course not. He surveyed the scene coolly, then said, "Before we leave for the day, I'd like to look over the vault."

"The vault?" Nessa thought he must be kidding.

"The famed vault where Frederick Vycor was murdered."

She considered him. The vault had nothing to do with the Beaded Bandits. He didn't seem the type of man who was impressed by a ghost story, yet she suspected he never did anything without a reason. So what was going on in his head?

He looked down at her. He had no expression on his face. None.

But she knew now that his impassivity meant only

that he was good at concealing his thoughts . . . his passions.

The heat of his body curled around her, enveloped her. Or maybe that was the heat of her own frustration she felt.

He raised his eyebrows. "What do you want, Ionessa?"

"Want? I don't want . . ." She couldn't even finish the lie.

She glanced at the tellers.

They had all counted their drawers. They were finished for the day.

She glanced at the door.

Eric was letting the last customer out.

She glanced at her wristwatch. 6:20 p.m. "As soon as the drawers are counted, the vault teller will place them inside the vault. Who tonight, I suppose, will be . . . Stephanie Decker."

Jeremiah strode up to Stephanie, who stood tapping her foot, waiting without patience for Lisa to finish the last transaction. "Decker, Nessa and I are going to tour the vault," he said.

"Tour the vault? You want to *tour* the *vault*?" Stephanie's voice hit the famed Stephanie high note, the one that made dogs howl. "Why? *Why* would you want to do that?"

Jeremiah stepped back as if she were spitting hissy all over his clean white shirt. "Is there a problem?"

"Mr. MacNaught will *not* approve."

Nessa exchanged glances with Carol, who was wide-eyed and edging away.

"Are you forbidding me?" He sounded mild, but beneath that, Nessa heard the steel.

So, apparently, did Stephanie. Her voice returned to the normal human range. "Of course not. I've cooperated with your investigation, and I will continue to cooperate in every way. Can you wait a moment while I finish bank business?"

Lisa gingerly slid her drawer toward Stephanie.

"Thank you, dear." Stephanie smiled so pleasantly at Lisa that the girl snagged her costume sprinting away.

While Stephanie verified the amount, the tellers picked up their things and called out farewells. They hustled toward the door like civilians trying to escape before the bomb squad detonated their latest acquisition.

As soon as Eric locked the door behind them, Stephanie crooked her finger at him.

He hurried over and stacked the drawers, then followed as Stephanie led the way to the vault.

She punched her code into the electronic panel. The round, deep steel door opened. "As you can see," she said, "I have my own personal code that opens the vault. Miss Dahl is the only other person in this bank who has her own code."

"If Miss Dahl has been deemed untrustworthy, why does she have access to the vault?" Jeremiah asked.

"Untrustworthy? What do you mean, untrustworthy?" Nessa couldn't believe he had said it.

"I understood there was a blot on your record," he said.

"That was a long time ago." Nessa should have known he had investigated her. That was what he did. But she felt as if he'd been digging through her underwear drawer without her knowledge, and she hated that.

"And I need to have someone here who can open the vault if I'm unavailable." Stephanie's outrage almost equaled Nessa's. "Really, if I needed assistance in running my bank, I would ask Mr. MacNaught."

If Jeremiah noticed resentment from either of them, he gave no indication. "Why wouldn't you be available?"

Eric muttered something under his breath.

"I'm ill sometimes, and I do take vacation—oh, why am I explaining myself to *you*?" Stephanie grabbed the drawers out of Eric's arms. "Give those to me."

He let go.

She staggered under the weight, then stepped into the vault and out of sight.

Jeremiah looked right at Eric. "What did you say?"

"I said, 'She's never here in time to open the vault.' That's what I said." Eric looked defiantly at Nessa. "Someone needs to tell them the truth, Miss Nessa. This isn't right!"

"Mr. Mac has nothing to do with the bank. He's an investigator," she reminded him.

"Maybe so, but he seems like he's got the chops to get things done," Eric answered.

Stephanie stepped out of the vault in time to catch Eric's last words, and the stupid boy betrayed himself with a blush.

"I've been thinking," Stephanie said. "Your point about the vault is well taken, Mr. Mac. Therefore, I think it might be wise if you and Ionessa signed in to acknowledge you were entering the vault." Picking up the clipboard with sign-in sheet, she offered it to Jeremiah.

He took it. "Why do you call her Ionessa?"

Stephanie blinked in astonishment. No one ever jumped her about that. "Because, um, isn't that her name?"

"She prefers Nessa. I wouldn't recommend muddying your reputation as a good manager by failing to remember a matter as important as your assistant manager's name." Jeremiah scribbled an illegible name on the list and handed it back.

"Of course, *you* would know *so much* about how to be a bank manager." Stephanie's scorching tones chastised him. "I'll have you know I graduated summa cum laude from Tulane, and never did any of my business classes have a lecture about whether or not I should remember the name of someone like—"

"I would stop right now." Jeremiah didn't raise his voice.

But something about his tone must have slapped some sense into Stephanie, for she broke off with a gasp.

"Don't." Nessa touched his arm. "Really. It's not necessary."

He looked down at her again, and this time he showed emotion. She couldn't read it. She didn't know if it was passion or possessiveness. But she did know he didn't give a damn about courtesy.

And Stephanie knew it, too.

He had betrayed too much to a woman so filled with spite, her eyes were muddy with it.

Stephanie's hand trembled as she extended the sign-in sheet. "Here . . . *Nessa*."

Nessa carefully wrote her name and filled in the time—six twenty-three p.m.—for both of them.

"Thank you, *Nessa*. Don't forget that the vault will close automatically at seven, and unless there's an override from the panel out here"—Stephanie tapped the electronic security—"it's secure until Nessa or I or someone with a code opens it in the morning."

"Thirty minutes is enough time for me to look around," Jeremiah said.

Stephanie smiled—my God, that was a bone-chilling smile—and backed away, clipboard in hand. "You don't want to spend the whole night trapped inside."

Eighteen

Nessa led the way through the round door into the dim vault.

Frederick Vycor's vault was long and narrow, about eight feet wide and fifteen feet long. The ceiling was ten feet high. A long counting table was fixed to the wall close to the vault door, and there Stephanie had placed the tellers' drawers. An entire unit of oak shelves was built into the opposite wall and stacked with bills—fives, tens, twenties, fifties, and hundreds, all banded and official.

Jeremiah slowly walked around the vault, looking at the walls, the ceiling, the shelves.

Nessa watched him, a half smile on her face. "What *are* you looking for?"

"I'm being a tourist, wanting to see the scene of a legendary crime."

She laughed. "No. Oh, no. Not you. Vulgar curiosity has never prompted any of your decisions."

"You think you know me that well?"

"I don't pretend to understand what makes you do

what you do, but I'm quite sure you don't waste your employer's time with frivolous pursuits."

"Quite right. I don't." He started the circuit again, his hands clasped behind his back, his gaze moving from point to point, assessing the vault. "What's the construction, do you know?"

"Word is Vycor had the walls poured in twelve inches of concrete and steel." She leaned against the wall, waiting while Jeremiah ran his hands over the far wall. "He was Hitler in his bunker."

"Hitler? Because he ran the bank by the rules?"

"Because he was a ruthless pig who never bent the rules."

"Do you bend the rules?"

He watched her as if he already knew the answer. "When it's the right thing to do."

"The right thing? As defined by you?" His tone goaded her.

She responded with rising ire. "As defined by someone who doesn't routinely kick puppies or foreclose on widows."

"For someone with your reputation, you're very quick to make judgments."

"With my reputation? What do you mean, *with my reputation*?"

"According to Mr. MacNaught—"

"The original puppy kicker himself!"

He began again, his eyes glowing with impatience. "According to Mr. MacNaught, you—" He stopped.

"I *what*?"

"Sh." Jeremiah held up his hand. His head turned slowly toward the door.

Then she heard it, too. The ticking of the timer. The smooth sound of steel hinges gliding toward . . .

They both sprang toward the door. They hit it precisely as the lock clanked shut with a solid clank.

"No!" Nessa slammed her hand on the cool steel. "Hey!" The sound of her fist was feeble, barely carrying to her own ear.

Jeremiah stepped back and glanced at his slim gold watch. "I have 6:50 p.m."

Nessa glanced at her watch. "So do I."

Jeremiah pulled his cell phone out of his pocket and flipped it open. "There's no cell service in here." He shut it again. "Of course not."

"I wonder if the power went out during the storm and the timer is off." Nessa rubbed her forehead with both her hands, trying to absorb the horror of getting into a fight with Mr. MacNaught's personal insurance investigator, then getting him stuck in the vault all night. . . . With her.

"Anything's possible. That is not, however, my first suspicion. I suspect Decker may have reset the timer."

Nessa remembered Stephanie's smile, the one that resembled a wolf about to dine on Nessa's entrails. "Of course. You're right. She hates me."

"I've begun to realize that. Nor is she fond of me."

Nessa gave a single, startled guffaw. "You kicked her out of her office."

Jeremiah didn't laugh in return. He didn't smile. He didn't move. He just looked at her.

And all she could hear was silence.

The walls were so thick. Stephanie had perpetrated the perfect practical joke. The bank was empty of customers. The tellers had left. Eric . . . poor Eric.

Stephanie could browbeat him into doing whatever she ordered, and if she said to leave without securing the premises, he would.

No one would miss them. Jeremiah and Nessa were locked in for the night.

The aunts would get worried and notify the police. The police would put out a bulletin. Everyone in New Orleans would know she'd gone missing. And in the morning when the door was opened—there wouldn't be one person who didn't know that Ionessa Dahl had spent the night with that tango-dancing Yankee insurance investigator, and no one in their right mind would look at Jeremiah Mac and believe they'd spent the hours counting money. Because men might be clueless about him, but no red-blooded woman could look at Jeremiah Mac and not think *sex*.

She couldn't look at him and not think *sex*. And the way he was looking at her made her suspect that the weekend away and the day spent apart did not, as she had hoped, mean he wasn't interested in her. It meant that he had briefly backed off and now would seize his opportunity.

She might be lonely. She might be horny. But here, in a vault so protected from sound she could hear nothing but the rush of her breath in her lungs, where the two of them were so isolated, she was very aware that sex with him was likely to be dark and emotional and far, far too addictive.

She pressed her back flat on the door and beat a useless, panicked tattoo with the flat of her hands. "What are we going to do?"

His gaze fixed on hers. He slid his jacket off his shoulders, draped it on the counting table. Strolled toward her. Leaning one arm on the door beside her head, he very deliberately placed his other hand on her thigh. The heat of his palm burned through the linen to her skin, rendering her . . . immobile. Caught in the net of his eyes.

She began to breathe slowly, deeply, trying to get in enough oxygen to maintain her hold on good sense.

When he began to crumple the material in his fingers, lifting the hem in a slow, bold rhythm, and the cool air washed over her bare skin, she realized there wasn't enough oxygen in the world.

He bunched her skirt at her waist and asked, "What should we do?" His voice rasped as he repeated her question. He used his large hand to span from the jut of her hipbone to the cotton-covered cleft between her legs.

A single thought sliced through her consciousness—out of a drawer filled with cheap, old panties, these were her oldest.

Good timing, Nessa.

"What should we do?" he repeated. His fingers stirred and stirred again, shocking her, arousing her. "What we have wanted to do since the first moment we laid eyes on each other."

Nineteen

For the first time, Nessa believed, really believed, Jeremiah's story about being an escort. Because right now, she would pay him to sleep with her. She'd seen the movies, she'd read the books, but nothing in her life had come close to the fantasy. Yet the way he touched her, so intimately, promised that sex with him would be all she'd ever imagined.

And when he slipped one finger beneath the elastic of her panties and lightly, so lightly, touched her clit, rapture hummed through her. With eyes wide open and every sense centered on her pleasure, she moaned. Faintly, but so clearly she heard herself, and knew he heard her.

There was no pretending. Not now.

His broad chest lifted in a long breath. He smiled, a dark, satisfied lift of the lips. Taking the narrow waistband of her panties in both his hands, he ripped it apart.

She gasped, startled by the implied violence.

She was alone with him. So alone. No one knew they

were here. And she barely knew him, this man with the battered face, this man who shrugged off a gunshot.

Did she have a choice?

Would he hurt her if she refused?

Would he hurt her if she yielded?

He saw her wariness, but typical man, he misread her. "Don't worry. I'll buy you new underwear." He dropped the shreds of her panties, and they fell around one ankle. "I'll buy you a hundred pairs of underwear, just for the privilege of seeing you in them."

Okay. He might not make conversation worth a damn, but he knew the right thing to say.

Gathering the hem of her skirt, one side in each hand, he lifted it to her waist and used it as a rope to imprison her against the door. Looking down at her bare legs, at her feet in their red heels, at the juncture where the small strip of curling hair barely covered her. He smiled that dark smile again, and sank to his knees.

"What . . . ?" Still he held her against the door, but she tugged against his restraint.

He used his body to separate her legs and touched his lips to her, a kiss so light she barely felt it . . . yet it sent a sizzle along her nerves.

Catching his hair in her hands, she lifted his face to hers. "I never allow anyone to do *that* to me."

"Never?"

"Never." Oral sex was too intimate. And it left her too vulnerable.

"Then it's a good thing I haven't asked permission."

She tightened her grip on his hair, fighting to keep his face turned up to hers.

"Remember how I worked my way through college?" he asked.

"Yes." She couldn't control him, and shuddered as his breath ruffled her hair and washed over her super-sensitive skin.

"I know what I'm doing. I can make you come right away, or I can hold you just on the brink for hours. I can make you so crazy with bliss you can't speak, or I can make you remember every touch, every lick, every time I graze you with my teeth and fuck you with my tongue." He kissed her again.

"No." He made her so horny, she was wet right now. But if she spread her legs and let him look *there*, taste her *there*, she'd be embarrassed and . . . "Just sex," she said. "Let's just have sex."

"No, Ionessa. It's never going to be just sex. Not with us." He looked her in the eyes. "I want you. I want to taste you. I want to smell you. I want my fingers inside you. I want to put my skin against yours and become one with you. I want to slide my dick into you and make you scream with pleasure. I want to make love to you in every way possible. . . . And then I want to do it all over again."

Her fingers forgot to hold him and fell away. "For a man who never had to talk, you do pretty well."

"It's you. You make me want to goddamn write poetry." His head dipped, and he kissed her *there* again. "But I'd be lousy at it, so you'd better let me do what I do best." He kissed her again. And again.

Finally, she realized he was waiting for permission. Permission . . . yet still he held her tethered against the door.

So that was the kind of man he was—unscrupulous and crafty. And she was locked in the vault with him. "Okay."

The word was barely a breath, but he heard her.

He slipped his tongue into her folds, delicately opening her to his exploration, and sighed as if in satisfaction.

The sight of him kneeling before her gave her a jolt of some emotion she should be ashamed to claim—she felt as if he were a supplicant, and she liked the idea that she held power over him.

Then he took her clit between his lips and sucked lightly, and delight slammed her against the cool metal.

Yes, there was power here, but it wasn't hers.

He used his teeth lightly, so lightly, yet each motion exposed a new nerve, and once that nerve was exposed, he showed her pleasure with his tongue and lips.

Her eyes slid closed as he assaulted her with all the expertise at his command, and proved he didn't lie—he knew how to take a woman to the brink of orgasm and hold her there while she writhed in desperation.

By the time he came to his feet, she'd been pinned to the door for hours, for years, wanting sex, wanting him, with a madness that touched her soul and would never completely be vanquished. She grasped his lapels and tugged him to her, kissing him fiercely, tasting herself on his lips and knowing that she had to have him—now.

"Unbuckle my belt. Unzip my pants." He took a condom out of his back pocket. "This is up to you."

It was so not up to her. She had no choice now but to do what *he* wanted so she could get what *she* wanted.

She fumbled with the belt, opening it only with his help, then carefully unbuttoned and unzipped him. His trousers dropped to his feet and he kicked them aside, and for the first time, she had an inkling why he wanted her to take the initiative.

The erection that lifted his boxers wasn't like any she'd seen before. Jeremiah was a big man, and this . . .

He observed her expression, every flicker of her eyelashes, every tremble of her lips, as she cautiously lifted the elastic away from his waist and lowered his underwear.

Her heart, already pounding, took a leap compounded by anticipation and fear. She didn't think this would be easy. . . . But he'd utilized every bit of expertise at his disposal to make sure she couldn't turn back.

He ripped the foil packet open and slid the condom over his dick, and the faint glisten made her think, *Lubricant*, and *thank God*.

She placed her hands on his shoulders; they trembled.

As he slipped his palms inside her thighs, the silence grew heavy and dark. He spread her legs wide, lifted her without seeming effort, positioned himself with his hips against her hips and his dick . . . his dick was hot and dark at the entrance of her body.

He pressed inside her.

She was tense, tight; she was making penetration difficult, but she couldn't help it. She hadn't had sex for so long, and never like this: half-dressed, standing up, with a man she barely knew, in a place hidden from the world, cocooned in silence and so aroused she wanted to scream.

Yet despite her body's resistance, he slid inside the first vital inches.

She caught her breath.

He wasn't brutal. Quite the opposite. But he was big. Too big.

She tried to get away, but he adjusted her. Lifted her. Lowered her. Pressed again, gained another few inches.

She groaned. He filled her, stretched her. This was too much.

He watched her, his green eyes so intense, lit by the light of his clever mind and his greedy desire.

She couldn't escape his invasion, not of her mind, not of her body.

She shook her head, denying him, and that made him thrust. For the first time, he moved on her aggressively. He pulled back and thrust again.

"No," she whispered.

"Yes." He thrust again and again, his penis rubbing inside her, his pelvis pressing against her, his hold tight and controlling.

She came. She didn't know how or why, but she came in a convulsion that made her use her legs and her arms to pull him close, all the way inside her. Maybe it hurt, but she didn't notice for the dark ecstasy that swept her along. It had been so long. . . . And it had never been this way. Jeremiah, with his insistence and his expertise and his size and his skill, made her one orgasm strike like lightning that lingered and lingered, growing and subsiding, and growing again until she gave up all control and screamed with the pleasure.

And when she screamed, he began the bright, driving rhythm that signaled his release.

She clawed his shoulders.

He pinned her against the door.

This was sex at its purest and most primitive. This

was fury and glory and a tempest of hail and heat, thunder, and finally . . . silence.

When it was over, they were both battered, panting, exhausted.

Carefully, he pulled out of her. He let her feet slide to the floor, and he held her while she regained her balance.

"Did I hurt you?" he asked.

"Yes." Her whole body ached. "But I don't care."

"Good. Because you marked me, too. And now we know what happens when we touch." He slid his fingers into her hair and lifted her face to his. "Neither one of us will ever be the same." For the first time since the door had slammed shut, he kissed her, a slow communion of mouth and lips.

Yet he didn't seem to realize they were done; he was kindling her, bringing her to heat again, as if they were two teenagers who couldn't get enough.

He broke off the kiss. Glanced around. "Stay here." Going to the shelves where the money was stacked and banded, he cleared them with a sweep of his arm.

She straightened, every bank officer instinct outraged. "What are you doing?"

One by one, he took the stacks, pulled the bands off, and scattered the bills over the floor. Ones, tens, twenties, fifties, hundreds . . .

She ran to him, caught his hand. "You can't do that."

"Watch me." The bills piled up, sliding over each other in a great jumble of wealth. When he had created a circle eight feet wide, he turned on her, a wicked gleam in his eye. "What other man can give you a fortune for your bed?"

She laughed. She couldn't help it. He was so absurd. "It's not yours to give, but—" Then it struck her.

She was still wobbling from their first time, and he . . . he was ready for more.

She held out her hand in a stop gesture. "We need to talk."

Twenty

Mac couldn't believe it. The most dreaded words in the English language.

We have to talk.

But he didn't have to argue. He had other ways.

Stepping close to Nessa, he looked into her eyes and pulled the pins out of her hair. "Yes, we do."

"What are you doing?" She lifted her hands and tried to stop him.

"It's half down, anyway. It looks untidy."

She bit her lower lip.

"Besides, I'd like to see it . . . curling over your shoulders. Do you know"—he dropped the last pin on the floor and ran his fingertips along her scalp—"your hair is as wild as you are."

"That's not true." As he massaged the back of her neck, her eyes grew unfocused.

"Okay. It's not as wild as you are."

"No, I mean . . . I'm not wild."

He chuckled deep in his chest.

Something about that sound apparently snapped

her back into the *now*. "I want to discuss what you know about my mistake seven years ago."

He unbuttoned the first button on her blouse. "At this very minute . . . you want to talk about what happened seven years ago?"

"Not what happened, exactly, but what you've heard and how you got the information."

"All right." He opened her blouse and looked . . . and looked. Nothing more. He just looked. He didn't have to fake his gratification, his awe . . . His gratitude. Women's breasts were one of God's finest creations, and these were *Nessa's* breasts.

They took his breath away.

Her chest rose and fell in a long sigh. "You're trying to distract me."

He glanced up at her, let her see the lust that possessed him. "Is that what you think?"

She stopped breathing. "Yes. I think that you . . . I think that you . . . um, distracting because you . . ."

"Your hair is down. Your shirt is open. I can see your breasts, and they're magnificent. I can see your waist and it's tiny. I know your legs are long and strong, and I know you aren't wearing panties. And you think I would rather not talk about how I found out you made a mistake in the bank?"

She must have seen the humor, for she started to laugh.

"Score one for womens' intuition!" He slid a hand in the cup of her bra and lifted out her breast. "I would rather taste this sweet nipple." Leaning down, he sipped it softly. "I would rather slide your blouse off your shoulders and follow its gradual descent down your arms." He brushed the material away and onto

the floor, and reveled in the silky skin under his fingertips. "I want to take off your bra, loosen your skirt."
Action followed each wish, until she stood before him
dressed in her red heels. . . . Only her red heels.

When she dressed this morning, had she realized the
kind of provocation those shoes would be? Never
again would he see a pair of red leather heels without
thinking of this moment, this passion, this woman.

He removed his shirt in record time. He stood naked
before her, scars and all.

As her gaze encompassed him, her laughter faded
completely.

What did she think? There was no mistaking him for
one of the pale, skinny guys with whom she'd grown
up. His muscle was formed, not of lifting weights and
playing tennis, but of hard work and peasant genes.
His scars were real, not the result of an accident, but of
cruelty and deceit.

She didn't shy away, but touched his chest and arms
with her fingers, stroking down to his elbows, and in a
choked voice, she said, "Nice."

Catching her hands, he turned her back to him,
lifted her by the waist, and urged her down among the
crisp new money. Bills fluttered as he settled between
her knees.

Since the first moment he saw her face on the video,
he'd been waiting for this—to stroke the globes of her
ass, to slide his hands up over her hips, her belly, her
ribs. He weighed her breasts in his palms, felt her sigh.

She leaned back against him, laid her head against
his shoulder, and relaxed.

Triumph burst through him.

She trusted him to care for her. To pleasure her.

In his office in Philadelphia, it had been easy to believe Ionessa Dahl got her way with a combination of cunning and sex. Now that he'd met her, it was clear that she never gave out what she promised with her lavish smiles and flirtatious blue eyes. No, she sent the men who worshipped her into battle while keeping herself pristine.

But she yielded to *him*.

He brushed her hair away from her neck, held her chin, and turning her face to his, kissed her.

Kissing Nessa—the penetration, the way she met his tongue, sucked on the tip—turned him wild. He made a sound deep in his throat, a growl of demand, and felt each muscle in her body grown taut.

Reaching over her head, she caught his hair in her fists and held him still, to kiss him as he kissed her, with tongue and teeth and lips. Boldness . . . from a woman obviously inexperienced, definitely modest.

He pressed his dick close between her legs, feeling her heat, overwhelmed by anticipation. Slashed by need, he wrapped his arms around her, struggled between the twin urges to plunge inside her . . . or torment her with lingering pleasure.

Lingering ecstasy. It had to be lingering ecstasy. This was a woman who'd enjoyed too little passion in her life, and he'd already been hasty once—he, who had been trained by a dozen females on how to give pleasure, and knew that for a woman, rapture involved time and patience.

Nessa deserved the best he could offer.

Their kiss ended slowly, and as they separated, he slid his palm up her spine to the base of her neck.

She stretched and mewed like a cat surprised by pleasure.

His grip on control slipped again. How did she do this, make him revert to being a horny teenager? And even as a teenager, lust had never goaded him so insistently.

Lingering ecstasy, he reminded himself. Because her constant wonder told him more than she probably wanted him to know. She'd never experienced a man who knew what he was doing. He was her first—and she didn't know it, but he would also be her last.

He attentively, languidly, slid her around and onto her back. Kneeling between her upraised knees, he placed his hands on either side of her shoulders, leaned into her. He smiled deliberately, wickedly.

Her beautiful blue eyes widened in alarm . . . and anticipation. "What?" she whispered.

"Do you know how beautiful you are?" It was a line he'd been taught years ago, but right now, he had never meant anything as much in his life.

She rewarded him with the most enchanting smile. "I'm impressed."

He was flattered but cautious. "I suspect you're not talking about what I hope you're talking about."

Her gaze glided down, then up again, meeting his eyes. "Oh, I'm impressed about that, too."

A comment that worked as an aphrodisiac, not that he needed one.

"But mostly I'm impressed because you complimented me, and you weren't even looking at my boobs."

The tiny hint of bawdiness from a woman who barely knew the word *damn* delighted him. "I can see them out of the corner of my eye, and as splendid as they are, they can't compare with the glory of your lips." He kissed her once, softly.

She pushed him back with a fingertip to his chest. "Is *that* one of the lines the ladies taught you?"

"No. Apparently, all it took for me to learn the art of conversation was the chance to be naked with you." In a leisurely fashion, he kissed her throat, her left breast, her right breast, her fingertips, her belly. . . .

With his thumb, he found her clit, and his lazy massage brought a low moan to her lips. She was damp and ready, yet still he dawdled, wanting to stretch her nerves to the breaking point. Her eyes were closed now, her lips parted as she panted. In the dim light of the vault, her skin was luminescent with rapture. Beneath her, the cash formed a green carpet that rustled as she moved in increasing restlessness. She held his shoulders, kneaded them. Her breathing increased; she was close to orgasm.

He knew with pride he had tended her fire, taking care not to let it die, and now she was alight for him again.

He sank down onto her, pressing his chest to hers, his groin to hers, mating them without penetration, wanting her to grow used to his weight, the way he felt on top of her, and to know the promise of pleasure.

He knew how to make her climax—it took only the slow press of his cock inside her, and she spasmed around him, shaking, coming on wave after wave of pleasure. She moved beneath him, meeting his hard, driving rhythm with a motion of the hips that made him grit his teeth. She clutched his chest in her arms, his hips in her legs, his dick in her pussy.

Her convulsive motion hurled him out of control and into insanity.

Groaning, he rose to his knees, caught her thighs in his hands, lifted her, and continued the torture. He thrust hard, filling her with himself, taking her, making her his. He couldn't stand any more, he couldn't hold it anymore. . . .

She arched her back, clawed at his thighs, cried out in ecstasy, while inside her, her muscles grasped him, milked him—and he came in great spurts. He shook with the effort of orgasm, desperate to finish, desperate to never finish, just . . . desperate.

Finally, he was done.

She was done.

He sank down on top of her, dropped his head on the floor next to hers.

And smelled the distinctive odor of new money.

Unwanted, the old cynicism clawed its way to the surface of his mind.

Man, if money was what it took to keep Miss Ionessa Dahl in his arms, he was ready to pay the price.

Twenty-one

Mac paced the vault in his rumpled shirt and wrinkled pants, looking for the entrance he knew existed somewhere. He'd tapped every wall, jiggled every air-conditioning grill—and found nothing.

He glanced over at Nessa.

Her suit was as bedraggled as his. She sat on the floor before the shelves, her head bent over the mounds of dollar bills as she counted them into bundles and slipped the bands back over them.

She'd taken off the red heels. Thank God, or he'd be on her again. As it was, he had to be very careful to not think about the fact that she wore no panties.

He glanced at the pocket of her jacket, where the plain white panties peeked out.

He would buy her silk and lace. Not that he needed it; as long as Nessa wore the panties, Mac would jump when she told him to. He just had to keep that information to himself or she'd use those red heels to walk all over him.

He had to get her out of here before morning. She hadn't said anything, but he knew damned good and well what would happen if Stephanie Decker opened the vault and discovered the two of them. In the conscripted world of New Orleans society, all hell would break loose. The gossips would have a field day. Not that affairs didn't occur and never raised an eyebrow, but an affair between straightlaced Ionessa Dahl and the rough-hewn Jeremiah Mac would be a tasty tidbit. And oh, shit, if someone decided to check into his background, his story of being an insurance investigator wouldn't hold up.

Somehow he didn't think Nessa would accept his deception lightly. For a woman he considered a liar and a thief, she had quite a strict code of morals. . . .

He leaned a hand against the wall. When he closed his eyes, he could feel what it had been like inside her. She hadn't been a virgin, but damn, she felt like one. Tight, warm, firm, yielding only to the most subtle love-making and the most powerful pressure.

His private investigators said she wasn't involved with anyone.

Mac now said she hadn't been involved with anyone for a long, long time. Which made him feel embarrassingly virile and soothed his worst suspicions of her.

Idiot!

Just because she didn't sleep with every dick on the street didn't mean she wasn't stealing him blind.

Although the amount really wasn't that much . . .

Abruptly, he straightened.

What was he thinking? Was he forgetting everything he'd learned the hard way? A thief was a creature to be despised, a sneaking, grasping, worthless soul who walked away from responsibility and left a wasteland behind him.

And if Ionessa Dahl was guilty, he would prosecute her to the full extent of the law.

The trouble was . . . he was no longer sure she was guilty.

"If you're not going to pace," she said in a mild tone, "you could help get this money back in order."

"I'm not pacing. I'm looking." But he sat down on the floor facing her and counted bills and banded them.

She sat cross-legged—a fact that did little to ease his rampaging libido—and she wasn't talking. Instead she sat with her forehead puckered, gaze on her hands, and did the work of the most menial teller. Clearly, she'd done it before, for she did it well.

Yet he wanted her to say stuff. Stuff like she always did, that kind of little patter that put him at ease and made him feel as if he was more than a businessman with a freakish grasp of numbers, more than a former escort to wealthy women, more than a bad seed that would best be destroyed. That skill she had of looking at him and loving what she saw—that was why he'd polished up the skills he'd learned to pay for his college. Nessa made him want to give her his best of . . . everything.

Weakness.

Yet also the truth.

Somehow, he needed to tactfully approach her about their love-making, remind her of her pleasure, and most important, discuss the continuing relationship.

"You enjoyed it," he said.

Possibly that hadn't been the best way to start.

With a faintly startled expression, she looked up from her work.

"The sex. You enjoyed it."

"Oh. Yes, I did." She looked down again. "Thank you."

"Thank you?"

"It is customary to thank the person who brings you pleasure, so—thank you."

"If that's the case, I should be prostrate before you."

That got her attention. Her eyes shone as she asked, "Really? *You* liked it?"

"All I can think about is—When can we do it again?"

Her gladness fell away. "I don't think that's a good idea."

Shit. "Why not? We both just agreed we are compatible."

"A professional relationship can't survive when the partners are involved. Things get . . . messy."

"Darlin', things between us are already messy. I nailed you against the door to the vault and again on a pile of money. And if it were up to me, I'd have my head between your legs right now. How do you propose to put that genie back in the bottle?"

"You *nailed* me?"

It had been too long since he'd had to watch his language around a woman, think before he spoke, and bite his tongue on every other word. Clearly, if he wanted to nail her again, he'd better start biting, and fast. "That was badly spoken. What I meant was, *you* nailed *me* against the door of the vault and on a pile of money, and I am abjectly, pathetically grateful."

She thought about it for an uncomfortably long time, then nodded. "As you should be. Nevertheless, it's not an activity I believe should continue." She glanced at his hands. "You count money like a professional."

"I put in my time in a bank," he said with ironic understatement. "Look, a love affair between the two of us doesn't have to be a problem. We can keep business and pleasure separate."

"Maybe you can. I'm not so coldblooded."

Another dreadful misstep. Tonight he would win first prize for messing up a good thing. "Neither could I, but I thought the argument might work." Dropping the bills he held, he caught her hands and did what any self-respecting man would do in these circumstances; he begged. "I'll do anything if you'll just give me another chance. I'll take you dancing. I'll cuddle all night, I'll read poetry in bed. . . ."

"Yes, yes, I know, you'll sing love songs, you'll rob a bank. You'll join the millions of men who make promises like that and don't follow through."

"Rob a bank?"

"Have you got a frog in your throat? You sound funny."

He felt funny.

Was this really how she got her accomplices? Had she been playing him all along?

He tested the waters. "I would rob a bank for you."

"One thing you should know about me." She sounded friendly enough, but she looked at him without a smile. "I hate a liar."

Was she checking him out? He didn't know. In his experience, treachery was very much part of the human makeup. And while he'd seen little evidence of hypocrisy in Nessa's personality, he'd been wrong before. Horribly, terribly wrong.

He touched the scars on his forehead.

The betrayals of the past had taught him a valuable lesson—it hurt more when the one who screwed you over was someone you trusted.

He looked hard at Nessa: at her sensuous lips, her long legs, her long, dark hair that felt like silk and smelled like flowers. And he realized that yes, she had started to work her way under his skin, convince him she was the person she appeared to be.

He wanted her again. He wanted her any way he could get her.

"You know, I've been thinking," she said.

Excitement and revulsion mixed in his mind. She was actually going to propose he help her rob his banks. "Yes?"

"The legend surrounding Frederick's Vycor's death was very specific. There was money scattered all over, but none of it was stolen."

"What?" His usual nimble mind wasn't making the adjustment. "What are you talking about?"

Patiently, she said, "There's no reason to mess with the money if you're not interested in taking it." She turned her head and looked at the shelves where the stacks of bills would be stored.

It was essentially a unit of bookshelves recessed into the wall. The back and sides were oak, with oak trim around the edges, and the shelves themselves were anchored solidly. "So I think the murderer couldn't get into the vault without disturbing the money. It's got to be heavy, but if a man could lift the entire block, the whole thing, out of the way, I think he would find the entrance to the vault is behind that wall."

*   *   *

Together they shuffled the massive shelves out of the way and found Frederick Vycor's secret bedchamber, with a rusty iron cot and a chamber pot resting beneath it. They followed a narrow, hidden stairway that crawled through the walls to arrive at the top of the house. A small door dumped them onto the roof, and from there they climbed down the rusty fire escape and onto the street.

It was night, thank God, and Nessa fervently hoped no one recognized them, for the dust and cobwebs of more than a century covered them from head to toe.

More important, in her opinion, was the fact that her clothes were crumpled and she looked like a woman who had been someone's *real* good time. And everything Jeremiah did and said made it clear which someone it had been.

He couldn't have been more unsubtle. He hovered. He worried about something that made him frown when he thought she wasn't watching. He *observed* her.

She hoped he didn't see how very much she wanted to get away from him.

"You wait here." He led her to a protected overhang on the building next to the bank. "I'll get a car."

"Mardi Gras," she reminded him.

"I've got strings I can pull, too." He got out his cell phone.

"What time is it?" she asked.

"Midnight." He placed his call.

Only midnight? Her whole life had changed in five hours? She waited until he finished, then asked, "May I use it? I need to call my aunts and tell them I'll be home soon."

He took her hand and folded the cell phone into her

fingers and held them. "Tell them you'll be home in the morning."

"Oh, God, no."

He pulled her close. "It's a little late to be shy."

"I'm not shy." Maybe a little. "But what happened in there . . . it wasn't me. I don't behave like that. I can't do that again."

"You're shocked at yourself." He sounded warmly, deeply amused. Or maybe pleased.

Whatever it was, Nessa didn't like it. "I'm not a prude."

"No, you're inexperienced."

"I'm not that, either."

"Who have your lovers been? College boys? Privileged guys from good homes? I told you, Nessa, I'm not like that. I learned my lessons from women who knew what they wanted and taught me how to please them. What we did in there was the tip of the iceberg. Come home with me, Nessa. I'll show you what it's like to make love to a man."

Had she really toyed with the idea of having a brief fling with this guy, then waving him good-bye and returning to her regularly scheduled life? Fat chance. One session with him left her blasted by passion.

Before she could fling out the same old, tired argument, he said, "Sure, we work together, but we won't be working together for long."

"No. We won't. But what would your Mr. MacNaught say about you sleeping with your assistant when you should be working the case?"

"I don't give a damn what he'd say."

But he looked disgruntled, and it was easy to see she'd struck a chord. "I'll go home."

"All right." He surrendered, but leaned close enough to kiss. "But I won't give up."

I never thought you would.

"Which one of us is going to tell MacNaught his bank's not secure?"

"We both will. To make sure he receives the e-mail."

"Yeah." While she called the aunts, a black town car pulled up, one with tinted windows and a chauffeur who spoke softly to Jeremiah, then held the door for them.

Jeremiah waited until the car was in motion before saying, "I'm going in early tomorrow to view the digital security and positively identify who shut us into the vault. Will you be there?"

There wasn't a doubt in Nessa's mind what she would see. "I wouldn't miss it. I want to see the look on Stephanie's face when she opens the vault and no one's there."

Stephanie.

Something about that name made Nessa jump.

"What's the matter?" Jeremiah wrapped his arm around her.

"I don't know." *They had forgotten something.* "I just had this sensation that somehow, we left evidence in the vault."

"I lifted the shelves out of the escape hatch. We stacked the money back the way Decker left it. We got into the hole. Handles were screwed into the back of the shelves, and I lifted them back into place. I promise, I didn't waver. The bills didn't fall out. The only thing we left in that vault was fingerprints, and they're supposed to be in there." He pulled her closer. "Stop worrying."

"You're right. Surely you're right." But for the rest of the trip and the rest of the night, a faint certainty nagged at Nessa.

They'd forgotten something very important.

Twenty-two

At eight thirty a.m., Stephanie Decker walked up the stairs to her bank. She tapped on the glass, and that little weasel, Eric, strolled toward the door—until he saw who it was, and then he hustled.

He was deathly afraid of her, and she smiled at the look of panic on his face. He got the key in the lock and the door opened so fast . . . what a beautiful moment.

She sashayed through the front door, dressed in her new Escada animal-print shirtdress with the black Armani jacket. Okay, they were knock-offs, but expensive knock-offs, and she'd spent the money because she knew she needed to look good for the cameras when the local stations interviewed her later. . . . afterward.

The tellers stopped chatting as she walked through the lobby. They stared at her wide-eyed.

As she headed for the vault, she gave them a cheerful little wave. "I'm going to get your cash drawers right now!" This was going to be so much fun.

She tapped in her code—she used the master code last night, so no one could tell it was her, and the digital video would only show her "checking" the timer—

and the lock on the vault door popped open. As she stepped inside, she squealed, "Oh, my God!"

"What is it?" one of the tellers yelled.

She didn't know which one. They were pretty much interchangeable.

But she didn't see anybody. She bent her head. She stepped inside.

They had to be here. They *had* to be. She'd shut them in. . . . They weren't here.

How could they not be here?

"Miss Decker, what is it?" One of the tellers was yelling from the door, but she didn't come inside.

Of course not. Everyone was afraid of old Mr. Vycor's ghost.

But Stephanie wasn't afraid of ghosts. She was afraid of people who were here last night, then disappeared without a trace.

"Miss Decker?" Oh, for God's sake, it was that queer teller, Jeffrey.

"What?" She shrieked. She darted her gaze over the table, the shelves, the floor. The shelves . . . what was *that?*

She hurried over, leaned down, and plucked at the wisp of white that was stuck between the oak of the shelves and the plaster wall. It was a cotton material with a hint of lace. She gave it a jerk.

The shelves shivered.

"Miss Decker?" Jeffrey yelled again.

She straightened up and as loud as she could, she shouted, "I'm getting your cash drawers. Go back to your station. I'll be there in a minute!"

"Okay!" He sounded disgruntled.

She didn't care. She gave the material another jerk, and this time, the shelves *moved*.

Another yank, and she held most of a pair of torn panties in her hands.

Her mouth hung open.

Panties. A woman's panties. *Nessa's* panties.

She'd been in here. She'd been screwing around in here with Mr. MacNaught's boy, Jeremiah.

Stephanie stared at the shelves. And they'd somehow gotten out without anyone knowing. As Stephanie stared at the shelves, a slow smile curved her lips.

She had Nessa now. For the first time since they had been working together, Stephanie knew that nothing that Nessa could do, no string Nessa could pull, could get her out of this corner.

Stephanie had been waiting for this all her life.

Nessa hovered by her desk, watching without appearing to as Stephanie stepped out of the vault, cash drawers in hand.

She looked positively benign.

Nessa looked at Jeremiah.

Arms crossed, he observed Stephanie. Then without a glance at Nessa, he disappeared toward his office.

Stephanie carried the drawers to the tellers, waited while they confirmed the amounts inside, and strolled toward her office.

Hastily, before Stephanie saw her staring, Nessa leaned down and pretended to lock her purse in her desk.

Something was wrong. Something was very wrong. Stephanie should have been staggered to discover Nessa and Jeremiah weren't locked inside the vault.

What had they forgotten?

"Ionessa."

Nessa jumped at the sound of that smooth, pleasant voice behind her.

The voice of the Stephabeast.

Stephanie continued, "When you get your things put away, come to my office."

Like a deer caught in the headlights, Nessa looked up into Stephanie's face.

Stephanie was smiling. Smiling big enough to be the shark out of *Jaws*.

Nessa took a long, shaky breath. She pocketed her desk key and followed.

Stephanie went to her desk, sat down, and folded her hands on the blotter. "Shut the door behind you, Nessa."

The way she rolled Nessa's name off her tongue made Nessa ever more nervous. Nessa had committed so many sins lately, but only one stood in the forefront of her mind. . . . The time she'd spent in the bank vault with Jeremiah.

"This morning, I got an e-mail from Premier Central's headquarters in Philadelphia." Stephanie pulled a paper out of the printer beside her desk. "From Mr. MacNaught himself."

Mr. MacNaught, the head of the bank, the man who looked like Danny DeVito. "Yes?"

"He has requested I remove you from work on the case with Mr. Mac and return you to your previous position as assistant manager."

Nessa hadn't expected that. "Why?"

Stephanie looked up from the sheet in her hand. "Excuse me?"

"Does he say why?"

"Mr. MacNaught has his ways of keeping track of what's happening in his banks."

Nessa looked Stephanie right in the eyes. "Yes, some people can be depended on to act as spies for the pure spiteful pleasure of it."

Stephanie flushed an ugly color of red, but her smile never wavered. "If there was nothing to report, no report would be made."

This time Nessa flushed. Last night, there had been plenty to report. She'd hardly slept for remembering what had gone on between her and Jeremiah: where, how often, and how deep.

But when she'd come in this morning, Jeremiah showed her the new digital security evidence. It showed them going into the vault, and in less than a minute, it showed them coming out of the vault. There was nothing to incriminate them—or at least, as Jeremiah said, nothing incriminating could have happened with anyone slower than Superman.

So Nessa was safe.

Wasn't she?

"Mr. MacNaught told me to tell you something else. He said that you seemed to be under the impression that someday you could advance in his bank. Apparently, you discussed it with Mr. Mac." Stephanie smiled again, a horrific smile. "He wants me to assure you that's not possible."

A sick feeling began in the pit of Nessa's stomach. "What do you mean?"

"Mr. MacNaught remembers very well the incident wherein you allowed an employee to waltz out of this bank with his cash. Mr. MacNaught wants me to

remind you that he takes being robbed very poorly."
Stephanie glowed with satisfaction and malice.

"I didn't rob anybody. I merely made a mistake."
Nessa's voice rose. "*You* did this."

Stephanie's smile disappeared. "I assure you, I did
not. Mr. MacNaught made the decision to allow you to
keep your job, but not advance, at the time of the incident." She relaxed back in her chair. "I simply made the
decision not to tell you."

"Because I was too useful working my rear off for an
advancement that could never come." Nessa stood up
and leaned across the desk. "That's it. I am not working for that bastard MacNaught, and I am not working
for you. I quit."

Stephanie came to her feet so hard her chair rolled
backward and slammed against the wall. She leaned
forward so she was nose to nose with Nessa. "You can't
quit."

"Watch me."

"I know what you did in the vault."

Nessa froze.

Stephanie opened her desk drawer and pulled out
Nessa's torn panties. She waved them in Nessa's face.
"You see these? I found them inside the vault. And you
know what that means?"

Nessa had a pretty good idea, but she wasn't going
to admit to anything.

"That means you and Mr. I-Gotta-Score-with-Nessa
were not only hiding in there, on bank property, hump-
ing like bunnies, but somehow you manipulated the
security evidence so that it appeared you had left the
vault when, in fact, you hadn't. Do you know what Mr.
MacNaught will do when I tell him *that*?"

"He'll want to know how we got shut in there before it was time for the vault to close."

Stephanie ignored that and continued her low-voiced tirade. "I don't know how you managed to get that vault open again so you could leave, but falsifying those tapes is a federal offense. So don't think you're going to leave me in the lurch here, *Ionessa*. You're going to work here at this branch of Premier Security until you rot."

Nessa felt the blood drain from her face. "There's no reason for Mr. MacNaught to believe you on the evidence of a pair of panties."

"If a specialist in security examined that tape, you know it would show the signs of manipulation. You know it would. Shall I send him that tape now, or shall I hold it. . . . For the rest of my life?"

Nessa felt sick. Betrayed. All these years of work and for nothing. Stephanie had locked them in the vault, an onerous offense, but Nessa had been an accomplice to a federal crime. And now she was trapped.

Desperately, she cast around in her mind for a way out.

Nothing. She could think of nothing. The only image that filled her mind was the picture of her, working too hard, watching Stephanie get the awards and rake in the bonuses, until she withered and died.

Stephanie saw the defeat in Nessa's face, and this time she didn't bother to waste a smile. Pulling her chair forward, she sat and pretended to busy herself with the papers on her desk. "By the way, you don't need to bother stopping by Jeremiah's office to inform him of your change in status. Mr. MacNaught has already done that. Now—you may go."

Twenty-three

Nessa stumbled backward, caught her balance, pivoted on her heel, and marched stiffly out of Stephanie's office. As swiftly as she could, and without glancing in, she walked past Jeremiah's office. She didn't want to see him. She didn't want to explain what had just happened. Like any sensible woman, she merely wanted to go to the ladies' room, lock herself in a stall, and sob.

But when she rounded the corner, there he was, standing by her desk.

Tall. Broad shouldered. Rugged. Not model-boy attractive, but dynamic. He commanded the eye—every woman in the lobby was staring at him. And he was focused on Nessa.

As soon as she got close, he asked, "What's the matter?"

"Nothing."

"Right." He took her arm in a firm grip and started toward his office.

She tried to twist it away.

He stopped. "I am prepared to make a scene right here in the bank with everyone watching. Are you?"

Of course she wasn't. If he made a fuss, she would have the kind of hysterics that would embarrass everyone in the bank except Nessa.

Nessa would be *mortified*.

So she let him guide her into his office and shut the door. He seated her in his desk chair, perched his hip on the desk, and said, "Talk."

She took a long, quivering breath. "Mr. MacNaught won't allow me to advance. Ever."

"Why not?"

"Because of that stupid mistake I made years ago." She twisted her hands in her lap. "I hate him. I hate Mr. MacNaught. I hope he gets genital warts."

"I think he's safe from that."

"Genital warts? I suppose. Who's going to sleep with *him*?"

Jeremiah rubbed his palms on his knees. "In this case, I'm going to have to agree with MacNaught."

She lifted her gaze to his and shot red thunderbolts from her eyes. At least she thought she did. She hoped she did.

Unfortunately, he appeared to be unblasted.

"I beg your pardon?" she said frigidly.

"You let a teller of dubious character walk out of this bank without checking her drawer because she appealed to your better nature. I do believe you when you say it was only a mistake."

She rose to her feet. "That's damned generous of you."

He plowed on, getting stupider by the word. "And yes, you've worked faithfully and not made another one. But you're soft. You're kind. Out of pure generosity, someday you're going to make another mistake, and if you're in a higher position, the mistake will be bigger, possibly even something prosecutable."

She stared at Jeremiah and realized—this was what he really believed. This was why he had distracted her in the vault rather than discuss the issue. Not because he was so swept away by passion he couldn't think, but because he knew she was going to be furious about what passed for good sense in his mind.

He scrutinized her as if he expected her to buy the whole load of manure. "Mr. MacNaught is looking out for himself and you."

"By golly, you're right. Mr. MacNaught has managed to get seven years of slave labor out of me while looking out for my interests. What a great guy!" She almost choked on her bile.

Speaking in a soothing voice, he said, "Look. I'll talk to him."

"Don't do me any favors."

"I'll explain you need a position that utilizes your gentler skills."

"No. Really. Don't do me any favors." He was making her feel cheap, as if she'd slept with him in the hopes of advancing her position.

He charged on. "Maybe in HR."

She had only one good nerve left, and he had just snapped it. "Human resources? What am I going to do in human resources? I'm good at finance, damned good at it. I understand the numbers. I know how to manipulate them. How do you think this bank has attracted so many investors? I take their profiles, help with their investments, and make them a fortune!" She flung up an arm. "I don't want to get stuck in human-freaking-resources!"

He looked taken aback, as if it had never occurred to him that a mere woman would want anything but a warm, fuzzy, people-related job.

"I want to *quit*." She paced across the room. "I can't believe I've worked extra hours, kept MacNaught's bank running at peak performance in the hopes that he'd notice, and all the time it was for nothing. I couldn't do anything that was good enough to wipe out the past." She stopped, stared at the wall, and took a quavering breath. "I have been such a sucker."

"So you're going to find another job."

"No, I . . . because . . . no. Just . . . no." She couldn't tell him about the panties. They'd fallen out of her pocket, but only a minute ago he'd proved he was the kind of guy who took responsibility for everything. He might try and make amends, and that would make matters worse. The last thing she needed was a guy with the conversational skills of a rock talking to Mr. MacNaught about what happened in that vault.

She shoved her hair off her forehead. She hurt all over. She felt as if she had the flu. She suffered from frustration and embarrassment—*sucker, such a sucker!*—and abruptly, she realized she couldn't stay here anymore. It didn't matter what Stephabeast did; Nessa had to get out. "I'm going." She walked toward the door, ready to throw a fit if he tried to stop her.

"Okay." He stood aside, and he had the funniest look on his face, half-knowing, half-angry.

She didn't know what it meant, but she didn't care. Right now, she only cared about Ionessa Dahl, sucker extraordinaire.

Going to her desk, she grabbed her purse and headed out the door, ignoring the startled tellers, the customers, Eric's stunned expression. Stepping out on the street, she looked around.

She didn't know where to go. She couldn't go home and face the aunts, and explain that her own gullibility had made it necessary that they continue working their boarding house until the day they died.

So where . . . ?

She pulled out her cell phone. She dialed a number. And when Georgia picked up, Nessa heard the roar of Bourbon Street in the background. "Can you meet me somewhere?" she shouted.

Georgia, bless her, didn't question Nessa at all. "Sure. Do you need me to come and get you?"

"No, just tell me where."

"I should have had a break about six hours ago. Can you get to that bakery? Deaux?"

"I'm on my way."

"Nessa . . . ? Do you need me to come and get you?"

But Nessa hung up. She stepped into the street, and the first cab she flagged down stopped for her.

If God was giving her a cab as compensation for all the crap she'd put up with all these years, God was going to have to do better than that.

She climbed in, and said, "Deaux Bakery."

The friendly-looking cabby took one glance at her face and took off like a rocket, scattering pedestrians and shooting through red lights. He got to Deaux in record time, and she gave him a magnificent tip.

Why not? She'd never be able to save enough money to spare her aunts from working for the rest of their lives. She might as well spend it like she had it.

She walked into the bakery and café, and Georgia waved her toward the tiny round table. Like any good cop, Georgia had her back to the wall and she faced the door.

Nessa must have looked like hell, because as she approached, Georgia came to her feet and caught Nessa in a bear hug. As Nessa clutched at her, Georgia whispered, "It's okay, Nessa. Whatever it is, we can fix it."

"No, you can't. No one can fix this. I've managed to get my tit into such a wringer—"

"Hey!" Georgia yelled at the waitress. "We need coffee over here, strong and black, and a plate of pastries and some pralines if you have them." She glanced at Nessa's face again. "And chocolate. Lots of chocolate." She shoved Nessa into a chair. Took the chair opposite. Leaned toward Nessa. "Now, tell me everything. Is it that man? Because if it is, I can take him out."

Nessa wanted to laugh. She really did. She just felt as if she'd lost the knack of it. "It's not him. It's me. That's what's killing me. I did this to myself." Slowly, then with increasing speed, Nessa told the whole ugly story.

At first, when she told Georgia about working for a promotion and being told it would never come, Georgia nodded as if she expected nothing different. And when Nessa told her about getting locked in the vault and gave her an abbreviated version of the events inside, her brown eyes twinkled. The story of the hidden entrance to the vault made her sit up straight, and the news that Stephanie Decker had found the panties made her groan in distress.

But when Nessa told her that Stephanie intended that she stay and work for her forever, Georgia made a vulgar sound. "Honey, that's blackmail, and blackmail is a crime. Haven't you heard that crime doesn't pay?"

"She's got me by the short hairs."

"All I have to do—and I'm more than glad to do it to that bitch—is suggest to the guys on patrol that Miss Stephanie Decker is a person of suspicion, and by the time they get done with her, she'll sneak out of New Orleans through the swamps at night and thank God she made it out alive."

Nessa leaned back in her chair. "You're trying to make me giggle."

"Is it working?"

Nessa thought. "Will there be a water moccasin in the swamp?"

"A six-footer and her babies."

Nessa nodded. "Then, yes, it is working."

Georgia's cell phone sounded, and she grinned as she looked down at it. As soon as she saw the message, the smile was wiped from her face.

"What's wrong?" Nessa grabbed Georgia's hand.

"There a robbery in progress at Premier Central Bank on Iberville, a block and a half from here." She started away, then as Nessa rose, she said, "Stay here." She ran out of the restaurant.

Nessa stared after her, then she ran, too.

Georgia wore a uniform and flat cop shoes and dodged through the crowd.

Nessa wore a business suit and pumps, and she used her two-inch heels ruthlessly to move people out of her way.

She lost sight of Georgia, then saw her twenty yards ahead as she drew her weapon and ran through the door at the bank.

Thirty seconds later, Nessa arrived, out-of-breath anxious for her friends inside. She charged through the door and into the lobby filled with frantic, milling customers and high-pitched female shrieks.

"A mouse!"

"There's another one!"

A small, gray, long-tailed creature scampered across Nessa's foot. She jumped. She looked down. Mice were everywhere, scurrying, dodging, panicked by the shrieks and the trampling feet.

No wonder people were screaming and running.

Then the crowd parted and she caught sight of Georgia standing, arms extended, weapon steadily pointed at the two tall, elegantly costumed, masked—and armed—robbers.

In a deep, husky voice, one of the robbers said, "Honey, you don't want to do that."

That voice. That familiar voice.

For the first time, Nessa heard, and saw, what the video had hidden from her.

Georgia shouted, "Put down your weapons slowly and raise your hands."

Nessa did the only thing she could do. She screamed, "A mouse!" and leaped toward her friend.

Georgia half turned.

Nessa knocked her off her feet.

Stupid. Clumsy. Awkward and a cliché. But it was the only way Nessa could think to stop her friend from shooting her great-aunts.

Her great-aunts . . . the Beaded Bandits.

Twenty-four

Mac's cell rang. He checked the caller ID.

Gabriel.

And Nessa had left the bank in a fury.

Opening the phone, he snapped, "MacNaught."

"They're robbing the Iberville Street bank." Gabriel's voice was cool.

Mac's voice was cooler. "After receiving disappointing information about her promotion, Nessa Dahl has left the premises."

"You don't know where she is?"

"Perhaps at the Iberville Street Bank."

"Perhaps." Gabriel waited a beat. "Bad news about security. My guy is locked in the john."

Mac's frustration level rose a notch. "Tell him to shoot his way out."

"He can't shoot his weapon. He doesn't know who's on the other side of the door, and no matter what you think now, you do not want a customer killed." Gabriel's voice was prosaic. "Anyway, he thinks there's a chair under the handle."

Mac made the connection at once. "He was in the john when those sonsabitches hit?"

"Yes, the thieves were watching for the right moment to strike."

"Whoever placed the chair should be on the tape."

"Whoever placed the chair is going to be in disguise, but we can do a lot with the high-def videos." Gabriel sounded satisfied about that, at least.

"What about the other security guard? The one I placed?"

Gabriel's voice turned cautious. "My guy's been trying to raise him on the cell phone. He finally got him, but the guy kept screaming—"

"They shot him?" Not that Mac wanted anyone hurt, but a little violence would finally get these cases the attention they deserved.

"Not exactly. The guy kept screaming, 'Mice!'"

"Mice?" Mac's gaze fell on the computer mouse on his desk. Naw, that didn't make sense. "What the hell does that mean?"

"I dunno, but we'll find out. The NOPD has one officer responding from a block away. She should be there by now."

"I'm going."

"I knew you would." Gabriel hung up.

By the time Mac got a cab, he'd received a call from Chief Cutter telling him an officer was on scene, and another telling him no shots had been fired and the robbers had gotten away with an unspecified amount of cash.

Mac walked into the chaos of the bank lobby to find two patrolmen at the door, three officers inside interviewing the witnesses, Gabriel's man on the phone, and his own security guard, a burly, 260-pound former LSU offensive tackle, standing on a desk.

In fact, four women were sitting on desks, one with her hand over her eyes while she sobbed.

The bank manager, Dave Bowling, hurried over. "Mr. Mac, we're trapping as many as we can, but I've got an exterminator on the way."

"Great." The shock had unhinged Bowling's mind.

Then Mac saw a small fluff of gray fur whisk across the floor.

Two of the women screamed. So did his security guard.

"Oh. *Mice*." Mac understood now. The thieves had brought in a cage full of mice and let them loose.

Brilliant. Just brilliant.

Georgia sat in a chair, an ice pack on her elbow, her eyes narrowed and furious as she listened to the police chief give her hell.

Another cop, a white guy with a lived-in face, stood behind her, massaging her shoulders.

Mac placed his hand on Georgia's arm. "You okay?"

"Just peachy," she snapped. "Sorry, man, I thought I had them."

"Shit happens."

"You don't know the half of it," she muttered.

"She got here before anyone else." The guy with the lived-in face offered his hand. "Antoine Valteau."

His accent was almost unintelligible to Mac, but Mac understood one thing—Antoine wanted Georgia out of the hot seat, and it was Mac's job to handle it. "I'm grateful to Officer Georgia Able for her service on the behalf of my banks and the people who work in them." Mac formally shook Georgia's hand.

Georgia looked up, her eyes suddenly full of tears. "She didn't realize she would knock me down—"

Mac went on alert. "Who? Who knocked you down?"

Chief Cutter thrust himself between them. "I suppose you want to know what went wrong?"

"No. I want to see it."

"Mr. Mac, I apologize." Prescott's security man walked up looking chagrinned and angry. "I had an itchy feeling that today was the day. I shouldn't have gone to the bathroom."

"When you gotta pee, you gotta pee." Mac looked around. There was nothing to be done here. "Send the file to Mr. Prescott, and tell him to send it on to me."

"Look, I need to review those tapes—" Chief Cutter began.

"And release them to the chief," Mac added.

The chief opened his mouth to argue.

Mac fixed him with a cold stare. "You are not bargaining from a position of power."

Chief Cutter shut his mouth.

Mac walked out the door.

Russell Whipple was in his bedroom, getting dressed for work, when the TV channel broke into *Days of Our Lives* with a bulletin.

The Beaded Bandits had robbed the Iberville Street bank.

He grinned.

Showtime.

Twenty-five

The sunlight flickered through the leaves of the great live oaks. The temperature hovered at a lovely seventy-two degrees. The rocking chair creaked as Nessa rocked back and forth, waiting on a porch of the Dahl House.

She didn't wait long.

A cab pulled up. Her great-aunts, the bank robbers, slid out. They wore their usual clothes: pants with elastic around the waist, flowered tops, sensible shoes. Their makeup was nothing special: some foundation, a little blush, a light lipstick.

They were giggling.

Hestia spotted her as they strolled up the walk, and nudged Calista.

Calista nudged her back, then, typically, tried a bluff. "Nessa, darling! What are you doing home at this hour? Are you sick?"

With great deliberation, Nessa rose to her feet. "You saw me. You know exactly why I'm here."

"We may have an idea, but why don't you tell us for sure?" Hestia was cautious.

"Do you know what I thought when I ran into that bank and saw you two? And realized that my great-aunts were the Mardi Gras bandits? My respectable, old-fashioned, kind . . ." Nessa couldn't find the words to express her horror.

The two women climbed the steps.

"We were hoping you didn't recognize us," Hestia said.

Nessa paced across the porch toward them. ". . . Waving guns!"

Calista turned to her sister. "I told you she did. Why else would she have knocked Georgia down?"

"In platform heels! Frightening people!" Nessa interjected.

"She could have tripped." Hestia sank down on one end of the porch swing.

"She's not usually clumsy." Calista sat on a chair opposite.

"Robbing . . . robbing the bank I work for!" Nessa raged.

Both of the aunts focused on Nessa.

"That was the point, wasn't it, dear?" Calista asked kindly.

Nessa's tirade came to an abrupt halt. "What do you mean, that was the point?"

"That bank has been unfair to you!" Hestia said.

"What has that to do with anything?" In the back of her mind, Nessa had been afraid of this. Afraid that they were robbing Premier Central banks out of misplaced loyalty to her.

"That made them the logical bank to rob." Calista managed to make it sound like a sensible choice.

"Why rob a bank at all?" Nessa asked.

"Because of Daniel's breasts, of course," Hestia said.

"Daniel's breasts?" Nessa's voice rose.

From behind the screen on the front door, Maddy said, "Hush, Miss Nessa, you don't want to tell the whole neighborhood."

Nessa whipped around. "Don't tell me you're in on this?"

"Don't yell at Maddy," Calista chided. "She has had nothing to do with our little capers."

Nessa whipped back around. "Your little *capers*?" She couldn't believe their insouciance. "Your little capers are federal offenses."

"Yes, but the Feds aren't worried about us. Capturing bandits who steal such small amounts won't win them any fame," Hestia assured her.

"Although Chief Cutter is getting irked with us," Calista reminded her sister.

"I know. He's worrisome," Hestia conceded. "We're having to get more and more inventive every year. But since we have a whole year to plan, we use the time to work out the details."

Calista beamed. "The mice were my idea."

"And a good idea, too!" Hestia high-fived her. "But wait until you see what I've cooked up for next year."

"No. No next year! No! And . . . why?" Nessa spread her hands out, palms up. "Why? Why?"

"I tried to tell you, honey," Hestia said. "Because of Daniel's breasts."

"But that was only the first year, sister."

Nessa whimpered in frustration.

"Let me explain." Hestia patted the spot beside her.

"I can't sit." Nessa stood stock-still, her fists clenched at her side. "I'm too anxious."

"It's all right, honey." Calista took the other end of the swing and patted the same spot.

Stiffly, Nessa lowered herself to sit between them.

Lifting her voice, Hestia called, "Maddy, you might as well come out, too."

Maddy opened the screen. In slow motion, as if today she were truly old, she walked to a wobbly old rocker, her own rocker, the only thing saved from Katrina, and sat. "Nessa, child, you want me to fix you a hurricane?"

Nessa knew good and well Maddy made her hurricanes with six different kinds of liquor. "It's not even noon."

"Sometimes, where your aunts are concerned, a good, strong drink is the only way to go," Maddy advised.

"We could open the champagne early!" Calista said.

"Champagne?" Nessa looked between the two of them.

"After a successful heist, we always celebrate with champagne." Calista's eyes sparkled.

"Not really champagne. It's sparkling wine," Hestia assured Nessa—as if that mattered. "But we have a reasonably priced brand dear Jacque Quinane recommended, which—"

"I don't care." Nessa held up her hand. "I don't care. I don't care."

"Honey, we don't want you to think we're stealing the money for ourselves!" Hestia said.

Nessa half laughed, but not in amusement. "Honestly, that never occurred to me. But right now, all I know is that it has something to do with Daniel's breasts."

"Exactly. That first year, I was walking down the hall upstairs and I heard the most dreadful muffled sobs coming from inside Daniel's room." Calista's lip quivered in remembered sympathy. "He had had an operation to give him breast implants. A backstreet doctor . . . honestly, I don't know what he was thinking."

"A backstreet doctor? One of those guys who isn't really licensed to practice medicine?" Nessa asked.

"That is just what we mean," Calista confirmed. "He'd paid most of it up front—"

Hestia poked Nessa with her bony elbow. "Up front. Get it?"

Nessa did not smile.

Hestia subsided with a sigh.

Calista continued, "Then he had a series of financial setbacks—remember when his father was institutionalized with Alzheimer's and his son got accepted to Stanford, all in the same week? Well, he couldn't pay the rest of the bill, and that horrible doctor turned him over to a collection agency. You know the kind I mean—like in *Rocky*, where they threaten to break your fingers if you don't pay."

"I understand." Nessa did understand. The picture was becoming only too clear.

"So those awful collection people were threatening to take his breasts back," Hestia said.

"Take them back?" Nessa was startled. "I thought you said they were implants."

"They were!"

"Oh." *Horrible.*

"So of course I told him we'd lend him the money."

"You didn't have the money."

"No."

"And you don't believe in borrowing." The only money the aunts had ever borrowed was to put Nessa through college, and they were still paying that back.

"For dear, sweet Daniel, we were willing to put aside our scruples," Calista said. "So we tried to get a loan."

"A loan? From whom?"

Calista's face set in grim lines. "Your bank."

"Premier Central?" Nessa heard her voice hit a new high. "Who did you talk to?"

"To That Woman."

"Stephanie Decker?"

Sitting straight and thin as a rail, Hestia took up the tale. "First, she asked why we wanted the money. When we told her it was a private matter, she asked all kinds of personal questions. Insulting questions. She made us fill out forms and—"

"And what happened then?"

"Then she looked at us and laughed—" Calista quivered with indignation.

"In our faces!" Hestia interrupted.

Calista continued, "And said the bank wasn't in the habit of throwing their money away on bad risks, and we should be grateful that Mr. MacNaught agreed to keep our niece on after she messed up so badly, that you were a sort of charity case for him, but of course it was impossible for you ever to expect to get much of a raise since you could never advance, so we might as well resign ourselves to being objects of pity throughout New Orleans for the rest of our lives."

"That bitch," Nessa said softly.

"Exactly what I said." Hestia nodded emphatically.

"We knew then you would have to leave the bank, but that didn't solve our problem of the money for Daniel," Calista said.

"We tried another bank, but while they were very polite, they wouldn't lend us the money, either," Hestia said.

"So we were watching *To Catch a Thief*—" Calista said.

"With darling Cary Grant. Marvelous man!" Hestia smiled.

"And I said—" Calista said.

"No, it was me," Hestia said.

"No, it wasn't, because remember? There was the scene with the fireworks, then the part where he was on the roof, then I said—"

"No, you forgot the part—"

Nessa interrupted. "One of you said, 'Let's rob Nessa's bank!'"

"That's right." Calista clapped her hands in pleasure. "We knew you'd understand."

The aunts started to get to their feet.

Catching them by their arms, Nessa brought them back down. "I don't understand, and you can't do this anymore."

"We're careful," Hestia assured her.

Ruthlessly, Nessa reminded them, "If I hadn't been there today, my best friend would have shot one of my aunts, maybe both of them."

That was the first Maddy knew of the details, and her hands trembled like leaves. "Miss Calista! Miss Hestia! I told you you'd stretched this stealin' to its limit!"

Very patiently, Calista said, "It's like that movie says, 'It'll all come out in the end.'"

"*To Catch a Thief* says, 'It'll all come out in the end'?" Hestia's brow knit.

"No, sister, *Shakespeare in Love*."

"That's right, I forgot." Hestia started to stand again.

"No! Sit down! This is not a joke!" Nessa's voice rose again. "This is serious. You scared me half to death, and look at Maddy! She's afraid for you! Maybe you can think you were justified the first year, but what about the next year? And all the years after?"

"Oh." Hestia settled herself again. "We gave Daniel the money, and his whole face lit up, and it made us feel so good."

"But we weren't going to do it again until the next year, the very day of our party, poor, dear Meghan Brownly came to the door with her grandmother's canapés, the ones the Brownlys have been guarding the secret recipe for three generations like it was the gold at Fort Knox." Calista was getting wound up. "And after all the years we've been friends—"

Hestia patted Calista's knee. "Hush, dear, Nessa's getting impatient again."

Calista subsided.

"Anyway, the reason Beth Brownly couldn't come was because she broke her top plate and she wouldn't be seen in public without her teeth, which I so sympathize with, even though I have all my teeth—"

This time, Calista patted Hestia's knee.

"Oh. Right." Hestia took a breath. "Poor Beth didn't have the money to pay the dentist, even though he was giving her a fifty-percent discount."

"It's that nice boy Grey Linney," Calista told Nessa. "He's always good to his elderly patients."

Hestia continued, "That same night, That Woman—"

"Stephanie?" Nessa clarified.

"Yes, Stephanie. She came to our party and she treated you like dirt," Hestia said. "At that moment we realized—God wanted us to rob the bank."

"God wanted you to rob the bank!" Nessa shouted. "Of all the absurd—"

"Hush, Miss Nessa. Hush, child." Maddy leaned way forward to pat Nessa's hand. "The neighbors'll hear."

"Have you been in on this the whole time?" Nessa demanded. "Because I expect more sense from you, Maddy!"

"Don't you sass her, Nessa!" Calista said sternly. "She didn't know anything until we gave her the cash to get her favorite chair fixed."

Nessa took in Maddy, rocking in the one chair that had been saved from the flood.

"She needed to have something of her own," Hestia said gently.

Like so much about Nessa's great-aunts, the whole explanation made horrible sense. And yet—"You have to stop."

"We're not hurting anyone," Calista said.

"We're helping dear people who need help," Hestia said.

"And besides, what are you going to do about it? Tell the police?" Calista shook her head in polite disbelief.

Of course, they had her. Nessa wasn't going to tell anybody.

This time, when the aunts stood up, Nessa didn't

stop them. They went into the house while she sat limply, staring at Maddy, her eyes filling with tears.

Maddy dug in her apron pocket and handed her a soft, worn handkerchief. "I know, child. When I realized what they were doing, I cried, too."

"They could have been killed. When I saw Georgia aiming at them, and Hestia aimed back, all I could imagine was the two of them in their coffins. . . ."

"I said that to those two girls. I said they would likely get shot if they didn't stop. And Hestia said, 'Miss Maddy, you're old, too. Would you really care if someone shot you dead today and ended all the aches and miseries?' And child, she had a point. Gettin' dead would sure beat this slow decline where I got to get up four times a night to pee and my belly growls like it's hungry, but I can only take three bites, and my knee swells in the summer, and every time I look in the mirror, I wonder who that old woman can be. It's lousy, I tell you, Nessa. When I lost my home, I thought I'd die. Not a thing left, barely a memory of my husband or my boy . . ." Maddy shook her head in sorrow. "When they gave me my chair back, my squeaky old chair, better than new, I know it's silly, but I felt like I could live the years the good Lord had assigned me."

"At least I understand why now." Nessa lifted her hands, looked at them as if they were a stranger's, and lowered them into her lap again. "They're stealing money and it's like a scholarship fund for the ones in need."

"That it is," Maddy agreed.

Out of the corner of her eyes, Nessa caught sight of a man standing at the end of the porch. She jumped;

subconsciously she'd known Jeremiah would show up soon.

But it wasn't Jeremiah. It was a tall, blond stranger.

Then as he walked toward her, she knew him.

It was Daniel. Daniel, dressed as a man in jeans, a T-shirt, and a vest. A vest that covered his paid-for-in-crime breasts.

The truth hit Nessa like a blast. "You're helping them." That was how the aunts managed the masks and the makeup and the . . . the . . . Nessa didn't know what he'd been helping them with. She only knew that this was the final blow.

He hung his head. "I am so sorry."

She didn't give a damn about his contrition. "How could you? How long have you . . . ?"

"Since the second year." He pulled up a chair, sat down close enough that his knees touched hers, and tried to take her hands.

She pulled them away. "I thought you were my friend."

"Don't, Nessa. I am your friend. When I realized what they were doing, I tried to talk them out of it, too." He glanced toward the end of the porch. "But I had about as much luck as you just did."

He'd heard it all, or at least enough of it to know she'd been soundly ignored.

"They won't stop," he said. "They were going to get caught or killed, and I knew they didn't have a chance with the wigs and the hats out of the attic."

Nessa kept her gaze level and cold. She folded her arms across her chest.

"Okay. You can be mad if you want. But, Nessa, those women have saved my life. I couldn't stand by while they were arrested or killed." Daniel looked wretched and guilty. . . . And defiant. "So I got my friend that makes masks for films—he's good, he works with Spielberg—and told him they were for a special Mardi Gras celebration at the club. When Miss Hestia and Miss Calista tell me it's time, I help them get ready, and then I go and do whatever needs to be done to distract the security guard."

"I saw you. On last year's security video. I couldn't quite place you. Because you were a man." Nessa pinched the bridge of her nose. "Don't you realize that you could get arrested or killed?"

"The thought has crossed my mind."

She lowered her hand. "So first Daniel figured it out, then Maddy. Any others?"

They shook their heads.

"But it stands to reason that if we put two and two together, sooner or later other people will, too," Maddy said.

"Especially with the pressure Mr. MacNaught is putting on the police chief." Nessa closed her eyes as she remembered. "Jeremiah is probably watching the video right now. If he figures out why I knocked Georgia down, I'll be arrested as an accessory to the crime, and who's going to believe me when I say I didn't know it was going on? I work for the bank. I know a lot about the security and the shifts for the guards. I have reason to hold a grudge. And I—"

"You what?" Maddy prompted.

"Nessa, you didn't sleep with Mr. Mac, did you?" Daniel sounded horrified.

Now it was Nessa's turn to be defiant. "Why not?

Isn't that what everybody wanted? Was for poor, lonely Nessa to get laid?"

"Not me." Maddy glared in old-lady indignation. "I wanted you to have some good man court you. I didn't want you to sleep with him. I still have some morals."

Nessa scrambled to make an excuse. "I didn't mean to do it, Miss Maddy. I just couldn't . . ."

"You couldn't help it?" Daniel grinned. "I'm glad to hear that. It's about time you had some passion in your life."

"That's not all I've got in my life." Nessa's low voice was tense and furious. "I've got two aunts who rob banks for excitement, and if I get arrested with them, who the hell is going to get them out?"

Twenty-six

Mac strolled up the front walk of the Dahl House. He stopped at the bottom of the stairs leading up to the porch and looked toward Nessa, rocking on the swing. "I'm beginning to know my way around New Orleans. I took the cable car from the bank, expecting to find you here. . . . And here you are."

"You could have called my cell." Nessa looked cool and composed. If he hadn't seen the video he would never have believed she had witnessed a robbery.

Maybe . . . planned a robbery.

"But I wanted to see you." He prowled up the stairs. "Wanted to see if you were all right after your harrowing experience."

She didn't say *What harrowing experience?* But she looked at him so blankly, she might as well have. "I never expected to see it happen right before my eyes."

"You were so surprised you foiled the officer who would certainly have ended the crime spree."

"Is one robbery a year considered a crime spree? I suppose it is, if it continues unabated." Nessa gestured to the chair opposite her. "Won't you sit down?"

"I talked to Officer Able, and she said she told you not to follow her." He sat on the swing beside Nessa, deliberately crowding her.

Nessa didn't react in any way. "I didn't listen. Maybe because I know the manager and the whole bank crew. Maybe because if I witnessed one of the crimes in person, I could solve it, spit in Mr. MacNaught's face, and get a new job. Mostly because I am so sick and tired of being the model employee and the model citizen." Nessa closed her eyes as if the tiredness had bled into her bones. "It's gotten me nowhere. So I ran after Georgia and into the crime scene."

"I watched the video repeatedly. You screamed about a mouse and jumped at Georgia. But I didn't see the mouse that scared you." He'd looked, too. Watched that moment on the security tape over and over again.

When she had run in the bank, she'd been nothing more than one of the onlookers. No one had given her any respect, paid her any attention, looked to her for instruction. Mac had seen that, and absolved her from guilt in the robberies.

Then a mouse had run over her foot. She had looked around the bank lobby, observed the situation. Jumped, screamed, ran at Georgia and knocked her down, foiling the possible capture of the Beaded Bandits.

And in that long, telling hesitation, she had once again roused his suspicions.

"In one stupid moment of fear, I messed up the biggest catch my best friend could ever have made." For the first time, Nessa's voice wobbled. "Georgia would have gotten a commendation. Maybe a promotion. Probably a reward. And I screwed it up for her."

Even now, Nessa stared blindly at the street before them, and he would swear she saw nothing.

"You're in shock." He slid his arm around her. "What do you think?"

"I think you're right." Turning her head into his shoulder, she burst into tears.

This was not theatrical crying. These weren't pretty tears. They wrenched from her in huge, heaving gasps that convulsed her body. She curled toward him as if agony gripped her.

Yet still Mac watched her with an assessing gaze, weighing her anguish against his suspicions. Her unhappiness seemed genuine enough, but he of all people knew how well people could pretend affection and regret, and what appears to be true is not necessarily so.

He had known Nessa would be uncomfortable and off balance about their tryst in the vault, so "Mr. MacNaught" had sent an e-mail to Decker to remove Nessa from the case of the Beaded Bandits, and tell her the promotion would never come through. Mac had pushed her hard, but he'd seen pressure work before, to squeeze out an unwilling confession or reveal a deep secret.

Maybe she was innocent—of the bank robberies, if not of criminal carelessness with his bank's money—and he had to be sure. He *had* to be.

Women liked him for his looks, his money, and his power. He had never cared what drove their passion; he wasn't interested in relationships, only satisfaction.

But Nessa was different. She was part of a close society with tight family ties. She seemed happy with her life, with her friends, yet the need to succeed drove her.

He understood that need; it was the force that drove

him also. But he was driven by bitterness and revenge, and she by loyalty and enthusiasm.

If Nessa was really what she appeared to be, he would give her everything—his heart, his soul, his confidence.

And if she lied . . . he would make her pay.

When her tears had slackened, he hugged her again. "Is there anything you want to tell me?"

"Yes." Her voice was small and shaky. "Do you have a handkerchief?"

He handed it over.

She mopped off her face and blew her nose. "I'll wash it for you." Leaning back in the swing, she sat on her backbone, stretched out her legs, and stared at the street. "What a lousy day."

"Why do you say that?"

"Let's see. I go into work, the meanest woman in the world does *not* act surprised, horrified, and guilty about locking us in the vault—"

"No, she didn't, did she?" In all that had occurred, he hadn't had a chance to follow that up.

"—And she tells me Mr. MacNaught has decided, because he's an idiot who believes every drop of poison she pours into his ear, that I'm not working with you anymore on the case and I'm back to being the bank's slave labor, and that I'm never going to get a promotion. Then I run away to talk to a friend, and while we're in the middle of a heart-to-heart, the Beaded Bandits strike, I do just what I'm not supposed to do, run to the bank, and find out . . ." She sat shaking her head.

"Find out what?"

She looked at him as if she'd forgotten he was there. "Find out I'm not the person I thought I was."

"Because you screwed up?"

"I sure did. I didn't think I could be more unhappy, and yet . . . here I am."

From inside the house, he heard the sound of heels on the hardwood floor.

With a slap of the screen door, Hestia stepped out on the porch.

To his surprise, Mac found himself rising to his feet. Here in New Orleans, especially with the Dahl girls, old-fashioned manners seemed natural.

Hestia accepted his courtesy as her due. "Mr. Mac, how pleasant to see you again. Nessa . . . child, have you been crying?" Her kindly face clouded with concern, and she hurried over and lifted Nessa's face. In a stern voice totally unlike her usual congenial tones, she demanded, "Mr. Mac, have you been making my great-niece cry?"

Like an impatient child, Nessa pushed her aunt's hand away. "No, it's not him. It's the Beaded Bandits."

"What about them?" Hestia asked.

"I saw them rob the bank today, and they make me very unhappy." Nessa sounded petulant.

Hestia drew herself up to her full height, a tall, thin, elegant elderly woman with white hair and patrician features. "Forget about them. They're not your problem."

"I wish I could," Nessa said.

Turning to Jeremiah, Hestia said, "Mr. Mac, any man who holds a woman while she cries deserves a home-cooked meal, and except for a few of the boarders who'll be in and out, we're dining alone tonight. Won't you stay and eat dinner with us?"

"I would love that. Thank you, Miss Hestia," Jeremiah said.

"Nessa, you go upstairs and wash your face. I'll tell Miss Maddy to set another place at the table. Mr. Mac, you can go into the library and pour us drinks."

Nessa glared at her great-aunt. How could she be so casual? Frustration made her want to do something she'd never done in her whole life—lie on the floor, kick her heels, and throw a tantrum.

Taking a compact out of her pocket, Hestia opened it and held it out to Nessa.

A glimpse into the mirror proved one thing—Nessa did not cry pretty tears. With an exclamation of horror, she fled into the house and right into the arms of Ryan Wright.

"Whoa, babe, slow down!" He steadied her, caught a glimpse of her blotchy face, and stepped back as if she had leprosy. "You okay?"

"Fine." Her voice was a little hoarse, and she cleared her throat. "What are you doing here?"

"I live here, remember?" He gave her one of his charming, boyish grins.

If Jeremiah was strong whisky, this guy was a wine spritzer with lots of ice.

"Skeeter and I came back and sacked out for a few hours. We've been playing on the streets night and day."

Skeeter stood by the door to the dining room, holding the instrument cases, his face glowing with sunburn and sweat already breaking out on his forehead.

She waved and smiled.

He bobbed up and down in greeting.

"Now we're going out again." Ryan wore a short-sleeved Hawaiian shirt that glowed like neon, showed off his buff arms, and would for sure get him the attention he craved. "We are making so much money. Those tourists are tossing twenties, and when we play 'When the Saints Go Marching In,' sometimes it's fifties and hundreds."

"That's great!" She edged toward the stairs. "I'd love to chat, but look at me. I had a little female upset and I need to go wash my face."

"I'm going to have so much money, I can buy this house."

"That is such good news. Not that we're selling . . ." She made it up two steps.

"Come on, man," Skeeter said.

Ryan kept up with her, talking fast. "What do you say? You could meet me tonight. You could watch us play, we could grab some drinks and dinner, and we could have some laughs."

"Thank you. That's very kind. But I'm busy tonight." Was he ever going to get the message? She'd already turned him down a hundred times.

"Come on. It'll be fun!"

"I don't go down to the French Quarter at night during Mardi Gras." She took the stairs slowly, trying to be polite, desperate to get away.

"I'll protect you."

"I know you would. I have complete confidence in you. But it's been an awful day, and I just can't." She fled up the stairs and down the corridor into her bedroom. Shutting the door behind her, she leaned against it and closed her eyes.

She was so sick of boarders. She had to get them out of her home.

Her eyes popped open in horror. And the more people who lived here, the more likely one of them would figure out that her aunts were the Beaded Bandits.

But surely none of them could imagine Miss Calista and Miss Hestia in the role. . . . But Jeremiah could. He was smart, he was ruthless, and investigating these robberies was his job.

And he was downstairs with her aunts right now.

Nessa dashed toward the bathroom.

When she opened the door a half hour later, she'd showered, washed and styled her hair, reapplied her ruined makeup, and changed into an orange top and a pair of linen trousers.

She didn't do the full grooming ritual to impress Jeremiah. She did it because the day that had started out with such promise had gone to hell in a handcart.

She shut the door behind her, headed toward the stairs, and met Daniel, now Dana, floating along in a pink satin V-neck cocktail dress with matching heels and his signature feather boa.

The sight gave her a jolt. She felt as if she'd seen him naked, without his Dana persona, and when he drawled, "*Como se va*, chère, look at you! So meticulously casual, yet so chic," she gratefully fell back into her comfort zone.

"Are you off to the club?" she asked.

"Tonight will be another big night, and, of course, since I took the afternoon off, I have to work."

They descended the stairs together, treading carefully, both sensitive to the atmosphere between them.

They heard Calista say, "Yes, some families are truly

troubled, but one must always give one's mother the benefit of the doubt. After all, how old was she when she met your father?"

"Screwed him, you mean?" Jeremiah said. "She was eighteen."

"He sounds like the worst sort of scoundrel to me," Hestia said.

"I am the last man to argue that."

"And he disappeared into thin air?" The disapproval in Calista's voice deepened.

Nessa clutched Daniel's arm. In a furious whisper, she said, "They're giving him the Interrogation." The questions they asked men they considered serious suitors. "What are they thinking?"

"They're thinking that that *thing* they did this afternoon has nothing to do with you and your happiness."

"They're crazy."

"They're eccentric."

"This is beyond eccentric."

"Okay. They're old and they don't care. How's that?"

"Fine!" She believed he was right. She just didn't like it.

Jeremiah's voice rumbled again.

With a glance toward the library, Daniel said in a low voice, "Best that I go out the back way, I think."

"I think so, too."

He offered his cheek.

She kissed it.

"Chin up, chère. We'll get through this." He departed with a swish of feathers, leaving her to hurry toward the library before the aunts could propose the details of the marriage contract.

She stepped in the door.

The aunts and Maddy had Jeremiah sitting in a chair, sipping a mint julep—ice, bourbon, and mint—while they led the charge to find out if he was suitable to court their great-niece.

He looked totally at ease.

He saw her first, gave her a brief inspection, and nodded. "You look better."

Great. He'd noticed she looked like the bottom of the bayou.

"I'll go check on dinner." In slow increments, Maddy got to her feet.

Jeremiah rose, too.

Maddy tossed commands like a general. "Calista, you'd best set the table. Hestia, open one of the bottles of wine we have left over from the party. You two"—she waved a hand at Nessa and Jeremiah—"you visit."

The old ladies whisked from the room.

Jeremiah smiled. "I believe I have their approval."

Nessa writhed with mortification. "Don't pay any attention. They're old-fashioned and like to know who I—"

"Am dating?"

"We're not exactly dating," she said severely. *Sex in the vault is not dating.*

The front screen door slammed open. Footsteps racketed across the hardwood floor, and two men's voices argued loudly.

"I think that's a dumb idea. Street musicians have to spend their time working the street, not putting the moves on every woman they meet, and if you think you've got a chance with Miss Dahl—"

"Shut up, man." Nessa heard a thump. "Just shut up."

"Ouch. That hurt!"

Nessa smiled weakly at Jeremiah. "That's Ryan. He plays the sax. And his friend, Skeeter. He plays the bass. Ryan boards here." *And embarrasses me to death.*

As if the musicians didn't even exist, Jeremiah still concentrated on her. "Will you go out with me tomorrow night?"

She stared at him, stricken by the realization that, no matter how sensible it was to no longer see him during their off time, she had to. She needed to know what his investigation was turning up. If he discovered something, she needed to try and divert him from the truth. She *had* to date him. Every night. Until the day he gave up this investigation.

A despicable plan, deceiving a man who was doing nothing more than his job. Yet she had no choice. She had to protect her family.

And the worst part was . . . she was glad. Glad because this gave her the excuse she needed to be with him. To get to know him, to look at his face, to bask in the sound of his voice . . . "Jeremiah, I would love to go out with you tomorrow night."

Twenty-seven

The restaurant was decorated in warm hues and discreetly lit by antique crystal sconces. Fresh flowers adorned the tables, and the maitre d' ushered Mac and Nessa into a sumptuous private alcove.

Mac made a mental note to give Mrs. Freytag a bonus, for she'd outdone herself with this place. He then nudged the maitre d' aside and held Nessa's chair. "It was rough getting a reservation here, but I've heard the food is the best in New Orleans."

"The best in New Orleans, and New Orleans has the best food in the world." Nessa lavished a smile at the hovering waiter. "How are you, Jean-Paul?"

The waiter wore a suit that cost more than Mac's, a thin, silly-ass mustache, and a supercilious smile. He clicked his heels and bowed, then flicked Nessa's napkin in the air and laid it across her lap. "I am fine, mademoiselle, and as always, it is a pleasure to serve you and your friend." His gaze fluttered over Mac, dismissed him, and returned at once to Nessa.

Taking Jean-Paul's hand, she said, "We missed you at the Dahl party."

"Sadly, during Mardi Gras, it is too busy for me to attend, but I sent my thoughts and my finest bread pudding." The guy had a corny French accent, and he fawned on Nessa in a way that made Mac slightly ill—and more than slightly jealous.

"It was gone as soon as it hit the table. When Mardi Gras is over, perhaps you can come and bring your waiters for one of Miss Maddy's home-cooked meals."

"As always, we would accept with the deepest of pleasure." Jean-Paul clicked his heels and waved at the hovering, suited female. "I leave you in Penelope's capable hands. If you have any desires, tell her and she will accommodate you at once."

Mac watched the interaction between the two with resignation. "You know all the waiters here?"

"That was Jean-Paul Lambert. He's the owner." Nessa gently mocked Mac's ignorance. "He came here from France fifteen years ago, opened this restaurant and two more, lost the other two in the hurricane, but refused to leave the city he loves. He's a wonderful man, he loves good food, and his chef is spectacular. We're in for a treat tonight."

Not, Mac realized, because of Mrs. Freytag's manipulations, but because of Nessa, who truly did know everyone in New Orleans. If she had planned the robberies on Premier Central banks, and everybody in New Orleans realized it, no one would betray her.

And that was the problem.

Because he didn't want her to be guilty, either. He wanted her to be exactly as she appeared—wholesome, charismatic, sexy beyond belief, and unaware of her effect on men. And of course, fatally attracted to him.

But he was too practical a man to dismiss her actions

during the robbery in the bank, so as soon as he had ordered the wine, he put his scheme into motion. "I've got to go back to Philadelphia."

"What?" She stared at him, her butter knife laden and halfway to her bread, her deep blue eyes wide with dismay—or with what looked like dismay.

"The robbery is over for the year. No one caught the thieves. There's nothing else for me to do."

"But there is! The thieves are still out there somewhere! Surely you've found more clues!" She watched him anxiously.

"No, no more clues."

"But I've introduced you to Chief Cutter—you could work with him some more and—" She caught herself as if embarrassed. Placing her knife on the edge of her plate, she leaned across the table and said softly, "I'm sorry. This is stupid. I'm not telling you the truth."

I suspected that. "Tell me the truth, then."

"I want you to stay because I enjoy your company."

If she was acting, he was her ideal audience. "I enjoy yours, too. I enjoy the places we go together."

"Yes, but you could take me to the swamps and I'd be happy."

"You should have told me that sooner." He grinned at her.

"Do you really think you've played out all your leads? You don't think you'll get back to Philadelphia and suddenly remember a suspect you should have questioned?"

"If I do, I'll come back."

"That would give me something to look forward to." She reached across and caught the hand he rested on the table. "I know Mr. MacNaught said I couldn't help you, but maybe I could look at the video of that last robbery and find something you missed."

Or she could get the chance to mislead him.

"I wish you could stay. Because the thing is . . . I think I might just"—her gaze clung to his—"love you." She jerked back in her seat as if her confession had shocked her. She pressed her lips together and waited, apparently terrified, for his answer.

The world had shifted on its axis.

He didn't know what he thought, what to say, whether to believe her or not . . . And yet, he did believe.

The Ionessa he thought capable of robbing his banks no longer existed in his mind. This woman, vulnerable and so real, had taken her place.

She loved him.

And he wasn't sure. . . . It was almost too difficult to imagine. . . . And was oh, so dangerous . . . but he thought that perhaps he loved her.

Turning his hand up, he twined his fingers in hers. "Maybe I could stay a little longer. To investigate."

"Good." Her gaze clung to his. "I'd like that."

Later that night, Jeremiah dropped Nessa off at the Dahl House. He kissed her long and hard, and in a husky voice, he commanded, "Sleep with me tonight."

"No. I can't."

"Why won't you sleep with me, Nessa?"

"It wouldn't be right."

He smiled a slow, painful grin. "What would make it right? A ring with a huge diamond, accompanied by a marriage proposal?"

"Do you think I'm that shallow?" She traced his jaw with her fingertips.

"I hope so."

She shoved him away. "Go back to the hotel, wicked man, and tempt me no more."

He stood posed on the top step of her porch. "A big diamond, a prenup, and a proposal that outlines all the reasons we should marry?"

"Get out of here!" Laughing, she pointed to the long, dark car that waited in the street.

He hurried down the steps and ducked inside, and she waved as his driver took him away.

Then she clutched her aching head in her hands.

When he said he was leaving, why had she objected? What had she been thinking? That was exactly what she'd been hoping—that he would leave. Because if he left, all her stress would dissolve. She'd have a whole year to dissuade her aunts from robbing the bank again. She'd be happy!

Except she wouldn't be happy, because she wanted Jeremiah Mac in New Orleans, where she could see his rugged face, listen to his rough voice, smell him. . . . He smelled so good, like clean male and good leather and great sex.

Her knees gave out and she leaned against the wall.

She'd told him she loved him.

And he hadn't believed her. Or maybe he did, but he didn't understand love.

Maybe . . . maybe, over the next few days, while he continued to search for the Beaded Bandits, she'd show him what love really meant.

Because one thing her great-aunts had taught her— love was a miracle.

And a miracle was exactly what Nessa needed.

Twenty-eight

Why won't you sleep with me, Nessa?

Because it's not professionally responsible.

Why won't you sleep with me, Nessa?

Because we have nothing in common in our backgrounds and we live miles apart.

Why won't you sleep with me, Nessa?

Nessa sat at the table in the Garden Suite at the Olivier House Hotel, barefoot, relaxed, sipping the last of a very fine Pinot Noir and waiting for the question Jeremiah had asked every night for the past week. She hoped with all her heart that the excellent dinner and fine wine didn't tap into her inherent honesty and make her blurt out the truth: *Because my aunts are the Beaded Bandits and it's bad enough I'm dating you to find out what's going on in the investigation, but if you ever find out about who they are, I won't have you say I slept with you to distract or influence you.*

That would be just ugly.

She also hoped that the next time he asked *Why won't you sleep with me, Nessa?* she wouldn't knock the dishes off the table, grab him by his collar, and have her way with him right there. Because it had been seven very long days and steamy nights since they'd been locked in the vault, and she was so horny that every time she took a breath, she thought of him. And every time she thought of him, her temperature rose another degree. And every time her temperature rose, she reminded herself who the Beaded Bandits really were and that a relationship with the man who was investigating them was impossible.

Then she took another breath and the whole cycle started over again.

Her aunts commented on her rosy glow, Georgia took note of her sparkling eyes, even Stephanie sourly mentioned that Nessa looked unnaturally flushed, like a syphilis sufferer.

Every day, that woman confronted Nessa's radiant face, and she hated it. Despite her best attempts, Nessa was not miserable. . . . And for some reason, the police force had not only ticketed Stephanie for two driving violations, but the animal control people had reported that her neighbors were complaining about her dog barking—and she didn't own a dog.

Nessa wondered how long it would be before Stephanie was sneaking out of town through the swamp filled with water moccasins. She hoped it would be soon.

Tonight, when Jeremiah had taken their dishes and put them outside the door, he came back and seated himself in the chair across from her.

He lifted his glass, took a sip, and instead of the usual *Why won't you sleep with me, Nessa?* he said, "There's no more leads to follow. So I have no choice.

I'm going to have to call this year's investigation a failure, and return to Philadelphia."

"B-but Mardi Gras is almost over. Only six more days until Fat Tuesday. You don't want to miss Fat Tuesday. We'll go to the parade!"

"As attractive as that sounds"—amusement quirked his cheek—"I've already fooled around too long trying to get into your pants."

She must be getting used to him, because she hardly flinched at all. "Is that what you were doing?"

"And eating too much good food, drinking too much fine wine, and kissing the prettiest girl in New Orleans as often as she'll let me."

Her toes curled at his tone.

Most guys disintegrated if they talked too long. Jeremiah was the only guy she knew who always started badly and got better.

"When are you leaving?"

"Tomorrow on the two fifty-three."

"Tomorrow? Afternoon? So soon?" She was shocked. "I thought we'd have time for . . ."

"For me not getting into your pants?"

"For me to get in yours." Okay. She'd had enough to drink, because normally she wouldn't have said it so bluntly. But if he was leaving, all the reasons she had for not sleeping with him were void, and . . . well, she was free. Free to do what she wanted, which was to attack him and make him show her all the details he'd learned during his long apprenticeship with women.

She put down her glass. She unfastened two buttons on her blouse. She stood and offered Jeremiah her hand. "Let me show you a reason to return to New Orleans someday."

He looked at her hand. Looked at her smiling face. Said, "If I'd known leaving would get you into my bed, I would have left four days ago."

"You would?"

"And returned so I could leave again."

She laughed, tossing her hair over her shoulders in a free and easy motion she didn't recognize as her own.

He rose as if pulled to his feet by an invisible tether, and she led him toward the iron spiral stairs. Halfway up to the bedroom, she couldn't wait anymore. Turning, she stood on a step above him, wrapped her arms around his neck, and kissed him.

The extra height made her taller; she liked that, liked kissing him at this angle. For the first time in their relationship, she felt in control. She caressed his earlobes with her thumbs, drew back and smiled into his face.

He looked up at her, and his eyes were green and intense. "Don't tease me, Nessa."

"I'm not teasing you." She opened his shirt and slid her hands inside. His chest rippled, the muscle definition strong and pleasing.

His jaw tightened. His green eyes glittered. Color bloomed over his cheekbones.

He unbuttoned her pants, put his hands on the top of her hips, and slid the pants, and the panties, down her legs. Pulling a condom out of his pocket, he gently pushed her down on the step. "I've waited too long,"

"I don't think so." She unzipped his fly and freed his erection. "I think you'll wait as long as I tell you to wait."

"Nessa, damn, please."

She kissed his penis lightly, then took him in her mouth, sucking gently.

He arched as if he'd been struck by lightning. "Nessa. For the love of God. You're torturing me."

Releasing him, she looked up into his face. "You don't look tortured." She ran one finger up and down the smooth, damp skin of his penis. "You look like a guy who's having the best time of his life."

"I . . . am," he said through gritted teeth.

She wanted to giggle.

Except she'd forced the lid on her need, and now it bubbled up, heating her from the inside out, making her feverish, her skin stretched so tight she felt sunburned.

Taking his hips, she turned him and pushed him down onto a step.

"If you want, we *can* go to the bed," he said. "We don't always have to do it in the most uncomfortable positions possible."

"Are you uncomfortable?" She climbed on top of him, braced her knees on the step on either side of his hips, and kissed his mouth.

"Yeah, I'm uncomfortable. The steps are digging into my back and my butt barely fits. . . ." he observed as she kissed his chest. "But I'm numb except where you're touching me."

"And that part feels good?" She kissed his nipple.

"Feels real good." He was barely able to speak.

She worked her way down his rippled belly.

He caught her under the arms, pulled her back up. He braced his feet on the step below, forming a lap for her to sit on. He gave her the condom and looked her in the eyes. "Next time, I promise I will let you do whatever you want me to. But I've spent three days with a hard-on—"

"Trying to get into my pants," she teased.

"Trying to get into your pants," he conceded, "so please, please put me out of my misery."

"Are you begging?"

"Pleading. Supplicating. Beseeching. Entreating . . ."

She grasped his penis in her hand, fit him with the condom, settled herself over the top of him, and slowly worked her way down onto him.

As expert as he was at making love, she was the opposite. She'd never done anything like this, she was pretty bad at it, and so aroused she was tight and swollen. It took her a while to get the method of holding him, opening herself, using her body's moisture, entering a little, pulling back, entering a little more.

All the while, he writhed beneath her, sweating, his jaw clenching, his muscles bunching and shifting beneath her. "Nessa . . . you have to . . . woman, damn, you make me . . ." His hands clutched the banisters in a desperate attempt to allow her the control she craved, but every time she withdrew, his hips surged upward. "Close . . . come on . . . sweetheart, this is . . ." Tears of frustration welled into his green eyes, glistening like emeralds.

When she finally managed to take him all the way inside, tears glistened in her eyes, too. She braced her hands on his shoulders. Took a long breath and *felt* him deep inside. And whispered, "It feels so good."

All motion ceased.

He stared at her as if she'd said the magic words.

She stared at him, breathless with excitement.

And beneath her, he exploded into action. Below her, he established a driving rhythm, his hips rising and falling.

She braced on the steps and levered herself up, over and over, meeting him fiercely, everything in her concentrated on one movement, one passion . . . this moment.

He twisted his hips, the motion feeding her need, yet holding climax at bay. Inside her, his erection rubbed every nerve, touched the deepest part of her. The fever between them rose and rose, higher and higher. She sobbed with frustration, needing, wanting the orgasm that teased and taunted.

Finally, he caught her hips in his hands, slammed her down and ground himself as deep as he could go.

And she came.

She threw her head back, moaning, convulsing over the top of him, while inside, his explosion filled her with heat.

And when they were finished, she took his hand, led him up to the bedroom, and they did it again.

Nessa and Jeremiah lay sprawled among the rumpled sheets, warm, exhausted, pleasured. His head rested on her rib cage, and she stroked his hair back and traced the scars on his face. "How did you get these?"

"How did you get these?" He kissed the underside of her breast.

"They just grew there." She smiled at him.

"I'm grateful they did."

He had evaded her question, but she wanted to know where he'd come from, what his dreams were. . . . Who he was. So she persevered. Stroking her hand across his chest, she said, "I love your body, too." She traced the scars there. "Did you get these the same place you got the scars on your face?"

"Do they bother you?" He dodged the question.

Out of frustration, she dodged, too. "Am I acting like they bother me?"

"You didn't answer me."

She sank her fingers into his hair, tilted his head, looked into his face. "There's a lot of that going on."

He didn't answer. Instead he scrutinized her, trying to see . . . something.

Did he sense that she hid secrets? Did he suspect that she had spent the week with him for ulterior motives? Did he see the guilt that scourged her soul, the guilt that she would rather be with him to spy on him than to not be with him at all?

She tried again, with a subject less personal. "Where did you grow up?"

"In a little town in Pennsylvania. A company town."

"You were poor."

"After the company went away, I was." He shrugged. "You know what that's like."

"I don't think I was poor, exactly. Just underfunded." From the look on his face, it was once again clear she'd skirted too close to painful facts. She continued, "My aunts were always there for me. But you said your mother didn't hang in there for you. Did you have to leave home?"

"Everybody's got to leave home sometime. And when I left home, I learned a few skills you've found a use for." He slid across the sheets to her face and kissed her, parting her lips, sharing breath, sharing passion. He whispered, "Does it bother you to know I was an escort? Is that why you're asking questions?"

"No! You just know so much about me, and I know

nothing about you, your background, what made you who you are."

"It doesn't matter, because I'm leaving tomorrow."

"Never to return?"

"You could visit me in Philly. In fact—" He started to get off the bed.

Delighted, she tackled him. "You want me to visit you? You'd let me see where you live?"

"Philly's different than New Orleans," he warned.

"Everything's different than New Orleans. You'd invite me to your home? Seriously?"

He wrapped his arms around her. "Seriously. There's a lot of stuff we have to talk about. But . . . in the morning. We'll talk in the morning."

He would, it appeared, share everything but himself.

Twenty-nine

The next morning, in the Garden Suite, Nessa drank her coffee and enjoyed a heady sense of satisfaction.

The night had been long, full of heated caresses, long explorations, husky laughter—her own—and one brief, desperate, betraying moan (his). Altogether, a fabulous experience that left her sitting in his robe, smiling lazily at the undercounter TV as it played the morning news. Political scandal, war, the latest crime on the streets . . . this morning, to her, it all sounded warm and fuzzy, a world as blissful as she was.

Jeremiah came downstairs, dressed in jeans and a polo shirt, computer in hand. With no preamble, he announced, "I've written a prenup."

"A prenup?" She smiled at the man who had made her feel warm, pleasured, sated. "For whom?"

He put the computer in front of her. "For us."

She still smiled, not comprehending for a long, long moment. Then, gradually, her smile slid away. "What do we need a prenup for?"

"It's practical for a man in my position, and it also safeguards your interests in case of my death, or in case the marriage fails." He spoke slowly, articulating each word. "However, I'd like to assure you that that's not my intention. When I enter into a deal, I work the deal to the best of my ability."

"Of course." In a daze, she thought he had missed his calling. He shouldn't be an investigator. He should be someone who negotiated contracts, ordered people around, overwhelmed opposition with his shock tactics. A general, maybe, or a CEO.

He continued, "Should we have children, I made it clear to my lawyer that after you and I discuss our beliefs and preferences in child rearing, the prenup will include the basics of our agreement. Whether or not the marriage is a success, I will not abandon my child and/or children."

She stared at the print on the computer screen, and it swam before her eyes. "I . . . can we stop for a minute? I'm not tracking here." She put down her coffee cup. "You want us to get married?"

"It seems logical." He manipulated the touchpad and brought up a different screen with two columns and numbered lists. "As you can see, I've created a list of pros and cons for marriage between us, and the pros far outweigh the cons." He pointed to the first item. "My business is based in Philadelphia, and I think you'll agree a long-distance affair between us is unsatisfactory."

Gee, just that morning, she'd been thinking a long-distance affair sounded pretty good.

"But it doesn't make sense for you to relocate unless you can hire help for your great-aunts, and if I understand your character—and I flatter myself that I do—

that kind of monetary commitment from me wouldn't be acceptable unless we were legally bound."

"You want me to live with you?"

"My next point." He pointed again. "Your aunts are older, and I believe you care a great deal about their sensibilities. You wouldn't feel comfortable living with me without marriage."

She said nothing. How could she? Her mind was empty of coherent thought.

"Would you?" he prompted.

"Would I what?"

"Be comfortable living with me unless we were married?"

"No, I . . . No, living with you isn't an . . . option."

"Exactly." He looked satisfied, a businessman pleased to know his analysis was correct. "Now, point three—"

She put her hand over his. "Wait. Please."

He turned to her, his brows raised in question, but she saw the intensity in his eyes. Yes, he approached the idea of marriage as a deal, but a very serious deal.

"When did you have a prenup made up?"

"I called my lawyer the day of the robbery and asked him to put together a mutually satisfactory contract."

"No. I mean . . ." She meant, when did he emotionally decide only marriage would do? But he sidetracked her. "Why the day of the robbery?"

"Until that day, I believed you to be a suspect."

He delivered that bomb with a phlegmatic attitude that sent shivers down her spine. "Wh-why? Why would you think that?"

"The robbers have someone on the inside at the

bank, someone who's feeding them information about the operations and the personnel. Because of the mistake on your record and your lack of advancement with the bank, I believed you had reason to carry a grudge."

"That's right. Mr. MacNaught told you. That bastard." She stared at her hands as she clenched them into fists on the bar.

He paused, cleared his throat, and said, "He's actually not so bad."

"I'm sorry if he's a friend of yours, but he has screwed me over so badly, I will never forgive him."

"Actually, he kept you on on the advice of his HR department, who believed that firing you over what would be perceived as a minor violation would play badly with the public, should you bring suit against the bank. It never occurred to him that he was doing you a disservice."

"What a pile of"—remembering that Jeremiah and MacNaught were friends, she finished—"nonsense. What is he even doing getting involved in something so far below his notice? The teller walked out with five hundred dollars! Doesn't he have anything better to do?"

"You'd be surprised at how often those kinds of errors aren't errors, but are deliberate. Mr. MacNaught does not like to be robbed." Jeremiah sounded a little clipped.

"Yeah, well, he should suck it up. After that teller incident, I don't like to be lied to, either, but people do it every day." An ugly realization scratched at her consciousness. "So you were investigating me."

"Mr. MacNaught believed, and I concurred, that you

were a suspect, but I realized almost at once you were innocent. But yes, I was investigating you."

She didn't like that one bit. "In the vault? Were you investigating me there?"

"In the vault, for the first time in my life, I behaved with a total lack of professionalism."

That appeased her a little, as did his slight smile, and the care with which he slid his robe off her right shoulder.

He used one finger to trace her collarbone, sending a chill over her skin. When her nipples tightened, he smiled. "I couldn't resist you, and I flatter myself that you couldn't resist me. Because you behaved with a total lack of professionalism yourself."

"Maybe that's what I do in the vault. I mean, if I steal money and direct robberies—"

"You hadn't been with a man for months. Years."

"What?" She was trying to find out what he really thought of her, get to the bottom of this investigation thing, and he was trying to distract her.

"You were so tight that I barely held myself back long enough to give you pleasure."

Okay. She was officially distracted. "Is that such a big deal?"

"Giving you pleasure? I think so."

"No. I meant—maybe some women are just tight."

"I learned a few things working my way through college, and one of them was how to tell—"

"All right!" She put her hand over his mouth. "I concede to your experience."

He spanned her wrist in his fingers and kissed her palm and her fingertips. "Am I right about your lack of recent experience?"

"Yes," she said between her teeth.

"I like women, and I've been with a lot of them, both during college and afterward. Does that bother you? Because I promise you, from the moment I walked into the bank and saw you, I knew there would never be another woman for me."

Time to drop the indignation about being investigated. She had lost control of the conversation, not that she'd ever had it, and he had her on the run.

But this was about more than sex. Unfortunately. "Is that why you want to marry me? Because you saw me and . . . and . . ."

"Fell in love? Yes."

She lost the ability to breathe. When her head started to swim, she took a gasping breath. "You love me?"

"I have always had a poor opinion of the possibility of maintaining a relationship for the length of two lifetimes. It seems impossible for the passions that set a relationship in motion to be maintained." He smiled ruefully. "Yet I have seen it done. If it's possible for other couples, then I believe the two of us, who are reasonable, mature, educated adults with common interests and even some factors of our background in common—we can also succeed."

He had in no way answered her question, but she wouldn't stop asking it. "You love me?"

He smiled ruefully. "I can't live without you."

"Then . . . would you like to propose marriage?"

He actually looked startled. "I did!"

She shut his laptop. "No. You showed me a prenup and pro/con list. As romantic as I find that, I would like my marriage to start with something more than a business proposition."

He look a long breath.

Oh, this was hard for him. She was so glad—proposing marriage was supposed to be hard.

Taking her hand, he slid to one knee, removed a ring box from his pocket, opened it, and asked, "Ionessa Dahl, will you marry me?"

She looked into his beautiful green eyes, inscrutable no more, but open and alive with passion.

Right now, she was the richest woman in the world.

He slid the ring on her finger.

She examined it. "Wow, it's so . . . big." The diamond was huge, the gaudiest thing she'd ever seen, set in platinum and surrounded by littler diamonds of merely a carat or so. The whole concoction was so big it could choke a hippo. It was so bright, she could signal commercial airliners with it. It was so shiny, she could use it as a skating rink.

And he was very proud of it.

"It's beautiful." Leaning over, she kissed his mouth and whispered, "Yes, I will marry you."

He kissed her back, his mouth hungry and possessive, and broke away only when she pulled back with a laugh. "My back is breaking."

"We can't have that. I have uses for you."

She wound her fingers around his neck. "And would those involve the big bed upstairs, or even the steps on the way up?"

He stood, dragging her up with him. "Let me show you." He took her hand and led her toward the bedroom.

And two words from the television caught her attention.

Bank robbery.

She stopped so quickly he almost jerked her off her feet.

"What's wrong?" He hadn't heard. His voice was still soft, indulgent.

"Sh!" She gestured roughly at him and turned toward the TV.

Local newscaster Arlanna Ramos stood inside the Premier Central Bank at the corner of South Villere and Cleveland, spewing facts at the camera as quickly as she could. "The Beaded Bandits have struck again, but what a change! This morning's robbery was brief and brutal—"

Vaguely, Nessa heard the phone ring.

Jeremiah walked across the room and answered, his voice low and intense.

Arlanna continued, "And while bank officials won't confirm the amount, an inside source has indicated over twenty thousand dollars was taken at gunpoint. Shots were fired, and while no one was hurt—" The camera panned back to show a teller sitting on a chair, crying and visibly shaking.

"My God." Nessa tore herself away from the television, ran for the bedroom, grabbed her clothes. "My God."

The aunts had struck again, and this time . . . this time, they had ruined them all.

Thirty

"As near as we can tell, $20,942 was taken—"

The bank manager's voice trembled as he imparted the news to Mac, but Mac wasn't really listening. His cool brain clicked the pieces together.

The polite notes that demanded money and offered advice . . .

The female voices that sounded so familiar . . .

The costumes that looked so real . . .

The Beaded Bandits weren't men. They weren't transvestites.

They were tall old women. They were Nessa's great-aunts.

And Nessa *knew*.

No wonder she'd slept with him. She'd been playing him like a fish, pretending reluctance, yet all the while, she hooked him and reeled him in.

What a fool he'd been. What an incredible fool.

He cut right through the manager's flow of words. "It's all right. I know who's doing it. They'll be arrested within the hour." He hung up while the manager was stammering his astonishment.

He flexed his hands. They were cold, his fingers icy.

He picked up the phone to call Chief Cutter, and call waiting beeped in.

Gabriel Prescott.

"What the hell is going on down there?" Gabriel didn't wait for an answer. "I'll be there this afternoon."

Mac glanced at the TV, where the meteorologist expounded on a storm front moving in. "Unlikely. Come in tomorrow. Today I need you in contact with the police and the bank." He didn't know why, but he felt driven to confess, "I know who they are, Gabriel. I have them now."

"Really?" Gabriel sounded cautious. "Don't leave me hanging."

Cool, good sense blew across Mac's heated mind. Gabriel hadn't believed Mac's theory that Nessa had been the mastermind of the operation, and today Mac had seen the shock and horror on her face. Certainly, she hadn't known about this robbery. Nor, if her performance last week had been any indication, had she known about that robbery before it occurred.

But once she saw her aunts in action, she had known—and that's when she started seeing him at night, smiling at him across restaurant tables, asking leading questions about his investigation, winding him around her little finger. And when he told her he was leaving, she screwed him senseless, not realizing he was already so blind and stupid in love he'd bought a ring and sweated over a marriage proposal.

Rage and humiliation clawed at his gut. He'd poured his heart out to Nessa Dahl.

All the while, she'd been laughing at him.

So he needed proof to convince Gabriel, and proof to

convince Chief Cutter and the whole NOPD that the old ladies they adored had set them up. "You'll know soon enough."

Hanging up, he stared at the phone. What he wanted most was to call Chief Cutter and rage at him for missing what was right before his eyes. But that wouldn't get Mac what he wanted. First, he needed to utilize the impeccable logic for which he was famous.

He called his secretary. "I need to know everything about the finances of the Dahl family in New Orleans, first names Hestia, Calista, and Ionessa."

"Yes, sir." Mrs. Freytag sounded cool and unflappable as always. "You do realize this is illegal?"

"I want it within the hour." He hung up, knowing without a doubt that she would have the information within thirty minutes. He strode into the bedroom to shave and dress—black suit, white shirt, red tie.

Today he would lose whatever anonymity he'd been able to achieve. The press would cast him in the role of ruthless invader—and he wanted to look the part.

Mrs. Freytag's call came as he finished tying his tie.

"Calista and Hestia Dahl have an account with Manhattan International Investments," she said.

"The amount?"

"One hundred and forty-two thousand, and seventy-six cents."

His temperature dropped another degree.

His breath was freezing in the air.

The Dahl girls had not a fortune, but a sizeable sum of money. Their whole helpless, disadvantaged act was just that—an act. They stole from his bank and invested the money. To collect that sum, they probably stole from other banks, too, in other guises.

And even now, he had hoped it wasn't true. Because some idealistic sliver of his soul still lingered, wanting to think Nessa was naive and wholesome, and her aunts were dotty and delightful.

But he had trained himself to look at the ugly truth straight on.

Those women were calculating thieves and skilled con artists—and they would be sorry they had caught Mac MacNaught in their nets. "Thank you. Mrs. Freytag, do we hold a mortgage on the Dahl House?"

He heard the keys click on her computer. "No. But we have their credit report from eleven years ago. . . . They applied for some kind of loan and were refused as a bad risk."

Nessa's school loans. "Find out if there's any kind of mortgage or loan using the house as collateral. Acquire it."

"Yes, sir. Anything else?"

"Notify Radcliffe. I'll need him and a team down here tomorrow morning."

"The lawyers?" The keys clicked again. "If I may ask, Mr. MacNaught, did you catch the Beaded Bandits?"

"No, but I identified them. It is almost over. I'll be in contact with you later." He hook-switched and dialed Chief Cutter.

He didn't get through at first. It took a minute of plain, cold language before the officer who guarded the chief's privacy connected them.

Chief Cutter spoke quickly, a man caught in a vise between duty and annoyance. "I know there was another robbery. I'm on the scene right now—"

"You're in the wrong place. Get in the car and drive to the Garden District."

"Why?" Chief Cutter sounded cautious.

"Because that's where the criminals live."

"You figured it out?" The chief's voice clearly doubted.

"Without a doubt." Mac's voice dipped below freezing. "You're going to arrest Miss Hestia and Miss Calista Dahl for the robberies at all the Premier Central banks."

Thirty-one

Nessa arrived at the Dahl House in time to meet her great-aunts opening the screen door and bustling onto the front porch.

Calista wore an apron.

Hestia's lipstick was smeared.

Those signs of disarray, more than anything, betrayed them to Nessa.

She stood before the steps on the porch, in the middle of the cracked, uneven front walk, and asked in anguish, "How could you, aunts? How could you?"

"Dear, have you heard what has happened?" Hestia's scowl puckered the wrinkles around her eyes, around her mouth.

Calista slammed the screen door behind her. "Someone robbed one of our banks in costumes like ours, took a lot of money, and fired at a police officer—"

In a chorus of indignation, both aunts said, "And everyone thinks it was us!"

Nessa stood frozen, her mouth half-open, feeling foolish.

Of course the aunts hadn't robbed that bank. They

would never steal that amount of money. And, remembering the white and shaken teller on TV, she knew they would never frighten anyone so desperately.

Nessa wanted to take it all back. Her anger, her sense of betrayal . . . the accusation.

But, thank God, the aunts hadn't seemed to notice.

The aunts came marching at Nessa, both tall, one thin, one plump, shoulder to shoulder, united in righteous anger.

Nessa fell back. "What . . . what are you doing?"

A cab pulled up at the curb.

Maddy came around the corner of the porch, hobbling as fast as she could. "Hestia! Calista! Girls, you can't do it!"

The aunts wheeled to face Maddy, and Calista said, "We have to, Maddy, we can't have everyone think we're violent and money hungry!"

"What are your intentions?" Nessa asked again, more urgently this time.

"We're going to tell the police the truth," Calista said.

"Are you crazy?" Nessa shouted.

"Chère, please remember, a lady's voice is always low and musical to the ear," Hestia rebuked.

"A lady doesn't rob banks, either," Nessa retorted.

"Actually," Hestia mused, "during the Depression, our Grandmother Hall kept the family out of the poorhouse and half of New Orleans fed with a little genteel larceny—"

Calista poked Hestia with a well-padded elbow.

Hestia's face turned stern again. "But that's not the same as taking the money to fulfill your own frivolous desires, which someone has done now."

A gust of wind swirled through the yard, making bark mulch dance across the sidewalk.

Maddy got to the top of the stairs and glared down at them. "Confessing your other crimes isn't going to make the police realize you didn't do this crime—it's going to make them put you in jail."

"We always knew it might come to that," Hestia said. "Although not for this reason."

"Please." Nessa stepped up to them and put her hands on their wrists. "This won't help the police find these thieves. It'll just confuse them and . . . and help the robbers get away." Specious reasoning.

Of course the aunts didn't buy it.

"Don't be silly, child," Calista said. "Once we point out the differences between our robberies and this one, that will clarify matters for the police."

In the distance, Nessa heard the sound of a siren. She jerked her gaze up to Maddy's dismayed face.

"The police will be able to focus on the real thieves," Calista continued. "Let's face it, those scallywags copied our well-thought-out operation, so they can't be too bright."

The sirens grew louder.

The sun disappeared behind a wisp of cloud, then came out again, then disappeared again.

"How do you figure?" Nessa asked through lips numb with fear. "You've been successful for years, *and* if these other thieves get caught, they can establish alibis for the times when you were robbing the banks instead of them. Copying your operation seems brilliant to me."

"If these thieves can't even make up their own

scheme, they have no pride in their work. Mere dabblers, and easy to catch," Hestia said dismissively.

Two police cars, sirens screaming, lights flashing, came around one corner. Another came around the other corner. They met in the street, nose to nose.

Nessa fought the urge to grab the aunts and tell them to run.

Neighbors came spilling out of their houses.

But Hestia placidly folded her hands before her apron. "Look, Calista, the police have come to *us*."

Nessa faced the street.

Two patrolmen jumped out of one car and pointed their pistols at the little clump of women in front of the Dahl House.

The cab driver got out of his cab, talking fast and furiously. "What you boys doin' to these nice ladies? Stop that!"

The patrolmen ignored him.

Looking wide-eyed and rebellious, Rav Woodland got out of the second car. He loosened his service pistol, but he didn't draw it.

Chief Cutter got out of the driver's seat of the third car. . . . And Jeremiah got out of the passenger's seat.

The sight of him, of his tall figure, held in stiff formality, of his stony expression, of his cool eyes, raking the four of them, passing over Nessa with exquisite indifference . . . she whispered, "Oh, God. Oh, God."

He knew.

Chief Cutter strode toward them, arms swinging, trying hard to smile reassuringly and instead grimacing as if he were in pain. And perhaps he was.

Nessa focused on him, focused to the exclusion of anything else, to the exclusion of Jeremiah Mac. In a tone that splashed him with acid scorn, she said, "Cutter, I'm surprised you've got the guts to come yourself. After all, you are an elected official."

"What do you mean?" Chief Cutter blustered, but he looked shamefaced.

Nessa leaned toward him, furious at the guns pointed their way. "You know good and well that the next cars to arrive will be the press, and they'll take photos of the police chief putting handcuffs on two old ladies and carting them away to jail."

Just as she predicted, a car pulled up and a guy with a camera leaped out, slammed the door, aimed a long lens, and started snapping photos.

The neighbors murmured and moved closer.

Chief Cutter's eyes shifted to her aunts. "Is that what I'm going to do? Am I going to arrest you ladies? Miss Calista? Miss Hestia?"

Jeremiah walked up behind him. "Of course you are."

"Shut up, Mac. Let the ladies answer." Chief Cutter never removed his gaze from the aunts.

Hestia moved forward and patted his arm. "I'm afraid so, Chief, but the important thing you have to know is—it wasn't us today."

"Oh, for shit's sake." Jeremiah walked away as if he couldn't stand to listen. Couldn't stand to look at them.

Hestia trotted after him. "Now, Jeremiah, I know you're disappointed in us. Nessa was disappointed, too, but we had good reason for stealing from Mr. MacNaught's banks."

Chief Cutter swiftly interrupted. "Ma'am, perhaps it would be best if you refrained from further comments until you've had counsel from a lawyer."

Hestia sailed on without pause. "Mr. MacNaught's banks not only have the highest profit margin and so are best able to take the hits, but Mr. MacNaught doesn't give to charity. We were helping him."

"By stealing the money and keeping it?" Jeremiah asked in steely disdain.

Thunder rumbled in the distance.

"We *give* the money away to the needy so Mr. MacNaught could receive a credit on his miserable, miserly soul." Calista caught sight of a reporter she recognized, realized she was wearing an apron, took it off, and handed it to Nessa. Fluffing her hair, she smiled at the cameras.

"That, and the fact we don't like the man because he has been so awful to our Ionessa," Hestia reminded her.

The Channel 26 News van pulled up and parked.

Jeremiah ignored that as if Hestia had never spoken. "Twenty thousand dollars is going to take care of a lot of needy."

"We told you, we didn't steal the money today," Hestia said impatiently.

Thunder rumbled again. The sun appeared, then blinked out again. From the west, Nessa could see a curtain of rain falling from a tall, gray cumulus cloud.

"Miss Calista, do you have an alibi?" Chief Cutter asked.

"Maddy was here with us," Hestia said.

Chief Cutter glanced at the tiny black woman and shook his head.

Maddy stomped her foot, and the loose boards on the porch rattled. "What, boy? You don't believe me because I'm old? Or because I'm a woman? Or because I'm black?"

In a pleading tone, Chief Cutter said, "Miss Maddy, you know none of that's true. You know why you're not a reliable witness."

Maddy challenged him. "Why?"

"Because you were employed by the family since before Miss Calista and Miss Hestia were born, and you've lived in the house since the hurricane." Chief Cutter shook his head again. "No one's going to believe you won't lie for them."

"You already have lied for them, by not telling what you knew of the previous crimes," Jeremiah said.

Maddy rounded on him. "Mr. Mac, you must have a lot of sin on your soul to have such a nasty opinion of me. And of them."

The neighbors nodded, and the local juvenile delinquent from down the street, Daniel Noel, lifted his fist over his head. "You tell 'em, Miss Maddy!"

The screen door slammed, and Pootie clomped out of the house, her short hair standing on end and the marks of her pillow on her cheek. She surveyed the turmoil with displeasure. "What the hell is going on here?"

"They're arresting Miss Calista and Miss Hestia for robbing the banks," Maddy told her.

Pootie turned on her like an irate wolverine. "Pull the other leg."

Maddy scrutinized their first, most reclusive boarder. "Look around."

Pootie's gaze swept the crowd and landed on Chief Cutter. "You're shittin' me. Have you lost what few feeble brain cells your wife hasn't knocked out of you?"

Chief Cutter's cheeks turned a mottled red. "She doesn't beat me."

"She oughta." Pootie saw Jeremiah next, and something shifted in her face, a comprehension. "Ohh."

With an authority he seldom flaunted, Chief Cutter asked, "Miss DiStefano, have you been here all day? Can you provide Miss Calista and Miss Hestia with an alibi?"

"Look at her," Jeremiah said. "She's been asleep."

"I'm afraid so." Pootie didn't bother to run her fingers through her wild hair. "Can't help you."

"Pootie stays up all hours of the night," Hestia told him. "It's part of her work."

"What does she do?" Jeremiah watched Pootie, but asked Hestia.

"We think it has something to do with the Internet." Hestia anxiously watched Pootie. "She has promised us it's not illegal."

Jeremiah snorted loudly.

Nessa wanted to smack him. He wasn't her dream man. He was her nightmare.

"We were on our way to the police station to confess, because whoever has done this, they've done a terrible wrong." Calista waved at the cab.

Jeremiah's lip curled. It was written all over his face—he thought they'd called it to help them get away. "Arrest them all." Now his gaze settled on Nessa, and the man who had held her this morning, who had given her a ring, who had clumsily confessed his love . . . had vanished as if he had never been. This man was hard and cruel and cold, a whose only interest in her was that of prosecutor for his foe. "Arrest them *all*," he said again.

"You can arrest Hestia and me. That makes sense," Calista said. "But why would you arrest Nessa and Maddy? They had nothing to do with the robberies."

"Accessories to the crime," Jeremiah said.

Hestia laughed lightly. "Don't be ridiculous! Maddy and Nessa are innocent. Do you really think Calista and I couldn't figure out how to rob a bank on our own? Why, we were collecting mice for months before this last robbery!"

"Please don't say anything else!" Chief Cutter was in agony.

"Hey!" Their next-door neighbor stood with her toes just over the property line and shouted. "What are you punks doing with Miss Calista and Miss Hestia?"

"That's Mrs. King," Hestia confided. "She's such a nasty old biddy—I hope she doesn't come over. She could make this very unpleasant."

"No, we wouldn't want this to be unpleasant," Maddy said, her voice heavy with sarcasm.

Nessa wanted to cry. The street continued filling with cars, reporters, neighbors running up from blocks away. The whole scene resembled a circus, and her aunts were the main attraction.

Yet the humiliation was nothing compared to the chill that Jeremiah's immovable presence created.

Nessa had to talk to him. Beg him . . . she'd done a lot of difficult things in her life. She'd kowtowed to Stephabeast. She'd placated furious customers. She'd faced the consequences when she let that teller steal the money. But nothing compared to the thick dread that filled her as she put one foot in front of the other and walked toward Jeremiah Mac.

He watched her come, his lids heavy over his green eyes.

She would have felt better if he showed emotion, any emotion, but there was nothing—no hate, no contempt, no lingering remnant of passion or love. "Jeremiah, please. They're old. They're eccentric. They didn't mean any harm."

"I'd have to disagree. It sounds as if they meant to teach MacNaught a lesson."

She bit her lip. "Yes, but it really wasn't much of a lesson, and it's nothing compared to what their suffering will be in jail. They don't understand what it's like in there—the drunks, the mentally ill, the lifelong criminals who will enjoy hurting them."

"They should have thought of that before they started on their crusade to discipline MacNaught." Jeremiah folded his arms over his chest.

"He's a rich man. A powerful man. He'll gain nothing from this prosecution. You know him. Intercede for them."

Jeremiah's mouth twisted in a nasty way, as if he'd bit into a rotten tomato. "You dated me to spy on my investigation, to mislead me when you could. You slept with me to distract me so they could rob the bank today."

"They *didn't* rob the bank today."

His voice was slow, low, and intense. "Lady, you have guts." Turning on his heel, he walked away, down the street, around the corner, and out of sight.

Nessa stared after him, stared at the place where he'd disappeared, her eyes and cheeks burning with humiliation.

A little more than an hour ago, she'd believed she

would marry him, bask in his love, love him in return. Then she'd seen the news, he'd seen the news, and their brief chance at happiness had evaporated.

Worst of all, he had tried to make her believe he was indifferent to her. But he wasn't indifferent at all.

He believed the worst of her. He despised her, hated her.

In the background of her consciousness, Nessa heard Chief Cutter say, "All right, Miss Calista, Miss Hestia. I'm sorry, but I have to arrest you."

The sun disappeared completely now. Lightning flashed, thunder boomed.

"Do you know what that is?" Nessa pointed at the sky and shouted to Chief Cutter. "That's heaven protesting the arrest of two of its kindest citizens."

"Chère, there's no reason to yell at Chief Cutter. He's only doing his job!" Hestia turned to the chief. "Will we get to ride in the patrol car with the lights flashing and the siren on?"

"There's no need for that." Chief Cutter got out a pair of metal handcuffs.

"But that would be so exciting!" Calista said.

"Sure. What the . . . heck. I'll turn on the siren and the lights." Chief Cutter sounded choked and hopeless. "Miss Hestia, I need your wrists."

Nessa kept her back turned. She couldn't stand to observe as Chief Cutter placed handcuffs on her sweet, eccentric, slightly mad and totally loveable old aunts. She heard the click of the metal as they shut—and a hard *thunk*.

She swung around and saw Chief Cutter standing, slack-jawed, while Hestia looked down at the handcuffs at her feet.

Calista hid a smile.

The crowd laughed jeeringly.

The cameras clicked and whirled.

"Chief, I'm so sorry." Leaning down, Hestia picked up the handcuffs and handed them to Cutter. "Calista has always given me such a bad time about my skinny wrists and narrow hands—I play the piano, you know, and was quite good in my youth. Put them on me again, and I promise they won't fall off."

Nessa put her hand on the jut of her hip. "Yeah, Chief Cutter, just in case anybody in the crowd didn't get a picture of you putting the handcuffs on one of the sweetest women in New Orleans, do it again."

"Nessa, there's no need to use that tone," Hestia said.

Chief Cutter signaled for Rav Woodland, and when Rav had loped over, he tried to give him the handcuffs. "You do it."

"No, sir!" Rav backed away, hands in the air. "My mama would slap me upside the head if she found out I put cuffs on Miss Hestia or Miss Calista."

"What do you think my wife's going to do to me?" Chief Cutter muttered. Then he raised his voice. "You're going to lose your job if you don't follow orders."

"I don't care, sir. I can't do it, and I won't do it." Rav backed farther away.

As Chief Cutter looked around in frustration, Nessa watched her aunts put the handcuffs on each other.

It was funny, in a horrible way, to see them catch Chief Cutter's attention and to see his reaction: the horrified start, the guilty glance around the hostile, grimly amused neighborhood.

"We're ready," Hestia chirped.

Calista proudly displayed the handcuffs to Nessa. "We've never been arrested before."

In a silence interrupted only by the wind-blown rustle of leaves in the trees, Chief Cutter took an arm for each of them. "We'll set bail as soon as possible, within twenty-four hours for sure."

"Bail," Nessa whispered.

How was she going to make bail for her aunts? She didn't have any extra cash stashed away for possible arrests!

Chief Cutter marched them toward his patrol car.

Hestia held her arms crooked so the handcuffs didn't fall off again.

Calista waved and made little chirping noises of encouragement at her friends.

And Nessa's heart sank with each step they walked away from her.

Finally, with the wail of child who had been abandoned once too often, she ran after her great-aunts and sobbed on their shoulders.

"It's all right, Nessa," they murmured in unison, patting her back. "It's all right."

A big raindrop splashed on the back of her neck. Another hit her cheek.

She grabbed for control. "You've got to go before you get wet." She kissed first one aunt, then the other, and helped them into the barred backseat of the police car.

As promised, Chief Cutter turned on the lights and the siren, and the aunts waved from the back window as they drove off.

Peripherally, Nessa knew the press had filmed the

farewell, and now they rushed toward her, microphones extended.

But the rain was coming down in earnest. The lightning flashed. The thunder boomed. And she couldn't talk. She could barely hold on to her bit of composure long enough to run toward the house. Toward Maddy. Toward safety.

She gained the porch, realized Maddy held the screen door open for her, and blundered through, feeling foolish, out of control. . . . And lost. So lost.

Her aunts, her security since she was barely five, were gone, in jail, and she didn't know how she would get them out.

Jeremiah, her lover, the man whose ring she wore, despised her.

She managed to get a few steps into the entry, braced her hand against the wall, and wept as if her heart would break.

She heard Maddy shut the front door against the tumult of rain and reporters outside. She heard Pootie clear her throat repeatedly. And still she couldn't rise from the morass of despair into which she had sunk.

Until she heard Pootie say, "I've got to go upstairs to check on a few things, but before I do, I think you ought to know—that man you think is Jeremiah Mac . . ."

Nessa caught her breath. Looked up. Saw the bitterly amused, twisted and dismayed expression on Pootie's face. "I *think* is Jeremiah Mac?" she choked.

"He's misrepresenting himself. He's the CEO of Premier Central Banks." Pootie clomped toward the stairway. "That guy is Mac MacNaught."

Thirty-two

That night, Stephanie Decker stood in her bathroom, creaming the make-up off her face and listening with half her attention to the local news, when a single phrase caught her attention.

". . . Arrested Calista and Hestia Dahl in their own home today for the robberies at Premier Central Banks."

Stephanie looked in the mirror, her eyes wide in her white, smeared face. "What?" She ran into the bedroom, tripped on the hem of her robe, caught the footboard with one slick hand, and hit the floor with a thud.

She didn't care. This was good. So good.

On the TV, Arlanna Ramos stood in front of the Dahl House, frowning as Chief Cutter put the handcuffs on the two elderly women. Nessa stood with her back to the scene, looking absolutely miserable. Furious. Helpless. Probably she was mortified, too. Stephanie cackled with delight. This was the best newscast ever!

Quickly, she grabbed a DVD, stuck it in the recorder, and pushed record. She wanted to save these memories *forever*.

Ooh. She'd have to write an e-mail to Mr. MacNaught. Not that he didn't know what was going on, but she had been incredibly successful in creating her own little slant and adding juicy details to the plain facts. Look at what she'd done so far. Discredited Jeremiah Mac to the point that Mr. MacNaught had told her to keep an eye on him, and gotten Nessa pulled off the job with him and back to the grunt work of running the bank. Which was exactly what the little slut did best, except for screwing the private investigator, which apparently she did exceptionally well, because he'd been sniffing after her all day and every night.

A drop of makeup remover slipped onto Stephanie's lip, and absent-mindedly, she licked it off. And shuddered. That tasted awful.

She had to decide when she was going to tell Mr. MacNaught about the panties. For it to be effective, it had to be before the investigator left. She could tell Mr. MacNaught about the secret entrance into the vault then, too, and he'd probably give her another raise. Maybe a promotion to a bigger bank. In fact, what she'd ask for was to be moved to some other city where no one knew her—

"... Mac MacNaught ..."

Hearing his name jerked Stephanie's attention to the television.

Arlanna continued, "Mac MacNaught, the president and CEO of Premier Central Banks, was on hand for the arrests."

But they were showing the wrong picture.

"The reclusive Mr. MacNaught made his satisfaction with the arrests quite clear."

Stephanie talked back to the TV. "Hey, stupid, you've got the wrong guy."

"Mr. MacNaught wouldn't stop to speak to the reporters, but he did take the time to exchange heated words with Ionessa Dahl, niece of the Dahl sisters and a Premier Central Banks employee."

"You've got the wrong guy." Frantically, Stephanie punched a new channel into the remote, landing on a local news report showing the same story and same man, Jeremiah Mac, and identifying him incorrectly as Mac MacNaught.

She was starting to feel sick to her stomach. She tried another local channel, then tried CNN.

Of course, that was dumb. The national networks weren't going to cover a story in New Orleans about two old ladies gone soft in the head and stealing—

"And today in New Orleans—"

Stephanie sat, stunned, and watched the same story unfold, and the same name flash under Jeremiah Mac's picture.

And she realized she'd been tattling about Mac MacNaught . . . to him. She'd been blackening his character . . . to him.

Her career with the bank was over.

But maybe an e-mail explaining that she did everything out of loyalty to the bank. Surely he would understand that.

And probably he didn't remember that part in a previous e-mail where she called him a nasty little lecher who spent his time in New Orleans going to parties and dancing with transvestites. . . . Wincing, she sat down at her computer and proceeded to grovel.

Thirty-three

In the morning, Mac woke with a grim sense of purpose. He'd been betrayed, but it wasn't the first time, and truth to tell, he'd expected it. After all, the people in his life had proved, time and again, that no one could be trusted.

So he did what he always did when he arose; he called his secretary. "Where's Radcliffe?"

"He and the team got rerouted to Houston, but"—he heard her clicking the keys on her computer—"their plane is landing right now, and they'll be in the city in time for the Dahls' bail hearing."

"Do we know when it is?"

"In Louisiana, a bail hearing must be held before the judge in forty-eight to seventy-two hours, and it seems there's a powerful push among the authorities and from the public to get the Dahl sisters released as soon as possible. So the hearing is set for this afternoon. When they finalize the time, I'll let you know."

"Do that. Did you acquire their mortgage?"

"Yes, sir."

"Start proceedings to foreclose."

"I . . . Mr. MacNaught? That's not possible. They're current in their payments," Mrs. Freytag said.

"During the transfer, the computer screwed up and records of their payments were lost."

Mrs. Freytag sounded startled and affronted. "Is that really necessary?"

"I'm sorry, Mrs. Freytag. I'm afraid I heard you incorrectly. Did you question my judgment?"

He could almost see Mrs. Freytag snap to attention. "No, sir. I'll take care of that right away."

With the efficiency that served him well, he used the rest of the conversation to catch up on the business in his office.

When Mrs. Freytag had brought him up to speed with everything that required his attention, he hung up, poured himself a cup of coffee, sat down on the bar stool, and stared hard at the chair Nessa had occupied only twenty-four hours before.

He had become what Nessa thought he was. The kind of banker who foreclosed on elderly, disadvantaged women.

He had a decision to make.

Nessa had proved treacherous, as treacherous as his mother and his father, as treacherous as he'd imagined.

But that didn't change the fact that the sex hadn't lessened his desire for her one iota. He was, he supposed, in love with her, or at least in violent lust with her, and as a man who prided himself on facing the facts, he knew he couldn't go back to his life and exist with any kind of satisfaction.

So he had two choices.

Live without her and find himself reduced to the kind of man she imagined Mac MacNaught to be:

miserly, miserable, and a caricature of Scrooge MacDuck.

Or absorb her into his life, knowing full well the kind of viper he took to his bosom, knowing he would have to spend the rest of his life waiting for the time when she'd strike at his heart and try to kill him.

There was no choice.

He'd live with her.

But on his terms.

Right now, he held the power. Nessa had to post bail, and his team of attorneys would make sure the bail was set high. She also had to hire an attorney for her aunts, and his team of attorneys would make sure the only lawyers that had a chance of succeeding would be the most expensive in the city.

At the same time, his lending company would demand immediate repayment on their mortgage.

If this case went to trial, the Dahl fortune would be wiped out.

Mac knew he hadn't misread Nessa's affection for her aunts. She would come to him again, offer herself and whatever else he wanted, and he'd negotiate carefully, paying her to be his mistress, to tend to his sexual needs, to show him affection and pretend she meant it. . . .

"No!" He stood up, abruptly offended at himself. No fake affection. Nothing but pure, clean lust. He didn't want her whispering that she loved him, he didn't want her clinging to him afterward, wiping tears from the corners of her eyes and claiming that was so good it made her cry. Thinking about how she made him believe he was the lover of her dreams, that he could someday hope to win her love . . . he felt sick to his stomach to think how she'd duped him.

But she knew a little of what he felt—by now, she had discovered his real identity. Yes, let her feel a little of the betrayal that bit at him.

He wondered if she remembered all the things she'd said to him about Mac MacNaught, and repented of them.

The doorbell rang, and when he answered it, a red-eyed, exhausted-looking Gabriel Prescott stood on the other side.

Mac stood back to let him in. "How'd you get here so soon?"

"I hired a plane to fly me in from Houston." Gabriel carried a small suitcase and a computer case. "I could *not* find a room in this city. Mardi Gras, they all said. Mind if I crash on the floor?"

"I'll have them bring in a cot. Or—no, maybe *you'd* better ask the management. Right now, I'm the most hated man in New Orleans." Thank God Mac had secured the Garden Suite for another two weeks before the news broke. If they could, the innkeepers would have thrown him out on his ear. The night before, after the video from yesterday afternoon had flashed from every television set, he'd waited two hours in the restaurant for his table at Brennan's—and he had had a reservation.

"As soon as I saw the reports on CNN, I remembered this." Gabriel pulled out his computer and put it on the table. He brought up a slice of video. "After the first theft, the police filmed the witnesses. This is Melissa Jude, the teller who was robbed."

"I know it's ridiculous." Melissa sat in a metal folding

chair, twisting her hands in her lap. "I know it's impossible. But it seemed as if . . . I think that they . . ."

"What is it, Miss Jude?" an off-camera policeman prompted.

She looked up, right into the camera lens. "The more I think about it, the more I think . . . those guys really were women."

Mac stared at the screen, bitterness rising in him. "That was what Melissa didn't have the guts to tell me."

"It was there all the time, right under our noses," Gabriel agreed. "When you proposed your theory, I didn't think you were right about Ionessa Dahl, but you were. She has been playing us and every possible law-enforcement agency for fools."

"I know."

"When I looked into those clear blue eyes on that video, I thought she must be the gentlest, kindest, purest soul in the world. You'd think I'd know better than to judge someone by the package."

"You'd think."

"Well." Gabriel dusted off his palms. "Let me get changed. I'll visit the banks. I want to talk to my men. I don't like this last robbery. Don't like it at all."

"There won't be another one. We have the thieves in custody."

Gabriel scrutinized Mac. "You're kidding, right?"

"It's obvious. The Dahl girls have been robbing my banks for years. They *are* the Beaded Bandits."

"Agreed. But not yesterday. Those were copycat bandits. The MO is only superficially the same, and look at the tapes! One guy is taller than the Beaded Bandits, and the other is shorter. And one's a chub."

Mac stared stonily at Gabriel, hearing the words but not wanting to comprehend him.

"You *have* viewed the tapes, haven't you?" Gabriel asked.

"No."

"You've viewed every other tape numerous times, but you didn't bother to view this one. What the hell . . . ? Do you like thinking the Dahl women committed this robbery, too?" Gabriel must have seen some flicker of betraying emotion in Mac's face, because he stumbled backward. "You do. You want them to be guilty of everything. What? Are you so used to the people you trust betraying you that you're more comfortable that way?"

Mac jerked his head back as if he'd been kicked. "What do you know about that?"

"Everything. I'm a security man, and you keep a low profile, but the information is out there if you look in the right place."

Mac stepped forward, fists clenched.

Gabriel stepped forward and met him.

The two men locked gazes.

Mac recognized a cold, harsh truth. Gabriel wasn't going to back down.

He stepped back.

If his capitulation was a victory for Gabriel, Gabriel didn't show it. "Okay. You don't look if you don't want to. You ignore the truth if you like. But you're paying me to see what you don't want to. I'll make sure the banks are secure, and I will make sure that camera is set up correctly and inconspicuously in the vault of Miss Dahl's bank. I figured if that hole had been open for a hundred years, we didn't need to worry about plugging it right away, but the way things have been going, the entire population of New Orleans is probably in there right now, smoking a joint."

"I'll order my car for you."

"If no one's talking to you, better let me do it." Gabriel cracked open his suitcase, gathered clean clothes, got changed, and got out of there.

Mac was relieved to see him go. Gabriel was right. Mac welcomed his ravaged fury—it was easier to bear the pain of Nessa's betrayal.

Nobody had ever betrayed Gabriel. No one had ever abandoned him to a street gang and stood aside while they kicked the shit out of him. . . . Mac did something he never did. With his fingers, he explored the scars on his face. Opening his shirt, he looked at the marks on his chest, touched each one.

Some scars left a record on his flesh. He used to believe they were the most terrible.

Now he knew better. The worst marks stained his soul.

A call from Radcliffe told him the law team had landed and were headed to corporate rooms at the Hilton, and then to the courthouse where they'd make sure the bail was set to the proper amount. The justice system in New Orleans was as corrupt as most; they foresaw no problem in getting their way.

In a few hours, Nessa would have to choose between letting her great-aunts rot in jail or coming to Mac for mercy. And he . . . he'd left her no choice.

Sitting down at his computer, he tried to work, but he couldn't concentrate. This betrayal had rattled him. Every time he looked at a spreadsheet, he wondered what Nessa was doing now. How Nessa would react when she saw him. He amused himself with scenarios of how she would fling herself at his feet, begging for mercy, while he pretended indifference and left his law team to negotiate her surrender.

But no. Mac couldn't leave his law team alone with her. By the time she was done with Radcliffe, he'd be a sweaty suit full of Silly Putty. Mac would do the negotiating himself. He'd enjoy letting her try her little wiles on him. . . . His glance flashed to the spiral iron stairway. His memory flashed to the shy little blowjob, to the smile she gave as she finished and glanced up at him. . . .

"God damn it!" He stood up and paced across the room.

Nothing about her was real. Not her smiles, not her eagerness, not her carefully orchestrated inexperience. He had to stop wanting to believe.

When the time came, he shrugged into his suit coat. He walked through the hotel. The doorman ushered him outside. His usual smile was not present, and Mac heard a sibilant whisper: "Bastard."

Figured. He'd seen the news report.

He turned to the liveried young man. "That's right, I am. In every sense of the word. Now get me a cab."

The doorman used his whistle.

The cab flew across the street and under the awning outside the building.

"Where are you going, sir?" the doorman asked.

"The municipal courthouse."

"Of course you are." He leaned down and murmured directions to the cabbie, who surveyed Mac with a cold eye, then faced the front.

Mac wisely fastened his seat belt seconds before the

cab careened out from under the awning and onto the street. Obviously, in the cabbie's desire to kill Mac, he didn't take into account that he would die also—or maybe he figured it was worth it.

Mac held on grimly, not caring that he had become the city's most hated resident. After all, he'd been that before. And this time he was big enough to hit back.

The street outside the courthouse was packed with press. The cabbie stopped at the corner. "This is as close as I can get."

Mac handed over the fee. "And this is as close as I can get to the exact amount." He paused in pretended surprise. "Oh, wait. It *is* the exact amount. No tip for you." He stepped out of the cab.

The press saw him immediately and swarmed like killer bees. They knew his name now, and shouted it at him.

"Mr. MacNaught, what do you hope to accomplish today?"

"Mr. MacNaught, do you intend to push for the full sentence?"

"Mr. MacNaught, will you take the Dahl sisters' age into account when arguing for their guilt?"

He pushed his way into the crowd, ruthlessly using his height and weight to make progress.

His lawyers formed a phalanx and moved toward him, and together they made it to the steps of the courthouse.

Radcliffe was shouting, "Mr. MacNaught has nothing to say at this time. Mr. MacNaught has nothing to say at this time."

Mac let him, but when they got to the top of the stairs, he turned and faced the cameras. Speaking directly into them, he said, "I am not moved by pleas of age or feebleness. These women are criminals who stole from me, and I will push for the full punishment of the law." Turning, he went inside.

He intended that Nessa should come to him and plead for her aunts.

That should bring her running.

Thirty-four

Inside the courtroom, Nessa watched as Mac MacNaught strode in, surrounded by obsequious lawyers dressed in the corporate uniform of dark suits and white shirts. The only way to tell them apart was that MacNaught towered above the little worms he hired to do his bidding. Obviously, the man always got his way.

Well. He was in for a surprise today.

He located her with his gaze. Looked steadily at her.

She held his gaze for a second. Smiled coldly. Smiled wider at his one unguarded, startled response. And turned to face the front.

Thanks to Pootie, she could post bail.

Last night, Pootie had showed Nessa the paperwork, explained that ten years ago, when Pootie moved in, the aunts had agreed to let her invest their precious savings. Pootie had taken the money, tended it, made sure it grew. At first, she'd tried to show the aunts the annual reports, but the aunts patted her hand and told her not to worry. "Like they figured I had lost it all or somethin'," Pootie had said hoarsely. "So I stopped showin' them and they never asked. I mean, I figured, What the hell? I lived here. When they needed the money, I'd get it for them. I just never figured 'em for bank robbers."

"You and me both," Nessa had said, right before asking for that job with Pootie's firm.

They'd immediately started training.

Now Mac seated himself across the aisle.

Nessa didn't need to look to know that. All the attention, all the bitter ire in the courtroom was focused on him.

And he was focused on her.

She didn't need to see him to know that, either. She could feel his brooding gaze.

The aunts came in, looking rested.

They'd been in their own cell, separate from the drunks and criminals, and obviously everyone in the jail had made sure they were well cared for.

The judge came in.

The courtroom rose.

The judge seated himself.

The courtroom sat.

The lawyers moved into position.

The court's prosecuting attorney argued that, considering the long-term series of crimes the Dahl sisters had committed and the large amount taken and vicious threats uttered the day before during the robbery, and the money that remained unrecovered, a significant bail be set.

Mr. Calhoun, one of the Calhouns, who had been the Dahls' attorneys for more than a hundred years, argued that the Dahl sisters were beloved throughout the city for their good deeds before, during, and after

Hurricane Katrina, had lived here their whole lives, and were not a flight risk.

The judge concurred and set the bail at one hundred dollars.

Nessa fought a grin at Mac's Yankee lawyers' outrage. Had they really imagined they could whip in here, fling their weight around, and change the way New Orleans felt about the Dahl sisters?

She stood up to go hug her great-aunts and take them home, but first she paused beside the row where Mr. MacNaught sat, stony-faced and cold. She dropped a ring box in his lap. "There's the ring you gave me." She smiled contemptuously into his face. "Thanks to Pootie and the investments she made, we can pay for my aunts' defense."

He reached out so swiftly, she didn't know he had her until he'd caught her hand.

"I'm not done with you."

"But I *am* done with you." She tugged at her hand. "You don't get it. I didn't do anything wrong except love my aunts."

"They're thieves. Everyone knows it."

"No one cares whether they are or they aren't . . . except you. Everyone here understands they're old and fragile and lack for excitement and want to make someone's life better, but they've got no money with which to do it. Everyone here in the city—in *America*—is rooting for them because they're doing something to make their own life better, and making someone else's life better in the process." She was saying too much, confessing her aunts' guilt, but what did it matter? Yesterday, they had confessed it themselves. "Don't you understand? They're Robin Hood. . . . And you're the Sheriff of Nottingham, only without Alan Rickman's evil charm." She jerked hard enough to free herself—or maybe he let go. But she stumbled backward, hit the bench across the way, and caught herself before she hit the floor.

He didn't move, but watched with cool satisfaction.

People were listening. People were watching. She couldn't wind up and hit him. Not like she wanted to. So she straightened the sleeves on her jacket.

"I have the lawyers, I have the money, I have the power." He listed his advantages, more sure of himself than any mere man had the right to be. "If necessary, I'll get this case moved to another venue to ensure a fair trial."

He would. "You are a loathsome pimple on the face of this fair earth."

"That's not what you said in the vault."

She heard the gasps and the murmurs.

The bastard had started the rumors circulating once again, and this time she'd be lucky if she didn't headline prominently in the *National Enquirer*—and her great-aunts in *Prisoner Weekly*.

He leaned forward, his voice pitched at a mere whisper. But she heard him. "When you're ready to admit defeat, come to me and we'll talk terms. And don't make me wait too long, Ionessa, for the longer I wait, the less lenient I will be."

"I wouldn't come to you if my aunts were sentenced to hang by their necks." She leaned forward, looked right into his eyes. "I would do what Dahl women have been doing for two hundred years—find me a rich old guy with one foot in the grave and the other on a banana peel. Then I'd take his money, pull some strings, get my aunts out, and *kill* the bastard who tried to make them pay."

Mac stared back at her, his face intent. . . . And openly, savagely hungry. In a low, dark tone, he said, "This is between you and me, and I warn you, Ionessa—don't go to another man."

For the first time, she saw through his eyes and into his soul.

Mac MacNaught was ruthless. He was dangerous. And he would keep what he believed was his.

Her heart pulsed hard in her chest and thundered in her ears.

She was his. She had given herself to him, and no matter how hard she tried, she still loved—

With a bang that made her jump, the doors of the courtroom slammed open.

Disheveled, wild-eyed, Rav Woodland ran in and shouted, "Premier Central Bank on Clairbourne Avenue has been robbed. A chase is in progress." He grinned right at Nessa, and flung his fists in the air in triumph. "Miss Calista and Miss Hestia are innocent!"

Thirty-five

It took two hours to sign the release papers, have Chief Cutter assure Hestia and Calista—in front of the TV cameras—that he would do everything in his power to make sure they were exonerated of all charges, and get in the limousine, a luxury for which Chief Cutter personally paid.

The people around the courthouse cheered as the limo slowly inched away from the curb, and the crowd grew thicker as the driver painfully maneuvered them up the street to avoid the worst of the Mardi Gras revelers. The tourists and locals pressed close to the car, screaming their approval at the aunts.

Nessa sat in the middle between her two aunts, and as they rolled down the windows, stuck their heads out, and waved at the crowd, Nessa met the driver's dark eyes in the rearview mirror.

He was big and dark-skinned, dressed in a formal suit with a bow tie, and his smile flashed as he said, "I tell you, ma'am, this is like drivin' the senior citizen prom limo."

"And I'm the prom chaperone." But Nessa couldn't

stop beaming. She would never, as long as she lived, forget the expression on Mac MacNaught's face when Rav ran in with the news and the courtroom burst into cheers. "Did you see the look on his face?"

"The judge, you mean?" Aunt Calista nodded. "Yes, he was absolutely astonished, and who knew getting the bail reversed involved so many details?"

Nessa could have cared less about the expression on the judge's face. It was the memory of Jeremiah's cool irritation that she hugged to her bosom, enjoying every moment of the mental replay: his astonishment, his frustration, and the low curse he muttered.

The jerk had enjoyed, wanted to hold her in his power.

Aunt Calista pulled her head in, her hands full of purple, gold, and green. "Look! Lagniappe!" As she draped beads around Nessa's neck, she caught a glimpse of Nessa's face. "Chère, are you all right? You look so fierce!"

"I'm just enjoying myself." Nessa smiled with all her teeth.

Hestia pulled her head in the window. Confetti showered from her hair, and she held two red plastic go cups in her hands. "That vendor gave me free hurricanes." She handed them to Nessa and Calista, then reached out again. Another was thrust at her, and she leaned back with a satisfied sigh. "I love New Orleans. There's no city like it."

"I love it, too." Nessa smiled as the heartbreaking notes of the blues drifted into the car. Yesterday morning, she'd been ready to leave her home and follow her man to Philadelphia. She'd never lived in the North. It would have been a whole new world, but for those few moments, she'd looked forward to it. Lately, she'd begun to feel claustrophobic in her home. . . .

She glanced at her great-aunts.

But if she left, who knew what Hestia and Calista would get up to?

Not that she'd had a clue what they were up to, anyway.

Yet it had seemed for a single, bright moment as if the whole world was opening before her, and she would share it with a guy she admired, liked, and loved. Which made the loneliness today so much more bittersweet . . .

Hestia asked, "Can we drive past that bitch Linda Blanc's house so she can see us?"

"Aunt Hestia!" Nessa was appalled at the language. Apparently, the copious amounts of alcohol in the hurricanes had relaxed her aunts. Relaxed her, too.

"Well, she is a bitch," Hestia said sulkily. "She told Betsy McBrien, who told Teresa Harper, who told me, that she thought we were guilty all along."

"You *were* guilty," Nessa said.

Calista took up the cudgels for her sister. "Yes, but our friends aren't supposed to say so!"

"And they are not supposed to use the word *felon* to describe us!"

The aunts had a point. But Nessa felt compelled to say, "Chief Cutter rented the limo for an hour. It took that long to work our way through the crowds, and we don't want to abuse his generosity."

The aunts' faces fell.

Yet Nessa couldn't stand to see their happiness diminished. Not today. "You've been through an ordeal, so I'll pay the extra. You deserve a treat." She hadn't yet told them about their newly acquired fortune. She thought Pootie deserved that privilege.

So the chauffeur drove into the Garden District and past the house where the bitch Linda Blanc resided. The neighbors gawked. Kids ran beside the car.

"Look, there's Linda!" Hestia pointed out a middle-aged woman wearing a floppy straw hat and gardening gloves, and using a shovel.

"She's working in the yard. Bless her heart, she looks sweaty and dirty and *awful*!" Calista crowed.

With as much astonishment as any of the neighbors, Linda stared at the limo, and when she recognized the aunts, she lifted her chin and turned her back.

The aunts kept their heads inside and waved as if the queen of England had trained them.

Then, as they headed toward the Dahl House, the aunts' dignity collapsed and they giggled like girls.

"That was so much fun!" Hestia said.

"Can we drive up our street, turn around, and drive back down, before we stop at the Dahl House?" Calista begged the driver.

"Yes, ma'am, I would be glad to do that for the Beaded Bandits," he said.

"Have you heard?" Calista chirped. "That nice boy Chief Cutter dropped all charges of larceny."

"Yes, ma'am, I did hear that." The driver grinned.

There was not one person in New Orleans, Nessa realized, who didn't believe the Dahl girls were the Beaded Bandits, and approved with all their hearts.

Well, except for Linda Blanc.

And Mac MacNaught.

They drove up their street. They made the turn to go back to the Dahl House.

And Hestia said, "I hear sirens."

"Really? I don't hear them." Calista stuck her head out the window again.

"But you know you need a hearing aid," Hestia said. "You're just too vain to get one."

"There is nothing wrong with my hearing, I just don't . . . oh, there they are."

The sirens were coming closer.

The aunts exchanged glances.

"You don't suppose they changed their minds?" Calista quavered.

"No, they didn't. For one thing, Chief Cutter can't afford that kind of negative publicity again," Nessa assured them. But inside, she cursed the phony thieves for bringing this fear on her aunts, and cursed Mac MacNaught even more on general principles.

As they drove back toward the Dahl House, three police cars went screaming past them and stopped at the curb by their walk. Officers leaped out of the cars. Nessa recognized Santino Leroy and her best friend, Georgia, as they raced toward the house, pistols drawn.

"They *did* change their minds," Hestia quavered.

"No, ma'am," the driver said. "They know where you are. They're looking for somebody else."

"A bad guy? In our house? Maybe one of the real thieves?" Calista craned her neck, then sat back, her hand to her mouth. "Maddy!"

"What?" Hestia grabbed Calista's wrist. "You don't think someone would hurt Maddy?"

Three of the officers fanned out. The other three walked toward the front porch.

Neighbors were pouring out of their houses, block-ing their view.

"Let me out," Nessa commanded.

The driver stopped the car.

She jumped out and ran up the street. "What's going on?" she shouted to Georgia.

"Miss Maddy called and said one of the fake robbers was holed up in your house," Georgia shouted back. "This time, when I tell you to stay back, Nessa, stay back. This is dangerous."

"I'll show you dangerous. My aunts will be danger-ous if you let somebody shoot Miss Maddy!" Nessa warned.

Georgia nodded grimly and prepared to circle the house, when the front screen door slammed open and a man dressed in a feather-trimmed ball gown stum-bled out. He looked like a pudgy, bedraggled Ginger Rogers, dodging Miss Maddy as she followed.

One officer vaulted up onto the porch from one side; Georgia vaulted from the other. They aimed their pis-tols and shouted, "Halt!"

Another police car screeched to a stop in front of the house. Chief Cutter leaped out and ran across the lawn.

Miss Maddy waved her cane and slammed it against Ginger's broad behind. "I have never"—*whack!*—"seen the likes of you"—*whack!*—"in such a getup. What do you think"—*whack!*—"your mama's going to say"—*whack!*—"when she finds out what you've been up to?"

The officers kept their weapons pointed at the sus-pect, but stayed well away from that cane.

The guy hooked the heel of his pump in one of the loose boards, and fell over hard enough to make the porch shake.

As he fell, Nessa caught a glimpse of his anguished face, with its smeared makeup and incongruously short hair. "*Skeeter?*"

Skeeter, big, dumb, breakfast-gobbling, bass-playing Skeeter, was . . . was one of the fake robbers?

Chief Cutter stood beside her. "You know him?"

"I sure do." She climbed the steps.

Chief Cutter drew his weapon and followed.

Miss Maddy stood over Skeeter, pressing the rubber tip of her cane into his chest. "Tell me the truth, boy. It's that wicked saxophone player who told you to do this, didn't he?"

Of course. For Nessa, the pieces fell into place. "Ryan Wright? That sleaze bucket set you up to this?"

Skeeter cowered from the two women and scooted backward. "Yes, ma'am. He wanted to rob banks like the Beaded Bandits. Said it would be easy if we pretended to be them, lived here, and used the clothes out of the attic."

"You stole Miss Calista's and Miss Hestia's clothes?" To Maddy, this was clearly the biggest sin.

"It seemed like a good idea. We planned it really carefully, and yesterday it went good. We got a lot of money, and no one got hurt bad. But today . . ." The big guy started hyperventilating.

Nessa and Georgia exchanged wry glances.

"We weren't supposed to do it again today," Skeeter whined, "but Ryan said it went so well, we should. On account of he has a real case of the ass toward the rich asshole who owns the banks. But he hadn't scoped out that bank or something, because right away stuff went wrong. There was this guy there, Gabriel Somebody, he had a gun and he shot Ryan, knocked his leg right out from under him. So Ryan shot back, but he hit the glass and shit went everywhere."

The women stopped advancing.

"Was anybody hurt?" Nessa asked.

Skeeter propped himself against the porch rails. "There was blood all over the place. One lady had a big piece of glass in her shoulder. There was this guy with blood on his face."

Nessa lifted an eyebrow at Georgia.

Georgia shook her head. "No one hurt seriously, but a lot of minor injuries."

Skeeter continued, "People were screaming, and Ryan ran out into the street. When I got out there, he was gone."

"Do you know where?" Chief Cutter asked.

"No! He left me there." Skeeter stuck out his lower lip, nursing a sense of ill use.

"Where's the money from the first robbery?" Chief Cutter's gaze swept Skeeter. "I'm going to guess you didn't spend it on clothes."

"It's all in Debbie Voytilla's bottom dresser drawer, under her vibrator collection," Skeeter said. "We figured Miss Maddy wouldn't bother to clean in there."

"That's the truth." Maddy shook her head. "I stay away from those private matters."

Georgia raised her hand. "I'll go check. It's a hard job, but somebody's got to do it." She headed into the house.

"Skeeter, what were you thinking, trusting Ryan?" Nessa asked.

"This whole thing serves you right, too." Maddy pointed her cane at him.

"I guess." Skeeter hung his head. "Once I got out on

the street, nobody was paying attention to me, so I caught a cab and came here, but then Miss Maddy spied me and right away she figured out what I'd done."

Maddy's wave of the arm encompassed his whole, quivering, stupid disguise. "I'm not senile yet."

Hestia and Calista struggled through the gathering crowd.

"When Miss Maddy saw you, what did she do to you?" As if Nessa didn't know, growing up in that household.

"She looked at me so mean-like, and told me to sit down and not move." Skeeter's teeth chattered as he remembered. "So I did it, and she called the police, and then I asked for a drink of water, and when she went to get it for me, I tried to sneak away, and she hit me with her cane." He rubbed his bottom.

"All right." Chief Cutter signaled his officers. "That should do it. Arrest him. Read him his rights. Take him away, and put out a bulletin for Ryan Wright." He turned to Calista and Hestia. "Can you provide a description? Is there perhaps a photo somewhere?"

"I don't know that I ever took a picture of that boy, but I certainly can tell you what he looks like," Hestia said.

"To show our gratitude, let us get your men a tall drink of iced tea before they go back to work," Calista said.

"Miss Hestia, Miss Calista, can we take a rain check?" Chief Cutter spoke toward the cameras that had gathered below the porch. "It's obvious now that these two men committed all the robberies and have always been the Beaded Bandits, and the NOPD will do

everything in their power to capture and punish the remaining bandit." He tipped his hat to Nessa and the
aunts. "Now, excuse me, but we've got a bank robber
to catch."

Thirty-six

"Miss Hestia, Miss Calista, would you sign an autograph for me?" Eight-year-old Jennifer Travers stood with her toes on the edge of the sidewalk in front of the Dahl House and held up a crumpled sheaf of wide-ruled school paper. "My mom says you're famous."

"Or infamous," Nessa murmured while the aunts signed their names.

"Now, Nessa, that's no attitude." Aunt Hestia waved at the photographers.

"All's well that ends well." Aunt Calista was less interested in their fans and more interested in the front screen door Maddy held open. "I am glad to be home!"

"Hurry on in here!" Maddy called. "You would not believe what has happened."

"After today, Maddy, I'd believe anything." But as the hours went on, Nessa seemed to have lost her sense of humor. She kept thinking of Mac MacNaught and the way he looked when Rav ran in with the news of the robbery.

He had gotten to his feet.

She had laughed in his face.

Then he'd taken a step toward her, and for one second she thought . . . she'd taken a step back. He looked as if, well, not as if he would hurt her, but as if he would grab her by the hair and drag her away to his cave. The memory made her squirm even now.

He might have lost this round, but she would see him again—and even before she'd known his true identity, she'd been conclusively shown that he always got his own way.

Not this time, brother.

Hestia, Calista and Nessa walked into the house.

The entry was cool and lovely, an oasis of peace after the turmoil of the court and the streets where the riot of Mardi Gras continued in an ever-greater frenzy. Flowers decorated the tables, and a glance in the library showed three arrangements decorating the mantel. "Nice flowers," Nessa said.

Maddy gestured them into the dining room.

"Oh, my," Aunt Calista breathed.

It looked like the annual Mardi Gras party, but more so. Food covered every last inch of the table and sideboard. Pies and petit fours, Jell-O molds and aspics, mushroom casseroles and gumbos, breads, biscuits, corn muffins . . .

"Who sent it?" Nessa circled the table in awe.

"Everybody. Neighbors, friends, relatives . . . people we never met but who heard about Miss Calista and Miss Hestia on the news. FedEx and UPS have been delivering food and flowers all day." Maddy joined Nessa in circling.

Aunt Hestia shook her head. "I haven't seen this big a spread since Mama's funeral."

"Let's see. It's Thursday. Lent starts next Wednesday.

Good thing, or we'd be bound to give it all away, and we don't know that many Protestants." Aunt Calista poked her finger into the icing of Mrs. Lerner's famous caramel cake and licked it clean. "It's good. Nessa, have a piece with us."

"I can't. I have to go quit the bank, and I want to get it over with before I celebrate."

Mac's deep voice spoke from the kitchen doorway. "That's impossible."

Nessa wasn't as surprised as she should have been.

He stood there, his suit coat open, his hands on his hips, a massive, overbearing, authoritative pain in the ass.

How did he get in here?

Knowing him, he'd jumped the fence. He certainly never respected the boundaries of civilization.

What was he doing here?

Telling her what she could and couldn't do.

No. Yesterday, in the front yard, he'd lost the right to tell her anything.

Remembering how she'd begged him for leniency for her aunts, remembering how he'd so cruelly rejected her, she stepped toward him in a fury. "I don't care whether Stephanie Decker has my panties or you've been in them. I *quit.*"

Maddy gasped. "In your panties? Ionessa Apollonia Dahl—"

Hestia and Calista bundled her out of the room before she said another word.

"Stephanie Decker has your . . . why would she . . . your panties?" Comprehension shifted in his eyes. "From the vault? Of course. That must be what she was apologizing about in that e-mail."

"Getting e-mails from her must be like Frenching a Hoover. She never stops sucking up."

"She's the manager of my banks, and that's where she's going to stay for the rest of her life. Unless she proves incapable of maintaining her high performance standards, and then I'm afraid she'll have to be demoted."

"How's she going to do that without me around?"

He circled the table. "You'll be around. You can't quit."

Nessa matched his movements, making sure his long arms could never reach her. "I really can. Do you know why? Because Pootie DiStephano is teaching me day trading, and I'm good at it. I'm going to work for her, and I don't need you and your crummy job anymore."

"You might not need my crummy job anymore, but you're not going to get from Pootie DiStephano what you get from me."

"I'd have to agree with you there. Pootie doesn't lie to me."

Picking up a pastry cheese stick, he eyed it. "It was necessary." He took a bite, and flakes broke off and dusted his lapels.

"It was necessary?" Nessa's voice soared like an opera singer's. "You came to New Orleans knowing who I was. You spied on me with your video cameras and your private investigators. You invaded my privacy before I even knew you were alive. You've been sitting up in that office in Philadelphia, having people say 'Yes, sir' and 'No, sir' for so long, you think you're some kind of god. You thought—you still think—that you have the privilege of making assumptions and playing games with my life. You decided I was a thief and you did everything in your power to prove it was true. And that was *necessary*?"

"I had to know the truth, and you were the logical suspect."

"The truth? The truth is that for years you've been screwing me over, letting me work toward an unreachable goal, and now you've screwed me in truth." She could almost taste her bitterness.

"It was good." He finished eating and dusted his front.

"It was *good*? What are you talking about—the cheese stick or the sex?"

"The sex." Once more, he stalked her around the table.

His caveman logic kept her incoherent while her rage built and built. Then it burst forth in a flood of indignation. "*Good?* If *good* was all I was looking for, I could get *good* on the street from a practicing gigolo. I could get *good* from Daniel. I could sleep with almost any guy and train him to be *good*. I thought I was making love to a man I knew, a man who had grown from poverty and abuse into strength and control. I thought you were a man I admired. And all the while, you lied to me in the most basic way possible—you lied to me about what you were. Who you are."

"It was necessary." He sounded like a broken record.

"To lie? No, it wasn't." She kept having visions of picking up the caramel cake and flinging it at him. Nessa's satisfaction would be overwhelming.

Miss Maddy's revenge would be dire.

"Why didn't you send one of your goons down here to investigate me?" He wasn't the only one who could be logical. "At least some person who hadn't devoted his life to believing I was a loser might have given me a fair shake and not tried to buy me with the biggest fucking ugly diamond on the face of the earth."

"You took the biggest fucking ugly diamond fast enough." He stopped chasing her and tasted his own bitterness, it seemed.

She laughed. To see his indignation was almost funny. "I thought it was *sweet* that you had such bad taste. I thought that proposal, which, by the way, was the worst in the history of the world, meant you had feelings for me you didn't know how to express. I thought I could show you how much I loved you, and over time you'd come to trust what we had between us. Stupid me!" She flung her arms up in exasperation. At her. At him. "I thought we were going to have a marriage, a relationship, and a love that would last for all time. Instead I find out that you are a bastard. Not because you're Nathan Manly's illegitimate son— which, by the way, you could have told me, but no, you had to let me find out from Pootie DiStephano, who knows an awful lot of good gossip once you get her going—but because you are a genuine, bona fide asshole who only loves two things: money and power. Well, Mr. Vycor the Second, have a lovely life sleeping in your bank vault every night, snuggled up to a bag of cash, because you threw away the best thing you ever had. *Me.*"

"I didn't throw you away. Nothing is over between us. You agreed to a contract with me." He spoke precisely, as if what he said made sense.

"A contract?" *What does he mean?* "The prenup? You have the guts to talk about the prenup?" She could hardly breathe from outrage. "I agreed to a contract with Jeremiah Mac. Not you. Never you. I told you, I hate liars. Remember that teller who lied to me, who told me she had a sick child, then waltzed out of the bank with enough money to ruin my career? It was my fault I let her do that. I take full responsibility. I didn't bother to hate her—that would be a waste of time. But I'm not *stupid*, and I learned to hate a lie told to hurt another person. Your lies were told to *hurt* me."

He shrouded his intensely green eyes with his heavy lids. "They were told to get at the truth."

"Then I hope you like the truth, because that's all you're getting from me." She walked toward the door.

His voice stopped her. "Does your truth include the fact that you lied to me, manipulated me into believing you loved me, to get information about my investigation? Or are we conveniently forgetting about that?"

I didn't lie about loving you. But she would never admit that.

When she resumed walking, he said, "My lawyers will block any attempt to clear your aunts of the previous counts of bank robbery."

She swung around. "What are you talking about?"

"Chief Cutter says he's going to prosecute that Skeeter person and the other guy for all the thefts, but you and I and everyone in New Orleans knows your aunts are the Beaded Bandits."

"I don't know that," she said quickly.

"Today, in the courtroom, you as good as admitted it. So one way or the other, your great-aunts will go to trial."

"You wouldn't."

But he looked implacable.

"You want me to beg."

"That would certainly be a pleasant bonus. Would you like to try right here and now?" He must know her pretty well, because he didn't wait for her answer. "Also, there are discrepancies in the books at the bank."

She couldn't believe he was so good at being a dirtbag. "So?"

"The discrepancies appear to originate with you."

"You are kidding."

"You have two choices. Be involved in an extensive audit, or show up at the bank Monday morning for work and figure out who's doing this to you."

"These discrepancies just popped up? I don't even believe you." Would he lie to keep her at the bank? Would he go so far to win?

Of course he would.

So she knew she would be at the bank Monday morning. "I have an ancestor, Althea Dahl, and she married her husband and killed him for his money. You know what?" She stepped toward him, so close he could grab her if he chose.

But something about her must have held him back— or maybe he was satisfied with his win.

"I don't want your money," she said. "I don't need your money. But I could feed you poison with my two hands and smile while I did it."

Thirty-seven

That night the party at the Dahl House was spontaneous, spectacular, filled with great food and drink, and everyone agreed it was one of the greatest ever thrown.

Which was why, at two o'clock in the morning, Nessa found herself with the aunts, washing the mountains of family china in the kitchen sink.

"I don't think Ryan is coming back." Calista stacked the dishes carefully. "So first thing in the morning, we're going to have to clean out his room and get it ready to rent."

"I'll look on the waiting list and see who's up next. People call and beg to stay here, you know," Hestia confided in Nessa.

"But it doesn't matter," Nessa said. "You two don't have to keep boarders anymore."

The aunts exchanged curious glances.

"Why not?" Calista asked.

"Because you don't. Because you've got money." Nessa could scarcely comprehend the burden that had lifted from her shoulders. "Didn't Pootie tell you? You have enough money to pay off the loan on the house and have leftovers. And if you leave those leftovers with Pootie, she'll keep investing them and you'll never have to worry about money again."

Hestia blinked at Nessa. "I know that. Pootie explained it all. But why would we not keep our boarders?"

"You'd have your house to yourself again. Think about it." Nessa smiled blissfully and dried another plate. "No more cooking breakfast, no more changing sheets—just the quiet peace of the Dahl House."

"And do what? Sit on the porch in a rocker?" Calista asked.

"Honey, peace is what you have when you die," Hestia said.

"And we're not dead yet," Calista added.

They weren't getting it. But Nessa could make them see. "I don't want to sound like Pootie the Second, but I'm tired of being pleasant to people. Sometimes I want to be alone to think and to just . . . be. Be messy, be silly, be naked if I want. I want to watch a chick flick in the living room without having Daniel make fun of me, or read a book without telling Debbie what I'm reading. And most of all, I want to sit down to breakfast and not talk to anyone."

"It sounds as if you hate having boarders." Hestia dug around in the soapy water, looking for anther plate.

"Oh yes," Nessa said fervently.

"But you see, the thing is, Calista and I like them. We thrive on the bustle, on having people around all day. We like caring for people. Miss Maddy likes it, too." Hestia grinned. "And we like supporting ourselves. Having boarders keeps us young."

Hestia had to be kidding. "But . . . you never had them before you took out the loan."

"We didn't know what we were missing," Calista said.

"But . . . you work like serfs feeding them and cleaning up after them."

"Serfdom is underrated," Hestia said cheerfully. When she saw the expression on Nessa's face, she said, "Listen to yourself, Nessa. *You* want to eat alone. *You* want to watch a movie. You're not talking about what *we* want. You're talking about what *you* want."

"You've been going through a lot of changes lately. Perhaps it is time you moved out." Damp dish towel in hand, Calista hugged Nessa.

Maybe it was the hour, but Nessa felt bewildered. "But . . . you could go on vacation!"

"We talked about that, but who would take care of the boarders? Miss Maddy's too old."

Nessa stared at the eighty-year-old Hestia and wondered when *too old* set in. "But . . . what are you going to do with the money? The money Pootie invested for you."

"Oh. The money." Hestia gestured carelessly, flipping bubbles across the kitchen. "Pootie's going to help us set up a scholarship fund—she calls it a charity fund, but you know Pootie, no sensitivity at all—and Calista and I will administer it, giving aid as we see fit. It's going to be so much fun!"

The aunts were going to give away their money. Their security.

They were keeping the boarders. Nessa had been working for seven years to get the damned boarders out of the house, and the aunts liked them.

And they had as good as told her to leave.

She had no direction. She had no home. And she certainly had no influence on the two strong-minded women who had raised her.

"You don't need to look like that, Nessa. Pootie won't let us be destitute." Hestia gave her a sudsy pat on the arm.

"You're right. Pootie's been taking care of your finances for years, and you didn't even know it. She's not going to let you down now." There was a bitterness in that, too, that despite Nessa's best efforts, it was Pootie who had saved them.

"Chère, come and put these dry dishes away." Calista set a stepstool for Nessa.

Nessa climbed up and carefully stacked the china on the top shelf of the cabinet.

"Now, what about you?" Hestia asked briskly. "You have a new job—in fact, you still have your old job. You're moving out this weekend. But what are you going to do about your young man?"

Nessa's back went up. "I don't have a young man."

Hestia sailed on as if Nessa hadn't spoken. "Calista and I were listening at the door while you two fought today."

"Miss Maddy said we shouldn't, but how else are we supposed to find out what's going on?" Calista asked.

"Then you know what he did." In the turmoil of the past few minutes, Nessa had managed to forget her resentment of MacNaught. Now it was back in full.

"He lied to you because he believed the worst of you," Calista recited.

"The bastard," Nessa mumbled, and reached down for more plates.

"Actually," Hestia said carefully, "I believe in this

case I should mention the saying about people who live in glass houses."

Nessa almost overbalanced. "What are you talking about?"

"I thought you knew it." Hestia frowned. "People who live in glass houses shouldn't throw stones."

"I know the saying, I just don't understand why you're bringing it up." Nessa looked down at her aunts' earnest faces.

"Dear girl, don't take this wrong. We're not reproaching you," Calista said.

"But you are as guilty as he is," Hestia added.

A chill swept up Nessa's spine and her hands and feet turned cold, while a flame burned her cheeks.

Calista started to hand Nessa a pile of bowls; then, as if she had second thoughts, she put them down on the counter. "It is possible to believe the wrong thing about a person, to believe with all your heart that that person, or persons, are guilty of a crime they didn't commit, even though you've known them forever."

"Why are you saying that to me?" Nessa asked.

"When you heard our robberies had been imitated, that violence had been done and twenty thousand dollars stolen, you believed that Calista and I were guilty."

The aunts hadn't referred to that moment when Nessa blocked their path and accused them of the bank robbery. Somehow, she thought—hoped—that in their dotty way, they hadn't noticed.

But of course the aunts weren't dotty, really, only immersed in their own happily eccentric world where once a year it was right that they robbed an evil bank and gave the money to one needy soul.

"You have lived with me and Hestia since you had

just turned five, yet you believed the evidence rather than what you knew of our characters."

Hestia said, "I'm not saying it is right for Mr. MacNaught to assume the worst of you, but with his background, that seems almost inevitable."

"His background?" Nessa couldn't believe they were having this conversation.

"He had a difficult upbringing, what with his father abandoning him and then his mother . . . dreadful! And no one to show him that there are noble causes and people of character." Calista couldn't contain her disapproval.

"Oh, cry me a river. I can't believe he had the guts to whine to you." Nessa almost spit in her wrath.

Hestia's usually pleasant tones grew sharp and stern. "He wasn't whining, Ionessa. He told us because we asked. Perhaps you should try talking to him rather than railing like a disappointed spinster after a three-day bacchanal."

Nessa caught her breath. Hestia *never* talked to her that way. Yet now her blue eyes were icy and disapproving, and Nessa stung as if she'd been slapped. "I'm sorry you think that, Aunt Hestia." But she was stiff and hurt, not really sorry.

"Nessa, come down here."

Nessa hadn't heard Calista give a command in that tone since she was a child. She climbed off the stool and stood between them, hating MacNaught for ruining her life, for turning her aunts against her, for everything that had gone wrong.

The two aunts placed themselves in front of Nessa.

Hestia started. "All your life, Calista and I have worried about the frightening restraints you've put on yourself and your emotions."

Calista continued, "When Jeremiah came along, we laughed for joy, because he cracked that shell you'd formed around yourself. For the first time, we saw how brightly the light of joy could shine in you."

"That wasn't joy, that was lust." If Nessa thought that would shake them, she was sadly mistaken.

Hestia nodded. "They're one and the same—pleasure not to be denied."

"I should have denied him."

"Should have?" Calista looked appalled. "For what reason? Life is to be lived, not shunted aside until all the days are aches and ashes."

"If I'd denied him, you wouldn't be mad at me."

"That's silly, Nessa. What we think isn't important to you," Calista said.

Hestia laughed. "Well . . . it's not important except when we have a great wisdom to share, as we do now."

Calista laughed, too. "Right. Your emotions are your emotions, and you have the right to feel each and every one of them."

Hestia cupped Nessa's cheek and looked into her eyes. "But dear, darling girl, not everything that has happened has been bitter, and this year's Mardi Gras events have opened new doors for you. You're learning a new job, and you're good at it. Sister and I have money we didn't imagine, and I know that lifted a burden from your shoulders. So explore your unhappiness, then straighten your shoulders, smile, and move on. And maybe . . . don't judge Jeremiah harshly until you've talked to him yourself."

"I did talk to him. This afternoon, remember? Do you know what he said? He said he was going to prosecute you for the robberies, anyway."

Calista tsked. "That poor boy. He's angry at the world, striking out blindly, trying to get attention."

"Is there nothing he can do that will make you see what an ass he is?" Nessa asked in despair.

Hestia turned toward the doorway. "Miss Maddy! What are you doing up?"

Maddy stood there in her red bathrobe and fuzzy slippers, and glared. "Are you girls going to stay up and chat all night long, or are you going to bed? Breakfast is coming blasted early in the morning."

"We were just telling Nessa to talk to Jeremiah," Calista said.

"I heard you. I've been listening for a while." Maddy peered at Nessa. "You gonna do it?"

"I don't want to talk to him." Even Nessa could hear the sulky tone in her voice.

"Of course not. You're enjoying your own private pity party far too much for that." Hestia pinched the same cheek she had stroked.

Nessa didn't want to admit it. Not now. Not about him. But the aunts had an instinct about people.

Did they have an instinct about Mac MacNaught?

"Miss Maddy's right. We're all tired," Hestia said.

"Of course Miss Maddy's right." Maddy made a shooing gesture toward the stairs.

"Let's go to bed," Calista said. "Nessa, tomorrow you can look for an apartment. This weekend you can move in. Monday will be the start of a new week, and a chance to clear things up with Jeremiah."

"His name isn't Jeremiah. It's Mac."

As the aunts drifted out of the kitchen, Calista said, "Jeremiah's his real first name, chère. Didn't you know?"

Thirty-eight

The next day, Gabriel took Mac through the changes they were making at the Chartres Street branch of Premier Central bank. "We'll work this weekend and next putting in new security cameras and upgrading the alarms. All the surveillance will be controlled remotely from a central point in the city. The only thing we can't control, of course—"

"Is the people. I know." Gabriel had reiterated that often enough. The human factor was always the unknown, and no matter how much security they installed, someone with enough intelligence, guts, or desperation could break through and take what they wanted. Lowering his voice, Mac asked, "What about the vault?"

"Let's talk in there." Gabriel waited while Mac punched his code into the electronic keyboard and led the way inside. The two men looked around at the tiny room, with the shelves hiding the secret passage, and in unison shook their heads. "This Vycor must have been as crazy as they come," Gabriel said. "No friends. No family. It's sort of pathetic, you know?"

"I know." *Mr. Vycor the Second*. Nessa's mocking voice echoed in Mac's mind. He was *not* Mr. Vycor the Second. He had friends.

He looked sideways at Gabriel. Maybe it was pushing it to call Gabriel his friend, but they'd been staying together in the Garden Suite. They didn't talk much, but then, they didn't have to. They understood each other, never got in each other's way, ate the same stuff, watched the same games. . . . It was almost spooky how much they had in common.

And Mac would have a family, too. A family with Nessa. Her great-aunts would be his . . .

He'd be related to thieves—but then, he was used to that. His father was Nathan Manly.

Nessa was coming in on Monday, or at least she was if she knew what was good for her. She'd want to know what discrepancies were on the books. He'd have to cook something up, because he'd lied; they balanced perfectly.

"Is there anything I can help you gentlemen with?" Stephanie called from the doorway of the vault.

The two guys glanced at each other.

"No," Mac said.

"Oh. Okay. Call me if you need anything."

They listened to Stephanie's footsteps retreat.

"That woman is really annoying," Gabriel said.

"That woman made some nasty mistakes and she's trying to keep her job. In fact, she's probably willing to fling herself across the tracks for me." Mac's mouth set in satisfaction. He would use Stephanie as the scapegoat for the books. She might not like it, but she would do it.

One problem solved.

Gabriel tapped the shelves. "Next Wednesday, I'm bringing in my top men to plug the hole. It'll be done overnight, and no one will ever know it was there."

"You can't do it sooner?" Knowing there was access to the vault gave Mac an itchy feeling up his spine.

"Not with Mardi Gras going on, not and keep it a secret. But next Wednesday is Ash Wednesday. Then the party's over. Everyone will be sleeping off a hangover. It's the best time to get this thing done."

The two men stepped out into the lobby.

Stephanie lurked in the background, trying to look interested and as if she were in charge.

The tellers and customers watched him from the corners of their eyes, hostility gleaming.

Gabriel shuddered. "Man. No one has forgotten what you said yesterday at the courthouse about the Dahl girls."

"I know."

"I'm surprised these people aren't getting a rope for a lynching."

"One more wrong move on my part, and I won't be able to buy myself a kind word."

"I told you I should have played the part of the insurance investigator." Gabriel contemplated Mac's hard face. "Do you have any more wrong moves to make?"

"I'm going to get what I want." He believed, with what he said to Nessa yesterday, that she'd come to him to make a deal. Every time the door opened, he expected to see her dressed in one of those dark suits that couldn't hide her curves and her red heels. And when he saw her, he'd know, and she'd know, he still held the power in the relationship.

He might be in love, but he was not a wimp to be controlled by a mere woman. They needed to establish that right away.

"Warn me before you piss anybody else off so I can step away," Gabriel said.

"You'll be the first to know."

"We'll be done with all the installations in three weeks." Gabriel glanced around the classically beautiful interior of the bank. "Unless, of course, we run into old wiring or a leaky pipe or termites."

"Which you will." Mac broke off the conversation.

Miss Maddy had entered the bank. She walked slowly, hunched over a cane. Her bones thrust at her fragile skin, and she shook with a visible tremor. For the first time, the tiny black woman looked her age. She glanced around as if bewildered by the size and bustle of the bank. Then she caught sight of him. Her black eyes widened, then narrowed. She started toward him, each step an effort that seemed her last.

Sadness clung to her like a cloak, and he realized that instead of coming herself, Nessa had sent their ancient cook to plead for her aunts.

The little coward.

At least *he* had some manners. With a long stride, he hurried toward Miss Maddy.

When she realized he was coming for her, she stopped in the middle of the lobby.

Damn Nessa. The old lady shouldn't be walking at all.

He stopped before her, gently took her hand. "Welcome to Premier Central Bank, Miss Maddy. What can I do for you?"

She said something, but her voice was so low and shook so hard, he couldn't understand.

"Come and sit in my office," he said. "I'll get you some water and you can tell me what you need."

She shook her head and tugged at his sleeve.

He leaned down.

She tugged again.

He bent almost double, putting his ear close to her face so she could speak right into it.

And she grabbed his ear in her bony fist and twisted.

The pain brought him right to his knees.

Her voice was just fine when she bellowed, "What in the *hell* do you think you're doing, talking about prosecuting two fine ladies like Miss Calista and Miss Hestia? You think two old women like them should be in jail with *tourists* and *drunks* and *Yankees*?"

He tried to shake her off, but she knew what she was doing. Her grip on his ear couldn't be broken, and it *hurt*. Hurt like a son of a bitch.

Of course, Miss Maddy was old, fragile, and small. He could have grabbed her arm. He could have knocked her down.

But he couldn't. He couldn't because the people in the bank hated him enough to plug him and sweep his body under the table, and picking on Miss Maddy would give them the excuse they needed.

Besides, he just . . . couldn't.

"You got no respect for your betters, boy?" Maddy yelled. "Your mama didn't learn you any different when you were growing up?"

"Those Dahl women are . . . thieves." Mac winced and squirmed.

"I've known those women since they were in dia-
pers, and I tell you, they never stole a thing for themselves." Maddy dropped her cane, leaned on his
shoulder, and shook his ear.

The agony almost made him black out.

"If you had a brain in your head, you'd know it.
Now, are you going to call your fancy-ass lawyers and
tell them they are to leave Miss Calista and Miss Hestia
alone, or are we going to stay here all day while you
whimper?"

The whole bank was laughing, and he could hear
Gabriel above the rest.

The security guard hovered nearby, clearly knowing
he should do something, but not knowing what.

Welcome to the club.

So Mac muttered, "I'll do it."

"What?" she shouted.

"I'll do it!" he shouted back.

She stopped shaking him. "You'll do that now?"

"Yes."

Maddy let go. "All right. I had hopes for you, boy,
and I'm gravely disappointed. *Gravely* disappointed. I
don't know if it's possible for you to get back in my
good graces. I don't know at all."

Slowly he rose off the cold marble floor. His ear was
ringing. His pride was dented.

The customers, tellers, and Gabriel were gasping in
hilarity.

The security guard was only grinning.

And Stephanie Decker looked like she'd swallowed
a whole lemon.

With her fists on her hips, Maddy looked him up

and down. "Do you have anything you want to say to me?"

He'd just been disciplined by a hundred-year-old woman. And there wasn't much he could say, except "I'm sorry, Miss Maddy. I won't use Miss Calista and Miss Hestia again in the battle between me and Nessa."

"That's good." Maddy nodded in approval. "Hand me my cane."

He picked it up. "But I'll use any other means to get her and keep her."

"Oh. Well." Maddy hooked her cane over her arm. "That's between you and her, boy. You and her."

As he watched Maddy make her way out of the bank, he realized—Maddy had just given her approval.

He had all the soldiers on his side. This was a battle he was going to win.

Thirty-nine

At 8:30 a.m. on Monday morning, Nessa walked into the bank and looked around.

Everything was as it had been twelve days ago. The Mardi Gras decorations still adorned the lobby. Eric still stood guard at the door. Five tellers still stood behind their stations. She locked her purse in the same desk.

Only one thing was different.

Mac MacNaught stood waiting for her.

He didn't do anything. He didn't say anything. He simply noted that she was there, glanced at the clock to confirm the time, and returned to his office. And projected death rays of disapproval while she got the tellers set up, met the steady stream of customers coming through the door, and worked up a first mortgage for a young couple from Metairie.

Stephanie was there, too, trying nervously to be pleasant and failing.

But Nessa hardly noticed, and certainly never felt a single twinge of anything but annoyance at Stephanie's skulking around. How could she, with Mr. MacNaught glowering in that office, which she knew he was doing even though she couldn't see him? The morning dragged, each tick of the clock scraping like glass across her nerves.

In fact, Mr. MacNaught was making the whole damned cadre of tellers nervous, and Nessa had half a mind to explain to him that he was ruining the formerly agreeable atmosphere in her bank.

She was so busy mentally composing scathing remarks that she jumped when, at eleven thirty, he appeared at her elbow and said, "I have to go to the Iberville Street bank. My security man wants to discuss upgrades to that system, too. If you need anything, give me a call."

"Uh, sure." She watched him walk away, and cursed herself.

The best scathing remark she could think of was *Uh, sure?*

How about, *What could I possibly need that you could give me?*

Or *Don't hold your breath until I call.*

Or *I'd rather die than take anything from you.*

That last was a little melodramatic, but it was better than *Uh, sure.*

"You okay, Miss Dahl?" Eric asked.

Nessa lifted her head from her hands. "Why?"

"You look a little . . . um, nothing. You look good." He backed away. "Real good."

Except for the fact that she kept remembering what her aunts had said to her—*Talk to him, listen to him*—she felt real good, too.

She did. Really.

She glanced around at the tellers. They were all

working furiously, not glancing in her direction, not chatting to the customers. Her regulars weren't talking, either, but standing stoically in line and getting out of the lobby as quickly as they could. A hush permeated the bank, the kind of silence one normally associated with a funeral home.

Something had changed, something that erased the friendly attitude.

She could blame MacNaught, but he wasn't here now.

She could blame Stephanie, but having the Stephabeast in the bank was like standing downwind from an outhouse, anyway.

No, Nessa was the one casting a pall over the bank, and she had to stop right now. She might still nurse a deep, dark, writhing, angry ball of resentment at Mr. MacNaught, but that was no reason to take it out on the tellers and the customers.

After all, tomorrow was Fat Tuesday. Outside, on the streets, *le bon temps* reached a frenzied climax composed of strong liquor, good food, and a fair amount of illicit sex. At the Dahl House, the aunts were preparing a special dinner from every rich, luscious ingredient that would be forbidden during Lent.

So she, Nessa, would put a smile on her face and stop grumping around—and while she was at it, she would watch Stephanie and see if she could catch her slipping a little cash into her pocket. If she was the reason Mr. MacNaught had forced Nessa to remain with the bank, Nessa would personally pull every dark root out of Stephanie's blond head.

The thought made her smile with genuine mirth, and at once the noise level in the bank picked up. The noon rush became animated as tourists hustled in and regulars came from their jobs. Nessa kept smiling. The tellers kept smiling. Stephanie slipped into her office and shut the door, which made the place positively jovial, and for the first time in days, Nessa felt . . . normal. In control of her life and her emotions.

She'd moved into an apartment this weekend, her first very own place, and this morning she'd gone out for breakfast.

She didn't have to tell anybody where she was going. She didn't have to explain that her pots and pans were still packed. She simply got dressed, went into the Quarter, ate, and came to work, and during the whole hour, she hardly spoke a word to anyone.

It was blissful.

She loved her aunts, but the constant chaos they loved had been chafing on her, and it wasn't as if she wouldn't still see them every night.

Moreover, she didn't have to work here forever. She had the job with Pootie who, only last night, had grunted, "Good," when Nessa made a buy.

The panties Stephanie held . . . well, the truth about Mac MacNaught had pulled the teeth on that little threat. In fact, if Stephanie wanted to keep her job, she'd probably better keep her mouth shut about MacNaught's sex life.

Furthermore, when MacNaught came back, Nessa would take matters in her own hands. She would force him to sit down and show her the discrepancies in the books, and *Nessa* would figure out the problem. . . . The bustle had died down, so Nessa headed for her desk.

The metal detector went off.

Something hit the floor.

Someone had dropped something. Or fallen down. And the marble floor was hard.

Nessa held her breath as she turned, expecting to hear some child's scream of pain, ready to run for the first aid kit—and instead saw Eric flat on his back, his eyes closed, blood gushing from a gash on his forehead.

A grubby, scowling Ryan Wright stood over him, gripping a semiautomatic pistol—and it was pointed at her.

Above the screech of the alarm, a horrible, awkward silence gripped the bank, and Nessa's first thought was, *Where's Mac MacNaught when I need him?*

Carol screamed, a good loud one.

Lisa yelled, "Everybody down!"

Everyone obeyed, tellers and customers, leaving only Nessa and Ryan standing.

In slow motion, she lifted her hands. "Ryan, what are you doing here? I thought you got out of town days ago."

"I did," he said between gritted teeth. "But my picture was everywhere. I couldn't catch a ride, I couldn't even get a sandwich. So I hid in the swamps." His voice rose. "Do you know what it's like in the swamps?"

Nessa inspected him. He looked considerably worse for wear. A scraggly beard covered his chin and neck. His clothes didn't fit and mud and stains covered them. Red blotches speckled his forehead and arms—mosquito bites. He looked like one of the homeless of New Orleans. No wonder no one had glanced at him twice. "I've heard there are water moccasins in the swamp. And their babies."

"I saw them." He scrubbed at one ankle with his other foot—chigger bites.

"You're a mess," Nessa informed him.

He scowled. "And it's his fault."

"Whose fault?"

"That bastard Mac MacNaught."

Briefly a memory surfaced; Skeeter saying, "Ryan's got a real case of the ass for the bank owner, I don't know why."

"Okay, I'm going to turn off the alarm for the metal detector." Nessa walked slowly toward the control panel. "We already know what set it off."

Ryan held the pistol in both hands and tracked her as she moved.

He was making her nervous.

He was pissing her off.

But she kept her voice calm and pleasant. "Robbing this bank doesn't seem like a good idea. I can guarantee at least one of the tellers has already set off the silent alarm. The cops are on their way. Why don't you put down the gun . . . ?"

"I'm not robbing the bank," Ryan said.

"Okay. What are you doing?" She shut down the metal detector and, except for the sobbing of one trembling teenager, blessed silence fell.

"I'm waiting for MacNaught to show up and try to rescue his sweetheart." Ryan's satisfaction permeated his tone.

Nessa found herself the center of every eye. She sighed. After this, the gossip would never stop. "That's why you're aiming the gun at me?"

"Smart girl," he approved.

"So it's a hostage situation."

"More points for Nessa!"

She had hated this guy from the moment she met him. Now she found herself loathing him. "Since it's me you want as a hostage, can we release the customers and the tellers?"

"I don't kill innocent people," Ryan said. "That's for the likes of Mac MacNaught and his father."

Using the voice she used to calm an irate customer, she said, "So everyone should very slowly stand up and file out the door."

"Everyone but you." Ryan smiled. "You need to go stand in the middle of the lobby so when MacNaught gets here, he'll see you right away."

"Can we let the people get out of the way first?" Nessa didn't wait for his answer. "Customers nearest the door go first, and please take your time. We don't want to startle Mr. Wright. Donna, as you go out, would you help the young lady? She seems to be hysterical. Jeffrey, Eric is stirring. You need to encourage him to leave if he can. You're all doing very well. That's right. Stay calm." Briefly, Nessa sent a thought to Stephanie in her office. But if Stephanie was too chicken to come out, then she could huddle under her desk until she rotted.

When the last customer and teller were out the door, he indicated the middle of the floor again. "Sit down and let's wait for your boyfriend."

Forty

"I wonder what's going on up there?" The driver of Mac's town car craned his neck. "Looks like something's going on at the bank."

Mac looked up from the alarm schematics Gabriel had given him. "At the bank? Like what?"

"I don't know. There're cops and an ambulance. They've got the street cordoned off. Probably somebody looked at their mortgage interest rates and had a heart attack." The guy laughed, caught himself, and coughed.

"That must be it." Mac bundled the papers into his briefcase. "Drop me off here."

Yellow police tape cordoned off the street. It didn't even slow Mac down.

"Hey!" one of the officers yelled, before recognizing him. "Mr. MacNaught, you got here almost as fast as we did."

"How about that?" He examined the area.

The tellers were standing on the street, crying. The customers were being interviewed by the police.

His heart began to pound.

Robbery? Maybe. More copycat Beaded Bandits. Maybe the return of Ryan Wright.

But where was Nessa?

He caught sight of Georgia. Yelled her name.

She hurried to him, talking as she walked. "That scumbag who pulled off the other two robberies came in with a semiautomatic pistol, knocked out your security guard, and took Nessa hostage."

His heart started pounding harder.

Ryan Wright was the human element Gabriel had been talking about. The guy so desperate he didn't care what happened, and he was determined to get his way.

"She got him to release the tellers and customers. The perp and Nessa are in there by themselves. We're lining up the SWAT team." Georgia used the cop voice, the authoritative one they'd trained her to use with excitable family members. "As soon as we can get a clear shot—"

"No." His blood cooled as he thought the situation through, made his plans. "We can't wait for that." Catching Georgia's arm, he asked, "Can you get me on the roof?"

"On the roof? Look, MacNaught, there's nothing being on the roof can gain you."

Mac looked Georgia right in the eye and in slow, precise tones said, "Mr. Vycor would disagree."

It took Georgia only a second to digest that. Another second to make the necessary leaps of logic. "I'll come with you."

"No."

"Mr. MacNaught."

"No. And I need a pistol."

"All right!" She grabbed his sleeve and started with

him toward the fire chief, who was standing by. "But I missed capturing the Beaded Bandits, and I'm making a big sacrifice here."

"Get in position. Keep your eye on Nessa. If you catch a glimpse of the son of a bitch who's got her—shoot to kill."

When the last person was out the door, Ryan waved the pistol at Nessa. "Now lock it behind them."

She took a breath. If she didn't lock it, if she gave it a push and ran outside instead, she could probably get out. She looked at the semiautomatic in his hand. Although probably not alive.

She looked outside, saw a cordoned-off area with police cars, fire engines, and flashing lights.

Good. The cops were here.

One uniform bobbed into view and gave her a thumbs-up.

Georgia.

The sight put heart in Nessa. These were her cops, her friends. They weren't going to let her get killed.

And in a darker, secret part of her mind, she knew that somewhere out there, Mac MacNaught walked the streets. He believed she was his, and he would not let her die.

With a decisive click, she locked the door. Locked herself inside with a world-class nutcase.

But this was Nessa's bank, and she knew its secrets.

"What are you doing?" Ryan asked as she strolled toward the vault.

"I figured you wanted the bank to fund your get-away, so I'm going to open the vault for you."

"Don't bother." Ryan limped after her, keeping

away from the door and close to the wall. "I'm not interested."

She punched her code into the electronic panel. Turned and stared at him as the door opened. "You're not interested? You were interested enough last week when you knocked off one bank and shot up another. There's a lot of money in there."

"I'm not going to go in and get it and let you shut me in, and I'm not going to let you go and shut yourself in, so you might as well get over to the middle of the floor, where your boyfriend can see you, and stay there." His voice rose with every word until he was yelling, half-hysterical with fury.

"All right." Nessa lifted her hands again. She walked to the middle of the floor, then glanced around. "Do you mind if I use my office chair? The floor's hard, and that's tough in heels. But I guess you know about that."

"Are you being funny?" The way his fingers tightened on that gun . . .

"No. I don't think so. I'm not feeling really humorous right now." She walked to her desk.

"Don't touch anything but the chair." Ryan sank into a seat along the wall facing the teller counter.

"No problem. It's not like I have my own pistol hanging around in a drawer. That's against bank policy. We would shoot the manager." As she talked, she glanced at her desk, seeking a weapon. Any kind of weapon.

The best she could do was the roll of quarters, which would be great if she had the arm of a professional pitcher. Actually, years of softball in school had taught her one thing—she threw like a girl. Last week was the only time she'd even come close to knocking someone silly, and those hail stones were a lot lighter than a roll of quarters. . . . The realization struck her. She looked up at Ryan. "Hey. In that alley. That was you who tried to hold MacNaught and me up!"

Ryan sneered. "Aren't you smart?"

"Why would you do that?"

"It was impulse. I saw that bastard. He was wearing an expensive suit. He had an executive haircut. He was with you. And I wanted to kill him just for the hell of it." Ryan projected a breathtaking hatred for MacNaught.

"Oh." Picking up the roll of quarters, she put it in the seat of her chair and started toward the middle of the bank. The wheels squeaked as they rolled across the marble.

"Right there," Ryan said, "where he can see you as soon as he comes through the door."

"Aren't you expecting a lot of MacNaught?" She seated herself on her chair, making sure she was easily visible from the vault. "What with being in the swamp, you may have missed the news flash, but I was a little upset when I found out he'd been lying to me about being an insurance investigator."

"Like that's the worst thing he ever did."

"I want to know a guy's real name before I sleep with him. Did he lie to you about his name before he slept with you?"

"Before he came along, you didn't used to be a bitch," Ryan said resentfully.

"I admit, he did release my inner bitchiness. But having you use me as a hostage is working it up, too." She rolled the chair back and forth, back and forth, working herself slowly closer to one of the customer-service centers stocked with pens and deposit and withdrawal slips. The marble block was antique, solid all the way to the floor. In case of gunfire—and unless she did some fancy talking, gunfire was inevitable—the service center would do as a barricade. "So I'm guessing you coming to New Orleans and robbing MacNaught's banks wasn't mere coincidence. You must have put a lot of planning behind it."

"I like to keep up with what's happening to MacNaught, so when I read about the Beaded Bandits, I thought, *Now, that's a plan I can get behind.*" For the first time, Ryan smiled in his familiar, smirky-guy way.

That's right, Nessa, keep him happy. "Where did you read about it?"

"On the Internet, in the *New Orleans Times-Picayune.*"

"I didn't realize you'd been here that long." He was shaking his head even before she finished speaking. "Why were you reading the *Times-Picayune?*"

"I did a Google search for MacNaught's name and found the story, and us guys in prison have a lot of time to read." He chortled at the look on her face, and said, "Assault and battery with intent to commit murder."

"What?" Even to herself, she sounded stupid.

"Isn't that what you were going to ask? Why was I in prison?"

"Yes. That was what I was going to ask." And suddenly she comprehended, where she hadn't before, the seriousness of the situation. Not that having a guy hold a semiautomatic pistol on her wasn't serious, but before, she'd been facing Ryan Wright, part-time street musician and full-time loser. Now she knew he understood violence, and if that grin on his face was anything to go by, enjoyed it. "You said you didn't kill innocent people. Are you going to kill me?"

"You're not innocent. You've been fucking Mac MacNaught."

No answer for that. "You're a repeat offender. You're going to go back to prison, maybe to death row."

"No. I am not going back to prison. And if you want to blame somebody, blame little Jeremiah, because this whole goddamn mess is his fault."

She twirled her chair in a circle, picked up the roll of quarters. "What *did* MacNaught do to you?"

"Him and his father. What a pair they were." Ryan's brief smile was gone. "And his mother. God, was she ever a whore. My dad used to say she got what she deserved, sleeping with that son of a bitch."

"You mean Nathan Manly?"

"Nathan Manly." He rested the pistol on his knee, pointed at her, and used his other hand to rub his leg. "Do you know where I'm from?"

"Somewhere up North."

"From Weathertop, Pennsylvania, home of Manly Industries."

Nessa was starting to understand. Deftly, she plucked at the paper rolled around the quarters.

"And do you know where Mac MacNaught is from?"

"Weathertop, Pennsylvania, home of Manly Industries?" She got one side of the roll free, and started on the other.

"Right you are. My dad was a good man. My mom always said so. He worked hard, for goddamn Manly Industries, and he drank hard, and he . . ." The pistol shook as if jolted by an earthquake.

"He hit hard?" Nessa guessed.

"All us kids would catch it every once in a while. A couple of bruises. No big deal."

No big deal, except Nessa felt sorry for the man holding her hostage.

And her aunts would want to know why was she listening to Ryan Wright and she wouldn't listen to Mac MacNaught.

Listen, God. I understand. This is a lesson. I recognize that. I'm learning.

"Everybody got a few smacks from their old man except the little prince, Jeremiah MacNaught. *His* father didn't live with him, because *his* father was married to someone else and had another kid with *her*. You know, I used to envy him? His father would show up once or twice a year and give him presents and take him through the plant. He never beat him. He wasn't around long enough for sweet little Jeremiah to get on his nerves." Ryan snorted.

"Then Manly Industries crumpled, the whole organization, and your father was out of a job."

"They didn't crumple. Nathan Manly stole the money, all of the money in that business, and it was a huge business, and left us destitute. Left the whole town and everybody in it on the breadline, not to mention a whole bunch of stockholders. So don't feel sorry for me. Feel sorry for poor little Prince Jeremiah."

"Because his father abandoned him." She'd been so eaten up with anger, she hadn't thought that MacNaught might have issues about people who steal, then walk away and never pay the price.

"No." Ryan couldn't have made his contempt more

clear. "Because everybody in that town hated his father, and his father was gone."

"So everybody in that town took it out on him." The scars on MacNaught's face and chest took on new meaning. *Assault and battery with intent to commit murder.* "What did you do to him?"

"I didn't do it," Ryan denied swiftly. Then he grinned. "But I helped my father get a hold of him. It was so easy. All the time, even after his father left, he was nice to me because he thought I had it rougher than him. That piece of shit felt sorry for me. So that day . . . it was in December, freezing rain falling—man, it was miserable! That day I ran up to him—he was with his mother doing Christmas shopping—and told him I needed help. And he told his mama to stay where she was, and came like a lamb to the slaughter."

"How old was he?"

"Thirteen. Big for his age."

"How many guys did your dad have with him?"

"Seven."

"So seven adult men beat up on a thirteen-year-old?" She slathered on the sarcasm. "Wow. Your dad was a hero!"

"He was! It was what everybody in town wanted to do. He would have gotten away with it, too, but the little prince's mother followed him, and when she saw what was happening, she ran and got the cops." Ryan showed his scummy brown teeth. "They arrested my dad, and because of Jeremiah and his goddamn mother, my dad got killed in prison."

Ryan's dad abused him when he was a kid, beat up on a thirteen-year-old, and Ryan was angry about his father's death. Blamed MacNaught for it. She didn't understand. She never would.

Picking her words carefully, she said, "If you're looking for revenge, this seems a precarious plan. MacNaught's going to leave this to the professionals."

"No, he's not."

"He's not a hostage negotiator."

"He's in love with you."

"Really, he's not. No guy in love would treat me the way he has."

"You're as dumb as any woman. He'll treat you however he needs to treat you to get you." Ryan's expression showed grim conviction. "I've watched you guys. I've watched him look at you. He adores you, and he's the kind of jerk who would do anything to protect his woman."

"Really." *Really?* "You think he adores me?"

"Why do you think I made another attempt at screwing you? Because if he thought he was losing you, he'd go crazy." Ryan wiped the sheen of sweat off his forehead. "He's going to come for you."

"But it still doesn't make sense." She twirled in a circle. Pushed herself back and forth. "What are you going to do if MacNaught does show up? Have him clean out the vault, order up a helicopter, and lift us off the roof? This is not James Bond."

"My dad always said I couldn't do anything right. Called me a faggot. Told me I was stupid. But I'll show him. I'm going to do what my dad couldn't do." Ryan held the pistol in one hand and used the other to pet the barrel. "I'm going to kill Jeremiah MacNaught."

Forty-one

Inside, the clock ticked on the wall.

Outside, Nessa heard sirens and shouting.

She stared at Ryan. "You're going to murder him? Isn't that the same as killing the goose that laid the golden egg? How are you going to get away?"

"I'm not. I can't live in the swamp. I can't get out of town. I'm not going back to prison. And my leg . . . I got shot last week. It's oozing and it smells. They're going to cut it off, I know they are." Ryan's face set in sullen lines. "So he's going to die. I'm going to die. And you—"

Nessa caught a glimpse of movement from inside the vault.

MacNaught had come to save her.

Ripping the last of the paper off the roll of quarters, she flung the coins on the marble floor.

They hit. They smacked. They rolled in all directions. The sound echoed in the empty bank.

Startled, frantic, Ryan leaped to his feet, pointing his firearm up and down, around and behind.

As hard as she could, Nessa shoved with her feet,

propelling the chair toward the service center. She dove for cover—and from the corners of her eyes, saw MacNaught. He knelt in the door of the vault. He aimed the cold black eye of a police service revolver right at Ryan. The pistol jumped in MacNaught's hands.

As she slid across the floor and behind the heavy marble slab, she heard the bark of a single gunshot, Ryan's scream, and a heavy thud.

Ryan's scream. He was the one who'd screamed ... wasn't he? If MacNaught was shot, she couldn't bear it.

Firm footsteps echoed through the bank.

She peered out from behind the counter, and there he was. Mac MacNaught.

Green eyes. Dark hair, mussed and falling over his forehead. Big bruiser of a body. Scars on his forehead. Scars that told a story Nessa could comprehend.

On the floor, Ryan lay unconscious, bleeding from a wound by his collarbone.

MacNaught leaned over him, retrieved Ryan's semi-automatic pistol, and stood.

Nessa scrambled to her feet.

MacNaught looked at her, and his relief and joy shone from him.

Ryan was right. MacNaught *did* love her.

"Ionessa?" His voice shook.

She'd never heard a sound as sweet.

She walked into MacNaught's arms.

He held her as if he would never let her go. "I thought I'd lost you. And I walked out of the bank without telling you—"

"I let you walk out and was such a—"

"Is it over?" a high, breathless voice said from the corner.

MacNaught jumped, freed himself, aimed the pistols. "Who's there?"

"Don't shoot me. Don't shoot me!" Arms up, Stephanie stepped out of the corridor and into the light.

"What the hell?" MacNaught stared incredulously.

"She was hiding in her office," Nessa said.

"She let you face him *alone*?" MacNaught's voice rose.

Stephanie's voice rose right back. "It wouldn't do me any good to get killed, too!"

Snarling like an angry bull mastiff, MacNaught gathered himself to spring.

Nessa pulled him back into her arms. "Stephanie's right. If I'd been in her office and she'd been out here, you would have wanted me to stay in there."

"But you wouldn't have."

"No. But you would have wanted it." Nessa could see Georgia standing outside the bank, gesturing. "The police want to come in."

"Stephanie, open the door," MacNaught ordered.

"My keys." In a panic, Stephanie slapped at her sides. "I don't know where they are."

"Here. Take mine." Nessa tossed them to her.

Stephanie's shaking hands missed by a mile.

In a low rumble, MacNaught said, "That woman is worthless. And he—" He glanced at Ryan.

"Do you recognize him?" Nessa asked.

"No. Should I?"

"His name is Ryan Wright, and he grew up in the same town you did."

"Ryan Wright. I don't know anybody named Ryan

Wright." MacNaught walked over to the prone body and turned Ryan's face to the light.

"He went to your school. His father worked at your father's firm, and when your father—"

That did it. "It's Russell Whimper. With a beard!"

"Russell *Whimper*?"

Stephanie walked past, keys in hand, but they rattled in her grasp.

"Russell Whipple, but he was always bruised or had a cast on his arm, so we called him Russell Whimper." MacNaught spoke with the confidence of a man who had left those days and that place behind. "His dad used to get drunk and beat the crap out of him, and Whimper would snivel and slink around school because he was so embarrassed. Poor kid. I haven't thought about him in years."

"He's thought about you—obsessively," Nessa said. "He blamed you for everything. When you were thirteen and they beat you up—"

Suddenly watchful, MacNaught looked up, into her eyes. "He told you about that, did he?"

"He bragged about it. It was his dad and his friends who did it. And Russell is the one who sprang the trap."

Reflexively, Mac's hand flew to his forehead. He stared hard at Russell, then shook his head. "He may have. I don't remember that day worth a damn. I only remember one thing for sure."

"Hold on!" Stephanie called to Georgia as she struggled to insert the key in the lock. "I'm getting it!"

"What do you remember?" Nessa asked.

"I remember my mother running away."

Startled, Nessa stared at MacNaught. "Running away? She didn't run away. She—"

"Look out!" MacNaught leaped. Grabbed her so fast he jerked her out of her shoes.

Shots splintered the air.

The glass front door exploded.

Stephanie screamed bloody murder and kept screaming.

MacNaught and Nessa rolled, and came to rest under the counter.

More glass shattered. They could hear shouts. "Police!"

Mac shoved at Nessa, pushing her out of sight behind the service counter.

She pulled at him, dragging him with her.

"It's okay!" Georgia's voice sounded like a bullhorn. "I got him."

"Got him? Wh-what happened?" Nessa stammered.

"I was stupid, that's what happened." Mac reclined on his back on the cool marble. "I thought Whimper was unconscious, and I didn't check him for weapons. When you looked back at me, he pulled a pistol out of his belt and aimed right at you."

"He said he wasn't going back to jail." Now that the danger was over, her teeth were chattering.

MacNaught clutched her, hanging on as if to warm her—or hold her in place. "Listen, Nessa, you've got to let me explain why I came to New Orleans."

He'd just saved her life. Twice. She didn't want to think about how he'd lied to her. "Don't you think we should talk to the police first?"

"No." He held her tighter. "I need to tell you *now*."

She recalled what her aunts said. *Listen to him.* But

now didn't seem the time. "If this is about how you hate thieves because your father stole all that money and abandoned you, I get it. I don't even blame you. I'd be mad, too. Not psychotically mad, not I'm going to sneak around and sleep with someone and lie to her about who I am mad, but mad."

"There's more to it than that." His voice sounded fainter.

"Look." Nessa put her elbow in his ribs and shoved her way free. "Georgia's yelling, Stephanie's still hysterical, my friends need me. You're the bank owner—you probably should talk to the cops and the press—"

"No, I only want to talk to you."

Cool air struck a damp spot on her stomach. "Someone must have dropped something, because—" She looked down at herself.

Red stained her shirt.

She looked down at him.

He was paper white, holding his left side while blood oozed from between his fingers.

The cops were all still shouting.

She screamed loud enough to drown them all out.

Within seconds, Georgia was there. "Hang in there, man!" She tried to pull Nessa away to let the paramedics get close.

MacNaught wouldn't let go of Nessa's hand.

"Not good. Not good!" One of the paramedics pulled open MacNaught's shirt. "What's your blood type, sir? Do you know your blood type?"

"O neg." MacNaught tugged Nessa close again. "Listen, I might not get another chance."

"I believe you. Whatever your reason was for being

a big fat jerk, it was good enough." *Not now, Nessa!* "I'm sorry I said it like that. You're hurt." *Maybe dying*.

He gasped a laugh. "But still a jerk."

She wanted to say no, he wasn't a jerk.

She couldn't. Not even if he *was* dying. "Is he going to be okay?" she demanded of the EMTs.

The EMT leaned over the gunshot wound with a flashlight. "He's going to be—"

MacNaught grabbed the guy by the wrist.

The EMT looked into MacNaught's eyes.

Some kind of manly communication occurred.

The EMT said, "He'll live. I'm almost sure of it."

Oh, God. It *was* worse than she thought. "Mac-Naught. Listen. You saved me and I'm grateful."

"To hell with your gratitude. I don't want your gratitude." As the EMTs started wiping at his side and wrapping him up, MacNaught panted from the pain.

Nessa took advantage of his silence. "Too bad. You've got it. You saved me, and I'm grateful. But that's not all I am. I'm mad and I'm hurt and . . ." Now she closed her eyes, trying to get the words out.

When she opened them, she found both EMTs, Georgia, and MacNaught staring at her.

"Guys, would you give us a minute?" MacNaught asked.

"Don't leave me with him. You need to get him to the hospital!" she called frantically.

They ignored her and obeyed MacNaught.

He took her hand. "Your aunts said I should tell you how I got this face."

"They said I should ask you."

"I was born a—"

She stopped him with her palm across his mouth.

Gently, he took her hand away. "I was illegitimate. Grandson of a dockworker. I hear it's not a big deal for most people if someone has a child out of wedlock, but it was in my mother's family." He winced and shifted. "Among the people they knew. Grandparents were ashamed. Hated knowing I was alive. Did as little as possible for my mother. All the time I was little, we were pretty much on our own. But Mom hung in there. Until . . ." He closed his eyes, and a tear slipped down his cheek. "I'll never forget seeing her running away."

She couldn't stand to see him like this—wounded and in anguish. "Now, listen, MacNaught."

His eyes popped open again. "First, you listen. I'm the son of two monsters, both of them willing to leave their child to God knows what fate. You're the child of an old family with a lot of pride and background and love. I know I shouldn't be shining your shoes, but I'm not like either one of my parents. I work hard, I don't run away when things get rough, and whether I should or not, I love you."

He'd said it before, but she hadn't thought he knew what it meant. Now . . . now she knew he did.

Plus he'd given a pretty long speech for a guy who might be dying, so she knew he wasn't, and understood that guy moment with the EMT was MacNaught telling him to keep her on tenterhooks.

She leaned close and spoke into his ear. "You'll do anything to win, won't you?"

"Yes," he said faintly—maybe because he really felt faint, maybe because she asked an uncomfortable question. Pulling a familiar ring box out of his pocket, he handed it to her. "Here. You can trade it in for one you like, but for right now . . ."

When she didn't immediately take it, he coughed weakly.

If he could scheme that well, he was going to live. But he really was shot, certainly in shock, and in need of medical attention. So she waved the EMTs over and kept it brief. "Russell told me. Your mother didn't run away. The only reason they didn't kill you was because your mom brought the police. MacNaught—your mother saved your life."

Forty-two

Nessa watched the staff from New Orleans Home Health Care settle MacNaught and his IVs and his monitors in the hospital bed in the study of the Dahl House.

Daniel stood with her, dressed in his performance costume and humming the theme from *The Godfather*. "Isn't it refreshing what a billion dollars can buy?" he murmured in her ear.

"It really is." Nessa rolled the gigantic diamond around her finger.

From out on the porch, they could hear Calista and Hestia calling to the ambulance team, "Thank you, boys. It was so sweet of you to bring him by. Are you sure you won't take more cookies? You have to help us eat them up! Remember, tomorrow is the start of Lent!"

The owner of Home Health Care, Morgaine Roux, was a tall, thin, gorgeous nurse with sculpted arms that clearly exhibited her experience in manhandling patients. She also had cold hands, a strong jaw, and a take-charge attitude that made Nessa think MacNaught got what he deserved by demanding his early release from the hospital. Morgaine checked all the monitors, leaned over the bed, and in a loud, slow voice, said, "There you are, Mr. MacNaught. And now you should rest."

MacNaught gradually opened his eyes. "I . . . was."

"Come, now." She straightened the sheets over his chest. "You couldn't have slept through the move."

Nessa grinned at Daniel and they tiptoed out.

"How long do you give her?" Daniel asked.

"About ten minutes." Nessa sat down on the stairs.

It was less than five when Morgaine came stomping out, muttering under her breath. Catching sight of Nessa sitting on the stairs, she said, "I pity you. He's going to run your life!"

As Morgaine walked out the door, Daniel grinned and said to Nessa, "Not so much, huh, chère?"

"I can handle him." Nessa stood and dusted off her rear.

"I think you can, too." Daniel scrutinized her jeans and chocolate brown T-shirt. "Love the shoes, darling."

"They are nice, aren't they?" Nessa smiled down at her new red flats. "I bought them last night."

"Did you have anything in particular in mind? Perhaps a little torment of your lover?"

Nessa widened her eyes and fluttered her lashes. "Why, Mr. Friendly, what do you mean?"

Daniel grinned. "That's what I thought. Dear girl, I have to fly. I have a long day ahead of me."

"But when it's over, there's another Mardi Gras behind us."

"Thank God."

Nessa wrapped her arms around his waist and

hugged him. "And you'll never have to help rob another bank."

"Thank God," he said with increased fervor, and kissed the top of her head. "Now, darling, you get in there before your Mr. MacNaught bursts a blood vessel, and I'll see you at church tomorrow!"

In a flutter of feathers, he headed for the door and met the Dahl sisters coming in.

"Good-bye, Daniel. Work hard," Calista said.

"Nessa, what did Jeremiah say to that woman? That Morgaine?" Hestia looked over her shoulder in puzzlement.

"He shouldn't send his nurses away," Calista said. "He was shot yesterday!"

"But not seriously injured," Hestia reminded her.

"He had to have two pints of blood, sister. That is serious."

"I know that, but the bullet struck no major organs."

While the aunts squabbled, Nessa walked into the study. With her hands shoved in her pockets, she stood and surveyed MacNaught.

He had an IV in one arm hooked into two bottles of fluid. He had wires coming off his chest to a heart monitor, and a clip on his finger to another monitor. He looked pale and profoundly irritated.

"I like the outfit," she said.

He looked down at the faded blue-and-red hospital gown bunched around his middle. "Thanks. Can you make these girls go away?"

Nessa cast a sympathetic glance at the two narrow-eyed nurses hovering in the background. "Is he in imminent danger of death?"

"If he keeps this up, he is," one of them muttered.

"Wait outside the door," Nessa instructed. "I'll call if he starts bleeding on the rug."

The nurses hustled out and were greeted by cries of delight from the aunts.

"Are they pushing cookies again?" MacNaught rasped.

"And pralines." Nessa strolled over, just out of reach. "If you pick on your nurses, I'll send you back to the hospital."

"The hospital won't take me."

"They will if I shoot you again."

MacNaught smiled crookedly. "Have I told you how smart you were to distract Whimper with the quarters?"

"No, you were too busy having a doctor probe your wound." She watched him closely, wondering how many details he remembered from yesterday. "Did you call your mom?"

"Yes. She was surprised to hear from me. Asked if I was sick, since I only call at Christmas."

"And you told her . . . ?"

"I told her I got shot, since I figured she'd find that out, anyway, but that I was okay." He watched Nessa closely. "I told her I called her with good news—I was engaged."

Lifting her hand, Nessa showed him the ring.

He smiled and relaxed against the pillows. "So what made you change your mind?"

"I did what my aunts said. I listened to you, and I re-alized that for good reason, you have issues about honesty. Then I figured out for good reason, I have issues about trust. I figured maybe between the two of us, we could work out our issues. I thought we'd better, since knowing you, you've probably made more enemies, and the next one might be a better shot." She was trying to keep it light, but unexpected tears sprang to her eyes.

"Don't cry. I'm fine. And from now on, I'll have you to charm my enemies."

She smiled tremulously. "You've got your own charms."

"If you're very careful, we can make love." He opened his arms.

Nessa looked around at the wide-open room, at the entrance where two nurses and two aunts were undoubtedly stationed. "If you're lucky, I'll hold your hand."

"Kiss and hug."

"You don't have to negotiate everything." But she laughed, walked close, kissed him, and let him wrap his arms around her. Gently she leaned her head against his chest and listened to his heartbeat. "Does that hurt you?"

"No." He stroked her hair back from her forehead. "I've been thinking about what you said yesterday. About my mother. Do you know, I've been very careful not to think of that time, and that's why I . . ."

"Never thought it through?" With care not to jostle him, she slid onto the mattress and rested against him.

They were both happier that way.

"When I was eleven," he said. "My mom got married. I didn't like my stepfather, and I don't think he much liked me."

"Because you were a big, clumsy, loudmouthed adolescent?"

"That might have been it. Plus, he worked at Manly."

Nessa could already see the setup. "And he got a hard time for getting stuck with Nathan Manly's kid."

"I guess. Yeah, probably." MacNaught took a long breath. "Then my real father skipped out."

"How rough was that?"

"All the time I was growing up, Dad—Nathan Manly—wasn't there very often, but when he was, he always acted like he loved me." MacNaught's hands paused as if he were thinking. "Looking back . . . I really thought he did. But when the company collapsed, he skipped out without a backward glance, taking all his money and abandoning me and my mom."

That kind of behavior baffled Nessa. "How could he?"

"Fathers do it all the time—run away with their secretary. In my business, I see it a lot. But I didn't think Dad ever would, and he really left us in the lurch. Manly Industries closed, and my stepfather was out of a job, stuck with a wife people called a whore and a kid he called a bastard. Times were tough, and I blamed my mom. For everything."

MacNaught was squeezing her too hard, but she just burrowed closer. She could feel the pain he was in and the anguish of those memories.

"I really don't remember much of the day they beat me up. The Christmas decorations, and the rain turning to ice . . . I think we went shopping because we figured no one else would and we wouldn't get spit at." Beneath her cheek, his heart sped up. "When that kid Russell Whimper came running to get me, I must have had some premonition of trouble, because I told my mom to go back in the store, and I went with him into the alley. . . . I think one of them hit me with a board or something, because I never saw them. Just smacked the ground, felt the boots kicking my ribs . . . looked up and saw my mom and thought she would save me."

"And she ran away."

"Yeah."

"To get the police."

"That does make sense, doesn't it?" He sounded disgusted with himself. "I don't know why that never occurred to me."

"Because you were thirteen and angry and hurt." She could imagine the hostility he must have felt. "Were you in a coma?"

"For a month, maybe, in the medical center in Philly, so when I woke up, Mom wasn't there. When she did get there, my stepfather was with her. He'd found a job in New York. They were moving. She was pregnant. I was . . . not kind."

Nessa looked up at him. "Rough times."

"I was such a dumb kid." He gazed at Nessa in perplexity. "I wish I could tell her. . . . Last night, I was going to. I tried. I tried to explain, but I just couldn't explain what I . . . how do you tell your mother something like that?"

Nessa got right to the heart of the matter. "Did she cry when you called?"

"Yes." He sounded as horrified as any man when faced with a woman's tears.

"Then I'd say she has an inkling." Nessa crawled up the bed so they were face to face. "The thing is, MacNaught, losing my parents was no picnic. Hestia and Calista both have suffered loss and anguish. The whole city of New Orleans is rising from the dead. I do understand that you hate thieves, and why. But you have to understand, that teller who lied to me almost destroyed my life. And I didn't steal from you, but you did lie to me. So let me make this clear—if you ever do it again, I will make you sorry."

"Normally, I don't tell lies. I'm known for my truthfulness—which people like Gabriel Prescott call tactlessness."

"I know it."

"I've never bought a woman a ring before, not even an ugly fucking one."

"I'm sorry I said that." Mortified, actually. "I don't usually say the F word."

"I've noticed. Me—I've never done a flow chart about how a marriage should work. I've never had my lawyers draw up a prenup. There's never been anybody for me but you. Gabriel saw me watching those videos of you, and I know he thought I was one perverted bastard." He cupped her cheek. "But when I saw your face, I fell in love, and I couldn't stand it. I loved my dad, and he walked away without a glance, and my mom waited until that gang was beating me to death before she walked away. Loving you wholeheartedly was too much of a risk. . . . But once I met you, I had no choice. Because, Nessa, you're as beautiful inside as you are out, and there'll never be another woman for me."

She smiled through tears. For a man who was lousy at conversation, he had a way of touching her heart.

"When your parents come down for the wedding, you and your mother can spend some time together.

Even if you can't quite tell her, by the time the baby comes, your mom will understand."

He jumped. "Are we having a baby?"

She smiled serenely. "I don't want to wait too long. The aunts aren't getting any younger, and Miss Maddy does love to hold a baby."

"That's a project I'm glad to work on." He kissed her. Kissed her deep. Kissed her hard. Almost knocked over his IV pole. "Son of a goddamn—"

"MacNaught!" Nessa grabbed and caught it. Sliding off the bed, she pushed her hair out of her face and backed away.

The nurses rushed in, clucking like hens. The great-aunts peeked in the door.

Pootie clomped in, smudges of black on her face. Without paying a bit of attention to Nessa, she said, "Mac! Plug-in for the automatic kettle in my room caught fire. Wiring in this place sucks. Better get that taken care of."

Debbie Voytilla came next. "Mr. MacNaught, something has to be done about that woman before she burns the place down over our heads!"

Bewildered, he raised his eyebrows inquiringly.

Nessa interceded with a firm, "Debbie, you need to talk to Aunt Calista and Aunt Hestia."

"He's a guy," Pootie said. "Guys take care of wiring."

Debbie glared at Pootie. "And of careless boarders."

Pootie laughed jeeringly. "He's not throwing me out. *I* have a lease."

"Nevertheless, Mr. MacNaught was shot yesterday. I think he should have twenty-four hours before he has to deal with the wiring in this house." Nessa gently guided the two quarreling women to the door, then settled herself in an overstuffed chair where he could see, but not touch, her.

Nurses. Aunts. Boarders. The whole city of New Orleans was interrupting Mac's private time with Nessa.

He realized—she was wearing red shoes. Like one of Pavlov's dogs, he responded with instant lust.

And the aunts hustled in.

He had to give vent to his frustration. But he was surrounded by women. "Darn it!"

Calista had a plate of pralines.

Hestia had a plate of cookies.

They put them on the bed beside him.

"Jeremiah, you sound so much better." Calista clasped her hands over her heart. "Last night, we thought you were at death's door."

Hestia beamed. "We're so glad. That you're better, we mean. Because we've been thinking."

"We?" he said cautiously.

"Calista and I. We've been thinking that it would be nice if you did some kind of promotion with the Beaded Bandits."

"Promotion?" he repeated stupidly.

"Yes, you know, like"—Hestia used her hands like a banner—"*If You're Opening a Savings Account at Premier Central Bank When the Beaded Bandits Strike, You Get a Toaster!*"

He could not believe the nerve of these Dahl women. "Nobody wants a toaster."

Nessa smothered her mirth behind her hand.

Hestia was not discouraged. "Then how about using the Beaded Bandits in your advertising? Like that furniture guy who yells at the camera and jumps in the air?"

"You know if you jump in the air, Hestia, your knee will give way," Calista said.

"We don't have to do precisely *that*," Hestia said. "I'm certainly not going to yell at anybody, but I know we could bring business into the banks. Jeremiah could pay us!"

"Toasters don't sound so bad now, do they?" Nessa said to Mac.

Calista must have noted Mac's expression. "Or we could raise money for a charity. You know, show up at the bank in costume and pass the hat."

In their faces, he saw the shape of his future world. In a conversational tone, he said to Nessa, "Do you know, all over the world, people are afraid of me."

"Why is that?" she asked.

"I'm known as a mean bastard."

Nessa sounded kind. "You would never know it now."

"No. You wouldn't, would you?" He looked at the aunts. "No mice."

"You'd let us do it?" Hestia clapped her sister on the back. "I told you it was worth a try!"

"No mice, no other living creatures of any kind," he said.

The aunts' faces fell.

"Well . . . but we were thinking of raising money for the animal shelter and using some of the poor homeless kitties," Calista said.

He put his foot down. "Kittens only."

"And the cute little puppies!" Hestia said.

How did his foot get stuck in this quicksand? "Kittens and puppies only."

"We have to start working on the schematic now!" Calista headed for the door, Hestia on her heels.

Nessa called them back. "Aunt Hestia. Aunt Calista. Don't you think you should start planning our wedding?"

Hestia waved an airy hand. "We already have it planned. We planned it when you were five."

Heads together, the Dahl sisters left the room, leaving Nessa and Mac staring after them in disbelief.

"They always intended to use the banks to collect money for the shelter, didn't they?" He had been thoroughly manipulated. "The rest of that was a ruse."

"When I was five?" Nessa said.

"I'm going to be knee-deep in puppy piddle, aren't I?"

"Knee-deep seems an exaggeration." Nessa rubbed her forehead. "I wonder what my wedding dress looks like?"

"I don't know, but you'll look beautiful in it." Mac held out his hand.

She came to his side and took his hand. "Thank you, MacNaught."

"My name is Jeremiah."

"Jeremiah." They smiled at each other.

Without looking around, Mac called, "Would you nurses scram for a while?"

Gabriel walked in. "Hey, bro. You're looking better."

Mac's exasperation exploded. "You can't come in. I'm trying to kiss my woman, and everyone in the city of New Orleans is visiting my bedside!"

"We're convivial people, we Southerners." Gabriel

grinned at Nessa and Mac's joined hands. "We like you to know we care."

Nessa tried to step away.

Mac wouldn't let her go. "The report on the security at the banks can wait."

"I'm here on a job. Just not that one," Gabriel said.

"Why don't you nurses go get a cup of coffee?" Nessa suggested. "Miss Maddy always has a pot brewing in the kitchen."

Nessa waited until the nurses had left, then perched a hip on Mac's bed. "What's wrong, Gabriel?"

Trust Nessa to see what Mac was too irritated to take in.

Gabriel's expression—serious, uncertain—meant something momentous had occurred.

Mac tucked a pillow under his head. "Sit down."

"I'll stand." Gabriel braced his feet. Squared his shoulders. Clasped his hands before him. "You're one of Nathan Manly's illegitimate sons."

Mac heard the unspoken words.

Gabriel knew a lot about Nathan Manly. Stuff he'd been concealing from Mac.

Gabriel continued, "A few months ago, I convinced Carrick Manly, Nathan's legitimate son, and Roberto Bartolini and Devlin Fitzwilliam, his two known illegitimate sons, to hire me to track down their remaining brothers."

"Jeremiah, you've got more half brothers!" Nessa said in astonishment.

"That doesn't actually surprise me. Nathan Manly wasn't known for his principles," Mac said.

Nessa clasped his hand tighter in hers and beamed.

"I've always wanted siblings. Now, honey, I have all of yours."

But Mac didn't know what he felt, really. Pleasure at having more brothers? In his experience, family wasn't a pleasure, and if Nathan Manly's other sons were anything like Nathan Manly, he didn't want to know them. "Do you know them, Gabriel? Are they good men?"

"I've handled the case personally, and I've come to know Roberto and Devlin well. They are good men. Married to good women." Gabriel stood rock still.

Typically, Nessa listened well, and picked the interesting statement out of Gabriel's speech. She asked, "Why did you handle the case personally?"

Gabriel answered to her. "Because there's a lot of interesting mysteries here. Why Manly destroyed his own company and stole the bankroll. Where he fled and why there's never been a trace of him. What happened to the money? And last but not least, how many sons did he produce?"

Mac studied Gabriel.

The guy looked like he was steeled for a punch.

"How many did he produce, Gabriel?" Mac asked.

"I know of five. Carrick, Roberto, Devlin, you"— Gabriel looked Mac right in the eyes. "And me."

Don't miss the DARKNESS CHOSEN series,
from New York Times bestselling author
Christina Dodd. . . .

A thousand years ago, a brutal warrior struck a terrifying bargain: In return for the ability to change at will into a coldhearted predator, he promised his soul—and the souls of his descendants—to the devil.

In *SCENT OF DARKNESS*, we met Jasha Hunter, the first brother to attempt salvation for his cursed family. Part human and part wolf, Jasha introduced us to this compelling world.

In *TOUCH OF DARKNESS*, we met Rurik Hunter, who shape-shifts into a hawk. Rurik, a learned archeologist, traveled Asia searching for clues that would allow his family some peace.

Read on for a sneak peek of *INTO THE SHADOW*, on sale in July 2008, when we'll meet Adrik, a sexy shape-shifting panther, who continues his brothers' journey to break the evil pact that has held his family in thrall for centuries—until a woman comes along who will change the course of destiny. . . .

The dream started as it always did, with a gust of cold Himalayan air striking Karen Sonnet's face.

She woke with a start. Her eyes popped open.

The darkness in her tent pressed on her eyeballs.

Impossible. Tonight she'd left a tiny LED burning.

Yet it *was* dark.

Somehow he'd obliterated the light.

No. No, it was a dream. Just like all those other nights.

But she could have sworn she was awake. She heard the constant wind that blew through this narrow mountain valley, whistling through the granite stones outside and buffeting the ripstop nylon canopy that protected her—barely—from annihilation. She smelled the stale scent of tobacco, spices, and body odor her cook had left behind. She felt the menacing cold slipping its fingers into the tent. . . .

She strained to hear his footfalls.

Nothing.

Still, she knew he was here. She could sense him

moving across the floor toward her, and as she waited each nerve tightened, stretching. . . .

His cool hand touched her cheek, making her gasp and jump.

He chuckled, a low, deep sound of amusement. "You knew I would come."

"Yes," she whispered.

Kneeling beside her cot, he kissed her, his cool lips firm, his breath warm in her mouth.

She hung suspended in time, in place . . . in a dream. Yet he kissed as if he were real, not a shadow in the night, and as he lingered, her body stirred, her breasts swelling, the familiar longing growing deep inside.

How many nights had it been? Two months? More? Sometimes he didn't come for one night, two, three, and on those nights she slept deeply, worn out by the hard work and the thin air at this high altitude. Then he'd return, his need greater, and he touched her, loved her, with an edge of violence sharp as a knife. Yet always she sensed his desperation and welcomed him into her mind . . . and her body.

This time, it had been almost a week.

He slid the zipper down on her sleeping bag, each tooth making a rasping noise, each noise making Karen's heartbeat escalate another notch. He started at her throat, cupping it, pressing on the pulse that raced there. He pushed the bag aside, exposing her to the cold night air. "You wait for me . . . naked." He pressed his palm between her breasts, feeling her heart beat. "You're so alive. You make me remember. . . ."

"Remember what?" He sounded American, without a hint of an accent, and at the times of madness, when she thought he must be real, she wondered where he was from and what he was doing here.

But he didn't want her to think. Not now. Greedily, he caressed her slight breasts, one in each palm. His hands were long, rough, callused, and he used them to massage her while with his thumbs he circled her nipples.

She made a raw sound in her throat.

"You're in need." His voice deepened. "It's been a long time...."

"I've been here."

"And that was my torment."

It was the first time he'd ever suggested he needed this as much as she did. She smiled, and somehow, in this pitch dark, he must have seen her.

"You like that. But if you've tormented me, I must torment you in return." His head dipped. He took one pebbled nipple in his mouth and suckled, softly at first, then, as she whimpered, with strength and skill.

He made her go crazy.

But, then—any woman who dreamed a shadow lover was already halfway to insane.

She grabbed a handful of his hair, and discovered how very long it was . . . and soft, and silky. She tugged at him, pulling his head back.

"What do you want?" His voice was a husky whisper.

"Hurry." She was chilled. She was desperate. "I want you to hurry."

"But if I hurry, I won't get to do this." He pushed the sheet down farther, caressed her belly and thighs. Lifting her knees, he spread her legs, exposing her to the cold, shocking her, making her suck in a startled breath.

"Let me see." He tilted her hips up. "Are you ready?"

His fingers glided from her knees along the tender skin on her inner thighs to the dampness there. With a delicate touch, he opened the lips and dabbed a touch on her clitoris. "I love your scent, so rich and female. The first time, it was your scent that called me to you."

Horrified, she tried to draw her legs together. "I bathe every night."

"I didn't say you smelled. I said you have a scent that calls to me." His nails skated up and down her thighs, pushing them apart again . . . and they were sharp, almost like claws. Almost a threat. "Not to any other man. Only to me."

"*Are* you a man?" The question slipped out, and she regretted it. Regretted injecting reality into the dream.

"I thought I had conclusively proved my manhood to you. Shall I do it again?" The hint of warning was gone; he sounded warmly amused, and the finger he pushed inside her was long, strong . . . and clawless.

The impact made her fling her head back, and when he pushed a second finger inside, her hips moved convulsively. "Please. Lover. I need you."

"Do you?" Slowly he pulled his fingers back, pressed them in, pulled them out . . . and as he pressed them in, he pinched her clit between his thumb and forefinger.

She screamed. She came. Orgasm blasted her away from this cold, bleak mountainside and into a fire pit. Her thighs clamped around his hand. Red swam beneath her closed eyelids. Heat radiated from her skin.

He laughed, one compelling stroke following another, feeding her madness until she collapsed, shivering and gasping, too weak to move.

He covered her with himself.

"I can't," she whispered, and her voice shook. "Not again."

"Yes, you will."

"No. Please." She tried to struggle, but he stretched out on top of her. Her head was buried in his shoulder; obviously, he was tall. His body, heavy with muscle, pressed her into the cot. His flesh was cool and firm. His shoulders, chest and stomach rippled with vigor, and his heart thrummed in his chest.

Power hummed through him, and he easily held her as he probed again . . . but not with his fingers.

She was swollen with need, and his organ was big, bigger than both his fingers. As he worked himself inside her, she whimpered, her body gradually adjusting to the width, the breadth, and all the while the aftermath of climax made her inner muscles spasm.

He held her wrapped in his arms, clutching her as if she was his salvation.

And she embraced him, her arms gripping him against her chest, her legs clasped around his hips, giving him herself, absorbing . . . absorbing all his ardor, all his need, knowing this was a dream and wanting nothing more.

When the tip of his penis touched the innermost core of her, they both froze.

Darkness held them in a cocoon of heat and sex and emotions stretched too tight for comfort.

Then their passion flashed bright enough to light the night.

He pulled out and pushed back in, thrusting fast

and hard, dragging her with him on his quest for satisfaction.

She held on, rapture flowing through her with the heat and intensity of lava.

The tempo built and built until above her his breathing stopped. He gathered himself, rising high above her, holding her knees behind him . . . then plunged one last time.

Ecstasy exploded her into tiny fragments of being. She came, convulsing with pleasure, until she was no longer an austere, lonely workaholic, but a creature of joy and light.

Unhurriedly, he dropped back on top of her, bringing the silk sheets and sleeping bag up to cover them. Reaching down to the floor, he pulled a large blanket over them . . . but no. She touched it with her hand and discovered fur, thick and soft. A skin of some kind, then.

Had he taken her on a trip back in time, back to a century where a man brought the woman he desired proof of his hunting prowess? Wasn't that a better explanation than madness?

As the perspiration cooled on their bodies, as their breath and heartbeats returned to normal, she realized—nothing had changed. She reclined on her narrow cot in her tent at the foot of Mount Anaya. The darkness still pressed down on her; the sense of wrong in this place still oppressed her. Tomorrow she would rise. He would be gone. And she would go to work, another day spent in hell. And she wept.